CHOMPIN' AT THE BIT
a horse play novel ~ book two

a novel by
A.D. RYAN

Copyright © 2016 A.D. Ryan

All rights reserved. No part of this book may be reproduced in any form or by any electronic or mechanical terms, including information storage and retrieval systems, without permission in writing from the author, except by a reviewer, who may quote brief passages in a review.

This book is a work of fiction. Names, characters, places, and incidents either are the product of the author's imagination or are used fictitiously. Any resemblance to actual persons, living or dead, events or locales is entirely coincidental.

Ryan, A.D.
Chompin' at the Bit / A.D. Ryan

(Horse Play Series ; 02)

ISBN 978-1533462794

Text and Cover design by Angela Schmuhl
Cover Image: Shutterstock, © Kiuikson

CONTENTS

Chapter 1. Road Trippin'	1
Chapter 2. Fun & Games	8
Chapter 3. Rehearsal	19
Chapter 4. Foiled Again	27
Chapter 5. Text, Interrupted	34
Chapter 6. My Past	42
Chapter 7. My Present	52
Chapter 8. My Future	63
Chapter 9. Worth the Wait	71
Chapter 10. The Morning After	79
Chapter 11. Me and My Big Mouth	87
Chapter 12. Home, Sweet … Intercepted	95
Chapter 13. Officially Outed	101
Chapter 14. Close Call	109
Chapter 15. The Perfect Gift	118
Chapter 16. One Thing After Another	124
Chapter 17. The Logical Next Step	130
Chapter 18. Mending Burned Bridges	137
Chapter 19. Suspicious BF is Suspicious	145
Chapter 20. Happy Birthday … to Me	153
Chapter 21. Things Aren't as They Seem	167
Chapter 22. Hot Tub Booze Machine	181
Chapter 23. Blackout	189
Chapter 24. Did We …? Didn't We…?	197
Chapter 25. Two Week Wait	208
Chapter 26. Distractions Never Work	213
Chapter 27. The Masters	219
Chapter 28. Fairytale Date Night	227
Chapter 29. Back in the Swing of Things	242
Chapter 30. Something is Amiss	253
Chapter 31. Under Wraps	260
Chapter 32. Campfire Tales	268
Chapter 33. Tripped up by Déjà-Vu	276
Chapter 34. Impulsive Decisions	284

ACKNOWLEDGEMENTS

While it probably doesn't seem like it, this is always the hardest part of any book to write. Regardless, let's get this party started …

I can never seem to thank my incredible family enough for being so freaking supportive of this hobby-turned-almost-career. You're some of my biggest cheerleaders and are always there to listen to whatever bizarre idea my brain cooks up next. You're all awesome, from my two tiny minions to my amazing husband, and my parents, who always encouraged me to follow my dreams—no matter how far out there and unattainable they might seem. I hope I am able to instill that same confidence and drive in my children that you so selflessly instilled in me. My siblings, you should know that you inspire me in so many ways.

Of course, I wouldn't be here without people who actually want to read the weird ramblings that fall out of my head and wind up on my computer. So, readers, thank you all for being awesome and for hounding me continuously for new books immediately after reading the latest one. It's that kind of pressure that drives me, and I love your enthusiasm!

Because my incredible street team and beta readers are given an exclusive first look into these books, you're seeing them at their most raw. You see the mistakes, and you're kind enough to mention them so I don't look like a total knob once Marla and Tiff see them.. so thank you for being so thorough and unafraid to tell me when I've messed up. I'm not too good for that constructive critique, and I'm so grateful to have you all on my side!

This is now the second novel that Marla at Proofingstyle has worked on, and I'm so happy that she was able to take me on. You're an incredible person, always professional with a quick turnaround. The attention and critique you offer is appreciated. I hope the stars continue to align and we continue to work together in the future.

And, Tiff, who's been here since the very beginning, first as a reader, then as a beta and editor: you're awesome. I am so grateful that you always seem to have time for me when you're not bogged down with work.

Again, thank you all so much for everything you do. I wouldn't be doing this without you all. You make it all worthwhile. Until next time …

1
ROAD TRIPPIN'
Madison Landry

"Okay," I said aloud to myself, standing over the small suitcase on my bed. "I've got pants, shirts, underwear, socks..." Turning around, I spotted the white garment bag hanging on my door. "My dress. Shoes ... I need shoes."

Jensen's sister's wedding was this weekend, and I was a mess trying to make sure I didn't forget anything. My nerves were even more rattled knowing I was going to meet the rest of his family for the first time. His father and I go way back, considering he's been the ranch's vet for the last couple decades, and I recently met his mother when Jensen started working on the ranch and he had to take me to the hospital after three subsequent falls from horseback. Not my finest moment.

Throwing open my closet door, I knelt to the floor and started leafing through the countless pairs of shoes that Willow had made me buy over the years. Some had lived a good life, while others were forced to suffer an eternity in the back of my closet due to the quarter-sized blisters they caused. *Evil shoes.*

"Hey," I heard Jensen exclaim behind me. "Is this your dress?"

The minute I heard the soft *tick, tick, tick* of the garment bag's zipper being lowered, I shot to my feet and launched myself across the room. "What exactly do you think you're doing?" I cried out, throwing myself between him and my dress.

Pushing his bottom lip out and batting his lashes, he pouted. "You won't show me?" His big blue eyes locked on mine, and I found myself captivated by him just as much as I had been when we'd met a few weeks ago. Had I not been exposed to this sort of mind-fuckery in the past, I might have easily been swayed and given him whatever he wanted. But I knew better.

"Nope." I was very assertive in my answer, and that just made him try harder. Wrapping his arms around my waist, Jensen lowered his face to mine, kissing me softly. But I held firm in my position. I knew what he was doing. Usually, he was pretty damn good at it.

This time, though, I remained firm. I didn't return his embrace (even though I wanted to), I didn't kiss him back (even though it killed me not to), I didn't respond to his seduction vocally (even though it took everything in me not to).

"It'll be bad luck," I said.

Apparently he thought that was pretty funny, because he lifted his face and smiled. "Madi, it's bad luck for the *groom* to see the *bride's* dress before the wedding," he countered smugly. "I don't recall there being anything against a man seeing his date's dress."

The left side of my mouth twitched with the desire to smile. Jensen and I weren't officially a couple. We'd both agreed that this was just casual fun, but I'd be lying if I said I wasn't hopeful that we could one day be more. Over the weeks, my feelings for him had developed, and there was no way I could rein them in. I was lost to him.

"Date?" I inquired, keeping the hope from my voice.

Jensen cleared his throat and furrowed his brows before shaking his head. "Right. Sorry. I just ... felt like that might be the easiest way to describe our arrangement."

My heart sank, but I didn't let him see that. Instead, I changed the topic back to a lighter one. "Well, regardless, you can't see the dress."

His smile returned, and he leaned in close again. "You'll have to give me a very good reason why not. And the bad luck thing is bullshit."

Truthfully, the only reason I had was that I didn't want

him to see my dress until I was in it. It was something Willow and I had discussed earlier in the week when I called and told her we would be in town Friday night. Then, before she even got the chance to ask, I booked myself in for hair and makeup at the spa on Saturday morning. She was more than a little pleased—I was actually surprised I could hear anything afterward, given the decibel she managed to reach.

I shook my head adamantly, trying to get him to believe the absurdity of my claim. "Mmmm ..." I hummed with mock-skepticism. "No, I'm pretty sure it applies to the best man's plus-one, too." I avoided the word "date" in hopes of bypassing another almost-breakdown from him. I was having way too much fun with him for it to end now.

Not surprisingly, Jensen wasn't buying it. Suddenly, he picked me up, shifted to the side and moved me out of his way before snatching my dress.

"Jensen Davis," I warned, holding my pointer finger at him as I stalked toward him. "Don't make me kick your ass."

The room was filled with his laughter as he took two steps back. "I'd like to see you try."

Waiting until he looked as though he wasn't expecting it, I lunged forward and threw myself against his chest, reaching over his shoulders for my dress. My attempts were futile, however as he was much taller and stronger than I was.

That was when I realized that if he could play dirty and use his sexy smolder, then so could I.

"Fine," I said softly, sliding down his body slowly, reveling in silent triumph when his body relaxed. Just a smidge. Smiling, I let my hand trail down his chest until it stopped at his abdomen and traced the line of his belt. His eyes locked on mine, and I looped my finger into his belt and started to release it.

Tilting my head up, we continued to stare at one another, and I moved minutely until our lips connected gently. Our kiss remained soft and tender as I slowly worked his belt free before moving onto the button on his jeans. It didn't take long before I was acting on desire and not distraction.

"Mmmf," Jensen mumbled, taking the hand that wasn't holding my dress and wrapping it around my wrist to stop me.

I sighed in defeat; this wasn't the first time he had denied us any major physical contact in the last five days. As the days went on, and the realization of him seeing his ex-fiancée again continued to weigh heavy on his mind, he withdrew. He assured me numerous times that nothing between us had changed, and he was always very open and honest about what he was feeling, but the truth of the matter was, I missed him—I missed *us*.

True, our relationship, if that's what it was, didn't start off like most. My dad had given him a job in an attempt to help him out after he'd fallen on hard times, and it made the most sense for him to live on the ranch, so he became my new roommate. The biggest problem with that was that I had recently gotten out of a particularly scary situation, and Jensen offered me a reprieve from that. He was a distraction, which was both good and bad.

Eventually, we couldn't fight our attraction to one another anymore, and we allowed ourselves to just give in. We still hadn't had sex, both of us agreeing that it would be best to take things slow and be responsible, but that didn't mean we hadn't been intimate in other ways. Our relationship had been progressing by leaps and bounds every day, but then it all came to a screeching halt.

On Monday, we fooled around a little, Tuesday a little less, and Wednesday and Thursday we snuggled on the couch and shared a few chaste kisses before retiring to bed. It felt as though the fire between us had begun to fizzle before it had even had a proper chance to ignite.

Biting my lip hard to keep my chin from quivering as rejection needled at me, I nodded in understanding having been through a couple days of this already. Jensen re-hung my dress on the door, his eyes registering nothing but his deepest apologies. "I'm sorry. It's not you."

His words were meant to comfort, but they didn't. Offering him a smile I knew lacked the reassurance he sought, I cradled his face in my hand and tried to push my own insecurities aside. "I know. You don't have to explain. I know seeing her is going to be hard on you." I paused for a beat, taking in his pained expression. "I just ... I want you to know that I'm here for you. No matter what."

Jensen pulled me into his arms and hugged me tightly. "Thank you."

With the air in the room suddenly bogged down with sadness and doubt that suffocated me, I decided to lighten the mood with a little humor. So, after wrapping my arms around his waist, I spoke. "And if she messes with you, I'll probably kick her ass."

I felt some of the weight in the room lift as Jensen genuinely chuckled, releasing me and holding my face in his hands delicately. "You're amazing, you know that?"

"I do," I quipped. He laughed again, his eyes sparkling more than I'd seen all week. "*There* you are. Welcome back."

Taking my hand in his, he led me to my bed and pulled me down onto his lap as he sat. "I'm sorry if I've been a total ass all week. Even just the thought of seeing her again gets under my skin." Dropping his eyes to our entwined hands, he brought them up and pressed his lips to the tips of my fingers. "Whatever it is about seeing her again that's got me feeling all sorts of fucked up ... just know that it's *not* because I want her back."

"You need closure," I whispered softly, moving my right hand and running it through his hair. "Seeing her and confronting her will bring you that after how the two of you ended things. Everything's going to be okay."

Jensen cupped my jaw, his fingers moving back until they twisted into my hair. Slowly, he pulled my face to his and kissed me. This kiss was different compared to the past few days; it was more reminiscent of the ones from before his anxiety started to kick in. Simultaneously, our mouths opened in a mutual effort to deepen the kiss, and my body twisted toward his as I wrapped my arms tightly around his neck. Desire washed over me, starting in my midsection and quickly blossoming, spreading outward until it completely engulfed me.

"Condoms," Jensen managed to say between frenzied kisses.

Keeping my left arm around his neck and resting my

forehead against his, I moved my right hand to tuck the hair that had curtained our faces behind my ear and nodded. "Yeah," I whispered, my heart fluttering as I came to the conclusion that we were finally going to make love. Shifting slightly, I made a move for my night stand where I had put the condoms I bought earlier in the week—just in case—but Jensen stopped me, causing my drumming heart to slow and plummet.

Sensing my distress, his eyes found mine again as he kissed me softly. "Pack them." Relief swept over me as I realized he wasn't saying *"no,"* just *"not right now."* I nodded slowly as my hope returned.

"I just don't want our first time to be rushed, and we have to leave soon if we're going to make it to the rehearsal dinner on time." Jensen seemed happy when I understood and smiled brightly before turning toward my clock. When he saw the time, he frowned. "We should get loaded up so we can hit the road."

Within fifteen minutes, we met in the hall where he took my bag to put it in my dad's truck while I grabbed my dress and followed him out. I locked up and turned to the truck to see Dad standing next to it.

"Hey, Dad," I said as I went to the passenger side. Jensen closed the back before rushing over to me and taking my dress from me, laying it flat on the backseat so it wouldn't get rumpled.

"You kids got everything?" Dad inquired.

Jensen nodded. "Sure do. You sure you don't mind us using your truck?"

"Absolutely. I won't need it, and it's definitely more reliable that that rust-bucket Madi refuses to part with."

I pouted. "It was Grandpa's truck. I love that thing."

Jensen laughed. "No you don't."

"Sure I do," I argued before releasing an exasperated breath. "We should be back Sunday night sometime. We'll both have our phones in case you need to get a hold of us."

"Nonsense." Dad shook his head and laughed. "You two have fun and don't even worry about things here. We can handle everything."

After hugging my dad, I got into the car while he and Jensen talked for a minute. They said their goodbyes and I waved at Dad before he started back for the barn.

"Ready?" Jensen asked, closing his door and fastening his seatbelt.

"Yeah," I said. "You?"

Smiling wide, Jensen took my hand in his and kissed the back of it. "I have been looking forward to getting away with you all damn week. I am more than ready to let the weekend begin."

FUN & GAMES
Madison Landry

Jensen let me pick the music, and we fell into a comfortable silence for the first part of our drive. About twenty minutes after hitting the highway, I glanced to my left to see Jensen's brow was furrowed in concentration. It would seem the closer we got to the city, the more stressed out he was becoming.

"Hey," I whispered, laying my head back on the seat and reaching over to place my hand over his on the gearshift. "Penny for your thoughts?"

Jensen smiled, but it wasn't his usual smile that made my knees weak. There was an edge of nervousness surrounding it. "I'm, uh, just thinking about tomorrow."

"Kaylie?" I inquired carefully.

Sucking in a deep breath, he shrugged. "Among other things."

"Will she be there tonight?" I had to admit, I was curious to see the woman who had betrayed Jensen in his hour of need. A part of me wanted to rub it in her face that her loss could be my incredible gain, but an even larger part of me wished that Jensen would be able to let her know that he was happier without her and was capable of moving on. Then maybe he could get the closure he needed.

"Um, I actually don't know. Lilah said she'd be flying out sometime this afternoon, so it might not be until later. I would be more than okay without having to see her tonight." He turned to me, his eyebrows knit together. "Would you mind if we changed the subject? I just ... I don't want to spend the entire drive talking about her?"

Squeezing his hand, I offered him a warm smile. "Definitely. What do you want to talk about?"

Jensen chuckled, his smile appearing a little more genuine and the corners of his eyes crinkling slightly. "You decide."

Pulling my bottom lip between my teeth, I tried to think of something to talk about. "Oh! I know!" I exclaimed, slipping my Chucks off and bringing my legs up onto the seat and crossing them. "How about a road trip game?"

I giggled when Jensen grew skeptical, cocking an eyebrow as he glanced briefly at me. "What *kind* of road trip game?"

"Ummm, truth or dare?" I suggested.

His laughter was infectious as it filled the car. "That's not exactly a car game," he pointed out. "Plus, how would we do the dares?"

I shrugged. "I guess it would depend on the dare."

As he stared at the road ahead of him, he contemplated my game choice. "You're sure you wouldn't rather play the license plate game or twenty questions? Hell, I'd even go for some eye-spy."

"Maybe later. Truth or dare?" I asked in an effort to get the game started.

"Um ... Truth. Yes. Definitely truth." I laughed as he convinced himself that truth was the "safer" option.

"What's your favorite ..." I paused for dramatic effect "... part of my body?"

"Oh, this is *dirty* truth or dare. I am so screwed," he said with a chuckle. "Okay ... I would have to say that my favorite part of your body is—"

"Be honest," I interrupted teasingly, arching my eyebrow.

He glared at me through the corner of his eye without moving his head. "Your eyes."

"Shut up! Come on, be serious." I laughed.

"I am. I guess it feels as though, when I'm looking into your eyes—no matter what it is we're talking about or doing—it's like you're letting me in. Almost like we're able to communicate without speaking." Suddenly nervous, he ran his fingers through his hair and laughed.

I stared at him for a minute as I absorbed his words and placed my hand on his forearm. "I feel that way too." There was another moment of silence where we smiled at each other before I continued. "Okay, your turn."

"All right. Truth of dare?"

"Dare," I said, curious to see what he would come up with.

I didn't miss the glint in his eye and the way his cheek dimpled slightly when he smiled deviously. "I dare you to ... tell me what you're most looking forward to this weekend."

"Um, that's not really a dare. That's a truth *disguised* as a dare," I pointed out.

"I fail to see the difference," he said with a coy smile.

He was a tricky bastard, I'd give him that much. "This weekend ... I guess I'm looking forward meeting the rest of your sister—even if that scares me a little too." Stopping for a quick breath, I smiled as I stared at him. "But I think what I'm *most* excited about is spending time with you. Alone. With no work or other distractions around."

"And we don't get that at home?" he asked.

"No, we do. It's just, at home my dad could stop by at any minute or we could get called out to the barn for an emergency. But I get you all to myself after dinner tonight. No distractions. After the wedding tomorrow night? Also mine. All day Sunday? Mine."

The corners of Jensen's mouth twisted up. "And what is it you have planned for me since you'll have me all to yourself?"

I shook my head. "Ah, ah, ah," I taunted. "One question at a time. Truth or dare?"

"Truth."

"Ugh!" I grumbled. "You're no fun! I had a really good dare too. Fine. Um, how many women have you slept with?" I asked the question quietly.

He didn't even flinch when he answered. "Two."

"Two?"

Looking over his left shoulder and turning on his signal

light before changing lanes on the highway, Jensen chuckled. "You seem to forget, I'm only two years older than you, and I was in a serious relationship for a couple years and then incarcerated for three — wait. How many have *you* been with?"

I knew what he was asking, but the way he worded it still made it sound like he wanted to know how many women I'd slept with, so I decided to toy with him. "Um, I've never slept with any women. Plus, you didn't ask if I wanted a truth or a dare." Not that it would have mattered; he'd have found a way to ask me the question with either choice.

"Okay, smartass. If you choose truth, I'd like to know how many *men* you've slept with. And, if you choose dare, then I dare you to tell me how many men you've slept with." He glanced at me for just a moment before turning his eyes back to the road, but in that brief second, I saw that he wasn't going to let this go. Not that I expected him to; it was only fair after I asked him.

"Four. My high school boyfriend — all of two times. Two guys in college, and then there was Dane. How is it you've only slept with two? I mean ... you have seen you, right?" I asked, stealthily tacking my questions on to the end of my quick ramble.

"Ah, ah, ah," he parroted my earlier words. "You didn't ask truth or dare."

Maybe this game was stupid. What the hell was I thinking? "All right," I conceded. "Tru—"

"Truth. I've always believed that sex is something that two people in a committed relationship do. It wasn't something to be taken lightly."

The use of past tense wasn't lost on me.

"And now?" I didn't ask truth or dare, nor was it my turn, but Jensen didn't seem to catch it.

Jensen sighed, concentrating really hard on the road and not looking at me, for whatever reason. "I've decided to just live in the moment. I lost a small portion of my life when I was locked up, and I'm not willing to sacrifice any more of my happiness for fear of missing out again."

God, I want to kiss him right now.

Jensen looked over at me and smiled, my lower half

suddenly reacting quite positively to his smolder and making me a little uncomfortable in my seat. "Not while I'm driving."

Apparently I still had to work on that whole brain-to-mouth connection—or lack thereof.

"Will you tell me about your family?" I asked, changing the subject.

Chuckling, Jensen glanced at me. "Is that a truth or a dare?"

I shrugged, wrapping my arms around my legs and relaxing my right cheek onto my knees again. "Neither."

"Bored with it already?"

Smirking, I said, "Meh, I guess without the real dares it's just not that much fun. It's basically just truth or truth."

"True," he responded, making me laugh loudly before he carried out my request. "Well, you've met my parents. We've always been pretty close. They're both actively involved in multiple charities, so there are always events and functions to go to. Fundraisers, galas."

"That's so cool."

"My mom hails from London. Occasionally you'll hear her native accent slip in, or she'll call you 'love,'" he explained, and I smiled.

"Lilah and I were born two years apart and fought throughout most of our childhood. We became close before I left for college." He paused, taking a deep breath before continuing. "But it wasn't until after the incident with Robert that we became even closer—even if she tells you it's all me refusing to give her space. Which is likely to happen."

"She sounds great." I was even more excited to meet her now. A part of me was a little envious, though; Dad was the only real family I had left. I loved him dearly, and we had a close relationship—as far as fathers and daughters went. But Jensen had it all: both parents, a sister ...

When the city skyline came into view, I lifted my head and dropped my feet back to the floor as anticipation filled my body. "What hotel are we staying at?" I asked, slipping my shoes back on as we entered the city limits.

"The Peabody," he said.

My eyes widened as I abandoned tying my shoelaces

and gawked at him. "Jensen, that's not necessary. It's so expensive," I told him. While a part of me has always wanted to stay at the Peabody, I knew we would have been just as happy in a room for half the price. Though, I'd be lying if said I wasn't a little *more* excited now.

"Don't worry about it. It's covered," he assured me with a sly smirk.

"What does that even mean?" I asked as he navigated the busy rush hour streets of downtown Memphis. Pretending he didn't hear me, he remained silent as he continued to make his way to the hotel.

It had begun to rain as we pulled into the hotel's parking lot. The sky above was still light, the sun just starting to set somewhere behind the darkening clouds. Jensen put the car in park and hopped out, grabbing his jacket from the back seat and holding it over his head as he came to help me.

"I don't know why I don't have an umbrella," he said with a laugh as he flung my door open and held the jacket wide enough to shelter the both of us from the rain.

Laughing with him, I wrapped my left arm around his waist and laid my right on his stomach, gripping his damp T-shirt as we ran for the doors. "Probably because it's Tennessee, and this is rare this time of year," I teased.

Once inside the hotel's doors, Jensen removed the jacket from over us and put it on. "Okay, I'll go grab the bags. Why don't you stay here and then we'll go check in." After placing a sweet kiss on the tip of my nose, he braved the cold wind and rain to retrieve our belongings.

While he was gone, I looked around the main lobby. It was absolutely stunning. The furniture was antique, fully restored and would have looked out of place anywhere else. It was obvious that their decorative inspiration was the original architecture. What I liked most about it was the beautiful hand-carved details below the open balconies that looked down on the lobby.

I was so immersed in the beauty of the main lobby that I almost didn't realize Jensen had returned. His hair was soaked from the rain, which had apparently gone from bad to worse in a matter of minutes. When I held my hands out for my stuff, Jensen disregarded me playfully and ushered me toward the front desk.

"Good evening," the desk clerk, Carlos, greeted us with a smile. "What can I help you with tonight?"

"We have a reservation under Davis," Jensen replied.

Carlos's fingers moved swiftly over the keyboard in front of him before his eyebrows furrowed. "It seems we've got more than one reservation under that name."

Shaking his head, Jensen apologized. "Right. Sorry. It's Jensen Davis."

A few more key strikes and Carlos smiled. "There we are! Looks like I've got you on the ninth floor with a breathtaking view of the city. Your room has a king-sized bed and Jacuzzi tub as well as a forty-inch flat screen television and a fully stocked mini bar."

As Carlos rattled off the features to our room, my jaw dropped more and more; Jensen had really gone all out when booking our weekend getaway.

"Sounds great," Jensen said. "Do you need my credit card on file for any charges to the room?"

Carlos looked at his computer monitor a little closer before shaking his head. "Nope. It looks like a Mr. and Mrs. Henry Davis have taken care of the charges for the three rooms."

I looked up at Jensen with wide eyes. "Your parents are paying for our room? No, Jensen ... I want to pay for half. This is going to cost a fortune."

"My father wouldn't allow for it," Jensen told me with a grin as Carlos handed him two electronic key-cards, one of which he promptly handed to me.

"Room nine-oh-seven," Carlos told us. "The elevator is just through this main foyer and to your right; the stairs are through the door down the hall from them. There is a community pool farther down that hall; though we ask that if you decide to go swimming, to ask us for towels up here as opposed to using the room towels."

Man, this place had a lot of rules.

"The restaurant is fantastic and serves a continental breakfast in the mornings until eleven a.m. If you have any questions or need anything at all, please feel free to call down to the front desk, and we'll do our best to meet your needs."

"Thanks," Jensen said, nodding his head in the direction the elevators were. "Shall we?"

Smiling my own thanks to Carlos, I followed Jensen to the elevator. As we waited for the doors to open I found myself growing more and more excited about the weekend ahead. I'd never been away with a guy before. The elevator doors opened and my heart thumped excitedly as we stepped in. I hit the button for the ninth floor and stood next to Jensen.

"Are you sure I can't take anything?" I asked, glancing over to see he had my suitcase handle in his right hand, his own bag slung over his left shoulder and my dress' garment bag in that hand.

"Nope. It's fine. I promise," he assured me.

As the elevator continued to climb, my excitement level rose right along with it. When the doors opened, Jensen waited until I stepped out into the hall first before following me. We followed the shiny gold-colored signs that pointed us in the right direction before finding our room. I slid the keycard into the lock until I heard the electronic lock disengage, and pushed the door open.

Sliding my hand along the wall next to the door, I found the light switch and turned it on. All the air was sucked from my lungs as I took in the gorgeous room we'd be staying in. I slowly walked forward, just barely hearing the door close behind Jensen, and I made my way for the bed.

"This is incredible," I said breathlessly. The walls were painted a very pale blue with white trim and crown moldings. There were two windows along one wall with floor-to-ceiling dark brown curtains that were open, letting what little light was behind the dark clouds into the room. The bed was huge, dressed in fluffy white linens and pillows that took up half the bed. A sturdy, intricate looking wooden headboard with a matching dresser and nightstands completed the room.

I just started to turn to Jensen when I heard something hit the floor behind me and strong hands ensnared my waist, completing my rotation before throwing us down onto the bed. I squealed playfully on our descent, and just as I suspected the blanket was so delightfully downy that it nearly swallowed us both.

Once on the bed, Jensen's mouth found mine, his tongue tracing the line of my lips as his left leg found its way between my thighs. Basking in the feeling of finally being in his arms like this again, I complied more than eagerly. I moaned as I opened my mouth and our tongues met, slowly gliding against each other as my fingers wove into his soft hair. Jensen's left hand moved down my body, a tremor of desire tingling in its wake until he gripped my ass and rolled us over so I was straddling him.

A strong feeling of longing settled between my legs, begging for an overdue release, so I pushed my hips forward in an effort to quell the ache for his touch. Both of us moaned at the friction—even with the two layers of denim between us—and continued to writhe against each other. I slipped my hands between us and started to unbutton the shirt he was wearing as he continued to guide me on top of him, setting the speed. With his shirt now open, my fingers danced over the hard lines of his chest and abdomen until I found his belt and started to unbuckle it. I moved fast, really hoping he wouldn't stop me this time, and had it open, along with his pants button and fly, only seconds later.

Jensen followed my lead, moving his own hands to the hem of my shirt before raising it up my body. I sat up once he reached my shoulders and finished pulling my shirt off before tossing it behind me. Jensen eyed me hungrily—like he wanted to completely devour me—and my body shook with exhilaration.

"Should I ...?" Knowing what I was asking before I could voice the question, Jensen nodded emphatically. I removed myself from his waist and went over to my suitcase, opening it to find the box of condoms I made sure to put in there. My hands trembled as my nerves took over and I fumbled with the box, dropping it with a sharp hiss when I gave myself a paper cut on the tip of my forefinger. Once the stinging subsided, I picked up the box and finally got it open before tearing off one of the foil squares and returning to Jensen.

He remained on the bed, his pants still on but undone, and he smiled at me as I moved to take my place over him. The foil square was still secure in my right hand as I leaned forward to kiss him again, and his hands quickly unfastened my jeans before he slid his right in and teased me over my panties.

"Oh, God," I gasped into his mouth as he pressed down hard, the white-hot desire I felt ripping through my entire body almost blinding me.

Slowly, Jensen swooped his fingers inside and began stroking me—no barrier of denim or cotton anymore, just skin on skin. I could feel the pleasure beginning to swell and build rapidly with every firm pass he made between my thighs, and my legs started to tremble the closer I got. My lips stopped moving against his, opening slightly as I panted shallowly and moved my hips against his hand.

My abdomen tightened in preparation of my climax and I could feel myself just barely teetering along the edge of pure rapture when my right leg felt a dull tingle on the inside. Then, it stopped as suddenly as it started before repeating.

"No, no, no," Jensen chanted quietly against my mouth, his fingers stilling. I kissed him softly and pushed my hips back into his still hand when the vibrating sensation ceased again. He waited about thirty seconds, and when nothing happened he slowly started moving again. I should have known it wouldn't last, though. The vibrating started once more, forcing Jensen to pull his hand from between my legs.

I whimpered at the loss of his touch and watched sadly as he reached into his left pocket and pulled out his phone. Rolling his eyes he connected the call. "Hey, Mom."

That one greeting officially signaled the end of our make-out session. *Damn.* I made a move to hop off the bed before Jensen smirked and held me in place. "No, we're in the city. We just got to the room, actually. Why?" he asked. There was silence on his part, and I could barely hear his mother's muffled words. "Oh, is it already that late? Damn. Yeah, just let us get ready and we'll be right down ... Yeah, we'll see you in a few."

With a groan, Jensen hung up his phone and tossed it onto the bed before double-fisting his unruly hair. "Ugh!" he cried out in frustration—frustration I, too, understood.

"Hey," I managed to croak out. "It's okay. We have all weekend."

He dropped his hands to rest on my thighs, and I closed my eyes as a tiny ripple of lust seeped back into my veins. "It most definitely is not okay. She couldn't have waited just a little while longer?" He grumbled, squeezing my legs and injecting a fresh shot of arousal into me.

I had to be the stronger person and stop this before it began again, making us even later for the rehearsal dinner. Opening my eyes was probably mistake number one though, because Jensen looked simply ravenous as he stared at my bra-clad chest and his fingers continued to send wave after delicious wave of lust through me. "Baby, I assure you, when we return to the room tonight, I promise to let you do whatever you want to me. But first ..." I forced myself back down his body until I stood at the foot of the bed and smiled resolutely at him. "We need to get ready."

Jensen stood from the bed, smiling. "Okay."

Placing my hands on his bare chest, I stood on the tips of my toes and kissed him delicately. "To be continued."

REHEARSAL
Madison Landry

Because we didn't have a lot of time, Jensen and I didn't talk much as we quickly changed out of our travel clothes and into something a little more formal for dinner. I traded my jeans for a knee-length black pencil skirt and a sleeveless royal blue satin top. I had just sit down on the bed to slip my black, open-toed sling-backs on when the bathroom door opened and Jensen stepped out, his face down as he concentrated on tying his tie.

"You almost ready, babe?" he asked, looking up just as I stood. Stopping dead in his tracks, his eyes moved up the length of my body, almost as though he were drinking me in. "You look ..." His words trailed off as he abandoned his tie in favor of staring.

Feeling the warmth of my blush fill my cheeks, I closed the space between us and picked up the blue satin fabric hanging around his neck. "Hey," I said softly, bringing my eyes to his as I started to work on his tie. "We match."

"So we do," he responded, placing a chaste kiss on my forehead while running his hands up and down the length of my arms. It was moments like this where I wondered if maybe his feelings for me were changing, too.

Making one final adjustment to the Windsor knot I tied, I smiled up at him. "There you go. I can now take you out in public," I teased.

"You're lucky we're running short on time, Madison. Otherwise I'd be forced to make you pay—*repeatedly*—for that," he threatened ... not that it was really a threat given the seductive inflection to his tone.

"I may just hold you to that," I quipped, winking at him. "Come on. Let's go."

With one last deep breath, I nodded, threaded my fingers with his, and allowed him to lead me to the door. When we exited the room, my anxiety over meeting his family reappeared, and I clenched his hand a little tighter with every step. He squeezed back softly, probably trying to signal I should let go before I cut off all the blood flow to his fingers.

The elevator ride seemed much shorter than when we first took it to the ninth floor, and I hoped the hallway had somehow gotten longer. I just wanted a little more time before getting to the hotel restaurant where we were to meet for dinner. No such luck. We arrived at the restaurant within minutes, and I found myself panicking before completely freezing outside the closed doors.

They sounded harmless enough from where I stood. I could hear muffled conversations and laughter, but this did nothing to assuage my fears. Fearfully, I raised my eyes to a concerned-looking Jensen. "What if your sister doesn't like me?"

Smiling, his eyes showed an unbelievable amount of understanding. "First, she's going to love you. Second, I don't plan on leaving your side all night."

"Promise?" I asked, my voice shaky.

Leaning forward, he kissed me lightly. "I swear to you."

I leaned my forehead against his and sighed as my eyes fluttered closed. "Oral contracts are binding, right?"

Jensen chuckled as I opened my eyes and met his sparkling gaze before he kissed me once more. "Yes."

Feeling some of my confidence return, I took another deep breath and nodded. "Okay, let's do this."

With my hand still in his, Jensen opened the door and instantly my eardrums were assaulted by a scream quite possibly higher than Willow's. Yeah, I didn't think that was possible, either. When my eyes located the source of the sound, I was shocked and stunned by the woman's beauty. Clearly, she had to be Jensen's sister, but she didn't look anything like

I had imagined. Her hair was a copper-blond color, not brown like Jensen's. It was actually very similar to their father's hair, and her eyes were a pale blue-green. She was definitely taller than me, but still not quite as tall as Jensen.

"Jensen!" she cried across the room, dropping the hand of a very large, linebacker-looking dude. It was probably safe to assume that was Kyle. "I've missed you!" Enthusiastically, she hopped up and wrapped her arms around his neck, but because he was still holding my hand, he returned her embrace one-armed.

"Hey, Lilah-Bean. You excited for tomorrow?" he asked sweetly as she dropped back to the ground. It was then that I realized there was a high probability that she had maybe indulged in a few cocktails. Her cheeks were a subtle shade of pink, her eyes glassy, and she was smiling ... a lot.

"Yes! Mom and I have been busy all day decorating the banquet room upstairs!" she told him animatedly, her entire body vibrating with excitement. "Oh! I can't wait for you to see it!"

"Easy, Lilah," the man I suspected to be Kyle said as he came up next to her. He held out his hand for Jensen to shake and beamed from ear to ear. His wide smile made him look slightly less intimidating as his cheeks indented with two of the deepest dimples I had ever seen. "Jensen, it's good to see you again." His big brown eyes drifted to me and his smile seemed to widen. "And you must be Madison. We've heard so much about you. I'm Kyle Lewis." He moved his hand away from Jensen and held it out to me.

I looked up at Jensen, who seemed a bit embarrassed by Kyle's candid confession, and reached for the outstretched hand in front of me. As soon as it lay flat against Kyle's, he yanked me toward him and wrapped me in the tightest bear hug I'd ever experienced in my life, forcing me to relinquish my death-grip on Jensen's hand.

After setting me back down, he wrapped his arm around Lilah's waist and pulled her tightly to him. "And this little looker is my soon-to-be wife, Lilah."

I smiled at her, but it fell shortly after as she appeared to be sizing me up. It wasn't until that moment that I realized her loyalties probably still lay with Kaylie. True, they were loyalties built on omission and lies, but there was a foundation there that I just didn't have, nor could I compete with.

Even though she kind of terrified me, I persevered, really wanting her to like me. "Hi, I'm Madison. It's so great to finally meet you." I held out a slightly trembling hand to her, but she didn't take it right away. Instead, she looked from me to Jensen, and then back again before her cold expression warmed and she smiled brightly. Sighing in relief, I felt my smile return.

"We're so glad you could make it, Madison. Jensen's been talking about you non-stop. It's nice to see him happy again." I was certain she meant nothing by it, but the "again" she tacked on certainly stung.

Sensing something was wrong, Jensen placed his hand flat against the small of my back. "Why don't we go get a drink?" he suggested quietly, nodding toward the bar.

Kyle and Lilah quickly became wrapped up in each other and didn't mind our exit. Jensen ushered me toward the bar and leaned against it as we waited for the bartender. I looked around at the slowly filling room and recognized almost no one. Jensen's parents were clear across the restaurant. Dr. Davis wore her caramel-colored hair up in a sleek chignon, and was all smiles as she and her husband spoke with another couple around their age. Kyle's parents, maybe?

As I continued to appraise the room, I noticed it was almost whimsical. There were plants and trees everywhere, expertly manicured to perfection. Each table was covered with a white table linen, three pillared candles of varying heights in the center, while six Chiavari chairs surrounded them.

"Sorry about her. She was upset about the breakup. Plus, she's been drinking. She's always a tad more sensitive to mood swings with a little alcohol in her," Jensen explained, drawing my attention back to him.

"No, it's okay. Honestly, I figured as much. I get it," I assured him.

When the bartender finally approached us, Jensen leaned in and asked for two glasses of champagne as I surveyed the room again. Paranoia had set in since meeting Lilah, and I had to wonder if any of these women were Kaylie. There were a few that I could have seen Jensen with; tall and gorgeous, some blond, some brunette.

A champagne flute appeared in front of me as Jensen leaned up against my back and whispered in my ear. "She's not here. I honestly don't think she'll show tonight."

"I wasn't—" I cut myself off as I turned around and met Jensen's knowing eyes. "Okay, so maybe I was. Can you really blame me, though?"

Chuckling he leaned down and kissed me. "No, I suppose not. Come on," he said, looking over my head. "My parents are waving us over."

"One more drink first," I said, bringing my glass to my lips.

"One more? You haven't even—" I tipped the glass in a very unladylike fashion and downed it, hoping to drown my nerves after the way Lilah greeted me. "Okay then." Laughing as I polished off my drink, Jensen turned back to the bartender and asked for one more. When I had it in my possession, he replaced his hand on my lower back and led me toward the far end of the large restaurant where his parents stood amongst a sea of people.

"Jensen!" his mother exclaimed, hugging her son. "And Madison. Oh, you look stunning." She pulled me into her arms and held me, and I couldn't help but close my eyes and absorb this moment. I could feel a slight burn in my eyes as I fought back tears, and I clenched them tighter to keep them from falling. The way she embraced me was overwhelming emotionally; it was how a mother would hug.

My mother died when I was two, so I didn't remember much about her. There were a few things that came to me in flashes, but I can't really be sure if they're memories or dreams. Throughout my childhood, I was close with Willow's mom, and she always treated me like a daughter. But for some reason *this* just felt different.

Her hand came up and smoothed my hair, almost knowing what affect this had on me. Thankfully, it helped and I was able to gather my composure and release her. "Dr. Davis, it's great to see you again."

"Madison, please, call me Janet," she encouraged, slipping her arm through mine and ushering me away from Jensen. I panicked, but only briefly until I turned and saw him and his father flanking us as we made our way to a large nearby table with ten chairs around it. "How was your drive in?"

"Um, it was good. It seemed to go by quick enough," I said, taking my seat to her left as Jensen sat on my other side, and his dad on Janet's right.

"How is your room?" she asked, sipping her champagne.

"It's great, Mom. Thanks again. Let me know if I can offer anything toward it," Jensen said from behind me.

Janet dismissed his offer by waving her hand. "Nonsense, darling."

As we sat and spoke, I hadn't realized my second drink had disappeared, but Jensen made sure I had another waiting. I could feel the dull tingle in my arms and legs as the alcohol started to take effect, and I found myself a little more social, always contributing something to the conversation. Occasionally, I'd glance over at Jensen and he would be smiling from ear to ear at me before leaning in and pressing his lips to my temple. Of course, just like every time his lips touched any part of my body, my mind went elsewhere.

I turned my body to him and smiled lazily. "Hey," I whispered, placing my hand on his knee.

"Hello," he responded with a smile of his own. "How are you feeling?"

"Ummm," I contemplated for far too long—a sure indication that I was well on my way to drunksville. "Pretty good, actually." I was trying really hard to annunciate every syllable that tumbled out of my mouth. "Though ..." I curled my index finger to invite him closer. "I think I might be getting a little drunk."

He chuckled, kissing my cheek before the faint scruff on his face tickled my jaw. "Yes, love, I think you might be."

I gasped, slapping his chest and drawing the attention of everyone at the table. "Oops, sorry." I waited for everyone to go back to their conversations before I turned back to Jensen. I giggled at myself, causing him to eye me curiously.

"Baby?"

My giggling ceased, and I snapped my head up. "No, no, no, no," I repeated in a loud whisper, leaning into him and cradling his face. "I like love."

Jensen's brows furrowed slightly. "Yes, love is good ...?"

"No, silly. I like when you *call* me love," I elaborated, running my hand over his jaw.

"Oh yeah?"

"Mmm hmm. You called me that when you scared Dane away." I giggled again as I remembered that first kiss. Not because the kiss was funny, but because Jensen's towel fell off and he accidentally (I think) exposed himself to me ... again.

"You're adorable," he confessed. "Dinner will probably be served right away. That should help sober you just a little. I should have made sure you'd eaten better before we left home."

"Mmm," I hummed. "You're always taking such good care of me, baby."

"Well, somebody has to," he teased as the servers arrived with our food. "Come on, eat something."

Because Jensen's family were also vegetarians, there were vegan options offered along with the standard meats for all the other guests. The food was delicious—which shouldn't have shocked me considering the hotel we were staying at, and soon I felt slightly less drunk, but still pretty damn loopy. As we ate, I looked around the table at everyone we were dining with. Janet and Henry were right next to me. Lilah next to her father, Kyle to her right. The Lewises sat next to their son, and his groomsman, Gavin, beside them. My eyes then drifted to the one empty seat at the table, and I glared at it, knowing who it belonged to.

"How was your dinner?" Jensen asked, tossing his napkin on his plate.

Breaking out of my trance, I turned to him. "Really good. Yours?"

"Also good. I'm going to grab a glass of cognac. Can I grab you anything? Coffee? Water?" he offered sweetly.

"Actually, a glass of wine." He arched his eyebrow skeptically. "I'm fine. I feel better."

"All right," he conceded before standing. "I'll be back."

"Oh, I'm actually just going to run to the ladies' room. I'll be right back." He pulled my chair out for me as I stood and kissed my cheek before we parted ways. I had to walk slowly considering the heels I wore and my still-slight inebriation.

I stumbled slightly on the tile floor, laughing foolishly at myself as I reached the stall farthest from the door. After finishing up, I moved to the sink and washed my hands before checking my makeup. I quickly applied a little more lip-gloss, feeling content with my appearance, and moved for the door. I was barely two feet from the washrooms when a hand ensnared my bare arm and yanked me into a darkened area of the hall.

Familiar lips were on mine before I could cry out, and my body instantly softened in his arms. The minute my back met the wall, Jensen released his hold on me, letting his fingers ghost up my arms until he cupped my face in his hands. Hidden from view of everyone in the restaurant, we quickly got lost in the moment as we kissed secretly.

Even though I was fairly tipsy, I didn't miss that there was something else behind this kiss. While almost every kiss we shared was intense and passionate in its own way, there was a different kind of eagerness that accompanied his affections. It was almost as if he had something to prove. But what? Honestly, I was in no condition to refuse him; I was terribly needy and just a little drunk—which was a terrible combination in most cases.

My desire from earlier exploded deep within me, and I pushed my hips toward his, feeling his arousal. I smiled against his lips before sliding my hands down and grabbing his belt loops so I could pull him against me. Groaning and pressing forward, his fingers curled and dug into the back of my scalp before moving quickly down my back and roughly grabbing my ass. He wriggled his fingers and I could suddenly feel cool air on my thighs as my skirt climbed higher and higher. I was about two seconds from grabbing his tie and pulling him into the washroom so I could do unspeakable things to him when ...

"Jensen?"

FOILED AGAIN
Madison Landry

Jensen closed his eyes and clenched his jaw in frustration as he pressed his forehead to mine. His fingers loosened against my backside before he moved his hands up to press—almost possessively—against my lower back. Breathing heavily, I turned my head away from his, moving my hands from around him to readjust my skirt. When my eyes found the source of our interruption, I saw a new face to accompany the voice I didn't recognize. Her eyes were ice-blue and her long hair a deep shade of auburn, falling as straight as a pin down her back. There was something about the way she avoided looking at me that pushed me toward a conclusion that made my blood run cold.

"There you are," she said, her voice confident to match her graceful posture and movements. Dressed to the nines in a form-fitted red dress, she positively oozed the stereotypical blue-blooded upbringing I assumed she had experienced. Her eyes finally found me, and she smirked—not smiled … *smirked*. "Who's this?"

My head snapped back and forth between Jensen and the woman whose name I had yet to learn—but suspected—before I smiled and pushed away from Jensen's still possessive hold on me. As I approached her, I extended a hand and offered her a smile. It wasn't a smile of kindness; it was downright arrogant. "I'm Madison. Jensen's date for the wedding. And you are?"

She took my hand, her eyes sizing me up before glancing

at Jensen. "She's pretty, Jensen. Not really your type, though, if I remember correctly. I'm Kaylie. An old ... *friend* of Jensen's."

"Oh, so *you're* Kaylie," I said with mock-realization.

"Madi ..." Jensen began to warn, coming up behind me and gripping my wrist.

"Yes?" I turned to him coyly, quickly recognizing the spark of lust in his eyes.

"We should get back to the party." Clearly I had recognized wrong. "I have to talk to Kyle, and my mother was asking for you before I came to find you." I didn't miss the way he emphasized that his mother was requesting me; there was definitely some kind of contempt directed toward Kaylie with his words.

"Well, I'd hate to keep Janet waiting." Slipping my hand into his and lacing our fingers together, I pulled Jensen back toward the restaurant.

"Yes, well, it's been a pleasure," Kaylie said, attempting to save face, even though I could hear the venom and scorn practically dripping from her teeth.

I stopped, a wicked smile on my face as I turned so I could view her through my periphery. "No, the pleasure's *all mine*."

As soon as we were free of her and back in the restaurant, Jensen pulled me into his arms and kissed me softly, careful to keep it quick so we didn't get inappropriately feelsy in front of a room full of people. "The pleasure's all yours, huh?" he inquired.

With a giggle, I shrugged. "So, that was her?" Jensen nodded, his smile falling slightly. "She seems ... nice?"

Jensen laughed. "Yes, well, I suspect she wasn't expecting that you would know who she was. I think it threw her a little." He paused for a moment, gripping my hips a little tighter. "What do you say we get out of here?"

Drunk or not, there was still something bothering me about why he kissed me the way he did. "Okay," I said softly. "But first ... I have to know if the only reason you want to leave now is because she's suddenly shown up? You don't feel like you've got something to prove to me, do you? Because you don't. We're not even—"

Smiling genuinely he moved a stray lock of hair from my face before tucking it behind my ear. A trail of fire licked my skin in his fingers' wake, and I sighed at the sensation. "While it's true I came to find you after she showed up, I assure you that she is not the reason I want to take you back to our room ... To our bed."

It felt as though my heart skipped a beat, and my cheeks hurt when my smile widened. "Okay," I said, taking his hands in mine and walking backward, forcing him to follow me.

"There you two are!" Janet called out to my right. Collectively, Jensen and I quietly groaned before turning to her. "You're not leaving so soon, are you? You must come have another drink with us."

Jensen looked at me, clearly not wanting to disappoint his mother. "One more?"

"One more," I agreed.

One more quickly turned to two, which quickly turned into Kyle, Gavin, Jensen, and me doing shots of Patron at the bar after Lilah and her buddy Kaylie retired for the night. In the course of the evening, I went from sober and nervous, to drunk and social, to full and tipsy, to shot-doing-laughing-so-hard-my-abs-hurt wasted, and Jensen had to hold me upright.

"Come on, little Madi," Kyle pleaded, holding another shot of tequila out for me. "You know you want to ..."

My vision had blurred substantially in the hours since Jensen and I had been pulled back to the party, and I had long-since abandoned my heels to keep from falling on my ass—again. "I dunno," I said, looking back at Jensen whose cheeks were slightly red and his eyes glassy. "I think Jensen's pree'y drunk."

"You two are lightweights!" Kyle boomed, thrusting the shot out toward me.

"Y'know, Kyle ... I don't respon' well to peer pressure," I informed him, taking the shot glass and holding it up before downing it like the pro I had become in the last ... um ... six? My three drinking partners followed suit so that I wasn't drinking alone. Noble, weren't they? I loved them.

All the drinking allowed me to forget about what's-her-name. Earlier in the evening, I'd caught her staring at us, but I would just smile and wave, and she'd roll her eyes and turn away. Drunk me gave zero fucks. I liked her.

"And I'd probably be a little more inclined to believe that, Madikins, if you hadn't succumbed to the last three shots," Kyle countered, holding up four fingers to the bartender. It was weird, every time he did that, there were just as many full shot glasses that follo—ooooh, it was all starting to make sense in my drunken state. Motherfucker.

"Hey, don't you have to get married tomorrow? I'ss, like..." I looked around the room for a clock or something before grabbing Gavin's left arm and yanking his wrist toward me. I had to lean in real close to make the three watches merge into one that I could still barely read. "Midnight-thirty. You're gonna need your beauty sleep." He handed me another shot glass, and I grimaced.

"One more and I'll let Jensen carry you caveman style up to your room," Kyle bargained, shoving another shooter in my direction.

"Fine. But only 'cause you're the groomy." The three men laughed, and we all held up our glasses in a silent toast and drank in unison. "Okay, boys," I announced, waving my arm dramatically in the air. "I'm going to bed because I have a hot date with an incredibly energetic woman in the morning." Both Kyle and Gavin choked on the swigs of beer they had taken while Jensen chuckled at their reaction. "What? Oh! OH! You boys, always with your heads in the gutter! I don't know how anyone puts up with it."

"Guess that's why you've made this date, huh?" Gavin ribbed playfully.

I narrowed my eyes at him. "You are not very funny, Mr. Piers. Ha! Your last name is 'Piers'! That rhymes with 'beers'!"

"Okay, you," Jensen said, still laughing behind me. "Let's get you to bed before you get talked into a few more shots and we have to take you to the hospital."

"Oh, pffft!" I exclaimed, bending over to retrieve my

shoes. Apparently, I moved too fast because I lost my balance and almost fell over. Jensen was there to catch me before I fell — he always was. *My hero.*

I couldn't stop giggling as he helped me upright and grabbed my shoes for me. He wrapped his right arm around my waist and held me steadily as he turned us from the bar. "I'll see you boys in the morning. Kyle, have a good sleep."

"I'd say 'you too', but I don't think you two will be doing much sleeping," he shouted across the emptying restaurant.

I turned my head quickly, causing the room to spin a little, and I opened my mouth to say something that was probably going to be highly inappropriate. Before I could utter a word, Jensen swooped me into his arms, and I giggled as he carried me from the room.

"Why'd you do that?" I asked through my laughter as he set me down in front of the elevator doors.

"Because you've been pretty open about a lot of things, and I don't know that, of all the people you've met tonight, Kyle is the one you want knowing about what we do or don't do in our hotel room."

"Don't do?" I questioned. "Are you saying you don't want to?"

Jensen snickered. "Not at all. But in your state, I'm worried you might not be feeling up to it."

The elevator doors opened, and I flattened my hands on Jensen's chest and pushed him forward until I had him pinned against the mirrored wall at the back. "I'm feeling jus' fine," I assured him before tilting my head up and standing on the very tips of my toes so I could kiss him.

Thankfully, he met me halfway and our lips moved slowly together. "Good," he said, breaking away from our kiss.

The doors opened and Jensen took my hand, quickly pulling me behind him down the hall to our room. I had to laugh when he dropped the key-card a couple of times. Finally, he got the door open, and we rushed into the room. He threw my shoes off to the side somewhere before gathering me in his arms and pressing his lips to mine.

Needing him naked, I slipped my arms between us and

started to tug on his tie. Simultaneously, his hands moved to the zipper of my skirt and slid it down slowly, each soft tick sending a yummy tingle directly between my legs. My skirt fell, creating a fabric puddle around my ankles as I quickly pulled the undone tie from Jensen's neck and discarded it behind me.

My fingers were a little clumsy from all the alcohol, making it a little more difficult to unbutton his shirt, so I appreciated Jensen's assistance as he ripped it off his body while our lips remained locked. Buttons flew in various directions, and I moaned like that same porn star I channeled the first time he ever touched me intimately.

My body was on fire as he slipped his hands beneath the hem of my shirt and started to raise it. Not that I wanted to, but I parted our lips and lifted my arms so he could finish his task. With me now in nothing but my matching black lace lingerie set, Jensen groaned and pulled me back into his arms before rushing us to the bed.

We fell into the down comforter, laughing as I struggled to find my way on top of him. Jensen overpowered me though and rolled me onto my back so he was pressed solidly between my thighs. He used his brightly tattooed arm to hold his full weight off me, his muscles straining against the inked skin. Through his dress pants, I could feel his arousal, and I pushed against him shamelessly.

"You need to lose the pants," I told him brokenly between shallow breaths.

Clearly, he didn't need to be told twice before he stood up and followed my orders, returning to me in his boxer briefs. "Better?" he asked, brushing his nose against mine before trailing light, teasing kisses down my jaw and neck.

"For now," I whispered, arching my back as Jensen kissed along the line of my right shoulder, pulling my bra strap down at the same time.

His lips travelled down the column of my neck, then over my sternum and toward my right breast while he palmed the left. I moaned, and Jensen groaned, pushing his hips forward again. "God, Madi. I want to fuck you."

I bit my lower lip, twisting my fingers into his hair, and

moaned again. "Make it so, Number One," I quoted Picard with a giggle that soon escalated to a full-blown laugh.

I felt Jensen's lips twist up into a smile against my breast and he released a chuckle. "That shouldn't be as sexy as it is."

His mouth descended on my body again, forcing me to swallow my laughter as more moans and sighs fill the room and I writhed against him. Pressure quickly expanded in my abdomen, my muscles tightening, the longer he continued to kiss and tease me. And then the tension released ...

... in the form of a hiccup.

Both of us raised our heads, and our eyes connected. Jensen had a goofy grin on his face, and I was just annoyed because I could feel the next hiccup building. "It's okay," I told him. "They'll go away." I hiccupped again. "Seriously."

They didn't relent though, and it was very frustrating. There we were, finally about to round third and slide home — *heh heh heh*, *"slide."*— and I had the worst case of hiccups! "Dammit!" I cried out before sucking in a deep breath, hoping that would work.

"I'll go grab you a glass of water," Jensen offered, climbing off the bed as I nodded.

He disappeared into the bathroom, and I pushed my half-naked body up toward the head of the bed, sucking in another breath as I lay back on the huge pillows. I heard the tap in the bathroom run for a moment. I assumed Jensen was waiting for it to get cold. Closing my eyes, I exhaled before hiccupping again, and sucked in another deep breath, holding it for as long as possible and questioning our luck.

5

TEXT, INTERRUPTED

Madison Landry

"Madi?" I could tell he was whispering, yet his voice still felt like jackhammers assaulting my brain. "Baby, here drink this."

My eyes fluttered open, and I saw Jensen sitting on the edge of the bed next to me. The room was bathed in bright light, forcing me to squint against it. Jensen held out a glass of water in his right hand, and his left was closed into a fist around something, palm down. As my brain struggled to put two-and-two together, I noticed I was under the blankets and half of the pillows were stacked on the bench at the foot of the bed.

Things were getting weird.

I pushed myself up to a sitting position, noticing I was still in my bra and panties, but stopped to hold my pounding head. "Oh, shit. My head feels like it weighs a ton … Not to mention the construction workers in there pounding the shit out of my brain. How does a hangover come on this quick?"

Jensen looked at me strangely, his right eyebrow arched with confusion—I think. "Madi, baby, it's ten-thirty in the morning."

"Bullshit," I argued, taking the water and opening my other hand beneath the fist he still held out. He dropped two Advil into my palm. "No, that's not possible. I remember …" Holding the glass of cold water and the pills in my hands, I wracked my memory for the events that led us here. "We were at dinner. Drinking, eating … Kaylie showed up, and then we went back to the party where Kyle and Gavin invited us to have a few drinks with them. Then we came back here and we …" That was when everything got a little fuzzy.

Jensen chuckled. "Intended to have the best sex of your life when you got the hiccups."

Yup, it all came flooding back, and that was when I only half-realized the light in the room was coming from the window. "Right. And you went to get me water. And now you're back, and I feel like I've been hit by a train."

"Let the Advil kick in. You'll be right as rain soon." Jensen used his hand to guide the painkillers toward my mouth until I took them. "When I came back with your water, I found you had moved up on the bed. I sat next to you and told you I had your water, but you didn't respond. You'd passed out."

I. Was. An. Asshole.

"Oh, God!" I said, covering my mouth with my empty hand. "I'm sorry!"

Jensen dismissed my apology with a quick laugh and a headshake. "Don't be. It was probably best we waited until neither of us was quite that drunk."

"Hmm, so does that mean tonight's a no-go too?" I asked teasingly. "I mean, it's a wedding. More free drinks … And I don't know Kyle all that well, but I guarantee you he's going to convince you to drink with him. You're easily swayed."

"Me?" he cried in disbelief, laughing. "Little Miss 'I don't succumb to peer pressure'? You outdrank me!"

"Lightweight," I ribbed, setting the glass of water on the nightstand. "Okay, I should shower before I go see Willow. What time do you have to go get ready with Kyle? Do you have some time to join me? I could make up for last night."

Looking quite pained, Jensen shook his head. "As much as I would love to take you up on that offer, I'm already a little late getting over there." He reached into his pants pocket and held out his keys. "Take your dad's truck to the spa. I've already let Willow know you'd be a little late. I'll be back here at two to pick you up."

"Thanks. I guess you should go then? Leave me all alone… Naked and wet …?" I could see his resolve beginning to break as I toyed with him a little.

"Madison ..." His voice was low and gravelly; I loved when he sounded like that. He leaned in, his eyes dark and stormy as he tried for a kiss.

In an instant, my fingers were on his lips. "Sorry! I haven't brushed my teeth yet! Don't leave until I have?" Finding a burst of energy, I leapt off the bed and rushed to the bathroom to brush my teeth and wash my face.

Jensen was just outside the bathroom when I flung the door open, startling me slightly. "I figured I'd meet you by the door so you don't try to entice me beneath the covers with you, making us both later than we already are."

I wrapped my arms around his neck and pressed my near-naked body against his. "And you don't think I could entice you anywhere? That sounds like a challenge, Mr. Davis."

Jensen leaned forward and touched his lips to mine before pulling right back. It was clear I wasn't going to win this one. "I'll be here at two. Call if you get bored or just want to talk. I'll see you in a bit."

Once Jensen was gone, I had a quick shower before I had to go see Willow. I was excited to spend a little bit of time with her today. After pulling on a button-up plaid shirt and jeans, I slipped my shoes on and grabbed my wallet and the car keys before leaving the room.

It took me just over fifteen minutes to get to Willow's spa, and when I walked in I was greeted by a familiar face I hadn't seen in months. "Well, there she is!" Brandon said, smiling wide as he pulled me into his arms. "How the hell have you been, darlin'?"

"Good. How are things with you?" I asked when he released me. His blond hair had been cut short recently, hiding the fact it was naturally curly, and his deep blue eyes held mine.

"Can't complain." He took a minute to look at me carefully. "Gee, Madi, I don't know that I've ever seen you this happy before. It looks good on you! When do I get to meet him? Y'know, give my opinion and all." Having known Brandon almost as long as Willow, I knew that he just wanted to get a feel for Jensen.

Brandon had always been an excellent judge of character. It was probably one of the reasons he made such a great therapist; being able to sniff out the truth usually meant he was able to help his patients much more effectively. He had concerns about Dane early on, and I was ashamed to admit I brushed him off, stating he was being ridiculous.

Hindsight really is twenty-twenty.

"Um, I don't know. Maybe we could meet somewhere for dinner before we have to head home tomorrow night?" I suggested, really hoping that worked for them; I really wanted Brandon to like Jensen. He was the closest thing I had to a big brother, and he was always looking out for me like one.

"Madi!" Willow cried ecstatically, walking out of the back room with two champagne flutes in her hand. Mimosas, most likely.

"Hey, Will," I said, wrapping her in my arms when she reached me and set down our drinks. "How've you been?"

"We're good! Business has been picking up this last week, and we're very excited about it." Willow grabbed our drinks, handing me one before looping her arm through mine and leading me back toward the stylists' chairs. "Madison, this is Georgia. She's from Italy and does amazing work."

Georgia stood next to her station and smiled at me. Her long chestnut hair was straight and pulled behind her shoulders and off her face. "I'm actually from New York, but I was living in Italy for the last couple years," she said, correcting Willow.

"Still from Italy, Georgia" Willow countered playfully, pushing me down into the chair.

"So, what are we doing today? What are you wearing?" Georgia asked, running her fingers through my hair.

"It's a cobalt blue sheath dress," Willow interjected before I could open my mouth. "It's a low V in the back and a V-neckline."

"Sounds lovely. So, were you thinking something up and off your shoulders and back? Or did you want to leave it down?" Georgia asked, looking at me through the mirror.

"Um, well, what if we pulled it off to the side ... so it was off my back, but still down? Is that stupid?" I really had no idea what the hell I was talking about.

Georgia smiled and shook her head. "Not at all. In fact, I've got just the style. Trust me."

I nodded, and Georgia turned me away from the mirror and toward Willow and Brandon as she started on my hair. "Sorry I was a little late this morning."

Willow shook her head. "Don't worry about it. As soon as I answered the phone this morning, I knew what it was about. Jensen sounded pretty rough." Willow laughed. "You two must have had a crazy night. Any details you'd care to share?"

Brandon squirmed slightly in his chair, causing me to laugh. "Actually, no. It turns out I passed out trying to rid myself of the hiccups." Willow exploded into a fit of giggles, and Brandon laughed pretty heartily as well. While I wanted to grumble and bitch them out, I couldn't; the truth was it was pretty damn funny. "Yeah, awesome, right? Poor Jensen, though."

My phone started vibrating in my pocket just then. "Sorry, Georgia, my phone's vibrating. Just give me a sec?" Georgia stopped styling my hair while I fished my phone out. As soon as I had it in my hands, she started working again.

"It's Jensen," Willow announced to the room. "You can tell by that goofy-ass grin she gets. I witnessed it more times than I can count that weekend I stayed with them."

> Hey. Just wanted to let you know I miss you. How's it going?

Smiling, I quickly tapped out a message in return. He missed me? That seemed ... deeper than we'd agreed on.

> Just getting my hair tugged and pulled, but it should look amazing. Miss you too.

I set my phone on the station's tabletop and turned back to Willow. "Sorry."

"No worries. So, Brandon said you wanted to do dinner tomorrow night? I think that would be fun! You guys should stop by the loft. We'll order in."

I was just about to respond when my phone vibrated again. Before I could grab it, Willow snatched it up and clicked a few buttons, smiling like a Cheshire cat the entire time. Brandon looked over her shoulder and chuckled before she pushed one more button and set it in her lap.

"What are you two doing?"

"Nothing," they said in unison. Schemers.

Glaring at them, I held my hand out. "Give me my phone, or so help me, Willow …"

Huffing and rolling her eyes, Willow handed me the phone, and I flipped to my messages.

> Tugged and pulled? Sounds kind of kinky?

> I'll show you kinky later… ;)

My mouth gaped open. "Willow!"

I was just about to text him back and tell him that that was Willow when my phone vibrated again, and Willow started bouncing in her seat. I could feel my cheeks flaming as I opened the newest message.

> Oh really? I look forward to it.

What was I supposed to say to that? Should I confess that it was Willow who sent that? Ultimately, I decided to leave Willow's involvement out as I tapped out the next message.

> Me too. It was a shame you couldn't join me in the shower this morning …

I closed my eyes tightly and hit send.

"Aw, look! Madi's sexting!" Willow exclaimed.

I laughed and waited for Jensen's response.

> Madison! That wasn't me! Kyle got my phone after I sent the first message!

"Oh, God!" I cried, dropping my phone to my lap and covering my mouth.

"Must have been juicy …" Willow guessed, leaning forward to grab my phone.

I shook my head, still pressing my hands tightly to my mouth. "No, it wasn't." I dropped my arms. "You were sexting Kyle. And then *I* continued it!"

Willow and Brandon's laughter filled the salon, Georgia joining them as she continued to do my hair. My phone vibrated in my lap again, even though I had yet to answer Jensen's last message. Terrified, I picked it up and read his newest text.

> I'm sorry. I didn't realize he took it! And I most certainly didn't expect you to respond.

Smiling, I tapped out another quick response.

> Actually, Willow stole my phone and responded first. It wasn't until "you" enjoyed what she had to say that I figured I'd try it.

His reply didn't take long.

> Well, even though I didn't start it, I did enjoy it. However, maybe we should keep track of our phones at all times?

I laughed, causing Willow and Brandon's curiosity to grow.

> Agreed. I should go though. I'll see you soon.

> Can't wait.

I turned my phone off and tucked it under my right thigh so it wouldn't distract me any further before I turned back to Willow. As Georgia put the finishing touches on my hair before moving on to my makeup, Willow suggested several meal options for dinner the next night.

"All right," Georgia announced, swiveling my chair to face the mirror. "What do you think?"

I leaned forward and took in my newly made-over appearance. The makeup wasn't overdone, which was nice. She used gold and brown eye shadows to make my hazel eyes pop, yet kept everything very natural looking. But my hair ...

it was stunning. She had pulled it all into a low ponytail off to my right, letting it drape over my shoulder, keeping my back exposed. It was styled in large, shiny curls, and she had styled a bow out of a few strands of my own hair to conceal the elastic that held my hair in place.

"I love it, Georgia! Thank you so much!" I exclaimed, hopping out of the chair and hugging her. I wasn't usually a hugger, but what Georgia had done definitely deserved one.

"Madi, you look fantastic!" Willow said happily. "Georgia, you did an amazing job."

After paying and tipping Georgia generously, I looked at the time and noticed that I only had just over an hour before Jensen was going to come pick me up. "Well, I guess I should go. I'll see you guys tomorrow night, though. Thanks again for squeezing me in, Will."

I hugged Willow and Brandon before I left the spa and drove back to the hotel. Once I was back in our room, I grabbed my garment bag from the closet and unzipped it. I smiled before I started to unbutton my blouse to get changed. I was definitely excited to show him the dress finally. It had been hard to keep it from him as long as I had.

I quickly folded the clothes I stripped out of and placed them into my suitcase before changing into a pair of sexy blue panties and discarding my bra—the dress' back was so low that a bra just didn't work. I grabbed my body lotion and moisturized before pulling the dress on. The satin was smooth against my skin as I positioned it and zipped the back up. Standing on my tiptoes, I did one rotation in front of the full-length mirror outside the bathroom and beamed as I took in the color against my golden skin tone.

After I was done gawking at myself, I found the shoes I wore the night before. Jensen was going to lose it.

It wasn't long before I heard the lock disengage and the door creak open. "Madi?" Jensen's smooth voice called out from just around the corner from where I stood. Turning in the direction he would inevitably pass by to head to our bed, I cleared my throat to get his attention.

The look on his face when he saw me was priceless.

6
MY PAST
Jensen Davis

"So, Madi seems great," Kyle said as he handed me a beer from the large fridge his penthouse suite had. His parents and ours went together to get him and Lilah the penthouse for their wedding. And it was spectacular.

I had just left the hotel room Madison and I shared to come and do the last-minute bachelor thing that grooms did while they got ready. I didn't want to leave her; she had made a very tempting offer before I left, and I so desperately wanted to accept after our failed attempt last night. But I couldn't. Well, I guess I *could* have in that respect, but I wanted our first time to really mean something because *she* meant something.

Even if I tried to tell myself she didn't.

Over the last few weeks, I'd like to think that Madison and I had grown closer. Even though, we may have started off on the wrong foot, there was something about her that intrigued me. She was different than other women I had dated. Clearly, in a good way; along with being beautiful, she was smart, funny and she didn't seem to take shit from anyone. Not anymore, anyway.

The energy between us was immediate; I felt it when I helped her up after she fell off her mount that first day. Even though my good deed was met with contempt from her, there was something in her eyes that told me differently.

Days of treading carefully around her followed. There were moments where she would let her guard down, and I would catch a very brief glimpse of who she really was, but just as quickly, that wall slammed back into place. Normally, I had no trouble reading people, so it was frustrating to not have any insight into what had happened to make her so jaded.

The day she told me about her ex's violent outbursts and infidelity, I felt an immediate bond between us. It wasn't that I would wish the betrayal of a significant other on anyone, but there was something strangely cathartic about knowing I wasn't alone. That neither of us was. Things changed between us after that. While Madison still put her guard up every time I started to take a new brick down, we were quickly becoming friends.

The sting of what Kaylie did behind my back would always be with me. How could it not? She destroyed a part of me the day she told me she had "taken care" of the pregnancy—our child—I'd also just learned of. As if I wasn't going through enough, serving a three-year sentence for aggravated assault after giving Robert exactly what he deserved. I never thought I'd be whole again, to be honest.

At least, not until I met Madison.

I looked up at Kyle as he stared at me expectantly before nodding and taking a swig of my beer. "She is."

Great was an understatement. She was actually the best thing to ever happen to me.

"You guys have a good night last night?" Kyle asked, waggling his eyebrows. It was ridiculous of him to even ask, because I wasn't a "kiss and tell" kind of guy. Ever.

I smirked, arching an eyebrow as I took another drink of my beer, and then sat back in the chair.

Kyle rolled his eyes. "Pussy," he grumbled. "We're *dudes*! We *share*!"

"Uh," I started to counter. "That's *women* who share."

"Fuck. Whatever. Dudes share too. Especially when it's about sex." He smiled impishly. "In fact, Lilah—"

I grabbed the cushion behind me and chucked it across the room at him. "Shut your hole, Lewis. That's my baby sister. She might kill me, but I'll give you a black eye and break both your legs before the ceremony." I wouldn't really, just like he wouldn't really tell me whatever it was he was going to tell me—at least, I hoped he wouldn't.

"You nervous?" I asked, trying to change the subject before he got it out of me that I had yet to "seal the deal," as he would say.

Kyle brushed my question off with a wave of his hands, scrunching up his face. "Pssssh, nah! This is gonna be a cakewalk."

I laughed. "Glad to hear it. Listen, man, I just wanted to thank you for taking care of Lilah. I know I gave you a hard time in the beginning, but I've never seen her happier than when she's with you."

"Whoa," Kyle said, clapping his free hand on my right shoulder blade. "Enough with the heavy."

Shaking my head, I smiled before bringing my beer to my lips and taking a drink. "You're right. However, that said..." I lifted my eyes to Kyle's. "If you ever do anything to hurt her—and I mean *anything*—I will end you."

While I knew Kyle treasured Lilah and had nothing but respect for her, I needed to be sure that she would never be hurt by another man again. Kyle knew about Lilah's past— hell, he'd woken up to her screaming in the middle of the night just about as much as I had—and he'd always been there for her. He never pushed her beyond what she was ready for.

Kyle's laughter boomed throughout the room as he flopped down on the sofa and kicked his feet up on the coffee table. "Jensen, I think you're failing to see the dynamics in our relationship," he joked.

"I know, but it needed to be said."

"All right!" Gavin exclaimed, joining us from the bathroom and grabbing the beer he had left on the table before sitting in the chair at the small desk. "What are you two pansies talking about?"

"Jensen just threatened to kill me," Kyle summarized.

Kyle and Gavin soon became engrossed in a conversation about Lilah's other bridesmaid, Bethany. Gavin was apparently pretty adamant about hooking up with her. While they talked, I pulled out my phone and sent Madison a quick text to see how her morning was before I excused myself to use the washroom.

The truth was, I hated being apart from Madison. Now that we had nothing to hide anymore, I never wanted to be without her. Ever. I had been so nervous to open up to her about my past, thinking for sure she'd kick me out or push me away, but she was surprisingly okay with it at all once she'd processed it. I couldn't have asked for a more caring and understanding person.

Which was precisely why I felt bad for acting like such a shit this past week. I hadn't intended for it to happen, but thinking about seeing Kaylie again had me struggling with my demons. Knowing my past helped Madison understand my stress. Was it fair to her? Absolutely not. Every time she tried to take things further between us, I'd freak out and pull away; for no reason other than my own anxieties of seeing my ex again.

I didn't love Kaylie. How could I? Not after what she did. Madison knew that. But I also didn't hate her, because hate would mean that I still cared for her on some level. Kaylie was just dead to me in every way. A ghost of a memory.

A ghost that haunted me more and more as the days to my sister's wedding drew nearer, because seeing her would remind me of the lies I told my family.

When Kaylie told me what she had done, I decided to tell my family that she had a miscarriage. I lied because Kaylie was the only friend Lilah had after leaving her entire life behind and moving from Chicago to Houston. Not to mention, I couldn't admit to myself that I didn't see her actions coming. It was denial, plain and simple.

Letting Kaylie walk away from me was easier than I thought—and not just because I was restricted to the visitor's area of the prison. This alone should have tipped me off on how clearly it wasn't meant to be.

Starting over once I got out, however, was much more difficult. I had built a life for myself in Houston with Kaylie. Sure, I was working for her father, but I was his right-hand man and practically ran that company for him. I moved across the country within days of being released, pissing Kaylie off since I hadn't "discussed it with her first." After she broke off all lines of communication three years prior.

Yeah, try to figure that one out. She was the queen of double standards.

When I arrived back in Tennessee a few weeks after my release, I felt a multitude of things—loss, heartbreak, fear ... It was almost too much to bear. Because of my recent release, nobody wanted to hire me—especially considering why I'd been convicted in the first place. I had no doubts that Robert used every resource he had to have me blacklisted at any company I might have had a shot with.

My sister and Kyle took me in without hesitation, and just as I was about to give up on ever being employed by anyone again, my father stepped in. When he told me about how Wayne Landry might be looking for a new ranch hand, I really had no other options. The last name niggled at me, but I couldn't quite place where I knew it from.

Originally, I thought about protesting, saying I wasn't quite sure what I wanted to do, but then remembered the predicament I was in and why. When my father pointed out that the job might be one I would enjoy and would be outside the city, well it sounded even more appealing. It would be much easier to try and put my past behind me if I tried moving forward.

Before I met with Wayne, I decided to do a little research on the Landry ranch and found out that it was the most popular ranch in the area and they had just started a massive expansion project this past spring to up their rescue and rehabilitation efforts. Then, there was his daughter. Madison Landry.

That was where I knew that name.

Madison Landry was a professional rider who had pulled out of the Master's Cup in Spruce Meadows when her mount for the last two years had been injured during training. She was good, too, from what I could remember. It had been a while since I'd had the time to sit and watch a competition, so I decided to Google her. There were countless links to her rides, another that showed her winning silver in twenty-fourteen with her mount, Halley's Comet.

My favorite links though? Her interviews. Not only was she a good rider, she was eloquent and funny, as well as beautiful. Her big hazel eyes were expressive, twinkling whenever she laughed or smiled at something the interviewer said. There was something that drew me to her, even then.

When I met Wayne for coffee in town for our first sit-down, I brought up a few additional ideas that might also bring in a little more revenue. He really liked my idea of running summer camp programs — which he would implement the following summer — and he also seemed really perceptive to the idea of hosting smaller competitions for the students. There were always people looking to sponsor events like that for a good cause.

He knew a little about my past from what my father had told him. Well, that and the background check he admitted to running on me. He knew about what happened in Chicago that led to my arrest — not a lot of people did, at Lilah's request — and he knew why I moved back. He seemed to show a lot of empathy, and I wouldn't know until my second day on the ranch exactly why he understood what I was going through. His daughter had been in an abusive relationship too.

"Oh, shit! She responded!" Kyle exclaimed excitedly, piquing my curiosity.

When I rounded the corner my eyes went wide as they fell upon the two men sitting side-by-side on the couch, huddled over ... son of a bitch! My phone! I was across the room in a flash, ripping the phone from Kyle's grasp as he laughed with Gavin.

"What the hell are you two doing?!" I shouted as I started flipping through my received — *and sent* — messages. The first one I saw was Madison's final response about how I didn't join her in the shower.

I looked up from the phone to see Kyle and Gavin wiping tears of laughter from the outer corners of their eyes as they continued to howl. They had been dirty texting *my* girl? What was worse was she was texting back ... thinking it was *me*. It bothered me that they had tricked her. I quickly tapped out a message to tell her the truth, because I knew Kyle would bug her about it later; this way, at least she was prepared.

I hit send and scrolled through the messages leading up to that last one and found myself smiling at them; apparently Madison was good at dirty texting. After a few minutes, she still hadn't responded, so I sent her another message to make sure she was okay. If Kyle fucked this up for me, I'd kick his ass.

I laughed loudly when Madison told me it was actually Willow texting, which caught the attention of Kyle and Gavin who came barreling into the room as I sent another message back.

"What's so funny?" Kyle asked, peering over my shoulder.

Kyle groaned. "Aw, man! Well that just took all the fun right out of it!"

After telling Madison I'd see her soon, I put my phone in my pocket and returned my attention to Kyle. "All right, let's get you ready to get married."

We spent the next little while tidying up before getting into our tuxes. I had just finished buttoning my shirt and adjusting my tie when there was a knock on the door.

"I'll get it," I announced. We weren't expecting anyone, so I definitely hadn't been counting on Kaylie standing on the other side of the door.

I held the door firmly so she wouldn't be able to enter the room. "What the hell do you want?" I demanded, glowering at her.

"Lilah asked me to bring this to Kyle," she said, her tone confident and unwavering as her eyes glanced behind me.

I looked down into her hands and saw a small black box wrapped with a shiny, silver ribbon. "I'll make sure he gets it." I took it from her. When my fingers brushed her hands slightly, my stomach convulsed as I fought the urge to wretch. I wouldn't let her see how deeply her mere presence affected me. She would never get the satisfaction.

I turned from her, ready to slam the door in her face without another word when her bony fingers wrapped around my wrist, sending my flesh crawling all over my body. "Jensen, can we talk?"

"No," I told her shortly. "We have nothing to talk about." Her fingernails started to cut into my wrist as she refused to let go of me. I glanced down at her hand before I looked back up and glared daggers at her. "You'd be wise to remove that hand."

"Or what?"

I yanked my arm free and leaned down until our faces were inches apart. Beneath my skin, my blood boiled with rage, and all I could hear was the loud pounding of my pulse in my ears. "Here's how today is going to go, Kaylie. We'll walk down the aisle to appease *my* sister. We'll smile for photos, break apart, stand by her and Kyle and watch as they get married. After that, we'll walk down the aisle once more before we congregate outside so people can talk to Lilah and Kyle about how gorgeous the ceremony was—or whatever the *fuck* it is people talk about at these things. Then, you're going to leave me the fuck alone. Are we clear?"

"Is this about *her*?" she inquired in an arrogant tone, her eyes narrowing in a way that made me believe she saw this whole thing as one giant competition. The sight of her made me sick. Every time I looked at her, all I saw was the woman who tossed our future away like trash without discussing it with me first. All I smelled was her betrayal.

I shook my head in disbelief, my nose wrinkling in disgust as I assumed her intent. "You leave Madison out of this," I snarled venomously. "Just …" I sucked in a sharp, irritated breath and pinched the bridge of my nose. "Just go."

After I slammed the door shut, I fisted my shaking hand into my hair and tugged violently, fighting the urge to scream in frustration.

"Whoa, Jensen," Kyle said, joining me in the entry. "What's got you so tightly wound? Who was at the door?"

"Kaylie," I ground out through clenched teeth, the pain from the force of my bite starting to tingle throughout my mouth.

Whispered curse words were heard before Kyle spoke up again. "Shit, dude. I'm sorry."

I shook my head, trying to force myself to remember

why I was here—Kyle and Lilah's wedding. "It's fine. She was looking for you. Lilah wanted you to have this." I tossed the box at him before taking a deep breath. "I need to get some air. I'll be out on the balcony."

Once outside, I leaned on the railing and took a few cleansing breaths. Even after all these years apart, it pissed me off that Kaylie still had the ability to get under my skin. It was frustrating, and I hated myself for letting her affect me this way. I leaned over the railing, clasped my hands together, and pressed my forehead against them. Eventually my heart stopped pounding angrily, and when I looked up, the sun glared off the roof of a truck as it pulled into the lot below. Actually, not just *a* truck. Wayne's truck.

I watched as the truck stopped in its spot and the door opened before Madison's denim-clad legs appeared. From the fourteenth floor it was hard to really see her, and all I really got a glimpse of before she disappeared into the hotel was that her blond hair had been pulled off to the side. Knowing that Madison was back at the hotel calmed me, and I felt any and all stress from my interaction with Kaylie disappear.

When I went back into the room, Kyle was showing Gavin the new watch that Lilah had given him. The patio door closing caused them to look up, and Kyle grinned. "You all right?"

I nodded once, returning his smile before pointing to his watch. "Let's see."

Kyle thrust his arm out as I approached, smiling like a four-year-old on Christmas morning. "Pretty sweet, huh?"

After he showed off the features of his watch—also listing the benefits of said features—we finished getting him ready for his big day before I decided to head downstairs. Just as I was walking out the door, Kyle called out to me.

"Hey, can you take this to Lilah for me?"

I took a breath and instantly felt my anxiety spike. "Um, sure." Kyle beamed and handed me the small jewelry box. I put it in my pocket before I slipped out into the hall and took the private elevator down to the ninth floor.

The closer I got to our door, the more excited I grew. Madison had kept her dress under wraps since the day she bought it — initially because she didn't even know what she bought it for. But even after I asked her to the wedding, she refused to let me see it. It was really very mean ... okay, not really.

As the door came into view, I grabbed my wallet from my back pocket and found my key. The smile that formed on my lips was almost painful as I wondered what I would find on the other side. I slid the key into the slot and waited for the green light before pushing it open. I made it three steps into the room when I heard her throat clear.

7
MY PRESENT
Jensen Davis

I turned sharply and found her in the narrow hall between the entrance to our room and the bathroom. Her hands were on her waist, her right leg bent so her left hip popped out, and her bottom lip was pulled between her teeth. The bright blue fabric of her dress really made her already sparkling eyes pop, and it hugged every damn curve of her body before resting right above her knees. The low neckline had me struggling against the urge to rush the short distance between us and ravage her.

"Wow," I said breathlessly. "You look incredible."

Releasing her lip, she started to rotate slowly ... taunting me. "You think?"

Holy fuck. As she continued to turn counter-clockwise in front of me, I noticed how the dress tightly hugged her ass before I noticed the silver zipper that stood out against the color of the dress. It ran the *entire* length of her dress. From top to fucking bottom.

Speaking of zippers.

I found myself more than just a little turned on, and was suddenly straining uncomfortably against my pants. Swallowing thickly, my eyes moved up her body as she completed her turn, and I smiled as I took in the detailing of her hair. While the dress screamed *sexy vixen*, the small bow fashioned out of her own hair was both adorable and classy.

I closed the space between us and wrapped my arms around her waist before I lowered my face to hers and kissed her softly. "Stunning. That dress is just ... *Damn* ..."

"Well, *you* look pretty damn lickable yourself," she whispered seductively, poking my chest for emphasis.

My lips found hers again, kissing her greedily as my fingers curled into the bare flesh of her back above her dress. Slowly, I moved them down until I had the zipper between my fingers and started to lower it.

"Mmmf," she mumbled into the kiss before pulling away. "And just *what* do you think you're doing?"

I shrugged, smiling crookedly because I knew it made her melt. "We've got about twenty minutes before we have to go." I said, moving the zipper another couple of inches while my other hand moved down and cupped her perfect ass. Her eyes fluttered shut for a moment, and I lowered my face to her neck where I started trailing the tiniest of kisses down and over her shoulders.

She moaned when my mouth moved down her chest and kissed the swells of cleavage that her sexy-as-fuck dress exposed, and I pushed my hips forward so she could feel what it was she did to me every damn day. "Jensen," she whispered through a breathy sigh.

The sound of her calling out my name spurred me on, and my hand left her backside before hiking the skirt of her dress up. Her skin was so soft beneath my fingers as they ghosted over her creamy, white thigh to the juncture between her legs. My thumb had barely grazed the fabric of her panties when she flattened her hand against my chest and pushed me away. The way her chest heaved as she took in several deep breaths and licked her kiss-reddened lips had me aching for her touch.

I tried moving forward again, but she kept me at arm's length and shook her head. "Sorry, baby," she cooed, taking a chance by reaching behind her with both hands and re-zipping her dress. "We have to go."

My eyes widened as she sidestepped away from me and grabbed a small black purse, dropping her phone and some of that lip shit that tasted like sugar into it. "But—"

Her eyebrow arched as she turned her head and eyed me over her shoulder. "You coming?"

"That's not funny," I told her, narrowing my eyes playfully as I realized she was likely getting me back in some twisted way for all of the unwelcome interruptions in the past twenty-four hours. It wasn't fair—especially since none of them were entirely my fault.

With a giggle, she shrugged and pulled the door open. "It kind of is." Once we were in the hall, she turned to me. "Like you said yesterday, you don't want our first time being rushed. So, let's enjoy the evening and then later, I'll let you do whatever you want to me."

"*Whatever* I want?" I repeated, several ideas coming to mind—some of which I wondered if she would actually allow.

Her head snapped back as she suddenly realized that "whatever" really could mean *whatever*. "Uh … within reason," she clarified quickly, and I laughed before pulling her back into my arms and kissing the tip of her nose.

"Come on," I said, sliding my hands down until they reached hers. She threaded our fingers together before turning toward the elevator.

We rode in comfortable silence down to the banquet hall, my thumb tracing lazy back-and-forth patterns over the skin of her hand the entire time. When we walked out, we were lost in a sea of people from last night's dinner. Kyle and Gavin were already in the room, Kyle schmoozing with guests and Gavin hitting on Bethany. It appeared that she was interested, laughing at his jokes and all. Mom and Dad found us shortly after we entered and came over to talk.

"Oh, Madison!" my mother exclaimed elatedly. "You look exquisite. That color is just … Well, it's simply marvelous." I smiled as I watched my mom pull Madison into a warm embrace. It was then that I found myself trying to remember Mom ever showing that sort of affection for Kaylie. I couldn't.

"Janet's right, Madison," Dad spoke up with an affectionate smile as he pulled her into his arms and hugged her also. "You really do look beautiful. Jensen's going to have to fight off all the single men."

They were both aware that Madison and I weren't together, but they treated her like we were. I was completely taken aback by their instant connection with her. I knew my dad had never been close with Kaylie, but I figured it was just because he was my dad and that would have seemed inappropriate. But as I watched my parents with Madison in that moment—and even thought back to how engaged they were in getting to know her better the night before—I knew that there was a reason they treated her differently.

They never really liked Kaylie. They only tolerated her because she was what I *thought* I wanted.

But they saw something different in Madison. Something I tried not to see because she didn't want more. They saw how happy she made me, and in turn, that made them happy and willing to welcome her into our lives.

Momentarily lost in my silent revelation, I hadn't even noticed that the three of them were staring at me expectantly. My parents both had a small amount of concern in their expressions while Madison seemed to hold a glimmer of knowing in hers. Unable to contain the smile that grew on my face, I leaned forward and pressed a firm kiss to her temple.

"I'm sorry. I must have zoned out for a moment," I apologized. "What were we talking about?"

"We were just wondering how everything went this morning with Kyle. He seems to be pretty relaxed," Mom said, gesturing to Kyle as he stood in a sea of people somewhere behind me.

I nodded, pulling Madison even tighter to me as I continued to bask in my happiness. "Yeah, it was great for the most part." They all eyed me curiously. "Oh, no. Nothing to do with Kyle. Kaylie stopped by to drop off a gift from Lilah."

The eye-rolls exchanged between my parents weren't missed. The contempt they seemed to be harboring toward her almost mirrored my own—almost like maybe they knew something.

Madison wrapped one of her arms around my back and rested the other above my heart. "So, when does everything start?" That was the thing about Madison; she was always so in-tune with my feelings that as soon as she sensed I was feeling a little off, she was quick to try and take my mind off of whatever it was that bothered me. It was almost like she cared more than a friend would.

"Soon, actually," Dad announced after checking his watch. "I should go and see how Lilah is doing. Jensen, why don't you remind Kyle of the time so we can get started?"

Nodding my response, I looked down at Madison. "I'll see you soon," I told her, cradling her face with my right hand before kissing her softly.

I watched as my mother stepped forward happily, looping her arm through Madison's. "I'll keep her company, darling." Madison returned my mother's gesture by bending the arm my mother held and placing her other hand on my mom's. My heart swelled at seeing Madison accept them as much as they accepted her.

After finding Kyle and Gavin, we went to the back room where we were to meet the ladies—well, *one* lady ... and Kaylie. Kyle was trembling, his dark eyes conveying exactly how much he was anticipating marrying my sister. His complete and utter devotion to her only further assured me that she was in the best of hands.

As Gavin and Bethany struck up their previous conversation, I went off to find Lilah. I knocked on the door to her private sitting area three times before opening it a crack. "Lilah?" I stepped in and found myself completely speechless. There, in the middle of the room, was my baby sister. She was absolutely breathtaking in a strapless wedding gown, its skirt full of hundreds of roses made out of the same fabric as the dress. The smile on her face only made her more radiant.

"Oh, Lilah," I said softly, crossing the room and hugging her tightly. "You look so beautiful."

Laughing, she returned my embrace. "Don't hug me too tight! You'll wrinkle me." Once we ended our hug, she did a twirl. "Do you think he'll like it?"

"I've already told you, he's going to love it," Kaylie said from right behind me.

Because I was still looking down at Lilah, I kept the scowl I felt forcing its way to the surface hidden. "Kyle would love you in anything. In fact, he'd probably be okay if you walked down the aisle in a burlap sack," I teased, completely ignoring Kaylie's presence.

"Ew!" Lilah exclaimed with a laugh, punching my shoulder.

"Oh," I said, suddenly remembering the gift from Kyle in my pocket. "Kyle wanted me to give this to you."

I handed her the velvety box and watched as she opened it. Her eyes lit up and she gasped, reaching down to touch the delicate necklace. It had three square-cut diamonds set in white gold; I think they were meant to signify past, present, and future.

Lilah picked up the necklace and examined it. "It's so pretty."

I had just taken the necklace to help Lilah put it on when Kaylie stepped forward. "Let me help you," she said, reaching for it.

My head snapped toward her, and I smiled while simultaneously glaring. "I got it. *Thanks.*" Lilah lifted her long hair as I stepped behind her and helped her put the necklace on, the bottom stone resting on the edge of one of her exposed chest scars. "There you go," I told her.

Dad stepped forward and looked down at her with a wide smile. "It's time, sweetheart."

Lilah drew in a deep breath and nodded quickly as she looped her arm through his. While I could see every bit of her excitement, I suddenly found myself dreading what I was about to endure as we exited the small room and waited to go back into the main hall.

I slowly turned around to find Kaylie staring up at me with a smug look on her face. She held her hand out, expecting me to take it, but I shook my head and walked past her to exit the room. I could feel her irritation as she followed close behind me. Standing in front of Gavin and Bethany, I placed my hands on Kyle's shoulders and gave them a squeeze.

The doors opened, and he sucked in a deep breath before proceeding down the aisle. When he reached the middle of the aisle I felt Kaylie's fingers weasel their way into the crook of my elbow before we started to follow. My jaw clenched, and I fought the urge to rip my arm away—*for Lilah*. That was my mantra of the day. Every second she was touching me was another I wished I was being burned alive.

Until my eyes found *hers*.

There, in the front row with my mother, was Madison. She had turned in her seat to watch as everyone came down the aisle, and the smile on her face made me forget all about my current frustration. Offering her a quick wink, I smiled back and, once we reached the end of the aisle, I parted ways with Kaylie and stood next to Kyle. Within a minute, Gavin stood next to me, and the music fluidly morphed into the "Wedding March." All the guests stood, Madison giving me one more gorgeous smile, and then everyone turned to watch what they were all here to see.

Kyle faltered slightly upon seeing Lilah, and I smiled; I don't think he took a breath until she was by his side and holding his hand. I wanted to give them my undivided attention, but I couldn't help my wandering eye from finding Madison time and time again. It was uplifting to see that she was unable to tear her eyes from me, as well.

The ceremony was beautiful; Lilah cried when Kyle said his vows, even if he snuck in a few jokes that only the two of them truly understood. All the guests laughed as well, pretending they were in on their private memories.

With Kyle and Lilah declared husband and wife, we made our way back down the aisle, and I didn't miss the look on Madison's face when I felt Kaylie's fingers dig into my arm again. Her eyes narrowed in annoyance, but the way her lips pursed and twisted up to the right was almost ... *devious*.

What could she possibly have been thinking?

The wedding party gathered outside the hall so the guests could congratulate the newlyweds, and as soon as I was free from my obligations to Lilah, I yanked my arm free of Kaylie's grasp and put some space between us. She didn't seem overly thrilled by my actions, but I didn't really give a shit. Moments later, guests started filing out, saying hi to the wedding party before moving on to Lilah and Kyle.

Curiosity struck me when I caught sight of Madison standing off to the side, her cell phone out in front of her as she snapped a picture and smiled at the screen. What the hell was she up to? Her eyes found mine, and she waved before startling slightly and returning to her phone. Was she texting?

Her eyes brightened, and she pulled her full bottom lip between her teeth as she slipped her phone back into her tiny purse and joined the masses in talking to the bride and groom. She approached Gavin first, and I couldn't help the jealousy that overcame me when they hugged. Thankfully their embrace lasted all of two seconds before she moved to his left and shook Bethany's hand.

"Hey," she whispered, taking my hands in hers when she stood in front of me. "Have I told you yet just how amazing you look?"

Beaming, I leaned my face down and brushed my lips faintly over hers. "No, actually. You have failed to adequately fluff my ego today. Shame on you."

She gripped the lapels of my tux jacket and stood even taller on the tips of her toes than her heels made her before planting her lips firmly against mine for a second. "Well, I apologize. Let me assure you that you are the most handsome man here." A throat cleared to my left, and I rolled my eyes, but Madison took it in stride and looked to Kaylie while smirking.

Reluctantly, I let go of Madison's hands as she continued, keeping the line moving, and stood in front of Kaylie. Her eyes moved up and down, assessing Kaylie's strapless purple dress before she spoke. "You look ... nice." Then her gaze shifted to Lilah and she held out her hands and smiled warmly. "And, Lilah! Oh, wow! You look absolutely radiant," she beamed as Lilah took her hands in hers.

Seeing Lilah smile at Madison as she gushed over her appearance was a nice change from how she initially greeted her last night. "Your dress ..." Madison continued. "Well, it's just absolutely stunning! It's from Monique Lhuillier's new spring line, isn't it?"

Monique who? I wasn't sure how Madison knew about whatever-the-hell she was talking about, but Lilah's eyes absolutely lit up, and she nodded emphatically. Madison cast me a sideways glance—complete with a slight smirk of triumph, and it was then that I realized she may have had a little outside help from Willow. She was trying to win Lilah over—and it was working.

"It is! When I was looking at bridal magazines, I saw this one and I just *had* to have it!"

"Well, it's gorgeous. And so are you. You're the most beautiful bride I've seen." Lilah and Madison talked about fashion for a few more minutes—well, Lilah talked, Madison mostly smiled and nodded, agreeing in all the right places and instantly dazzling Lilah. It was just one more reason for me to think that Madison was absolutely amazing.

Kyle smiled at her as she approached. "Well, I was relieved to hear you weren't quite as hung over as I expected," he teased, pulling her to his chest. The waves of animosity rolling off Kaylie were enough to chill a person to the bone. She was not impressed by how easily Madison had worked her way into my family's hearts, and it pleased me even more.

Once all the guests had their chance to talk with the bride and groom, Devon, the photographer, came over and spoke to Lilah and Kyle before ushering us all outside for a few pictures. Madison was more than willing to tag along, so I wrapped my arm around her, tucked her into my side, and we walked.

"Okay, so why don't we get the bridal party there in front of the garden?" the photographer suggested as he took a few steps back and eyed the area for his shot. "We'll get the bride and groom in the middle and the bridesmaids and groomsmen to either of their sides.

As we all moved into position, I saw Madison appear to Devon's right and cock her head to the side. "Just ... one sec," she said before rushing forward to stand in front of Lilah. She knelt down and fixed the skirt of her dress before standing up and combing away a few stray hairs. "There. Perfect." She took a few steps back and tilted her head again, seeing something that she didn't quite like. "Y'know what? I think the girls are too close to you. Your dress is so full on the bottom that I think they should maybe shift to the left a few inches.

The guys should mirror them ... for symmetry."

"She's right," the photographer announced. "What's your name?"

Madison moved to stand next to him, smirking slyly at me before turning to face him. "Madi. I took a few photography courses in high school, and I dabble as a hobby."

"Excellent. Well, thank you."

"Anytime." That glint in her eye had returned, and I knew she was up to something more. What, though? I had no idea.

The photographer snapped a few pictures of the group before Madison suggested some other poses where the bridesmaids and groomsmen were spread out, standing away from the bride and groom. When the photographer seemed pleased with those shots, Madison leaned in and whispered something to him. He smiled and nodded before coming over to us. "Okay, we're going to do a few shots of the bride with her family, the groom with his, and then bring the two families together."

"What about the rest of us?" Kaylie asked, seeming a little desperate to be in the pictures.

Madison stepped forward and adjusted my tie for me before addressing Kaylie without looking at her. "Oh, I think you're finished." I held back a shocked laugh. "We're going to focus on Lilah and Kyle now."

"We?" Kaylie repeated snidely.

I glanced down to find Madison looking up into my eyes and winking. "What are you doing?" I whispered, still not one hundred percent certain I knew what she was scheming.

"Just making Lilah's day one she'll want to remember. No regrets," she replied softly, running her hand along my jaw. "The truth always has a way of coming out, and I don't think she'd be so forgiving if she knew. In fact, she'd probably regret involving her in what should be the happiest day of her life." My body froze as I stared in awe at the woman standing before me. "If it were *me* and I found out something like that, I'd hate to see the constant reminders of a friendship based on lies in our wedding photos."

Before I could question the "our" she used, suddenly

wondering if it meant she wanted more, she continued. "In fact," she said softly. "I think you should consider telling her. Not today. But soon, before she finds out some other way." A small smile graced her face. "Just think about it. The longer you keep it from her, the more you risk her being upset with you, too."

"Madi!" I heard my mom call out. "Why don't you join us in this photo?"

The smile fell from her face and her jaw dropped in shock. "Wha—Janet, no. This is a family picture. I couldn't possib—"

Cutting her off before she could finish, my mom rushed over and grabbed us both by the hands, pulling us over to where Lilah, Kyle, and Dad stood. "Madison, you're with Jensen. You're a part of this family now," she expressed as we walked past Kaylie. They knew what Madison and I had was casual—they were very open-minded—so I could only assume they were needling Kaylie.

A frustrated growl escaped my ex as soon as the words reached her. When I turned to glance at Kaylie, her face was almost purple.

"Get closer, Madison!" Lilah exclaimed, tugging her closer to her side. I moved in to stand behind Madison and wrapped my arms around her waist before placing a lingering kiss on the top of her head. That was the last straw for Kaylie, as it would appear, because she let out a loud huff and stormed off toward the hotel.

"Okay, everyone," the photographer said, putting the camera up to his face. "Smile!"

8
MY FUTURE
Jensen Davis

"Here you go," I said, coming up behind Madison as she sat at our table in the hall. I set her third glass of wine down in front of her. Dinner had just ended, and the DJ was gearing up for Kyle and Lilah's first dance as a married couple.

"Thanks," she whispered, shifting toward me as I sat next to her.

"Are you having a good time?" I asked, really hoping that Kaylie being here wasn't upsetting her. She *seemed* to be doing okay, but Madison always had a way of guarding herself and pretending everything was fine.

She nodded, her eyes shining with enthusiasm. "I really am. I thought things would be awkward, but I think everything is going well."

"My family seems quite taken with you," I said, unable to contain my smile.

She nodded. "They're great. I'm glad Lilah seems at ease around me now."

"Speaking of ..." I said, still curious as to how that happened, and cocked an eyebrow inquisitively. "Monique Lhullier?"

Pulling her bottom lip between her teeth, she blushed furiously. "I took a picture and sent it to Willow."

"I knew it."

She laughed, bringing her glass to her lips and taking a swill of it. Once she swallowed she continued. "I was willing to try anything, short of selling my soul, to get your sister to like me. And the dress looked like the perfect icebreaker. Willow was beyond jealous that I was seeing a Monique Lhullier dress in person. She's pretty nuts."

"Well, Lilah seemed receptive to your efforts, so I'd say your idea was genius," I complimented.

Taking another sip of her wine, she shrugged. "I don't know why you're so surprised," she said, feigning pompousness before erupting into a giggle.

Laughing with her, I leaned forward and kissed her softly before capturing her gaze and pulling back. "So, are you going to dance with me tonight?"

"I told you I don't dance," she replied seriously.

Arching an eyebrow, I glanced down at her wine and challenged her admission. "Unless you're drunk," I countered, reminding her of her words from a week ago when I caught her dancing with abandon in the living room. I knew she was already starting to feel the effects of the wine; she wasn't drunk, but the blush that filled her cheeks would indicate she was well on her way.

"Hmm, good point ... However," she whispered, leaning in extra close, her lips brushing my right ear lobe. "If I were to get *that* drunk, there's a good chance I won't be up for whatever it is you have planned for later."

"Well, in that case," I said, pulling back and taking her glass from her hands before drinking the rest of her wine.

Her eyes widened, watching in disbelief as I polished it off and set the empty glass on the table. She had just opened her mouth to say something that was sure to be snarky—it was one of the things I loved most about her—but was interrupted by the booming voice of the DJ.

"Ladies and gentlemen, I'd like to introduce you to ... Mr. and Mrs. Kyle and Lilah Lewis!" The room exploded in applause and everyone stood as they watched Lilah and Kyle walk back into the room for their first dance. A soft melody floated through the room as Kyle pulled Lilah into his arms, and they were both beaming from ear to ear during their entire first dance.

Across the room, I spotted Kaylie on the edge of the dance floor. She raised her champagne flute in a silent salute to me, and I rolled my eyes, bringing my attention back to Madison. She watched, completely enraptured, as Kyle spun Lilah around on the dance floor and sighed as she leaned her head on my shoulder.

Cameras flashed all around the room as the song came to a close and Kyle cradled Lilah's face and kissed her tenderly.

"Okay, ladies and gents," the DJ announced as the song slowly morphed into one I recognized. "The bride and groom would like you all to join them on the dance floor before we kick this party off right!"

I kissed Madison atop her head as it remained on my shoulder. "Dance with me?"

She giggled softly. "I told you, I can't dance ... especially in these shoes. And you drank all my wine."

A slow song started playing, and Madison looked a little wistful as she listened to the lyrics. Shifting slightly in my seat, she was forced to raise her head. "Dance with me?" I repeated, dropping to my knees before her. Her eyes fluttered, and she gasped when my hands found the back of her right calf and trailed down to her ankle. I lifted her foot off the floor and slipped her sexy heel off before moving over to the other and doing the same thing.

"Jensen, what are you—"

Cutting her off before she could finish her question, I repeated, "Dance with me." That time it wasn't a question. I put her shoes under our table, took her hands in mine and stood up. Even though she still hadn't given me an answer, I pulled her to her feet and walked backward to the dance floor, forcing her to come with me.

"I can't—"

Before she told me again that she couldn't dance, I wrapped my right arm around her waist and took her right hand in my left. Then I lifted her slightly until she stood on the toes of my black shoes, and slowly, I began to move my feet back and forth, dancing softly to the rhythm of the music.

"Well, what do you know," I said playfully, pulling our joined hands between us and placing them over my heart. "You *can* dance."

"Who knew," she quipped back, tightening her grip on

my shoulder as I flattened her hand between mine and my chest. "Thank you for asking me to come with you. I'm having a great time. Even if we have yet to ..."

Her words trailed off as the music played on around us, and we continued to sway simply within a couple feet of the wooden dance floor. "I'm glad you're having a good time." I told her, smiling and pulling her body impossibly closer to mine.

As the music began to fade, I lowered my face to hers at the same time she raised herself up onto the tips of her toes, and our lips united in a tender kiss. There was something about this kiss that seemed different than all the others. I couldn't quite place it, but a shiver worked its way down my spine when Madison's left hand found its way to the nape of my neck, teasing and twirling the short hair there.

"Okay!" the DJ's voice said loudly through the sound system, pulling Madison and me from our own little world. Loud dance beats filled the room, and hoots and hollers could be heard over the bass that vibrated through the walls and floorboards beneath us. "It's time to kick this party up a notch!"

"How about another drink?" I asked loud enough for Madison to hear me. She nodded, stepping down off my feet and taking my hand in hers as I led her back to our table. "Okay, you stay here and I'll be right back. Wine?"

"That would be great," she replied, her eyes following me as I backed away and made my way for the bar.

The line was longer than I expected and was moving pretty slowly since there was only one bartender. As I waited, my eyes scanned the room to find Kyle and Lilah in the middle of the dance floor with Gavin and Bethany, dancing up a storm. Suddenly, they all looked in the same direction before Lilah pulled Kyle toward her and pointed across the room—at Madison. Kyle grinned from ear to ear and ran across the dance floor to where I left Madison and grabbed her hands.

Smiling, she shook her head furiously, and her pink cheeks deepened in hue as she tried to refuse him. She even pointed to me standing here as if trying to tell Kyle I would be back soon. If I knew Kyle, though, he would have none of it. Eventually, he got her out there.

She was still barefoot as Lilah took one of her hands and started dancing with her. They both started laughing and hopping around to the beat of the music. There was only one other time I ever saw Madison dance like that—and she didn't know I was watching at first.

Finally, I made it to the front of the line and ordered myself a beer as well as Madison's wine before making my way back to the table. On my way, I passed the DJ's table, and I leaned in to ask for a very specific request. He looked at me strangely for a minute, but nodded once he located the song I wanted him to play. After thanking him, I found my seat and sipped my beer while I watched Madison move on the dance floor.

"Hmmm," a familiar voice hummed behind me.

I didn't have to turn around to know who it was; the hairs standing on the back of my neck from her ice-cold energy was more than enough of an indication. "What do you want?" I demanded snidely, refusing to acknowledge her with a glance. Instead, I focused on Madison.

"Ever since last night, I can't help but wonder what it is you see in her," Kaylie commented, pulling her chair closer to me until I could see her through my periphery.

"I don't see how my relationship concerns you," I snarled, pulling my beer to my lips again and smiling when Madison turned around and saw me. I knew she saw Kaylie the minute her eyes narrowed, but she quickly let the emotion pass.

"Jensen we both know that what you have with her can't possibly be real." Kaylie laughed, and I found myself biting my tongue before I said something to her that I knew would cause a scene. "I mean, her accent is charming and all, but ... look at her."

What was it she expected me to see? Because all I saw was my girl having the time of her life ... with my family.

I paused for half a second when I realized I'd considered her "my girl." It was the first time I'd thought of her as mine. What we were doing—or planned to do was just supposed to be casual. When did that change?

"The two of you come from different worlds, Jensen. You have nothing in common. Before your little stint in prison, you'd been places and done things that others could only dream of doing and she's ... Well, she's so ... *unrefined*." She pronounced the word as though it left a sour taste on her tongue, and I felt my earlier rage return and boil like lava under my skin.

I tried to keep my wits about me, taking another drink of my beer before setting it down and smirking at her. "Well, Kaylie ..." I stood up fluidly and arched an eyebrow at her. "We can't all be born with sticks up our asses, now can we?"

Satisfied with Kaylie's jaw dropping to the floor at my retort, I turned and walked away from my past to go find Madison. My present, and hopefully, if my revelation didn't spook her, my *future*.

Apparently my timing was impeccable, because as soon as I stepped onto the dance floor, the music changed into the request I made. I smiled wickedly, waiting to see Madison's reaction to the song. She didn't disappoint. As soon as she recognized it, she quickly turned to find me standing less than a foot away from her.

She closed the gap between us and smirked. "I don't suppose this is a coincidence?" she asked, arching an eyebrow at me in question as "I Wanna Dance With Somebody" began. It took me back to the night of our first official date, and I grinned at her.

"Not entirely," I said to her in response, chuckling as I moved another small step toward her. "Dance with me?"

Madison shook her head sadly and shrugged, taking a step back and eyeing me coyly. "I'm sorry, but I can't."

With rosy cheeks and eyes alight with glee, she just held her finger up toward the roof as the chorus played and giggled. "Because I wanna dance with somebody who loves me," she said, cockily paraphrasing the song.

In less than a second, I had closed the gap between us, my heart pounding in my chest so frantically I thought I might have to be revived if I didn't get it under control. Her breath shuddered as I wrapped my arms around her and lowered my face to hers. Not sure what to expect, her eyes drifted from mine to my mouth as her tongue peeked out to moisten her bottom lip.

Brushing the tip of her nose with mine, I moved and placed a feather-light kiss upon her lips before capturing her stunning eyes again. "What if you would be?" I whispered.

She inhaled sharply, her eyes glistening slightly as they darted between mine in disbelief, and she pulled back. "Wha- what?"

"I love you, Madison."

She didn't return the sentiment, her wide hazel eyes flitting between mine. I'd spooked her. I considered trying to take it back, but then realized I didn't want to.

"I know we agreed that this would be casual, and I tried to keep it from happening, but, Madi—"

She didn't let me finish, pressing her lips to mine firmly. Once my own shock lifted, I moved a hand up to cradle her face, and when my thumb brushed her cheek, I felt a tear. I brushed it away as I pulled my lips from hers, and she moved her face into my hand, placing a kiss on my palm before bringing her eyes back to me. "I love you too, Jensen."

In a moment that can only be described as the most perfect one I'd ever experienced, our lips collided passionately, and the rest of the world fell away. My arms moved down her body to encircle her waist, and I lifted her until our faces were level.

Madison pulled her face back, panting lightly. "Do you think anyone would notice if we disappeared?"

"I don't know that I'll care if they do," I told her honestly, setting her back on her feet and taking her hand in mine.

We made a quick stop at the table where Madison scooped up her purse, and I snatched her shoes before we rushed out of the room, the anticipation for what would finally happen tonight fuelling us. Out in the hall, guests had gathered, probably in an effort to escape the loud music so they could talk at a comfortable level. Thankfully no one tried to stop us as we continued on our way to the elevator.

Madison's hand trembled in mine as we waited for the doors to open, but when I looked down at her, I was met with nothing but a wide smile and pink cheeks. A low *ding* sounded through the hall, and I gave Madison's hand a light squeeze as the doors opened. It was unfortunate that there were several hotel patrons inside; I was quite looking forward to ravishing Madison—just a little. Instead, I controlled my primal urges and guided her inside the elevator, positioning us back against the wall.

"Nine, please?" I requested since there were several people blocking the buttons.

It didn't escape my notice, or surprise me when a few of the men's eyes followed her. In an act that proved to be a touch possessive, I released her hand and wrapped my arm around her waist, securely tucking her into my side. Thankfully she didn't seem to mind as she returned the gesture in kind and wrapped her arm around me. Sharp, pleasurable jolts of energy shot through me as she started moving her hand down my back before slipping it up under my suit jacket. Her fingers trailed along the waist of my pants before trailing lazily up my spine, and soon my hand was mirroring hers, occasionally tickling the bare skin above her dress before tracing the zipper down over her ass.

The doors opened on the sixth floor, and a few people stepped off. From beside me, Madison groaned, her hand fisting the back of my shirt in what I suspected was frustration. I leaned down and kissed the top of her head. "Three more floors," I whispered softly, and ran my hand over her back lightly in hopes of calming her.

There were no other stops between six and nine, so when the doors opened on our floor, I ushered her through, keeping my hand on the curve between her lower back and ass. With her shoes clutched in one hand, I kept my other on her as we rushed through the hall to our room. When our door came into view, Madison opened the clasp on her small purse and pulled out the key to unlock the door. Together, we rushed into the room, the passion now blanketing us entirely as I tossed her shoes to the floor and forced the door closed faster than it would have closed on its own.

ID
WORTH THE WAIT
Madison Landry

The sound of the door closing and the privacy lock sliding into place made my body vibrate with anticipation. A fresh surge of adrenaline was pumping through my veins, mixing with the three glasses of wine I'd had with dinner; I couldn't stop replaying the scene downstairs over and over in my mind. It was ... perfect.

He told me he loved me, and I never even saw it coming. I thought he was only in this for the casual sex we still hadn't had. I couldn't pinpoint when exactly he flipped, but I was so glad he did.

Jensen turned toward me, and the look in his eyes was intense ... wild ... *ravenous*. I shivered, my mind simply buzzing with the possibilities of what was to come. Without turning from him, I dropped my purse to the table behind me, and within seconds, our bodies collided, our mouths uniting with fervor as Jensen's strong hands grasped desperately at my back.

Moaning, my lips parted slightly, and I twisted my fingers into Jensen's hair. His arms tightened around me, hands flattening and moving up until his fingers curled into the bare flesh above my dress. When his short nails bit into my skin, I whimpered—loudly—and started shifting my body in an effort to feel him ... *all* of him.

"Oh God, Madi," he murmured against my still moving lips, walking forward until he had me sandwiched between his hard body and the wall. "*Fuck*. I want you so badly."

I groaned softly in response to his words of desire as they pulsed through my body, settling between my legs. I couldn't wait to finally make love to him, but first ...

My hands moved down his body slowly, stopping once I reached the waist of his pants and moving along until I reached his hips. From there, I slid my hands down and into his pockets before finding what I was looking for and removing it.

Jensen pulled his face back from mine and looked down as I held my hands between us. "What the hell are you doing?"

Taking several labored breaths, I pressed a few buttons on the touch screen of his phone and shut it off before tossing it on the table with my purse. "Eliminating any and all distractions," I told him breathlessly.

He hummed appreciatively. "That's my girl."

My knees trembled; it was probably a good thing he still had me pressed between his body and the wall. "I am, you know," I whispered. "Yours."

The elation in his eyes was contagious, and his smile was wider than I'd ever seen it. I tilted my face up to kiss him at the same moment he whispered, "I love you so much."

Our lips pressed together, this time moving slowly—passionately—as his hands ensnared my hips and pulled them toward him. Feeling how I affected him only excited me more, and my body shook with anticipation.

At a painfully slow pace, his hands moved up my body until his fingers tickled the bare skin of my back. Instead of gripping me tightly, though, I felt cool air waft over newly exposed areas of flesh as he slowly lowered the zipper of my dress.

His hands stopped moving once they hit the swell of my ass, and I started to grumble against his mouth in protest. Well, that was until his hands made their way around to the front of my body, travelling north until he palmed my breasts over the slackened fabric of my neckline.

"Yes!" I gasped, throwing my head back against the wall with a light *thud*.

Jensen's lips journeyed down my jaw, stopping once he

found my throat where he began kissing and nipping playfully at the sensitive skin. My body was on fire as his fingers pressed deliciously into the bare skin of my cleavage. The sounds that escaped Jensen could only be described as animalistic as he curled his fingers, the tips disappearing beneath the satiny fabric and brushing my hardening nipples.

My entire body tingled as Jensen moved his hands back to my waist, pulling me away from the wall. Our lips reconnected as we walked, and I brought my hands between us, hastily tugging on Jensen's tie before tossing it to the floor as we made our way toward the king-sized bed. The backs of my fingers grazed his chest as I quickly worked on unbuttoning his shirt and he groaned into my mouth as I released the final one from its eyelet. My hands made two—or five—passes over the planes of his muscular chest before they found his belt. In a flash, I had released the buckle and had his pants open. His skin shuddered as my knuckles tickled his lower abdomen, and my breathy giggle against his lips was met with a light chuckle and headshake from him.

Without warning, Jensen gathered me in his arms and rushed us to the bed where he sat on the edge as I stood before him. His hands were still firmly planted on my hips, his fingers digging in and pulling me toward him as our kiss became frantic—needy.

Completely lost in a frenzy of lust, my hands moved up Jensen's bare chest and over his shoulders beneath his shirt. I pushed the fabric down over his arms until it wouldn't go any farther. Groaning, almost reluctantly, he released his hold on me, and I all but tore the clothes from his arms. Now free of the confines of his shirt, his hands found me again, and I sighed as his fingers searched for the zipper so he could finish what he started only minutes ago.

With my fingers back in Jensen's soft and unruly hair, the zipper traveled over the curve of my ass. I shuddered when Jensen finally reached the end of the line, and the entire dress loosened around my body. Placing one last, lingering kiss on his lips, I dropped my hands from Jensen's hair to allow my dress to fall to the ground at my feet.

Silence shrouded us as he gazed upon my near-naked

form. Slowly, he placed his hands on my thighs, resting them directly below the curve of my backside, and his fingers started curling and clawing into the muscular flesh there.

"You're so fucking beautiful," he told me, moving forward to pepper my naked upper body with dozens of feather-light kisses. His voice was so low and gravelly I almost didn't recognize it.

A sharp gasp escaped me when his fingers started moving inward where he proceeded to gently stroke and tease me over the lacy blue fabric of my panties. The pressure he used switched between tender and firm as he ran them back and forth between my legs before finally slipping beneath the lace. We moaned collectively when he came into contact with my bare flesh, and he continued to stroke and tease me. I could feel my pleasure building rapidly, and I struggled with the urge to jump him. As much as I wanted to finally have sex with him, I also wanted to savor every second. Every touch, every sound ... I wanted to remember it all, and it seemed evident from the way Jensen's eyes moved over my body that he wanted the same thing.

And then I couldn't take it anymore. I needed him. Now.

With his legs still hanging over the edge of the bed, I slowly inched forward, forcing Jensen to remove his hand from between my thighs as I lifted one leg at a time to straddle him. My fingers moved lightly along his shoulders until they wound themselves back into his hair, while his lips travelled across my warm skin, stopping when he reached my right breast. Bringing his left hand around, he firmly gripped the soft flesh and drew my nipple into his mouth. That same, shameless porn-star moan bubbled to the surface when he swirled his tongue around it. His lips twisted up into a cocky smirk against my chest before he kissed, licked, and nipped a quick trail over to the other side.

Needing more than just his mouth on me, I drove my hips forward desperately while tugging on his hair to force his face back to mine. Even though I expected it to be, this kiss wasn't as frantic as before; his lips were tender against mine, parting slightly when my tongue lightly traced his lower lip.

With a quiet groan, he deepened our kiss until our tongues slid languidly against each other. I continued to move my hips back and forth above him, and he moaned with what I hoped to God was pleasure—I was assured seconds later when he met my movements with an upward thrust of his own.

His strong hands moved down my back, gripped my ass and pulled my hips against him again. "Oh, God!" I gasped into his mouth, pulling his hair and unabashedly grinding myself down onto his lap again. "I want you so much. Make love to me."

Jensen nodded slowly, holding me firmly before standing up with my legs still around his hips. I was confused at first until he turned and set me back on the bed. He stood before me for maybe half a millisecond before I was swiftly pushing his pants and boxer briefs to the floor. My heart started pounding with excitement when he kicked off his shoes, stepped out of his pants, and removed his socks.

After his last article of clothing had been tossed aside, I inched my way back toward the headboard so he could join me on the bed. My back pressed against the cool pillows as Jensen climbed up onto the bed, easing himself between my legs. His gaze was intense as he hooked his thumbs into the sides of my panties and tugged them down my thighs. Our eyes remained locked, and I lifted my hips to aid him. The fabric slid smoothly down my thighs, his fingers ghosting over my skin with them. My breath shuddered when I watched him drop the scrap of blue lace to the floor.

With our bodies bare, Jensen lowered his weight on me, and all I could hear was the sound of my own heart pounding wildly in my ears as he began to move above me. His motions were slow—*controlled*—as we maintained eye contact, and moaned every time the tip of his erection grazed my sensitive flesh. Wrapping my legs around his waist a little tighter, I watched him clench his eyes shut—almost as though he were fighting with himself. In hopes of bringing him back to me, I placed my hands on the sides of his face and pulled his lips back to mine.

Our kiss was slow, but deep, and I met every one of his

gentle thrusts with one of my own; and still, I needed *more*. I pushed my hips up a little more eagerly, and ...

"Fuck," Jensen gasped, breaking our kiss and ceasing all movement above me as he entered me slightly.

Even though I was on the pill, I knew there were still repercussions of what we were doing—unprotected. But I didn't want to stop; he felt so fucking *good*. There was conflict in his eyes as he remained motionless, and while I *knew* I should be the strong one, I couldn't stop myself from tightening my legs around him in an effort to bring him closer; it was like my brain had checked out completely.

"Oh, God," I moaned.

"Shit, Madison ..." His eyebrows pulled together and his head shook.

Smiling softly, I dropped my feet to the bed and shifted away from Jensen—doing what he was struggling to do—before reaching into the night stand to grab one of the condoms I'd put there last night before dinner.

He pushed himself up onto his knees as I rolled over and fumbled with the damn foil packets again—unable to find the loose one from last night in my impatience. When I was finally successful, I got up onto my knees in front of him and tore the packet carefully. Smiling, I crawled toward him and lowered my hands between us and *slowly* lowered the condom down his length as I leaned in for a kiss.

When my hand reached the base of his erection he hissed, moving his right hand over my thigh and inward until he was stroking the sensitive skin at the juncture of my legs. Once again, his fingers worked slowly; each pass he made left me panting until I could feel myself teetering on the edge of bliss.

"I want you, Jensen," I said breathlessly.

A low growl resonated from somewhere deep inside him, exciting me. Before I knew what was happening, Jensen threw me back onto the bed, and I cried out with a playful giggle as he repositioned himself between my thighs.

I lifted a trembling hand and pushed a few stray pieces of hair away so I could look him in the eyes. "I love you," I told him softly.

My heart soared when he smiled back, his fingers gently stroking my jaw and trailing up to my temple before he kissed me softly. "I love you, too."

With our feelings out in the open, he slowly moved forward, and we groaned in unison as he entered me. No words could describe the emotions that went through me in that moment. Our eyes locked once more as Jensen moved slowly above me, my climax rapidly culminating within me and threatening to wash over me sooner than I was hoping.

Moving quickly, I pulled his face back to mine and kissed him hard. Everything we felt for one another amplified in that moment as our kiss quickly escalated and our hips moved together. His breathing became shallow and every thrust made him groan and whisper the occasional profanity into my mouth.

My moans grew louder with every pulse of his hips, and my orgasm started surging through my body, my muscles tensing in preparation.

"Jesus," Jensen muttered softly, pulling me out of my euphoric state enough to hear the soft knocking.

At first, I thought it was coming from the door, and I could feel annoyance quickly replacing pleasure. It wasn't until I *really* focused on its origin that I realized it was coming from above me. Every time Jensen pushed into me, he was hitting his head on the headboard.

It shouldn't have surprised me that the two of us couldn't even have sex without something stooge-like happening. I mean, really. If you looked back on our track-record, it was full of entertaining mishaps — mostly at my expense. Thankfully he didn't stop though; he merely slowed and glared at the headboard.

Then, a look of revelation registered in his eyes, and they glinted deviously as he leaned down to kiss me softly. I felt nothing but his love for me as his hands left the side of my head one at a time. We were still kissing passionately when the wooden headboard creaked, causing me to open my eyes and look above me.

Reaching up, his hands gripped the top of the headboard tightly — using it for leverage as he continued to thrust his hips forward and …

I cried out, my short nails digging into the flesh of his muscular back as Jensen picked up momentum in our new position. Soon, my entire body tightened and released around Jensen, pulling him over the edge with me.

Breathing heavily, Jensen released the headboard, dropped to the bed, and wrapped his arms around me as he pushed deep inside me once more, groaning as he came. We both laid there, panting hard, our sweat-dampened bodies pressed tightly together as they started trembling in the wake of our orgasms.

Feeling his lips twist up into a smile against my skin, Jensen kissed my neck before pushing himself up onto his elbows and smiling down at me. "Are you okay? I didn't … I wasn't too rough, was I? Your ribs are okay?"

Even though I was pretty sure my entire skeletal system was nothing more than a puddle of goo at this point, I managed to nod my head with a sly look in my eyes. I hummed softly, rocking my hips up into Jensen's again. We both groaned in post-orgasmic delight. "That was incredible."

"Agreed."

"What do you want to do now?" I asked, lifting my head and kissing Jensen softly before letting it drop back onto the downy pillow.

He seemed to contemplate my question for a moment before smiling. "Well, we have yet to take advantage of that Jacuzzi … and, it is our last night here?"

Arching my right eyebrow, I smirked devilishly. "I think that sounds like a great idea."

Placing one last kiss on my lips, he stood from the bed. As the tub filled, he called down for a bottle of wine before leading me to the oversized tub. The next couple hours were spent drinking wine and making love before passing out wrapped in each other's arms.

10
THE MORNING AFTER
Madison Landry

"No, she's still asleep," Jensen whispered as I breached consciousness. "I'm going to let her sleep a few extra minutes, and then we'll come down to meet you all for breakfast." There was another brief pause as my eyes fluttered open and focused on the pale blue wall ahead of me. "Yeah. We'll be down in about an hour ... See you then."

I heard a light *click* as he set his phone on the bedside table, and the bed shifted slightly beneath him. I was lying facedown on the bed with my arms up under the pillow and didn't have to turn around to know he was watching me; I could *feel* his eyes on me.

"You sure like to stare a lot," I mumbled into my pillow before propping myself up on my elbows and turning to face him. Fuck me if he wasn't the most gorgeous man on the planet.

The duvet was pulled up to his hips as he lay on his left side (naked from the waist up, I should add), his arm propping him up as he stared at me. His lips twisted up into a smirk as he chuckled lightly. "Did I wake you?"

I shrugged. "Not really. I think I was waking up anyway. Who was on the phone?" I asked.

"Mom. Just reminding us to meet them for brunch." When his eyes fell to the sheets and I saw *his* cheeks turn pink, I smiled. He was so adorable. "She wanted to tell us last night, but she hadn't noticed we'd snuck away."

I was no longer focused on how adorable he was, but by

the very real possibility that his mother knew we had ... that we had snuck away to ... *Shit!* There was no way in hell I was going to be able to face her.

Jensen's eyebrows pulled together with worry the longer I stayed silent. "Love?"

I shook my head, still freaking out inside. "Sorry. Was she ...?" I paused for a minute. "Was she upset that we left?"

"Nah. Quite the opposite. She felt pretty horrible about us not really getting a lot of time to ourselves this weekend," he explained before moving across the bed and pulling me into his arms. "How was your sleep?"

"Phenomenal," I said, curling up against him with my head on his chest. The heat of his naked body against my own was too much to ignore. "So ... We have a whole hour before we have to go downstairs?"

When I tilted my head up to look at him, I was met with a cocky smirk. "Well, aren't you just insatiable?"

I shrugged. "What can I say? You're like an addiction I can't feed fast enough."

"You're twisted," he said with a laugh, pressing his lips into the top of my head. "Why don't you go hop in the shower?"

Slightly disappointed that he was ignoring my lame attempt at seduction, I frowned. "Okay," I said, pulling out of his warm embrace and crawling off my side of the bed. Completely naked, I walked about three feet from the end of the bed toward the bathroom before turning around and smirking. "You sure you don't want to join me?"

In a flash, the blankets were thrown from the bed and Jensen had me hanging over his shoulder, carrying me to the bathroom where we spent the next thirty or forty minutes ravaging each other in the shower. It was unclear if our glowing complexions were from the hot water or the lovemaking — perhaps a combination of the two — but, honestly I didn't care.

Because we had spent so much time in the shower, it didn't leave me a lot of time to do much of anything with my hair, so I added a bit of mousse and blow-dried it into loose waves before applying a touch of mascara and lip-gloss.

I couldn't tear myself from Jensen's side the entire walk to the elevator or the ride down to the ground floor. And I didn't want to. Based on the way Jensen had his arm wrapped tightly around me and kissed the top of my head on several occasions, it would seem he felt the same way. It was the happiest I'd been in my entire life; the constant smile on my face would attest to that.

When we arrived at the restaurant downstairs, everyone was already seated and laughing. We were about ten minutes late—which wouldn't have been so bad had Kyle not turned to call us on it.

"Well, well, well," he boomed, drawing the eyes of everyone at the table toward us. "Look who finally decided to grace us with their presence."

I was certain my body temperature went supernova as my cheeks filled with a color that was sure to be blinding. Jensen didn't say anything to deter them from thinking what I knew they all were. Instead, he chuckled and pulled the seat next to his mother out for me before kissing her cheek.

"Sorry we're late," he apologized into her ear before taking his seat on my other side.

Janet brushed our tardiness off. "Nonsense. I trust you both slept well?"

"Yes, very. Thank you," I said quietly, returning her warm smile before looking across the table to see Kaylie glaring daggers at me. Her attitude was really starting to piss me off. For the first time since Jensen and I started seeing each other, I felt more than confident in our relationship. Something changed over the last few days, and I no longer felt uncertain about our future.

Feeling pretty smug, I placed my hand on Jensen's thigh beneath the table and turned to him. "What are you having, baby?" I cooed. Through my periphery, I was pretty sure I saw Kaylie roll her eyes—wouldn't have been the first time in the last twenty-four hours; my stunt with the photographer pissed her off too.

"Um, I'm not sure yet, love. What are you in the mood for?"

I rested my head on his shoulder and looked at his

menu. "Pancakes, I think. It's been a while."

Jensen nodded and closed his menu. "Yes, it really has been. I think I'll have the same."

"So, Madison," Henry interjected. "Jensen tells us you've been coaching a few young riders?"

I nodded, turning to Henry. "Yeah. After I got hurt, it's all I was really able to do. I used to do it before I got into competing, and I never really realized just how much I missed it until a few weeks ago."

"You used to compete?" Lilah spoke up, garnering a disapproving glance from her maid of horror.

I nodded, reaching for the mimosa in front of me, and was just about to answer when Jensen shocked me by speaking up. "She did, and she's quite the rider. She won silver in the Masters a couple years ago." My jaw dropped as I stared at him; I knew he was aware that I had competed, but I had no idea he knew specifics.

"That's so cool!" Lilah exclaimed as I continued to gawk at Jensen. "I haven't ridden in years."

Refocusing on the discussion, I turned to Lilah and smiled. "Well, come out to the ranch sometime. We can go for a trail ride. It'll be fun."

Aaaand, one more glare from Kaylie.

"Do you think you'll compete again?" Lilah asked.

"Um," I pondered. "I'm not sure, actually. Halley's injuries were pretty substantial, so I guess it would depend on her progress and your father's medical opinion. I wouldn't mind it, but I really enjoy working with the horses we have, and I've also found somewhat of a prodigy in one of the girls I coach. She's quite amazing given her age. I think she could go far."

Lilah and I talked at length about her visit, and the entire time, Jensen's hand moved up and down my back as he engaged in a conversation with several others around the table. When breakfast arrived, there was a moment of silence as we all took the first few bites, and then the conversation started up again. I wasn't shocked—nor did I really care—that Kaylie had remained pretty silent through most of the meal. Her and Lilah talked a little, she even laughed at something Kyle said to Gavin. As I studied her, I could *see* how Jensen found her attractive; she was quite beautiful—on the outside anyway.

The longer I focused on her, the more annoyed I became, because all I saw was a phony sitting there with Jensen's family, pretending that she didn't betray every single one of them in some way. It was disgusting, and I really hoped that Jensen would take my advice and tell his family the truth about her before she had a chance to get her hooks into them any deeper.

Jensen must have been able to sense my shift in moods because he leaned in and kissed my temple. "You okay?"

"Uh, yeah. I just need to go to the ladies room," I whispered. "I'll be right back." I placed a gentle kiss on his lips before excusing myself.

After using the facilities, I washed my hands and gave myself a quick pep-talk before applying a little more lip-gloss and exiting the fancy-schmancy restroom. I made it all of two steps before I halted dead in my tracks, definitely not expecting what I found blocking my way.

"Kaylie!" I said, startled, as I moved to the left a step so she could access the washroom. It frightened me a little when she stepped *with* me, though. I was no good at one-on-one confrontations.

"You realize it won't last, right?" she said, her tone sounding awfully bitter.

Good at confrontations or not, I wasn't going to stand there and listen to her venomous words. Shaking my head I shifted to walk around her. "Think what you want, Kaylie. He's moved on. Deal with it."

"Where do you think you're going?" she asked, wrapping her scrawny fingers around my bicep. "I'm not done talking to you yet."

"Funny," I snapped, yanking my arm free of her grasp. "Because I've said all I have to say to you."

"You've known each other a few weeks." My head snapped back toward her, curious to see where exactly this was going. "You're *a phase*." Her nose curled up into a sneer as she spoke. "A rebound. What he and I had was—"

"A fucking joke," I interrupted with a dry, humorless

laugh. "After what you *did* ..." I shook my head and took a step back. "I honestly don't know why he hasn't told anyone the truth about you."

Kaylie laughed, and I really, *really* wanted to punch her in the throat. "You think that because you've spent one weekend with them that you've managed to worm your way in? I have a history with these people, *Madison*. Actual relationships wi—"

"Based on lies! And from what I could tell, his parents seemed to enjoy my company over yours all weekend," I retorted arrogantly.

Kaylie's eyes moved back and forth rapidly between mine, almost as though she was unsure what to say; I should have known better. "You think you know me?"

Crossing my arms tightly across my body, I arched an eyebrow at her. "Oh, I know you. You're a selfish, manipulative bitch. Did you give any consideration at all to how he would feel? You didn't even give him a choice."

I watched, slightly afraid, as Kaylie's eyes widened and her face went red; there was a very good possibility she was about to explode. "What about *me*?" she shrieked, a little louder than I'd have liked. We didn't need an audience. "I never wanted kids. Ever. I couldn't be saddled with such a burden—especially with him sitting in a prison cell for three years. So yeah, I got rid of it when I knew he couldn't stop me."

"What?"

My heart skipped a beat, and I gasped as I quickly turned to face our uninvited spectator. When I saw Lilah's angry face, her wide eyes moving between Kaylie and me, I panicked. My hands were sweating as I turned to her completely. "Lilah, I—"

Her hand flew up to silence me as she focused her fierce eyes on Kaylie. "You did *what*?"

For the first time, I saw real fear in Kaylie's eyes. She stepped forward, holding out her right hand to Lilah as she spoke. "Lilah, honey—"

"Save it!" Lilah barked, making me jump in fright. She lowered her head but kept her enraged blue eyes on Kaylie.

"What. Did. You. Do?"

Then Jensen entered the small hallway, and my heart sank. This was all my fault. If I had just walked away, Lilah wouldn't have found out this way. Tears of regret burned my eyes as I dropped them to the floor, completely ashamed.

"Hey," he said softly, glancing at each of us curiously. "What's going on in here?"

Lilah's eyes left Kaylie's, and she glared angrily at her brother. "Oh, nothing really." Sarcasm dripped from every word out of her mouth, and I bit the inside of my cheek to keep quiet; I had already done enough damage. "I just walked in on Kaylie telling Madison that she terminated the pregnancy. Is that true, Jensen?"

Glancing up, I saw Jensen's eyes widen as he looked to me for an explanation. I couldn't look at him — couldn't respond. Instead, I choked back a sob and mumbled a quiet apology as I rushed from the room, through the restaurant and out the main doors of the hotel until I collapsed on the front steps. He was going to hate me after this.

I sat there crying for a few minutes, cursing myself for opening my big fat mouth at all instead of just walking away like I had originally intended, when a voice spoke behind me. "Madison? Sweetheart?"

Sniffling, I looked up to see Janet above me. She settled in next to me and wrapped her arms around me. I melted into her embrace, feeling the need to spill everything that just happened like word vomit. I held it back because I knew I'd already done more than enough to this family. "Oh, honey, what's wrong?"

Her hand began to move softly over my hair in an effort to calm me as I bawled into her shoulder. "I just did something horrible," I blubbered.

"Shhh," she said softly, wrapping her arms around me even tighter. "Do you want to talk about it?"

I shook my head, my breaths becoming more ragged the longer I cried. "I shouldn't have said anything to begin with," I sobbed brokenly.

Janet's hands stilled and she forced me up until she was staring directly into my eyes. "Does this have something to do with Kaylie?" I nodded once—apparently I found it impossible to lie to any member of the Davis family, and I was pretty sure if she asked me specific questions, I'd tell her everything.

"Mom?" Jensen's low, emotionless voice cut right through my heart, and I closed my eyes tightly, unable to see the look of disappointment on his face. "Can I have a word with Madison?"

11
ME AND MY BIG MOUTH
Madison Landry

This is it, I thought, clutching my hands together tightly in my lap to calm the shaking that had suddenly taken over my entire body.

"Of course, dear." With a smile, Janet wrapped me in one more hug, and I responded to it by hugging her back—quite possibly tighter than normal because I was afraid it would be the last time. Giving me one more firm squeeze, Janet pulled out of our embrace and stood up before leaving Jensen and me alone.

I turned until I was facing forward again, my eyes focusing on the pavement as I toed at the step my feet were on. Behind me, Jensen huffed before sitting next to me, his body right against mine. "So?" He nudged my shoulder with his, indicating I should start talking.

"It was an accident," I whispered hoarsely, wiping the tears from my cheeks with the back of my hand. "I'm so sorry. She just … confronted me and started saying all this stuff about me being a phase. I didn't mean to say anything, I swear." I dropped my face into my hands. "God, you must hate me."

"What?" he said, completely shocked, as he grabbed and twisted me to face him. I still couldn't meet his gaze until he placed his hands on my face and forced my eyes to his. "Madison, I could *never* hate you."

"But I—"

Jensen sighed. "Did something I've been too chicken-shit

to do. I'm not angry with you, baby. I'm angry with myself."

Feeling relieved that he wasn't upset with what I had unintentionally done, I threw my arms around his neck. He held me for a long while, occasionally placing a kiss in my hair before he pulled me away from him. "Wait ..." I froze. "She said you were a phase?" I nodded slowly before he cupped my face in his hands again. "You know she was just trying to get to you, right?"

"Yeah," I replied quietly.

"I love you, Madison. I'm not going anywhere." His eyes held mine as he leaned in to kiss me, wrapping his arms around my waist and pulling me to him.

Sighing, I tightened my hold around him, hoping that I was able to convey just how much I loved him too. Even though I had accidentally outed Kaylie, he was able to forgive me; I only hoped his sister—

That was when I panicked. "Lilah!" I gasped into his mouth.

Jensen pulled his lips from mine and arched an eyebrow questioningly. "Not exactly the name I expected."

"Oh, God, she must be so upset." I pulled out of Jensen's embrace and folded in on myself again.

Jensen shook his head. "Not with you, love. Mostly with Kaylie ... and me."

"Your parents?" I asked, turning my head to look at him.

He let out a dry laugh, running his hand through his hair. "My father assures me that while they didn't know with one hundred percent certainty, they suspected something."

"I still can't believe I did this," I whispered.

Jensen stood, pulling me to my feet with him. "From the way Lilah tells it—or rather, how she screamed it—*you* didn't say anything that would have slandered Kaylie. She said that before Kaylie said anything about terminating the pregnancy, she thought that maybe I had told you that Kaylie was a bitch—or at the very worst, that she maybe cheated on me."

What he said confused me for a moment because that wasn't how I remembered it—at all. Quickly thinking back on everything that was said between Kaylie and I, I realized that he was right. I was elated that I hadn't been the one to break the news by sticking my foot in my mouth—as I was so prone to doing ninety-nine percent of the time—but I still felt partially responsible.

"You still seem upset, love." Jensen stopped me once we were back inside the hotel and looked down at me.

"I should have just walked away from her. I shouldn't have said anything at all. Even if I wasn't the one to out her, I engaged her. You should be furious with me," I told him.

Jensen shook his head adamantly. "Nope. I'm not. While I'll admit, the timing wasn't exactly ideal; I can't say I regret that they all know now. I only wish I'd have manned up when we first ended things. I could have avoided this altogether."

He wrapped his arm around me. "Come on. Don't worry yourself over everyone being upset. They're not. I promise." His words fell flat the instant we were outside the restaurant and could hear the violent shouts coming from within.

"You were my best friend!" Lilah shouted. "I comforted you after you and Jensen broke off the engagement, consoled you while he was away ... And the whole time you were keeping something like this from me?"

Even as we pushed the doors open, we couldn't see them, but I still tensed. Jensen tightened his grip around my waist protectively. From the sounds of it, Kaylie and Lilah were still near the washrooms off to the left, but there wasn't a doubt in my mind that everyone in the restaurant could hear their heated discussion.

"It was nobody's business, Lilah!" Kaylie rebutted, garnering a very unladylike snort of disagreement from Lilah. "I have a right to decide what I do with my body."

"Nobody's business?" she cried. "Nobody's fucking business? What about Jensen's right? That was *his* child, too. He deserved to have a say, regardless of his situation at the time!" Lilah let out a frustrated cry before there was a deafening pause. "You know what?" Her voice was surprisingly calm when she continued after a few beats of silence. "I'm not going to continue this discussion here. Or anywhere, for that matter. As far as I'm concerned, you are no longer my friend. Don't call. Don't email. Just don't try to contact me at all, because I won't respond. You are dead to me."

Lilah emerged from the little hall near the washrooms, and I froze, unsure what to expect from her if she was that angry with Kaylie. I gripped the back of Jensen's shirt and tried to prepare for the worst.

She glanced quickly at us and forced a smile on her face. "Let's get back to brunch, shall we?"

"Lilah—" Jensen started to say before she cut him off with a sharp glare.

"No. I'm not going to get into this any further. We'll talk—at length—afterward." And with that, Lilah breezed by us and rejoined the table.

To say the rest of our meal was awkward was an understatement; there may as well have been a large pink elephant sitting in the empty chair across from me. Everyone glanced at the empty spot at least twice, but no one addressed it.

"So," Gavin said, breaking the uncomfortable silence. God bless him. "Where are you guys going on your honeymoon?"

I looked across the table, being sure to avoid the empty seat, and looked at Lilah and Kyle. Kyle genuinely smiled and wrapped an arm around Lilah, who still seemed a little upset but kept her game face on. "Greece, actually," he said, squeezing his new wife to his side before releasing her. Our plane leaves tonight."

For the remainder of the meal, everyone at the table talked while I pushed my cold pancakes around on my plate. Jensen's hand on my thigh brought me out of my silent funk, and I turned to him with a small smile.

"Not hungry, love?" he asked softly.

I shook my head and set my fork down. "Not really."

After everyone finished eating, we stood, saying our goodbyes to those that were leaving the hotel to head home. As I stood to the side while the Davises and the Lewises spoke, Kyle approached me and wrapped one of his massive arms around me.

"You know that what happened wasn't your fault, right?" he said under his breath, and I looked up at him with wide eyes. "She won't be upset with you. In fact, I'd be willing to bet that this will bring you two closer." He offered me a dimpled grin and a wink. "Trust me."

"Thanks, Kyle."

Giving me one last hug before he pulled away. "Anytime. Keep your chin up, Madikins."

Jensen was back by my side soon enough, pressing a kiss to the top of my head. "Should we go and grab our things before we get charged an extra night?"

"Sure," I told him with a smile.

We had both just turned to leave when Lilah appeared in front of us. "Wait," she said, her eyes moving back and forth between us both. "Can we talk?"

Inhaling deeply, Jensen nodded. "Yeah." He turned to me. "Why don't you go on up to the room?"

I just started to pull away when Lilah spoke up again. "No. Madison should stay. I mean, if not for her, none of this would have come out."

Ouch.

Lilah must have realized the impact of her words, because her eyes widened with remorse. "Oh, no. That's not how I meant it at all. I'm *glad* I know. Yeah, it sucks, but I'm glad."

Lilah led Jensen and I back to the table, and we sat there for a moment until their parents and Kyle joined us. Once again, we sat in maddening silence, waiting for someone to begin. Thankfully Lilah was that person.

"So, spill it, Jensen."

"What's there to say that you don't already know?" he replied, leaning on the table and clasping his hands in front of him. "Kaylie aborted the pregnancy when I went to prison. She told me, and then I never heard from her again."

I looked around the table to see that Henry and Janet both seemed unfazed by this news while Lilah and Kyle looked as though they were hearing it for the first time. Lilah sat with her arms crossed over her body, her hard eyes steeled on Jensen as he fidgeted very uncharacteristically and Kyle's brows were knit together as he absorbed everything.

"Right," Lilah continued. "But why didn't you tell us? We're your family, Jensen. God! I had her in my wedding party. She's in my pho—" A look of revelation flashed in Lilah's eyes as she turned to find me smiling both apologetically and sheepishly. "This is why you suggested the change in some of the pictures."

I shrugged. "I just wanted to make sure it was still a day you could look back on fondly. I didn't want to interfere. Really."

"No. *Thank* you." Lilah's eyes flashed back to Jensen. "Back to you."

Nodding, Jensen continued. "After Robert ..." Lilah's eyes widened with what looked like paranoia as she looked between Jensen and me. "Well, you only really hung out with Kaylie. The two of you had gotten so close. I guess I just didn't want to add any more stress to your life."

"Okay," Lilah replied slowly.

"I understand why you felt you had to keep it to yourself, darling," Janet interjected. "But, you shouldn't have had to bear that burden alone. We would have found a way to deal with everything."

"I know. I *know*. I'm sorry. I really thought it was better this way," he agreed in frustration, fisting his hair in his hands. For the first time since the incident, I found myself comforting Jensen in his time of need by running my hand up and down his back.

"Look," Henry said, speaking up for the first time. "We're not angry—" Lilah snorted her disagreement. "Lilah ..." he warned.

She rolled her eyes before letting her hands fall to her lap. "Fine. I'm not *mad*. Just hurt that you felt you had to keep this from me. I never would have helped her through the breakup—especially knowing she likely didn't care for you if she was capable of doing something so abhorrent."

"You're right, and I'm sorry. I never meant to hurt you, Lilah." He raised his eyes to her and smiled. "I promise I'll never keep anything like that from you again."

Even though I knew his comment wasn't about me, there was a part of me that wanted to smack him and feel offended that he'd even think there was a possibility of something similar happening again.

Realizing the same thing, Jensen turned to me with an apologetic look in his eyes. "Shit. I didn't mean to imply—"

I cut him off. "It's fine," I assured him weakly.

We sat there for a few more minutes while Lilah asked a few more questions which Jensen answered willingly. It wasn't any easier to hear the second time around. I hated to see him so hurt over what Kaylie had done to him, and I vowed in that moment to never cause him the kind of pain that she had.

Eventually, Lilah and Jensen found their way back to a good place. It still upset her that he kept something so huge to himself, but she understood. We'd been sitting there for an extra two hours, and it wasn't until Henry alerted us of the time that we decided we should grab our luggage.

Once back inside our room, I did one more quick check of the washroom for anything we may have forgotten in the shower before returning to the bedroom. Jensen was seated on the end of the bed with his head in his hands.

"Hey," I said softly, stopping in front of him as he sulked. "You okay?"

Raising his head and moving his hands to encircle my waist, he looked up at me. "I think so. It's just been an ... *intense* morning."

Still remorseful because I couldn't apologize enough for today, I ran my fingers through his hair. His head rolled back, eyes closing as I used varying pressure on his scalp to try and soothe him. "Are you still up to going to Willow and Brandon's for dinner? We don't *have* to." I wanted to go—more than words could express, but if Jensen wasn't feeling up to it after this afternoon, I wasn't going to push it.

When his eyes met mine, I knew his answer. "Would you be upset? I'm just ... drained." His fingers tightened on my hips.

I forced a smile. I'd be lying if I said I wasn't mildly disappointed, but I understood. "It's fine. Willow will understand. We'll plan for another time."

"I'm sorry, love."

I shook my head. "No. It's fine." I moved to turn around so I could finish checking the room for our belongings when

Jensen pulled me back until I fell into his lap.

"Hey. You forgot something." With a smirk, he pressed his lips to mine and kissed me softly. I was hesitant at first, considering everything that had happened, but just like every other time we were in close proximity, I was quickly dazzled. Putting everything I had into the kiss, I placed my right hand on his neck as our mouths slowly moved together, and I sighed into his slightly open mouth.

Jensen fell back onto the bed, taking me with him, before I propped myself up and broke the kiss. It wasn't often I stopped things from progressing—okay, so it was *never* me who stopped things from progressing—but I knew one of us had to. "Um, I think your dad would prefer to not be charged for another night. We should pack up and get going."

"Are you turning me down?" he asked, quirking an eyebrow.

I kissed him chastely on the lips and giggled. "I guess I am. But only because I'm trying to save your dad another four-hundred dollars here."

Jensen and I wandered through the room, checking and double-checking that we got all of our belongings before he took our bags and led the way to the elevator.

12
HOME, SWEET ... INTERCEPTED
Madison Landry

"It's good to be home," I announced, pushing the door open and walking through. The drive back from Memphis was better than I thought it would be; it was almost as though the events of that morning had never happened.

Willow was a little disappointed that we couldn't go for dinner, but after I explained everything, she understood, and we made plans to get together another time. Jensen couldn't apologize enough.

I heard our bags drop to the floor behind me before strong arms encircled my waist and soft lips were on my neck. "Mmm hmm," Jensen hummed, the sound vibrating against my skin.

My entire body tingled with every pass his lips made over my neck. When his fingers snuck beneath the hem of my shirt and started trailing along my stomach, I shivered and turned quickly to plant my lips on his. The way his hands moved up my body, occasionally curling his fingers into my skin, had me sighing. My entire body was set aflame as his hands continued upward, stopping only once he found my breasts. I was starting to think he was obsessed with them. Unable to take it anymore, I quickly reached for the bottom of his shirt and started to tug it off of him.

Just as Jensen released my chest so I could pull his shirt off and have my way with him, there was a knock at the door. There had to be some kind of law that stated we were to be interrupted every single time we rounded second base in this house. And, if there was, I wanted it overturned. Stat.

It didn't take a rocket scientist to figure out who it was without opening the door. My father always had impeccable timing.

"Welcome home," I groaned quietly, effectively ending our kiss. "Would you mind taking the bags to our rooms? I'll see what my father wants."

"Sure." He leaned down and brushed his lips over mine and along my jaw, the scruff on his face scratching my cheek until he stopped at my ear and whispered, "Don't take too long."

My entire body quivered as he moved around me with our bags. It may have taken me a minute to come to my senses as the heat from his smoldering eyes lingered, rendering me frozen. Another knock snapped me out of my trance, and I stepped forward to open the door.

"Hey, kiddo," Dad greeted with a big grin. "I saw you guys pull up, and I just wanted to see how your weekend was."

I narrowed my eyes playfully. "Dad, did you miss me?" I teased.

With a laugh, he shrugged. "I guess you could put it that way." He cleared his throat nervously. "I also just wanted to let you know that you should feel free to sleep in a bit. We can handle the barn tomorrow morning."

"You sure? We don't mind—"

Before I could finish, Dad interrupted. "Yeah. It's fine. Take a couple extra hours. We'll manage."

"All right. Thanks." I wrapped my arms around my dad's neck and hugged him. "I missed you, too, old man."

Dad chuckled, hugging me back. "Okay, smart aleck. You get to bed. I'll see you both in the morning."

"'Night, Daddy," I said sweetly, kissing his cheek.

After saying goodnight, I closed and locked the door before turning off the lights on the way to my room to change into something a little more comfortable. My suitcase was on my bed when I arrived, and I smiled, knowing that Jensen was likely waiting for me in his room. I suddenly found myself debating my wardrobe choices for the night before realizing that there was really only one option.

I approached my dresser and opened my underwear drawer, moving everything around until I found ... nothing. I opened several drawers before moving over to my suitcase and opening it to see if maybe I absent-mindedly packed it on Friday. *Nope. Nadda.*

"Madison?" Jensen called from across the hall.

I ran my fingers through my hair and tried to think back to where I could have put it; I was *sure* I put it in its usual hiding spot in my underwear drawer. "Yeah?"

Deciding to wait until morning to continue my search in favor of being in Jensen's arms, I grudgingly pulled on a tank top and a pair of shorts before rushing across the hall. With wide eyes I stopped in his doorway, instantly recognizing the light blue shirt he wore. He sat on top of his duvet with his back against the headboard and his hands behind his head. My eyes moved up to his face—only to find him grinning cockily.

"That's mine," I growled, stalking toward him with narrowing eyes. If I was being completely honest, it looked good on him; the fabric wasn't too tight, but I could still clearly see his muscular upper body beneath it. I liked seeing him in it—but I still couldn't believe he'd snuck into my underwear drawer and took it back!

I crawled up onto the bed, moving slowly to straddle his thighs as he continued to smirk and eye me smugly. "You want it?" he asked, moving his hands from behind his head to the tops of my bare thighs. I nodded sharply, and Jensen's fingers squeezed delightfully before he forced himself upright.

Our faces were inches apart and my breathing increased as I yearned for his kiss ... his touch ... My breasts brushed his chest with every breath I took, and I found myself aching for him in every way. "Then take it," he demanded before crushing his lips to mine.

I wasted no time in ridding him of *my* shirt before fisting his hair in my hands and kissing him again. Hard. My hips moved against him, feeling every solid inch of him between my legs through the thin fabric of our pajama bottoms. A familiar warmth expanded in me, stretching outward as his hands moved over my hips and slipped into the back of my shorts to grip my ass firmly, and I rocked against him eagerly.

Needing to take a breath, I pulled my lips from his, smiling and meeting his burning stare. I reached for the hem of my tank top and lifted it over my head. It confused me when I lowered my face back to his and he pulled back slightly.

"What are you—?"

His head shifted to the right slightly, and he smirked. "Just making sure there's no knocking at the door ... no phones ringing. It seems we're prone to being interrupted," he joked.

Shifting my hips softly, his eyes fluttered, and his fingers dug into the flesh of my backside. I laughed, leaning forward and pulling his earlobe between my teeth before whispering, "I assure you there will be no further interruptions. Make love to me, Jensen. In our bed."

Jensen sat up slowly while simultaneously pulling my hips forward. When my mouth opened in a breathless moan he kissed me, his tongue sweeping over mine in a way that left my body quivering. As we kissed, Jensen was working really hard to shove my shorts down over my ass, trying to get me naked. His attempts were futile given our current position. In an effort to keep our bodies close while getting into a position that we could work with, I wrapped my arms around his neck and shifted to the right. He followed, removing his hands from my shorts and pressing himself between my legs.

My head touched the cool pillows behind me, and I moved my hands down his body until I reached the waist of his pants and slipped them in the sides. I was able to force them down a couple inches, and from there, I hooked my feet in and pushed them the rest of the way. Never breaking away from my lips, Jensen kicked his pants off frantically, and I slipped my hand between us until it was wrapped tightly around his solid length.

He hissed a sharp breath between his teeth as I began to move my hand up and down his shaft, varying the pressure I used on each pass and running my palm over the head. In a flash, Jensen sat up and started tugging my shorts down until the position of my spread legs wouldn't allow for any more.

Smiling slyly, I lifted my legs straight into the air between us. The way his eyes traveled down my lean legs before him, settling on my ass—which was completely exposed to him—made my breath shudder every time I inhaled.

I had just begun to drop my feet back to the bed on either side of him when he reached out and slapped his hands around my ankles, holding them firmly in place. "Wait," he rasped. Whenever his voice sounded like that—all deep and commanding—my body reacted very, *very* positively. Without saying another word, he leaned over. My gaze followed as he opened his nightstand and grabbed one of the condoms he must have pilfered from my suitcase, quickly rolling it down his length before aligning us.

All it took was a shared look between us, and he placed my legs on his shoulders and pushed his hips forward slowly. The sensation of him filling me caused my eyes to close for a moment, and I moaned long and low.

When his hips rested against the backs of my thighs, he pulled out before thrusting in rapidly. I cried out as he triggered that delightful little hot-button that was very rarely stimulated during sex prior to now. Seeing just how much I enjoyed how that felt, he pulled away before burying himself inside me once more. A new profanity escaped my mouth every time he moved, bringing me closer and closer to the heights of pure ecstasy I yearned for, but instead of biting my lip to silence myself, I cried out to encourage him.

He grunted, slowing his pace before allowing my legs to fall to either side of him. His blue eyes were wild with passion as he leaned forward and kissed me deeply, working his arms beneath my body until he lifted me off the bed and onto his lap.

In this new position, our bodies were mashed together, my legs practically wrapped around him as he thrust up into me, meeting the gentle rocking of my own hips. Feeling my orgasm approaching quickly, I threw my head back, panting and gasping for air. Torrid kisses littered my glistening neck before his breath caressed my skin.

"I love you," he sighed against my neck, wrapping his arms around me tighter and pulling my body down onto him again. "I love you." He repeated his affections with every upward movement, and my abdomen tensed with my impending release.

"I love you, too," I said breathlessly, dropping my face to stare deep into his eyes as my climax closed in on me. I pressed my forehead to his, locking eyes as we quickened our pace. With a moan, my eyebrows knit together as I clung desperately to his body.

My body trembled, and I unraveled in his arms. "Jensen!" I gasped as his arms tightened around me and he threw me back down to the bed.

My body was still numb, my skin all tingly and warm as his hands moved up my torso, his movements more manic as he raced to join me in post-orgasmic bliss. I watched as his eyes locked on mine, his lids hooded in lust as he came.

His arms and legs shook against me before he collapsed more of his weight on my chest, both of us breathing heavily. "That was ..." he panted. "Wow."

I laughed. "Yeah. That about sums it up," I responded, taking in one shuddering breath after another.

Once our breathing returned to normal, Jensen excused himself, kissing the tip of my nose sweetly before exiting the room to discard of the condom. It wasn't much longer before he was back in bed, his chest pressed to my back. We had every intention of going to make a light dinner before turning in early, but before we knew it, we both passed out. It wasn't surprising after an emotionally turbulent day.

13
OFFICIALLY OUTED
Madison Landry

The smell of breakfast pulled me from sleep just enough to realize I was lying in bed alone. Sitting up, I pulled the white sheet tightly to my chest and ran my fingers through my hair as I searched for my tank top and shorts. When my eyes fell on my shorts hanging half-off the end of the bed while my top was in a heap at my feet, I smiled fondly at the memory of the night before.

My happiness was short-lived as I stood, and felt a dull ache in my abdomen. It didn't last long, but I knew instantly it wasn't the last of them; being a woman sucked for three to five days out of the month. At least I could be thankful it held off until *after* our weekend away. I quickly changed and went to the bathroom to clean up before joining Jensen in the kitchen.

"Hey," he said, turning to me with a smile. "I was just about to come wake you. The eggs are just warming in the oven while I finish with the toast." The toaster popped, and he put the two slices onto an awaiting plate and buttered them.

I stepped farther into the kitchen, stretching up onto my toes to kiss his cheek before moving around him to grab the cup of coffee he had waiting for me. "Thanks for cooking."

"My pleasure, love." Jensen grabbed one of the oven mitts and grabbed the eggs from the oven, placing them on the potholder next to the plate of toast. "Okay, breakfast is ready. Dig in so we can get to work."

Jensen and I dished up and took our places to the table, eating our first few bites in silence. As we ate, I thought about our weekend away. The way his parents seemed to welcome me with open arms definitely put my mind at ease—even if there was a miniscule part of me that was initially afraid to even compete with Kaylie in their eyes. Upon meeting them and seeing how they were around her, I soon realized that there was something missing in that dynamic entirely.

From Henry's forced smirks when she would say something during photos, to Janet's occasional eye-roll she didn't think anyone would see ... It was obvious that they didn't think very highly of her at all. They also didn't seem very shocked by the revelation that Kaylie had aborted their grandchild, and I had to wonder why.

"Babe?" Jensen said, placing his hand on my knee and pulling me from my thoughts.

"Hmm?" I smiled and looked up at him.

His eyebrows pressed together, almost curiously, and he smiled. "What are you thinking about so intently?"

I set my fork down. "About the weekend." Jensen smiled happily ... until I continued. "Your parents didn't seem too shocked about what happened."

Jensen didn't say anything.

"It just sucks, you know? They'd have been great grandparents," I whispered with another small shrug.

Jensen bobbed his head up and down a few times in agreement. "In time. Lilah wants babies as soon as possible. They'll get their chance."

He turned back to his food and picked up his fork, seeming a little down again. I wanted to kick myself in the ass for even bringing it up without thinking how it would affect him. I was so damn nosy.

Knowing I had to fix it, I reached across the table and placed my hand on his forearm. When his eyes met mine, I winked. "Well, I'm still bound by an oral contract to supply you with three children and a dog, so, there's always that."

The corners of his blue eyes crinkled as his smile stretched across his face, and I sighed in relief when he laughed. "Thank you," he whispered, leaning over to kiss me softly. It was likely he was thanking me for lightening the mood more than he was for agreeing to give him the kids his ex wouldn't. "Okay, we should finish up here and get out to work. You have a session with April this morning, right?"

"Mmm hmm," I mumbled around my most recent bite of eggs.

"Do you know who you want her to ride yet?"

I nodded, having given this a lot of thought the week before. "Yeah, I want to try her out on Max. Having trained him, I have a feeling they'll be good together."

"Do you want me to bring him in while you prep for your session with her?" he asked, scooping another bite of eggs onto his fork.

"Sure. That would be great. Thanks."

After cleaning up, we quickly got dressed and headed out to the barn hand-in-hand. We had no reason to hide.

"Good morning, you two!" Dad exclaimed, drawing the attention of Tom and Jeff to our arrival. "You ready to work? There's still quite a bit to do before our new boarders show up in the next few days." He noticed our joined hands, but all he did was smile.

"Okay, well you boys have fun with that, I'm going to go and see if Jill is using the indoor arena for her lessons so I know where April and I will be." I looked up at Jensen. "I'll see you later."

The dull cramps returned, and I winced before turning away. Of course Jensen noticed it. "Are your ribs bothering you again?"

"No," I told him honestly. "They feel great. It was nothing to worry about. I promise."

A look of understanding seemed to flash in Jensen's eyes, but being a gentleman, he didn't ask for any more clarification. "All right. I'll see you at lunch. Have a good morning."

"You too." Outside the arena entrance, I did a quick check of the lesson board and saw that Jillian was in a session. I gripped the handle to the large sliding door and opened it a crack, yelling "Heads up!" before opening it enough to slip through.

Jillian looked over to me with a weak smile while her

two students trotted around the arena. "Hey, Madi. How've you been?" Her voice was uncharacteristically monotonous.

"I've been good. You okay?" I inquired as I moved next to her.

She shrugged. "Yeah. Remember that guy I told you about?" I nodded. "Well, he broke up with me this weekend."

"I'm sorry to hear that." I really was.

"Meh. Sure, it sucks, but everything happens for a reason, right?" Jill laughed lightly, shaking her head as if to clear it. "Blah! Enough of that." She turned to her students for a quick second. "Okay guys, you can slow to a walk and change direction on the diagonal." With a smile, she looked at me again. "What's up?"

"Oh, I have my first private with April today, so I was just wondering if you were using the indoor arena for your next lesson?"

"I can. April loves riding outdoors, and it's gorgeous out there. Take advantage of it."

"Heads up!" a familiar voice boomed, and I noticed Jillian's eyes brighten.

I turned to see Jensen slip into the arena, closing the door behind him before he jogged toward us. Jill leaned into me and nudged me with her elbow. "He's so hot, huh? I realize I just broke up with Tyler and all, but I think there was something betwe—"

His eyes were on me as he approached, the blue of his irises absolutely captivating as he reached out for my hand. "Hey, I forgot something," he whispered softly as he tilted his face down and kissed me sweetly. My entire body felt tingly, and I hummed appreciatively as our lips parted

It was like we were alone in the arena as the entire world slipped away around us. Nothing else mattered when his lips were on mine.

Beaming, he released his hold on me. "Good morning, Jillian. I didn't mean to interrupt." He smiled at me again. "I'll see you at lunch."

"Yup." Jensen exited the arena as I turned to find Jillian gawking. "Um, Jill?"

She shook her head and blinked a few times. "Sorry. I

had no idea. I didn't mean to ... Holy crap!" I laughed at her inability to string a sentence together. "How? When?"

"A couple weeks, actually," I confessed with a warm blush creeping up my face.

Jillian's eyes and smile widened. "Good for you!" Her smile instantly transformed to one a little more devious. "Does he have a brother?"

I shook my head. "Brother-in-law. Sorry."

"Too bad." We both watched her students for a moment as they rode around at a steady walk. "Okay, you guys can pick up a trot. Good job, Vicky!"

"Well, I'll leave you to this. I'll talk to you later," I said, making my way for the exit.

Jill waved. "Sounds good. Have a good lesson!"

When I stepped back into the barn, I heard nothing, which could only mean the guys had all gone outside or to the other barn since they were beginning to get it ready for new boarders. While all the time we had spent on the new expansion was extremely exhausting—and very expensive—it didn't quite feel real until now. It was all very exciting to know that our successful little operation here was beginning to blossom again.

I started setting up a jumper course in the outdoor arena for April to practice on, and by the time I had the jumps set up, she showed up with Max. He was a ten-year-old chestnut gelding, and one of the best I had trained. If today went as I'd hoped, I would let April and her mother know that he was for sale.

As they approached the arena, the deep caramel color of his coat gleamed and his flaxen mane bobbed and shone in the sunlight. "Good morning, April," I greeted as I opened the gate for her.

"Hi, Miss Landry!" she replied enthusiastically before stopping in the center of the ring and tightening the girth behind Max's front legs.

"Please, call me Madi," I told her with a laugh. "How are you today?"

"Oh my gosh!" she exclaimed, gracefully mounting the large Thoroughbred gelding. "So excited! When I told my girlfriends I was training with *Madison Landry* ... O. M. G. They were totes jealous!"

Oh, to be fourteen again.

I watched April warm Max up around the arena. It didn't take long before April's mood shifted from giddy to professional. She took instruction well, always nodding and accepting my constructive criticism on her posture or how she corrected Max's form.

"Okay, let's try the low combination to get Max warmed up for the course. I'll just set up a few cross rails, and then we'll raise them bit by bit." I raised the poles into the cups before addressing her again. "How high have you jumped with Jill?"

"Um, two and a half feet, I think?" she said as Max trotted past me.

I nodded, brushing the dirt from my hands onto my jeans. "And how did that feel? Were you comfortable with it?"

She nodded. "Yeah. But I'd like to try three."

"Well," I said with a light laugh, loving her enthusiasm. "Let's see how you do with two and a half first, okay?"

As I expected, April and Max were amazing over the low rails. They went through the combination a couple times before I raised the poles, and after I felt they were ready, I instructed them on the course. I had set up a brush jump, a couple of oxers and a combination. Max handled it like a pro. He and April were perfectly matched.

After completing the course at two and a half feet, and seeing Max clear the rails by at least a foot each, I figured we could raise it another half a foot. I wasn't wrong; April handled Max very well, and he finished the course again with ease before our time was up.

"All right, you can cool him down. You both did so well today!" I praised her. "What did you think of Max?"

April loosened the reins so Max could stretch his neck as she removed her feet from the stirrups and raised the leathers to criss-cross them over Max's withers. "He's amazing! I've ridden quite a few horses while here, and I loved them all, but he's different. Better. Smoother."

The smile on my face widened as I watched her lean forward to pet his neck affectionately. He snorted happily and shook his head, enjoying the attention. They made a couple laps around the arena while I cleaned up the course, returning the standards and poles back to the far corner. I was just putting the last jump standard in place when I caught a mess of brown hair walking toward the new barn. Raising my hand, I waved at Jensen and fought to contain a girlish giggle when he winked in return.

April dismounted, and I walked with her back to the barn. She had just tethered Max to groom him when her mother approached. "Hi, sweetheart! I saw a little bit of your riding, you were spectacular."

"Thanks, Mom!" April squealed. "This is Max. Isn't he awesome? I *love* him."

I smiled, running my hand down the front of Max's face before turning to April's mom. "I knew he'd be right for her. You know, Mrs. Peters, I trained Max myself. He's a great horse, and I feel he's perfectly suited to April." I nodded my head toward my father's office while April fed Max a few carrots and removed his saddle.

I opened the office door and gestured for her to enter first. Once inside, I raved about how well April did during her lesson and how much potential she had to go far in the industry. Mrs. Peters didn't seem too surprised as she sat in the chair across from me.

"As I mentioned last week, I think April could go far in this business. It's a lot of hard work, but she's open to suggestions to better herself and she's amazing. It's not just riding. There's certification to get her into the pro circuits, and she'd need a permanent mount. One she feels comfortable on."

"And you think Max is that horse?" she deduced.

I nodded once. "Even after just one session, I do."

"How much are we talking?"

It didn't take much to sell her on Max's pedigree and worth, and soon she was handing over a check and signing the paperwork. April had herself a new mount.

Before leaving the office, we spent a few more minutes discussing the cost of board and her additional lessons. With everything in order, I walked Mrs. Peters out of the office to tell April the good news. She let out a squeal that pulled Max's focus, and then hugged her mom and me.

"So, you're free to come out to the barn whenever to ride him, but you still have to follow the rules set for everyone. You must be respectful of lesson times and stay close to the grounds should you go for a trail ride. There are marked trails for the riders here, and we need you to make sure you stay on them. It's a safety and liability issue." April nodded, her eyes still wide with disbelief as I rattled off things she already knew. "I want to see you twice a week, once for a riding session and the other will be for textbook work. If you're serious about this, there are a lot of things that need to be learned in order to certify you."

"I am! I swear I am!"

I smiled. "I know you are. You still have a couple years, but I think in that time, we can get you into a few of the local competitions — in fact, Mr. Davis had made a suggestion to my dad about us hosting a few a year. They would be excellent practice for an aspiring young rider."

"Yes! All of it! Yes!" Her eagerness reminded me of my own enthusiasm when my grandfather told me everything I was telling her.

We set up her bi-weekly sessions before I left the two of them with their new gelding. I offered to take him back outside for them when they were ready to head home, and after releasing Max back out to his paddock, it was time for lunch. I was excited to tell everyone about Max's new owner and our newest prodigy.

14
CLOSE CALL
Madison Landry

When I arrived at Dad's for lunch, everyone congratulated me on selling Max and securing April's extra training. It only took one question from my dad to bring me down from my high.

"How much did you get for Max?" His expression was static as he stared intently at his poker hand while Tom placed his bet.

I stood next to Jensen at the counter where he was cutting vegetables. While I knew for a fact that Dad often offered deals on some of the horses we sold to our current clientele, I wasn't sure how he would feel about the discount I gave Mrs. Peters—especially considering how much this renovation was costing us. I only hoped he would see the light at the end of the tunnel when it came to the additional funds in board and extra training we would be getting for taking April on a little more.

Jensen's eyes were on me as he waited with Dad for me to respond, and I grimaced slightly before mumbling, "Fifteen."

Dad's eyes slowly rose from the cards in his hands before he turned his head to me. "Madison, you do realize that Max's pedigree *alone* appraises him at fifteen thousand, don't you? The years of training that went into him easily raise his value."

"Yeah, I know. But think about it. We're taking April on once more each week ... plus the money we'll get for his board now. It's just, he's ten. He's never competed. Sure, he may have champion bloodlines, but he's not a champion yet. And he won't be unless we get him someone who wants to make him one." I shrugged. "And April does."

Jensen smiled at me before returning his attention to the vegetables he was slicing on the cutting board. I reached across and swiped a sliver of red pepper from the pile and popped it in my mouth. "I'm sorry I didn't consult you on it beforehand."

With a sigh, Dad conceded. "Nah, that's okay. I guess I see your point." He returned to his poker game just in time for Jeff to lay his cards down on the table.

"Royal flush!" he announced before sweeping the pile of loose coins and bills toward him. Tom and Dad groaned simultaneously, throwing their cards down on the table like children.

"Okay," Jensen announced. "Lunch is almost ready." He turned his attention to me. "You hungry?" There seemed to be some kind of hidden connotation in his voice, but I knew it really wasn't the time to act upon it. Of course, my mind was pretty much one-tracked lately, so it was likely just me hearing inflections where there were none.

"Famished. What's for lunch?" I inquired, peering over his arm to see what he was making.

Jensen smiled. "For you and me, roasted bell pepper and feta wraps. And I cooked up a little of your dad's left over chicken from last night for theirs." He nodded toward the stove where he had two skillets going. In one was a combination of red pepper, mushrooms and purple onion strips sautéing, and in the other was the same, but with slivers of chicken cooking along with it.

"You're kind of amazing in the kitchen," I admitted happily.

When his lips twisted up into a smirk, I knew I should have thought before speaking—as usual. He lowered his head until he was right by my ear and whispered, "Only 'kind of'?"

My cheeks instantly warmed, remembering our kitchen interlude a little over a week ago, and I pulled back with a tiny gasp. "You're terrible," I whispered, poking his abdomen with my pointer finger before washing up for lunch.

"Maybe," he snickered. "But you love it."

"I don't know why ..." I teased before another sharp pain radiated in my abdomen. Up until now they had been relatively dull—almost non-existent—which could only mean the beginning of that bitch, Aunt Flow, was imminent. *Whore.*

I put my hand on my hip and put pressure on the cramping area, drawing Jensen's concerned eyes to me. "You okay?"

The cramp passed, and I smiled at him, hopefully assuring him. "Yeah. Fine, thanks. Do you need any help?"

Shaking his head, Jensen lifted the skillet with chicken and used the tongs to place equal portions onto a small bed of spinach in the center of each wrap. Then, he topped them all with some feta cheese and wrapped them tightly. "Would you take these to the guys?" he asked, picking up the plates and handing them to me until I had both hands full and was balancing the third on my forearm.

"So, Madison," Dad spoke up as we all ate. "Your birthday's coming up in just under two weeks."

"Yeah. So it is."

Jensen looked up from what he was doing. "It is?"

"September twenty-second," I replied.

"Well, what did you want to do?" Dad continued. He was always holding out hope that I'd want to do *anything* to celebrate, but I liked my low-key traditions.

After swallowing my last bite, I wiped my hands on my napkin. "Um, absolutely nothing—like every year. Save for our tradition."

"Tradition?" Jensen inquired.

"Yeah, ever since I learned how to ride, Dad would always bring me out here and we'd go for a long trail ride on my birthday. Every year. We've never missed one."

I looked up at my dad, who was looking a little embarrassed due to my outing his softer side. "It's my favorite part of the day," I added softly.

"Mine too, kiddo."

"So that's all you do? No party? No cake?"

I shook my head. "Nah, not since I was in middle school. I was never big on parties."

"Well, what do you want for your birthday?" Jensen prodded, nudging my knee with his beneath the table.

Dad choked a little on his food as he fought back a laugh. "Oh, Madi doesn't do gifts."

"That's ridiculous," Jensen said, shaking his head like such a thing was impossible.

I shook my head. "No, really." I told him. "I have everything I need. Everything." His eyes locked on mine, hopefully picking up my meaning. "It's ridiculous to spend money on frivolous things. No gifts. Please." The look in Jensen's eyes told me he wasn't ready to comply.

"So," Jensen said, trying to understand. "No party. No cake. *And* no gifts?"

"Right. Easy peasy." I stood up and started to clear the empty plates away before putting them in the dishwasher. I turned back to everyone and smiled, trying to get the discussion *off* my birthday. "Can we train outside today? It's gorgeous out," I asked Tom as we put our shoes on.

He nodded. "Yeah, I think that would be fine. Why don't you go and catch Starla, and we'll get started in about thirty."

Jensen stayed at my side as I grabbed Starla's halter and lead. "Mind if I tag along? Your dad doesn't need me for a bit, and I've missed you terribly."

How could I argue with that? I couldn't, plain and simple. "Sure. I'd love that."

I laced my fingers between his, and we walked happily out to the far paddock, thoroughly enjoying each other's company. "So," Jensen began. "Do you want to go for a trail ride tonight? Maybe before dinner."

"Sounds great," I said as we entered the paddock together. Starla stood near the center, ears flicking as I clicked my tongue, and she wandered over, making my job easier.

"So, I'll get Halley and Ransom ready for six then?" Jensen said on our way back to the barn so I could tether and groom Starla.

I smiled wide. "Perfect." Jensen leaned down and placed a sweet kiss on my lips before backing away.

After getting Starla tacked up, I led her to the outdoor arena. Tom was hard at work setting up a few jumps, and I grew nervous for my ass when I saw him take the rainbow planks out. Starla had only ever jumped a basic rail, so it was likely she would refuse this one—I just hoped I could stay seated. Phantom pains ripped through my ribcage as I predicted the outcome.

During our warm up, Starla's ears perked forward as we walked past the awaiting rainbow jump, but she didn't shy away from it or seem skittish. I grew hopeful. Once she was warmed up, we moved into a trot. For such a young horse, she was incredibly docile. Her transitions between gaits were almost always seamless, and she was such a smooth ride. We actually got pretty lucky with her, because her parents were a bitch to train; we actually retired her dam as a permanent brood mare because she was so feisty. We hoped her foals wouldn't inherit that trait. Starla was her first filly and was proving to be a delight.

"Lookin' good, Madi," Tom praised. "Why don't you move her into a steady lope for a few laps, and then we'll take her over a few low cross rails."

"Sure." All it took was a gentle nudge for Starla to transition into a canter. We circled the arena a couple of times before I moved her down the center and over the one foot cross rails that Tom had just set up. As expected, Starla took them with ease, and I was ecstatic.

"Good, Madi!"

Patting Starla's neck, I circled around to take the short jumps again when I caught sight of Jensen, Dad, and Jeff taking a break to observe my session. Jensen's eyes were trained on me, a smile spread wide across his face while Jeff and Dad spoke amongst themselves, casually glancing over once in a while. After two more times over the rails, Tom set the rainbow planks to the same height and instructed me to give them a try.

Confidence filled me knowing how well Starla was doing today, and I turned her in the jump's direction. When we were a stride away, I started to shift forward in my saddle in preparation for her to leap forward. My conviction was short-lived, and my heart leapt into my throat when she refused, shooting me forward. Thankfully, I was able to tighten my legs and grip onto her mane before flying over her head ... but just barely.

I heard Jensen curse, and I cringed. Here I had just gotten myself healed—barely over a week ago—and I was already close to being on my way back to the ER.

"Damn it," I muttered, irritated with myself for not seeing it coming. With my panicked heart pounding, I righted myself in the saddle and backed Starla up a few strides to turn her around and try again. "You can do this." I wasn't *just* talking to Starla.

This time, I paid attention to Starla's body language as we approached. Her ears perked forward and her neck tensed, pulling her head back a little; she was scared—which was to be expected of anything unfamiliar. She refused again, but this time I wasn't nearly as close to falling off as before. Of course, that didn't stop Jensen from hopping the fence and rushing toward me.

"I'm fine," I said through clenched teeth, my frustration clear in my tone as I turned Starla sharply. I didn't back her away like before, thinking that maybe by doing that the first time I confused her and made her think she was done with it. She needed to be exposed to it.

"Madison," Tom interjected just as Jensen opened his mouth to speak. "Why don't you take her over the cross rails again?"

I shook my head adamantly, steering Starla back onto the track so we could circle around and try the rainbow again. "No," I stated firmly. "She's going to do this."

As we approached the jump again, Starla still seemed nervous, but not nearly as much. Her ears were still straight forward, but she didn't throw her head up this time. Her final stride spread out, and I sucked in a breath while leaning forward, paying close attention to the cues she was giving me, and we sailed over the low multi-colored planks.

It wasn't until she landed that I expelled the breath I had taken, allowing myself to relax. She did it, and I managed to stay on through it all. Starla maintained her lope as we circled around to do it again. When I looked toward the center of the ring, I saw Jensen had joined Tom. While Tom looked pleased that I had stuck with it and made her go over it, Jensen looked bot relieved and terrified. I couldn't blame him, not after what happened his first few days here.

"I'm taking her again," I announced. "She needs to do it more than once." No one disagreed with me, but Jensen looked like he was about to pass out. He really shouldn't have been so stressed about it; Starla took the jump without even second guessing it now that she knew it wasn't going to bite her.

I had her take the rail twice more before Tom spoke up again. "Great job, Madi. You can cool her down now. She did really well."

I slowed Starla to a walk and gave her a little more rein so she could relax her neck. I leaned forward and patted her neck, being sure to drag my hand up and scratch her shoulder as I sat upright again.

"You scared the shit out of me," Jensen said, appearing beside me as I walked Starla around the arena.

I looked down at him as he reached out and rubbed Starla's neck. "Sorry. I couldn't make her *not* take it though. It would have sent the wrong message."

"No, I get that. But you *just* got better. It's likely all it would have taken was one fall to fracture your ribs again." Jensen sighed, reaching back and gripping the back of his neck. He was way too tense.

"Right. But it's a risk one takes when riding. You know that," I countered, letting him know that his falling off was just as likely as mine. Okay, maybe not *just* as likely, given recent events. But he could fall off — if he wasn't perfect.

"I suppose," Jensen mumbled.

I put the reins in my left hand and reached out with my right to run my fingers through his hair as he kept pace with Starla and me. "Look, she took the jump, and more importantly, I *didn't* fall off. I'd say that's a pretty successful day, wouldn't you?"

"Yeah," he conceded, an impish grin quirking the left side of his lips up. We moved to the center of the arena where

I dismounted and stood before him. "I have to go out to the far paddock to check on the horses out there. Your dad said there've been a few coyote sightings and he wants to make sure the horses out there are okay and that they aren't coming near the grounds."

I nodded. "Okay. Be careful."

He pressed his lips to mine. "You too. See you in a bit."

The rest of the afternoon was pretty humdrum. I taught the afternoon lessons as agreed upon by Jill and me while she worked on her invoicing for the last week. Time seemed to fly, and before I knew it, it was five and we were beginning to bring the horses in for the night.

By seven, the stalls were full of happily feeding horses and Jensen was just tightening Halley's girth for me. I stopped by my dad's office before we headed out and knocked softly on the open door.

"Hey, kiddo," he said, raising his eyes from the computer screen. "What's up?"

"Just wanted to let you know that the horses are in and feeding. Jill is in with her seven o'clock lesson, and Jensen and I are going to take Halley and Ransom out on the trails," I informed him. "You okay with that?"

Dad smiled. "Yes. Thanks for letting me know. You two be careful."

"We will." With one last wave, I walked briskly to the end of the barn where Jensen was waiting for me.

He handed me Halley's reins, and we stepped out into the cool evening air, mounting our horses before hitting the trails. The breeze was nice on my bare arms, and it wisped through my loose hair as we found the farm's first marked trail.

"So, you really don't want anything for your birthday? We could invite Willow and Brandon over and—"

I shook my head before cutting him off. "Nope. I'm quite content to just have a quiet dinner with you and Dad, and go on my father-daughter trail ride."

He didn't protest, merely looked at me like I was crazy and nudged Ransom into a trot. We walked the trails as the sun began to set, talking about the possible coyote problem.

"Did you see any signs that they were close to our land?"

Beside me, Jensen shrugged, seeming a little unsure. "Well, I *think* the prints I saw could have been from a coyote or a large dog. I can't be too sure. I got all the horses moved to the paddocks within the grounds in hopes we can keep them safe through the winter. Have you ever had a problem with coyotes or even wolves before?"

I shook my head. "Not that I can recall, but we had a dog up until a couple years ago. I think it's an Alpha-male thing, and it kept the wild dogs at bay."

"What happened to the dog?"

"Oh, he was ancient. He was my grandfather's. Best dog ever," I said, fondly remembering Shadow. "He was this gorgeous Doberman/German Shepherd cross."

"Have you ever thought of getting another dog?"

I hummed contemplatively. "Um, sure. I would love another dog; I guess we've just been so busy around here that I never really thought about it. I always wanted a German Shepherd. They're so loyal and are by far one of the best guard dogs out there, based on my experience."

Jensen grinned. "I had a shepherd as a kid. She was the best."

"So yeah, maybe when things settle down, I'll start looking for a dog," I said with a shrug. "Hopefully it'll help with the wild dogs loitering about."

A smile slowly crept across Jensen's face, but before I could ask him what he was plotting, he nudged Ransom into a gallop. With a laugh, I urged Halley forward with a squeeze and chased him through the trails until we came to the river and slowed to a walk, laughing.

The sound of the river flowing was soothing. We allowed Ransom and Halley to lower their heads for a drink before we walked along the bank, talking and taking in the scenery. It was all so peaceful and serene. It was the perfect end to a pretty great day.

15
THE PERFECT GIFT
Jensen Davis

Madison groaned, pulling the blanket up over her face to block out the sun that was starting to brighten the room.

I raised my arm and turned over slightly to slap the snooze button before resuming my previous position, enveloping her warm body. "Good morning, love," I whispered, placing a soft kiss just behind her ear. "Did you sleep well?"

"Mmm hmm." Her voice was muffled beneath the thick comforter.

Kissing her again, I hugged her a little tighter, her ass coming into contact with my groin. There was a brief moment where I contemplated ravaging her, remembering once the fog of sleep in my brain cleared that we couldn't. "How are you feeling?"

With another groan, Madison pulled the blanket from her face, causing her hair to stand on end due to the static electricity of the down duvet. I chuckled, raising my hand to tame her flyaway hairs. "My lower back is killing me, actually."

Slowly, I lowered my right arm down her body, stopping just above the curve of her backside. Then I slipped my hand beneath *my* shirt that she was wearing, pressed my thumb into the muscle there and began to rub in a circular motion. It never once occurred to me that my overwhelming need to take care of her in whatever way she needed would backfire on me and torture me further—until she started moaning and telling me how good it felt. I really had to fight the urge to thrust my hips forward against her ass with everything I had.

"Do you need any Advil?" I rasped, suddenly eager to get out of bed, yet not easing the pressure or stopping because I needed to be touching her. Like I said: torture.

She turned her face to me and kissed me quickly on the lips. Her cheeks were pink, and I couldn't help but wonder if maybe she was getting herself a little worked up a moment ago as well. "You're sweet. I have some Midol in my medicine cabinet. I'll grab some when I go to get ready," she assured me.

"Okay. What do you want for breakfast? I'll go and get started on it," I offered as she pulled herself out of my arms.

I smiled as she stood, watching my T-shirt fall over the tops of her thighs. Even though I bugged her about wanting it back—because I did—I definitely loved seeing her in it. I wasn't sure if it was just the fact that she was completely wrapped up in something that belonged to me, or if it was because she loved that it was both mine and a nerdy Trekkie shirt. Whatever the reason, I would gladly give it to her for keeps—but would never willingly tell her that.

"Omelets?" she suggested quietly.

Nodding, I sat up and swung my legs off the bed to pull my flannel pants on. "Okay. I'll go brush my teeth and get started on them."

Not wanting Madison to have to wait, I grabbed my toothbrush and snuck into the ensuite washroom that the spare room had and took care of my morning needs before breakfast. As I looked around the half-bath ensuite, I could tell it was added on after the initial construction of the home. Usually, a one-story farmhouse as old as this one was pretty basic.

In my time living here, I could tell that Madison had likely put a little bit of money into the home to make it hers. The newer hardwood floors and carpet would attest to a renovation in the last five years, as well as the addition of this washroom and the fully renovated basement suite.

As I stood in front of the mirror looking around, I found myself wondering why Madison never took this bedroom upon moving in. Not only was it bigger and brighter due to the two large windows on the walls that formed the outer corner of the house, but it had a private washroom.

I kissed Madison on my way to the kitchen where I placed the frying pan on the stovetop and turned the burner on to warm. I gathered all the ingredients for our breakfast, took them to the island, and began to prepare everything in a mixing bowl.

I had just poured the egg mixture into the frying pan when Madison emerged in jeans and a tank top, wearing a zip-up hoodie overtop to guard her from the morning chill. Her long blond hair was pulled back into a ponytail, and she smiled as she reached for the coffee. It had just finished brewing, so I hadn't yet had the opportunity to pour it for her.

While I continued to look after breakfast, Madison poured our coffee before taking hers to the table and sitting in her seat. One look over my shoulder told me she wasn't feeling one hundred percent yet, and I couldn't help feeling the deep-rooted desire to usher her back to bed to sleep it off.

"I'll be fine, Jensen," she said, pulling her foot up onto the chair so her thigh rested against her chest. "As soon as the pills kick in, I'll be right as rain." Her voice sounded a little hoarse to me, as well, and I worried she might be getting sick.

When our omelets were ready, I plated them and took them to the table where we powered through them before I went and got dressed for work. Our morning was no different than any other as we cleaned out the stalls before going our separate ways. After doing a walk-through of the grounds, checking the troughs, I grabbed straw from the shelter. I slipped on my work gloves, grabbed the twine that held the bale together, and lifted it with ease before taking it about forty feet to my left and into the new barn. According to Wayne's huddle with us this morning, we had several new boarders showing up in the next couple of days, so he wanted me to make sure the stalls were ready for when they arrived.

After laying the straw on the floor of four of the thirty stalls, I grabbed another bale for four more to restock. With the eight stalls we expected to fill padded with fresh straw for the horses, I ran over to the other barn for a couple bags of oats for storage as well. Madison was nowhere to be seen as I walked from one barn to the other, so I assumed she was either busy with Jillian or maybe in her father's office doing some paperwork.

The main barn was empty, and as I passed by the arena door, I could hear Jillian's loud voice as she disciplined one of her morning riders for trailing to close to another rider.

I walked the length of the barn aisle toward the feed storage room, and just as I rounded the corner, I gasped sharply. I didn't mean to, but it caught me off guard to find Madison in there. Finding her there wasn't the reason I responded the way I did, though. To be honest, my reasoning was actually pretty ridiculous and the product of an as-of-late under-sexed brain.

There was nothing overtly sexual about Madison standing up on the stepladder, her body stretching long as she reached for a nearly empty bag of alfalfa pellets, but I was on the verge of sporting major wood, regardless.

I stood there, staring at her as she struggled to reach that damn bag. A gentleman would have offered to get it for her, but I was frozen in place, my eyes moving up her lean, denim-clad legs, over her tight little ass until my gaze locked on a two-fucking-inch sliver of skin between her jeans and tank top. Depraved thoughts of licking the exposed flesh suddenly crossed my mind, and it wasn't until she spoke that I snapped out of it.

"Are you seriously just standing there?" she snapped.

Shaking my head and forcing my eyes to hers I apologized. "Sorry. I, um … No, there's no excuse for that. I'm just sorry. Here, hop down, I'll grab it." I held out my hand for Madison so she could step down carefully, the gentleman in me finally bitch-slapping the horny pervert into submission — for the time being, anyway.

"We're going to need more. That's all we have left," Madison said as I stepped up onto the ladder and snatched the bag from the top shelf. "Oats too."

"I'll head out to the feed store before lunch. Can you think of anything else we might need?" She shook her head. "Okay, if you think of anything, let me know."

"I will." She took the bag of pellets from me and smiled. "And thanks for helping me. Even if it did take you away from ogling my ass." The little vixen was trying her hand at being a tease again. Well, two could play at that game.

Impulsively, I pulled her toward me, turning our bodies until I had her sandwiched between me and the wall. "I mean it, Madi. If you think of *anything* you might need ... You let me know."

Her big eyes widened as they danced between mine, the light picking up the flecks of green, and her breathing quickened. With my body pressed right against hers, I could feel her heartbeat—or maybe it was mine. "Jensen, what are you doing? I was just teasing. We can't ..."

I smirked before leaning down and kissing her softly. "Maybe not today," I whispered, my lips ghosting over hers. She exhaled a shaky breath as I parted our bodies. I was pretty sure her knees were trembling as she flattened her empty hand against the wall, bracing herself.

Feeling pretty satisfied with myself—and pretty damn frustrated at the same time—I smiled. "I'll head into town now. Maybe I'll stop at the diner and grab something for lunch. Will you see what the guys want and give me a call?"

"Sure. But this isn't over."

Chuckling, I stepped forward and kissed her. "Wouldn't be any fun if it was, now would it?"

I climbed into the truck since I knew my bike wasn't the best option if I had to load up on feed. I missed riding my bike and decided to see if maybe Madison might want to go for a ride sometime. The drive to town was quiet due to the stereo not working—I'd have to remember to take a look at the wiring later and see if I could figure it out.

My shopping trip didn't take long since I already knew what I needed. After paying the cashier, I loaded up the truck, and just as I climbed behind the wheel, my phone rang.

"Hey, Madi."

"Hey. Just talked to the guys. My father would like a cheeseburger with fries—he's trying to clog his arteries, I swear. Tom and Jeff both asked for a turkey club on white with a side of fries. And I'll have a spinach salad. If you could ask them to throw some egg and a little cheese on there, that'd be awesome."

"Sure. I'll see you in a bit then. Love you," I told her, unable to contain the goofy grin on my face; people walking by had to think I was absolutely certifiable.

"I love you, too. See you soon."

We hung up, and I drove to the diner to put the orders in. While I waited, I decided to walk along the sidewalk of the strip mall where the quaint little restaurant was located.

Next to the diner was a card shop, next to that, a small, independently owned bookstore, then a small children's clothing store. After passing the last window of the kid's clothing store, I stopped, staring directly into the window of the next little shop. A wide smile broke across my face and my mind was made up. Closer to Madison's birthday, I would be coming back to buy her birthday gift.

16
ONE THING AFTER ANOTHER
Jensen Davis

The next few days were ... *long*. The monotony of the everyday didn't help either. Madison and I would wake up—me extremely turned on from the way she would sleep against me. The first and second nights she slept with her back to my chest, and I thought that was bad enough. Well, the third night, she rolled over sometime in the night and draped her leg over my body. That wasn't enough to wake me, however; it wasn't until she started sighing breathlessly and moving her hips that I awoke with a start.

I wanted to believe it was an innocent dream, but once she started saying my name, I knew it was more. She was going to be the death of me. I tried to ignore it, but the longer I waited for her dream to end, the more aroused I became.

It was common knowledge that you weren't supposed to wake a sleepwalker. But what was the rule for sleep ... um, sex? No, what she was doing wasn't sleep-sex; it was grinding and moaning and touching ... *Oh, God.* Her soft hands started moving over my chest, my skin breaking out in goose bumps even though I was anything but cold.

"Madi," I whispered, pressing my lips into the top of her head and running my fingers along her back. "Baby, you're dreaming. Wake up."

With a quiet snort, Madison's head lifted from my chest. Even in the dark, I could see her blink a few times as if trying to fully breach the surface of consciousness. "Jensen? What time is it?" Propping herself up on her right arm, she used the back of her left hand to rub her eyes.

"It's about two in the morning. You were sort of talking in your sleep," I explained, kissing her temple before easing her back down onto my chest.

I could feel Madison's forehead furrow against my lips. "I was?" Then she gasped.

Laughing, I rolled onto my side, gently forcing her head to the pillow as my eyes captured hers in the dark room. "I figured I should wake you before my brain was no longer in control," I explained, trailing my right hand along her face, pushing a few strands of hair behind her ear.

Her eyes fluttered before locking on mine again. "God, I want you so much. I hate this." I had to laugh again because she was adorable when she pouted.

"Soon enough." I brushed the end of her nose with my own before leaning in to kiss her. I kept the kiss short and sweet in an effort to keep our mounting sexual frustration from escalating any further. If it did, I couldn't guarantee we wouldn't spontaneously combust.

"We should get some sleep. We have to be up in a few short hours," I whispered against her lips.

Madison hummed moving forward and snuggling into my body as my arms encircled her. "I love you too, Jensen."

The next morning I awoke to Madison staring at me. She was lying on her side, her head propped up by her left hand.

Closing my eyes, I stretched my body. "Good morning," I groaned. "How was your sleep?"

"Pretty good." There was something in her eyes that intrigued me. I was about to ask her what was going on when she leaned forward and kissed me. She tasted minty fresh, telling me she'd been up for a bit. "I'm happy to report that tonight you'd better be prepared to have your world rocked, Jensen Davis."

Her voice was still a little rough, but she assured me it

was just a cold. She'd been drinking tea with honey, hoping to soothe her throat, but as she pressed her forehead to mine, I wondered if it might be a little more serious.

"You're hot," I told her.

Smirking, she hummed and rolled closer to kiss me again. "You're not so bad yourself," she said, the rasp in her voice lending an added air of seduction.

Before she could kiss me, I sat up and placed the back of my hand to her forehead. "No, love, you're burning up."

"Jensen, I'm fine."

Using both hands, I cradled her face and used my thumb to check her lymph nodes; growing up with a doctor for a mother taught me a few of the basics. "Your glands are swollen. Open your mouth, please?"

"No," she said with a laugh. "You're overreacting. It's just a little cold."

"Does it hurt when you swallow?"

She quirked an eyebrow, and went to pull the sheets back from my legs. "Let's find out."

"Damn it, Madison, just answer the question."

With a huff, she rolled her eyes. "Yes, *doctor*. Sometimes—though not always—it feels like I'm swallowing glass." She paused. "But it's been better."

I wasn't sure I believed her. "Please open your mouth." She did as I asked, and I immediately saw the white spots on her tonsils. "I can't be sure, but it looks and sounds like you might have strep."

Madison released a heavy breath. "Figures."

"It's highly contagious, but if your dad will let me take you in to see my mom, we should be able to get you on antibiotics right away."

I flew out of bed and got dressed while Madison slipped across the hall to her room and did the same. Catching this early would require a far less aggressive antibiotic. I only hoped we hadn't let it incubate too long.

Wayne was just leaving his place when we strolled up the walkway, and he understood once I explained my suspicions. He handed us the keys to his truck, and I ushered Madison into the passenger seat before we flew down the highway.

I called to see if my mother was in the clinic, but she wasn't. She was actually in the city with my father. Madison suggested just going to a walk-in clinic, and while I was hesitant, I figured there'd be no harm in that.

We had to wait over an hour before Madison's name was called, and then we were in the exam room for another twenty minutes before the doctor finally showed up. He was an older man, standing around five-six, with a rounded belly and gray hair. His wire-rimmed glasses sat low on his nose as he looked down at the file in his hand.

"Miss Landry," he greeted. "What seems to be the problem?"

"My boyfriend thinks I might have strep," she replied, clearing her throat with a wince.

The doctor looked toward me, then at Madison before feeling her throat. She winced when he asked her to swallow, and she seemed just as reluctant to open her mouth as she was when I asked her earlier. He asked her if she'd been coughing, to which she replied no, and he took her temperature, shaking his head when he read the thermometer.

"Well, Miss. Landry, your boyfriend was right. You're scoring at a four."

"Out of?" she asked, sounding hopeful.

"Five. Your temperature is sitting at one-oh-one, your lymph nodes are swollen, there's white exudate on your tonsils, and lack of a cough. I want to run a rapid-strep test just to confirm, though."

Confused by the list of her symptoms, Madison said, "Okay?"

The doctor took a swab of Madison's throat and did what he had to with it. Waiting for the results was agonizing, but finally, the line appeared, signaling a positive for strep.

"I'm going to prescribe an antibiotic," he informed her, writing down on his prescription pad. "Take them until the bottle is empty. You on the pill?"

Madison blushed. "I am."

His light blue eyes glanced up over his glasses at the two of us. "Be sure to use a backup method of birth control if you're engaging in sexual relations. Antibiotics can hinder the effectiveness of the pill."

"We use condoms as well," I spoke up. "But good to know. Thank you."

He tore the scrip from his pad and handed it to Madison before leaving the room. We followed shortly after, hitting up the pharmacy right next door and picking up the pills.

"Sorry I was so resistant," she said, after taking her first dose.

"It's okay. I'm just glad we got you in and on some antibiotics now rather than later."

We arrived home around eleven. Wayne saw us pull into the drive and came over to see us as we turned toward the barn.

"How you doin', Madi?" he inquired.

"Jensen was right," she told him. "It's strep. The doctor gave me antibiotics to take for ten days."

"Well that's a relief. Hopefully they kick in soon and you can get back to feeling like your old self," he said, placing a hand on his daughter's shoulder. "Tom said you can forego training today, and I think it would be best if you take it easy for a few days until your throat feels better. There's some paperwork I can leave for you if you need something to do."

A smirk toyed at the right side of Madison's lips, and she glowered at him while shaking her head. "Gee, you're a peach."

Wayne laughed. "Anything for my little girl," he teased.

"Is there anything left to do in the barn?" Madison asked.

Wayne shook his head. "Everything's been taken care of."

Madison looked at her father, then me. "I know you both want me to take it easy, but would either of you object to me riding Halley for a bit?"

Wayne glanced my way, and I shrugged. "I don't see why not," I responded. "Just take it easy. Don't over-exert yourself. I wouldn't want you to exacerbate the issue."

"Sounds good."

While Madison went off to catch Halley, I made the

rounds to ensure that the troughs in all of the paddocks were full. The sun rose high in the cloudless sky, and by noon, it was obvious that we were in for another scorcher.

On my way back to the barn, I saw Madison on Halley in the outdoor arena. She'd shed the sweater she put on that morning before we went to the doctor, and then nudged Halley forward, circling the arena. I waved and then left her to the rest of her session.

When I got back into the barn, Jillian came out of her session looking for someone to help her bring a few extra standards inside for her next lesson. We walked outside together toward the back of the barn where the extra standards were kept and we each took one and hauled them to the arena door. The task effectively killed a little more of my morning, and by the time I helped Jillian move the standards inside, it was almost lunchtime.

Madison was already at her dad's, cooking some soup. The guys hadn't arrived yet, so I approached Madison and gave her a kiss on the cheek.

"You know, this whole 'being infected' thing is a total drag," she grumbled in a hoarse voice. She sounded worse than this morning.

"I agree, but if you just take the antibiotics and rest, you should be better in a few days."

She set the spoon down and turned to face me, pouting. "I sure as hell hope so."

With a smile, I nodded. I was just about to say something completely inappropriate when the front door opened, and the guys came sauntering in. So, instead, I kissed her on the forehead and got started making sandwiches.

17
THE LOGICAL NEXT STEP
Jensen Davis

By Saturday, Madison was starting to feel a little better. She had about seven days left of her antibiotics, but even after two days of rest and drugs, she was starting to sound better.

"I'm glad you're feeling better," I told her, my hands moving up to her hips and gripping them before I quickly rolled toward her. Madison squealed in surprise as we unexpectedly fell off the bed and onto the floor, where I pinned her beneath me. My lips quickly descended on hers, tender kisses quickly turning frenzied as my hands traveled under the shirt she wore to fondle her tits.

That got her attention—but not in the way I had hoped. Laughing, she struggled beneath me, pushing on my arms to remove my hands from her chest. I had no intention of abandoning my post, though.

"Hey now," she breathed. "We should save all of this energy for tonight. There's no time this morning."

I released her chest from my hands and flattened them against the cool hardwood on either side of her head. "Are you trying to kill me?"

Her laugh echoed in the small room as she shimmied away from me before pushing herself to her feet. "Last I checked no one died from blue balls."

"Maybe not," I replied dryly, standing up after her. "But it doesn't make it any less hard." Yeah, she heard it; apparently her Freudian slips were contagious. "Forget I said that."

"Mmm," she purred, her eyes drifting down my body and her lips twisting into a cocky smirk. "Wish I could."

If I didn't put a stop to this conversation—and fast—I knew that it would make it even more difficult to wait until tonight. It was already five-forty-five in the morning, and if we didn't grab a quick bite to eat, we would be late.

I wavered briefly between being responsible and accepting whatever punishment Wayne might dole out for us being late. Responsible won out—barely—and I smiled wickedly at Madison before standing up and throwing her over my shoulder.

She laughed, lightly slapping my ass as I carried her down the hall toward the kitchen. "I can walk, you know!" she exclaimed, not relenting her assault on my backside. Her weight shifted on my shoulder and her hands flattened on the small of my back briefly. "Actually, never mind. I think I like this view. I think this should be my regular mode of transportation from now on."

"And let you get lazy?" I teased, slapping her ass and making her squeal again before I sat her on the island and started looking for something quick to make for breakfast.

As the eggs cooked, I diced some watermelon, cantaloupe and honeydew into a bowl and added some sliced strawberries and grapes. When it was done, I turned and put the bowl next to Madison as she remained on the island and returned my focus to the eggs. After plating them, I turned around to find Madison popping a grape between her lips. It really shouldn't have been as fucking sexy as it was, but that horny bastard inside of me sure as hell thought it was.

Madison smirked slyly, chewing slowly as I cleared my throat and walked our plates to the table. Behind me, I heard Madison's bare feet hit the ground as she padded across the kitchen floor and set the bowl of fruit on the table before taking her seat.

Breakfast was mostly quiet—save for the soft moans Madison made every time she would slide a piece of fruit into her mouth. She was doing it on purpose to torture me further; to build anticipation. Little did she know it was unnecessary, and if she continued to do so, there would be a very good possibility that I would have to pull her aside at some point in the day and do things to her that were probably illegal in parts of the world.

Once we met up with Wayne and Tom in the barn, it didn't take long to muck out the stalls. After our regular chores were done, Madison went to work with Halley, freeing up her afternoon to train with Tom.

I had just finished when my cell phone vibrated in my pocket. Wiping my hands on my jeans, I reached for it and smiled when I saw it was my sister. "Hey, Lilah. How was Greece?"

"Amazing! You were right." Lilah and Kyle had asked my opinion on where to go for their honeymoon early into their engagement, and since I had done quite a bit of travelling around Europe after graduating high school, I thought that Greece would suit them perfectly.

"Is Madison around?" she asked.

I frowned. "You mean you'd rather talk to her than me?"

"Pretty much," she teased, giggling. "Nah, you know I love you. I was just wondering if I could see if she was doing anything this afternoon. I want to get to know her a little better, and Kyle got called to work, so I have the afternoon free."

"She's out riding right now, but I'll get her to call you as soon as she comes in, okay? I'm sure she'd love it if you came over."

"Sounds good. I guess I'll talk to you in a bit. Thanks."

When I stepped out of the barn after hanging up with Lilah, I was shocked at just how stifling it was. Using the back of my arm, I wiped the sweat from my brow as I rounded the corner of the barn after finding the outdoor arena empty.

The sight before me didn't help my rising body temperature—or cock—*at all*. I stopped dead in my tracks, completely stunned into silence as I took in the sight before me.

There, on a patch of grass about mid-way down the outer wall of the building, was Madison and Halley. Halley was tethered to the old hitching post and Madison's back was to me as she held the hose over the large mare's back. The sound of her laughter rang out whenever the spirited horse would throw her head up and splash her. Of course, because I was a man, I immediately noticed that the white tank top Madison was wearing was absolutely soaked through. It reminded me of our water fight in the wash stall a couple weeks ago, and was just as physically stimulating as it was then.

Something primal stirred deep within me, and I found myself behind her in a matter of seconds.

"Oh!" she cried, startled, when my hands found their way to her hips and turned her around. I clearly hadn't thought it through entirely before acting, because I was suddenly drenched as well. I couldn't be disappointed, though, because the cold water washing over me on such a hot day was refreshing.

"What are you doing?" she asked, giggling as I backed her against the outside wall of the barn and kissed her neck. The hose fell from her hands as she wound her arms up around my neck, teasing the short hairs there while I continued to kiss the soft skin of her neck.

"Do you have any idea how damn sexy you are?" I growled, lifting my head to look her in the eyes. "Seeing you like this—"

Madison's lips twisted up into a knowing smirk. "Oh, I get it. It's the wet shirt, right?" She briefly looked down at her chest, her bra clearly visible before raising her eyes back to mine.

I shrugged one shoulder and chuckled quietly. "Maybe just a little." I kissed her again, meaning for it to just be a gentle peck on the lips, but as soon as our lips were pressed together, Madison's fingers twisted into my hair, holding me in place. Her tongue slipped out, tracing my lower lip until I complied with her tacit request.

We soon got caught up in the lust that shrouded us, tugging and pulling at one another after days of very little physical contact. The entire world didn't seem to fucking matter as I moved my hands down her torso and up under her wet shirt until I was groping her tits again. She moaned against my mouth, rocking her hips forward to meet mine.

There was a soft nicker to my left before cold water briefly splashed our legs, reminding us where we were. Madison and I looked over at Halley who was pawing the ground, hitting the hose every once in a while and splashing us again.

"Cockblocker," Madison muttered to the mare with a headshake.

"She must be in cahoots with the rest of them," I said with a laugh, pushing myself away from Madison and the wall. "So, my sister called and wanted to talk to you. Says she has a free afternoon and wanted to know if you were free to hang out?"

Madison looked a little shocked as she picked the hose back up. "Uh, yeah. I have to meet with April for a certification class, but after that? Totally clear."

Smiling, I pulled out my phone and dialed Lilah's number, handing it to Madison.

She looked a little nervous, which was understandable, given what happened last weekend. Soon, her eyebrows relaxed, and she sighed with what looked like a small breath of relief. "Hey, Lilah!" A pause where I assumed Lilah spoke. "Um, yeah. I could free up some time. Did you want to go for that trail ride I promised? Yeah? Great! Okay, I'll see you then!" She hung up the phone before beaming up at me. "Your sister's coming over, and we're going to go for a trail ride. I thought I'd take her down by the river."

"Good," I said, smiling back at her as she handed me my cell phone. "I've actually got a few errands to do in town today, so I'm glad you'll be busy with Lilah."

Her eyes narrowed suspiciously. "What errands? We have enough feed. It can't be an errand for the ranch, which can only mean it's a personal errand, in which case I feel compelled to know — what with my birthday coming up this week and all. A birthday I specifically told you no party, no cake, and no presents for."

The woman was good at reading the situation and the people around her. However, I wasn't ready to give up my plans for my afternoon, so I laughed it off, bending over to plant a soft kiss on the top of her head. "You're being paranoid. I'm getting the oil changed in my bike."

"Oh. Well, okay then. Glad we came to an understanding," she said, nodding her head once as if to affirm her point.

Little did she know ...

"All right, I'll let you finish up here so you can meet up with April before Lilah gets here. I'll see you in a bit."

Two hours later, Lilah's red mustang pulled into the driveway. She parked in the parking alley on one side of the barn and climbed out. Smiling, I rushed over and pulled her into a hug. "It's good to see you," I told her, setting her back on her feet and noticing how tanned she was.

"Lilah," I heard Madison say behind me. "I'm so happy you came by today. Are you ready to go pick out your horse?"

"Okay, you ladies have fun. I'm going to head into town for a bit. Call if you need anything." Placing one last kiss on Madison's lips, I jogged toward the house and hopped onto my bike. Her birthday wasn't for another five days, but I planned to make it her best one yet.

I made a few stops around town before the one little shop I came across earlier in the week. Smiling as I looked in through the window again, I pulled the door open and walked through the main foyer. I knew that it was a smaller, independently owned shop, and that was actually what I preferred. Had I gone to one of the bigger, well-known chains for this sort of thing, I would have been paying out the ass, and Madison would have none of that. She would prefer no money to be spent on her, but that wasn't going to happen.

I moved slowly through the aisles between the clean glass cases, peering in and admiring everything I saw. While I knew what I was doing went against what Madison said about birthday gifts, there was a part of me that wanted this to show her just how serious I was about us. It was the next logical step in our relationship.

Everything I looked at varied in size, color, and shape. I had a basic idea what I was looking for, but nothing was really popping out at me. When I was in town earlier that week, I really liked what I saw in the window display, but they had since changed it. I was suddenly regretful for not making my purchase then.

"Can I help you?" a woman asked from behind me.

Turning quickly, I smiled. "Yeah. I'm looking for something for my girlfriend." It suddenly occurred to me that, while that's exactly what Madison was now, it was the first time I'd ever said it out loud. I liked hearing it.

"Big step. Been together long?" the sales lady asked.

"Just a few weeks," I replied, looking back into one of the glass showcases. "Actually, I walked by on Tuesday, and I really liked the ones you had in the window."

Her eyes brightened. "Come with me, they're closer to the back. I'm Rhonda, by the way."

"Jensen," I replied.

As she led me farther into the store, I couldn't help my eyes from taking in all of my other options. I would have bought out the entire store if I could afford it ... and if I knew with absolute certainty that Madison wouldn't kick my ass into next week. Of course, as soon as my eyes fell upon what I initially came here for, all of the others were forgotten.

"Beautiful, aren't they?" the woman asked.

"Very," I said, kneeling down to get a closer look at them all. It was hard to decide; other than their varying sizes, they were pretty much identical, and I could see Madison with any one of them.

After a lot of contemplation and holding each one to inspect and get a feel for them, I made my decision. "So, would it be too much trouble to pay today and come back Thursday? It's for her birthday, and it's hard to keep anything from her."

"Yeah, that shouldn't be a problem. I'll mark it 'sold,' and you can come by whenever. Just make sure you have your receipt in case I'm not in when you come back." She handed me my credit card and receipt after marking down the details of our arrangement. "It was a pleasure doing business with you, Mr. Davis."

"Thanks, Rhonda. I'll see you next week." Feeling good about Madison's birthday gift, I exited the quaint little shop, excited to present Madison with my little surprise.

It was a big step, but I was more than ready to take it.

18
MENDING BURNED BRIDGES
Madison Landry

After Jensen left Lilah and me alone, I turned back to her with an elated grin. "So, let's go find you a horse." Lilah beamed, falling into step with me as we went into the barn. "When's the last time you rode?"

"Oh, it's been years," she replied, her eyes roaming around the expanse of the facility. "This place is huge! I mean, I knew it had to be from what Jensen said, but I just never imagined … It's amazing."

Before grabbing a couple of halters and leads, I showed Lilah around. I took her into the viewing gallery where we each grabbed a soda from the fridge and sat to watch a bit of Jillian's lesson. Lilah was completely enraptured by the experienced class as they maneuvered around the small indoor hunter course.

"I'll have to make sure you're here next time we use the cross-country course. There are uphill banks, a drop fence, and a few corner rails. I even convinced my dad to have a coffin put in." Lilah's head snapped to me, a completely horrified look on her face, and I laughed. "Oh no! A 'coffin' is an obstacle found in a lot of cross-country courses. You go over the first hill, and at the bottom of it is this ditch—usually filled with water—and the horse has to jump it before climbing a second hill. It's actually pretty fun."

"Well, they should call that a 'ditch' then. 'Coffin' sounds dark and ominous," Lilah joked, returning her eyes to the lesson and taking a sip from her soda can.

"Actually, there is a ditch obstacle, but it's totally different. We have one of those, too. Seriously, I'll have to show you one day." I loved that Lilah seemed to be taking an active interest in my line of work. While I knew she had past experience with horses, as Jensen did, it was exciting to help her remember how much fun the sport could be.

When the lesson ended, Lilah and I made our way back to the barn. "I think I'll put you on Starla. She's young, but she's incredibly well-tempered; I think you two will complement each other nicely."

I led Lilah out to Halley and Starla's shared paddock. After catching Starla, I handed her off to Lilah and caught Halley. We took them to the outdoor hitching post and Lilah came inside with me where we grabbed my brushes. As I brushed Halley for a second time that day, her coat gleaming in the sun from her bath earlier, I had to smile every time I'd catch a glimpse of Lilah with Starla. She was talking to her and would laugh freely whenever Starla would nudge her with her muzzle. This would cause Lilah to lose her balance and stumble a few steps back time and time again.

Once the mares were brushed, Lilah and I went back into the barn to drop off the grooming equipment and grab our tack. I showed Lilah where Starla's saddle and bridle were before grabbing my own personal equipment, and we met back outside.

"Okay!" I exclaimed, making the last adjustment to Halley's girth before going over to check Starla's. "I'm just going to make sure it's tight enough. Starla can be tricky; she hates a tight girth, so she puffs out her lungs making you think it's tight. Then, as soon as you get on, she expels the air and the saddle slips. I'm sure *she* thinks it's hilarious."

I lifted the left saddle flap and gripped the girth strap closest to Starla's shoulder before leaning into her lightly. I waited a beat, and when I saw her breathe out, I pulled the strap upward, smiling victoriously. Now that that strap was tightened, she wouldn't be able to fight the second one. Tricky horse.

"There you go. Do you need a leg up?"

Lilah pulled her stirrups down the leathers, measuring

them against the length of her arms to make sure they were right for her height and hummed. "Umm, no. I think I can manage."

I was a firm believer that riding a horse was a lot like riding a bicycle; if you had done enough of it earlier in your life, it could be permanently engrained into you and should come almost as naturally as breathing. Seeing Lilah mount up in one graceful movement only proved my theory—that or she was just as perfect as her brother. Actually, that was probably *exactly* it.

Within minutes, Lilah and I were on the trails. The ride to the river was about forty-five minutes long, giving Lilah and me a lot of time to talk. She told me all about her honeymoon—well, maybe not *all about*. I didn't need to hear about the sex parts ... even though I was fairly certain Kyle would have found a way to talk all about it if he were here.

"We stayed in Athens," Lilah said. "It's absolutely stunning. On the first day, Kyle and I went to Acropolis ... Jensen was right. It was breathtaking."

"Jensen's been to Greece?" Was that jealousy in my voice? Why, yes. I believed it was.

Lilah nodded beside me. "Yeah, he backpacked all through Europe fresh out of high school."

"Did he go alone?" Yeah, that bitchy, green-eyed monster was starting to rear her ugly head; sometimes I just couldn't contain her.

Lilah inhaled deeply and shook her head. "Mmmm. Nope. Not alone." It didn't take me long to decipher the tone in her voice as one of disgust. It was then that I realized that Jensen didn't travel Europe with a *woman*, but he likely went with Robert.

Neither of us said anything else, letting the awkwardness fill the air between us for a moment before the steady rush of water could be heard as we neared the Tennessee River. Until Jensen introduced me to our little picnic paradise, this used to be my favorite place. There was nothing more calming than the sound of the water or the way the breeze would pick up the clean, fresh scent and wash it over you.

"Oh wow," Lilah said breathlessly. "This is beautiful."

Taking a deep sigh of contentment, I nodded my agreement. "Do you want to walk along the bank of the river for a bit? Just, you know, enjoy the scenery." After nodding, Lilah and I urged our horses along the riverbank, walking side-by-side and talking.

"So, Mom and Dad haven't stopped talking about you since the wedding."

I could feel my cheeks warming, and I tried to keep the silly smirk off my face. "I'm sure you're exaggerating."

"No, really," Lilah told me with conviction. "And actually, I'd like to apologize."

Stunned, I looked at her as my eyebrows pulled together. "Apologize? For what?"

"Uh, because I'm a raging bitch?" Lilah snorted, and I laughed in response.

"Not at all!" I declared. "Why would you even say that?"

Lilah rolled her eyes, suddenly serious. "Come on, after how I treated you when we first met? I was a bitch, and I shouldn't have been."

I shook my head, my eyes falling to my hands, which were tightly gripped around Halley's reins. "No. I understood. You were friends with her. That's where you felt your loyalties should have been. I was the new girlfriend and a threat to them getting back together."

"See, but that's just it. I *knew* they would never get back together," Lilah said surely as we walked out from under a canopy of low-hanging branches and into the sun. "He was so angry with her when they broke up. I honestly thought it was about his time away. I thought she was going through hell while he was locked up, when in reality she brought everything on herself. God, he must hate me for taking her side all this time."

"Not at all. He thought he was protecting you from more—" With a strangled squeak, I cut myself off from finishing that sentence. I wasn't sure if Lilah knew just how deep my knowledge of her past stemmed, and I didn't want her to be upset with Jensen for telling me.

Her curiosity had already been piqued, however. "More what?" I shook my head, trying to brush off her probing question and redirect her focus. But, like her brother, she was stubborn. She halted Starla and kept her eyes locked on me.

One look told me she wasn't angry, just confused and curious. I sighed with defeat as I halted Halley and waited for Lilah to move Starla up next to me. "I know about Chicago." She opened her mouth to say something, and her bottom lip quivered slightly. "Don't ... be upset with him. It was after my accident. He had said something about my injuries looking familiar."

"Oh." Her voice was quiet and raspy, and she shifted her eyes to her hands as they fidgeted with the reins.

"I asked. He told." Bravely, I reached for her hand nearest to me, squeezing it gently until her eyes found mine again. "He didn't tell you what Kaylie did because you'd already been through so much. He couldn't bear the thought of hurting you more. Sure, it wasn't the smartest plan—but his heart was in the right place."

Lilah nodded, squeezing my hand and allowing her lips to turn up into a slight smile.

"He was actually afraid that you and your parents might be upset with *him*," I confessed.

The smile fell from Lilah's lips again before she spoke. "Of course he would think that," she huffed. "Obviously we're not mad at him. Sure, we were upset—but not at him. What upset us was that he kept something so huge to himself. He was forced to grieve the loss of his child *alone*. No, I'm definitely not mad at him. I'm mad *for* him."

Jensen would be so relieved to hear that.

Lilah laughed just then, her stoic mood lifting at something unspoken. "It's funny," she started. "I never noticed them welcome Kaylie the way they did you." I laughed softly at her words, drawing another quizzical look from her. "What?"

"Jensen said the same thing," I explained, remembering the conversation we had the morning after we came home. "He also said he thought maybe your parents suspected what Kaylie had done ..."

Lilah clucked her tongue, encouraging Starla forward; I followed suit, happy that we seemed to be able to have this conversation openly. True, it wasn't how I had planned this afternoon to play out, but it was somewhat of a relief to finally move toward closure on the entire thing.

"After the two of you left, I was still pretty pissed—more at the entire situation than anything. It was then that Daddy told me that he already suspected what Kaylie had done." I nodded, not wanting to interrupt her at all. "I had never been so upset with him in my entire life. I mean, he practically *knew* and didn't say anything?"

"I'm sure he had his reasons," I whispered, coming to Henry's defense.

She nodded. "Oh, he did. And once I calmed down, his reasoning was quite sound. When Jensen told them that the wedding was off, Daddy was immediately suspicious. He and Mom never liked Kaylie much—as I mentioned—but Daddy said Jensen was more upset than they'd ever seen him… and he'd been sentenced to three years in prison, you know?"

"I do."

Lilah nodded. "He was so sure to tell her before the trial that they'd make it work, so their breakup just came out of left field. That was when Daddy tried to use his pull at the hospital to get Kaylie's medical records, but he was unsuccessful. It turned out Kaylie had thought everything through and had the procedure done under the radar—paying off anyone involved. He didn't give up until his medical license was threatened if he didn't stop digging. Kaylie's doctors and lawyers were pulling the 'doctor-patient confidentiality' card since they knew she and Jensen were no longer together."

"Wow." There was nothing else to say. So, Jensen's parents had known—for the most part, at least. They just lacked confirmation. "Well, I can't say I'm unhappy that you all know for sure now. I wanted Jensen to tell you—maybe not when it came out—but you definitely deserved to know."

Lilah smiled again, her eyes lighting up as they met mine again. "And I want to thank you for that. And for being sure to manipulate the photos at the wedding. You have no idea how much that means to me."

"I'd do it again." I turned to Lilah with a warm, sisterly

smile. "What do you say we head back now? Jensen should be home soon. Did you want to stay for dinner?" I asked, turning Halley back in the direction of the ranch.

Following my lead, Lilah's lips turned down into a pout. "I wish I could, but Kyle should be home for dinner. Rain check?"

"Definitely," I assured her.

Our ride back to the ranch was good. We talked more about Lilah's honeymoon. She told me I absolutely had to go to Greece, even going as far as to tell me she'd make Jensen take me. Through my laugher, I assured her that in no way was I going to accept such an extravagant gift. While I was beginning to enjoy being doted on, I didn't want to be that girl who expected lavish gifts from her boyfriend. Now, if we planned it together and both saved up for it, that would be a different story.

As we walked leisurely along the trail next to the gravel road, I smiled when I saw a familiar motorcycle coming from the opposite direction. "Look, Jensen's back."

We knew he would reach the barn before us, so we continued at a leisurely pace, giving Lilah more riding time since she didn't get to do it often. We reached the grounds, dismounted, and were entering the barn just in time to see Jensen leaving the arena.

"How was your ride, ladies?"

"Really good. How's the bike?" I asked, loosening Halley's girth.

For a brief moment it looked like my question confused Jensen—which, in turn, confused me. "Oh," he responded before I could question his odd behavior. "It's good. Running smooth. Lilah, you want to stay for dinner?"

I wondered briefly about the change in topic. What the hell was he up to?

"Madison already offered, but I can't. Kyle will be home for dinner. Another time, though?"

With a smile, Jensen nodded. "Definitely. Well, I'll let you ladies finish up here. I need to go talk to Wayne before I start bringing the horses in with Jeff."

Jensen kissed me softly before knocking softly on my

dad's office door.

"Come in," I heard Dad say. *"Jensen. Back so soon?"*

"Yeah," Jensen replied, his voice so low I almost didn't hear it. "I wanted to have a word with you in private ... if you have a minute that is?"

"Sure, sure! Come on in and close the door."

That was the last I heard as Jensen glanced over at me once more before stepping into the office and closing the door.

19
SUSPICIOUS BF IS SUSPICIOUS
Madison Landry

Things were ... *strange*. What could he possibly want to talk to Dad about? And why would it have to be in private? If it had anything to do with the ranch, it was just as much my business as it was my dad's.

Lilah and I had just finished grooming our horses when the door to Dad's office opened and they stepped out laughing. This behavior only piqued my curiosity more. Wayne clapped his hand on Jensen's shoulder. "Well, I wish you luck, son."

With what, I found myself wondering. My question went unanswered when they ended the conversation and Jensen made his way over just as Lilah and I closed the two stall doors.

"You taking off now?" he asked his sister.

Lilah nodded, wrapping her arms around Jensen. "Yeah, but I'd like to come back more often. I'd forgotten how much fun this was."

I pushed my curiosity aside for the moment to acknowledge Lilah. "Why don't we plan for every Saturday? And if Kyle isn't working, he can come out for dinner afterward."

"Sounds great! I'll talk to him and see," Lilah said, her excitement reflecting in her eyes.

Jensen took my hand in his and we walked with Lilah out to her car. "Okay, you drive safe."

"Please," Lilah scoffed playfully. "You're the maniac in

the family."

Laughing, I nudged Jensen's side. "I'm going to have to agree with her."

Grumbling something about "women always sticking together," Jensen opened Lilah's car door for her and waited for her to step in. It was nice to see his chivalry wasn't focused solely on me.

After Lilah left, Jensen turned to me, wrapped his arm around my shoulders, and led me toward the barn where the guys had started bringing the horses in. "You had fun?"

"Yeah, we did. We talked about some stuff."

"Well, that's pretty vague," he teased, his fingers lightly digging into my ribs, tickling me.

I giggled while shrugging and bending my body, both trying to stay in his arms while also trying to get away from his merciless attack. "Well, we need to keep some mystery between us," I said through my laughter. "Or else we're going to become pretty damn boring."

His fingers stopped moving against my side before he swiftly turned me to face him. "There's nothing boring about us, love," he assured me, his gorgeous blue eyes burning into mine with an intensity that had me struggling against the one urge I had right now.

"Um," I sighed breathlessly, not breaking our gaze. "I'm going to head in and shower. Maybe start dinner. You okay to finish up with Jeff?"

"Of course. I'll be in soon." With a smile that made my knees buckle and my heart flip flop (while other parts of my anatomy trembled and pulsed with anticipation), he kissed the tip of my nose and backed away from me.

"Sounds good."

Back at the house, I promptly showered and then changed into a pair of black yoga pants and a blue, thin-strapped tank top. After turning the radio on in the kitchen, I perused the fridge and cupboards for inspiration. I eventually settled on vegetarian lasagna, so I put a pot of water on for lasagna noodles, cooked up the sauce in an over-sized skillet, and steamed some fresh spinach. I was just putting dinner into the oven when the door opened.

"It smells amazing in here," Jensen exclaimed, coming up behind me and burying his nose in my neck. His lips started kissing that spot just below my ear that sent my entire body into a tizzy. "Mmm, but you smell even better."

"You are so cheesy," I said with a light laugh, crossing my arms around myself until they overlapped his hold on me, and we swayed back and forth to the music coming from the radio. I hummed. "This is nice, though." My eyes fluttered closed as we continued to move, and his lips ghosted the length of my neck and shoulder.

"What do you say we find something to do until dinner?" he suggested, breath fanning over my skin and making me shudder.

"Well, I have to put the garlic toast in right away, so you should go shower." I brought my right hand up and placed it on his stubbly jaw, turning my face toward him and kissing his cheek. "Plus, I'd hate to allow you your dessert before you've had a chance for dinner," I teased.

Turning me until I faced him, he tried to argue his case by pressing my body between his and the fridge. There I was, sandwiched between his hot body and cool stainless steel, completely ready to succumb to him with a whimper. Our lips hovered less than half an inch from each other's, and his warm breath tickled my skin as his eyes probed mine. The jerk was teasing me; building up the anticipation even more.

"You're right." He stepped away from me, and I let out a huge breath I hadn't even realized I'd been holding, looking at him pleadingly.

"I am?" I squeaked.

Not another word was spoken as he smirked, turning and rounding the corner to the bathroom. The level of sexual frustration was almost unbearable, and before I even realized what I was doing, I found myself right outside the bathroom door. I pressed my ear up against the door and listened for when the shower started so I could slip in. Breathing heavily, my hand rested on the knob, ready to turn it when I realized that *this* was exactly what he wanted.

With my resolve firmly back in place, I took a step back and retreated. The air was infused with the heavenly scent of our dinner by the time Jensen re-emerged, wearing nothing more than his black pajama bottoms and a white T-shirt.

"Just in time," I told him happily, pulling dinner out of the oven while I pretended that his pre-shower attempt at seduction hadn't almost worked. "The bread will take about ten minutes. Would you mind setting the table?"

"Not at all." I soon regretted asking for his assistance when I stood from putting the bread in and felt his body deliberately brush up against mine. "Oh, sorry," he said, his lips brushing my ear and his voice low and raspy with lust.

Everywhere his body connected with mine was like live wires crackling and sparking to life under my skin. My heart raced, and I felt warmth spread all over my body. Then, he was gone, placing the plates on the table. He was toying with me. Testing my willpower. Well, two could play at that game.

"Is it me, or is it hot in here?" I asked, opening the freezer and grabbing an ice cube. It wasn't a total lie; it was hot in here, what with the unseasonal warmth outside and the rising temperature from the oven being on—among other things raising the heat in our kitchen.

"Yeah, I guess a litt—"

By the time he turned around, I had already started running the ice cube over my neck. I had seen this in a movie once and wondered how it was supposed to be sensual. I mean, didn't one take cold showers to essentially turn *off* their arousal? The expression on Jensen's face seemed to be telling me otherwise, only encouraging me to continue to run the melting ice over any exposed flesh I could.

It wasn't until my body registered the chill of the cube that my nipples reacted strongly to the cold. Jensen definitely noticed, his stormy eyes lowering to focus on my perky breasts. That was when I understood the connection.

"You okay, baby?" I asked, my voice soft and—hopefully—seductive. "You're looking a little ... *warm.*" Smiling, I held out the half-melted ice cube. "Would you like to borrow this?"

He was across the room in a flash, his chest heaving and grazing my hardened nipples with every breath he took. My heart pounded harder than before—I wasn't even aware that was possible without needing to seek medical help. The way his eyes burned into mine—almost like he was staring directly into my soul—made my knees tremble, almost buckling underneath me.

Soft and slow, the fingers of his left hand moved up my right arm, barely touching yet leaving goose bumps in their wake, until he cradled my face in his hand. My eyes darted between his and his soft pink lips, my tongue poking out to moisten my own as I anticipated a kiss so torrid and frantic it might make me spontaneously combust. Capturing my eyes once more, his thumb stroked my cheek and he moved forward until his lips were a hairsbreadth from mine. The innocent gesture sent my body into full-on hormone overload, and I was half a second away from pulling his face to mine ...

Until the oven timer went off.

Knowing exactly what he was doing (because Jensen Davis was the master of all things cockblocky) he smirked, his lips still so close to mine I felt him do it. "I think the bread's ready," he whispered, stepping away and leaving me wanting him even more.

The cocky smirk on his face told me he was entirely aware of what he was doing to me as he pulled on an oven mitt and removed the garlic bread. After he turned off the oven, I watched through my periphery—still unable to move from where he left me—as he cut the loaf into slices and plated them.

"What's wrong, Madi?" he inquired, his voice dripping with mock-sincerity.

My resolve had been completely obliterated, but that wasn't to say I couldn't piece it back together in time to give him a taste of his own medicine.

Forcing a smile to my face, I turned to him. "I'm fine, baby. Just ... *hungry.*"

The sexual tension between us was thick, and the time spent silently eating didn't seem to help ease it. As we ate, Jensen sang his praises about my lasagna, and I thanked him, unable to take my eyes off his mouth. The things I imagined him doing to me were extremely vivid, making it hard for me to sit still.

Hoping to at least get the kitchen clean before we lost ourselves to blind passion, I jumped up from the table after dinner to put a little space between us. I worked quickly putting the dishes into the dishwasher, and as soon as I closed the door, strong hands were on my hips. He turned me around so quickly that I likely would have kept going—or fallen over—had he not stopped me just as suddenly.

Plunging my fingers into his soft hair, I pulled his face to mine and kissed him. As our tongues swirled with one another's, his fingers curled and clutched at my back in an effort to pull me closer. Breathless moans filled the kitchen as pleasure rolled through me, and his hands began to move over my body, memorizing every swell and every curve. Moaning softly into his mouth, I shifted my hips forward, feeling the solid bulge not-so-hidden by his flannel pants.

Slowly, I moved my hands down his back, my fingers dancing over every muscle covered by the soft cotton of his shirt until they found the hem. Jensen's lips left mine just as I started to pull the shirt up his body, and I had barely gotten it past his ribs before he scooped me up in his arms and rushed us to his room.

Setting me back down on my feet, he finished removing his own shirt before pulling me back to him, his mouth descending on my neck and shoulders.

I moaned in response to his touch, my hands now pressed flat on the naked planes of his back as they moved downward. When I reached the waist of his pants, I slipped my hands in and pushed them down over the curve of his ass, gasping when I realized he wasn't wearing any underwear.

"Why, Mr. Davis," I started to say as his pants fell to the floor, "you seem to have forgotten something."

Jensen kept his hold on me, raising his face from my neck to look at me, grinning impishly. "I figured it was just one less thing for you to take off," he quipped, stepping out of his pants, the forward momentum of his body backing me toward his bed. His hands rested above the curve of my ass again, fingers slipping into the back of my yoga pants and squeezing until his short nails bit deliciously into my own bare skin.

Smiling slyly, I looked up at Jensen. "I guess great minds really do think alike."

Groaning, he slowly pushed my pants down my legs and his fingers trailed lightly back up over my backside as I stepped out of them. His hands didn't stop there, though; they continued up my body until they were under my shirt, raising it over my ribs and tossing it to the floor before kissing me again.

A ripple of pleasure worked its way through my body, settling between my legs, and I deepened our kiss. My tongue was insistent against his as he lowered our bodies to the mattress and grabbed a condom from his nightstand. I whimpered when he stopped kissing me (again) and watched as he sat back on his heels to roll the latex down his length. I was suddenly all-consumed by my own eagerness of being with him like this again. It had been a long fucking week.

Opening my legs to him, he nestled between them, his erection resting against my warm, sensitive flesh. I groaned with need, pushing my hips up to his and forcing our bodies to finally surrender to passion. He reclaimed my mouth and started moving in time with me; every downward move of his matching my upward one and vice versa. Occasionally he would tease my entrance, causing my entire body to hold steady and await the sensation of him inside me. It was just that though — a tease. *Fucker.*

He knew what he was doing to me; his devious smile against my lips wasn't belying that. Eventually, he couldn't stand it anymore.

He broke our kiss and locked eyes with mine. "I love you, Madi," he whispered softly, brushing my hair off my forehead.

"I love you, too."

Raising my head off the bed and cradling his face in my hands, I pressed my lips to his as he slowly eased his hips forward, entering me. As soon as we were joined, his slow pace increased until we were both teetering on the edge. Breathless moans, dirty affirmations of pleasure, and whispered declarations of love filled the room as our bodies continued to move with one another, seeking out the euphoric bliss we had both been without for the last several days.

My abdominal muscles started to tense as my release became imminent. Sensing this, Jensen shifted his body slightly and slipped an arm between us until his thumb started using varying degrees of pressure to stimulate me externally. It was then that I let go, crying out as my body stiffened and shuddered through my orgasm.

His actions were his own undoing just as much as they were mine, and soon he collapsed most of his weight on me, refusing to separate us just yet.

Not a word was spoken for several minutes, our tender caresses and loving glances speaking volumes more than any words could express. Jensen was the first to break that silence when he brushed the sweat-dampened hair from my forehead, tucked it behind my ear and kissed me sweetly.

"I've never loved anyone the way I love you, Madison. I wanted you to know that." My lip quivered, and happy tears formed in the corners of my eyes. "I don't know what I'd do without you now that I have you."

Smiling, I ran my right hand over his slightly stubbled jaw. "Lucky for us you'll never have to find out."

20
HAPPY BIRTHDAY...TO ME
Madison Landry

"Happy birthday."

My eyes fluttered open, squinting against the sunlight streaming through the window, and I turned around to see Jensen coming into the room. In his hands was a tray with a small vase of flowers, a glass of orange juice, and what looked like a very tasty stack of chocolate chip pancakes.

"What's this?" I asked in that raspy morning voice that (I hoped) everyone got, sitting myself up. I had a few days of antibiotics left, and I'd hate to get sick all over again.

"Breakfast in bed for the birthday girl," Jensen replied excitedly, setting the tray over my lap. The smile on his face was wider than I'd ever seen. My cheeks hurt for him.

"Jensen, I asked you not to make a fuss," I reminded him, only mildly serious because this was actually the sweetest thing any guy had ever done for me. As I looked over the tray of food, my eyes fell upon an envelope perched against the small flower vase.

"That better be just a card," I warned, my tone low and menacing as I reached for it.

Jensen chuckled but didn't say anything to inform me otherwise as I opened it. The front of the card was simple with *"Happy Birthday"* written in big colorful font against a white background, and I smiled when all I saw was his handwriting on the inside. The cheeky bastard was starting to show me that he knew his way around a loophole. It only made me grow increasingly suspicious.

Technically I'm not breaking any rules with this card. I couldn't let you start your birthday off without telling you again just how much you mean to me. Happy birthday, Madi.

Love, Jensen

"Thank you," I gushed, setting the card on the tray as I contemplated what to eat first.

Jensen joined me on the bed and watched as I dug into my food. "You're not eating?" I asked, covering my mouth so as not to show off the bite of melon I'd just taken. Classy, I know.

"I'll eat in a bit. I'm content to just sit here with you." He winked at me and clasped his hands in his lap as he leaned back on the headboard.

It was weird—him watching me. "You don't expect me to share, do you? It's my birthday."

Jensen laughed. "Oh, so *now* you're okay acknowledging your birthday. When my pancakes are involved."

"I never said I didn't want you to acknowledge it. Just no parties or gifts," I clarified before taking a bite of pancake.

"Don't forget the cake," Jensen teased.

Nodding, I quickly amended myself. "Right. Mustn't forget the cake."

There was a devious gleam in Jensen's eyes as he continued to watch me, and a part of me suspected he was up to something. Over the last week, I'd walked in on many-a-phone call only to have him quickly say goodbye and hang up. I never questioned him about it though, because I was probably just being paranoid. At least I *hoped* I was; I'd hate having to castrate him.

"That was delicious," I told Jensen after swallowing my last bite. "Thank you."

Pleased, he hopped off the bed and took the tray. "Okay, you should get up and get ready. It's almost ten-thirty, and your dad will be here within the hour to take you on your trail ride. I've taken the liberty of packing the two of you a lunch and have several bottles of water in the fridge for you to take as well."

"That was really sweet, but Dad and I should be back in a few hours. I doubt we'll be gone long enough to need lunch."

Jensen shook his head. "Nope. Me, Tom, and Jillian have everything covered here. You and your dad are going to spend the day together. You'll be home for dinner."

I was fairly certain I was no longer being paranoid. "Jensen Davis," I said, climbing out of the bed and narrowing my eyes at him. "What are you plot—"

"Baby," Jensen crooned, pulling me into his arms—probably in an effort to throw me off the scent. "You and your dad work so hard. The two of you deserve some time off to just enjoy the day. Consider this my gift to you."

"Ah-ha!" I cried, pushing out of his arms. "I said no gifts! You *are* up to something!"

Rolling his eyes, Jensen shook his head. "Whatever you say, love." It was neither an admission of guilt nor denial. He was deflecting. "Go on. Get ready."

Jensen left me in the bedroom, my mind still reeling with thoughts of him having bought me something so extravagant that he needed to get me out of the house.

Maybe I was being completely ridiculous. I mean, aside from the phone calls I'd walked in on—and heard nothing incriminating—there was no concrete proof that he was scheming. Maybe he really did just want Dad and me to have a day off together. My heart warmed at his kind gesture, and a smile spread across my face as I went to go get dressed.

When I entered the room, I realized that I hadn't slept in my bed since before Dane showed up. It got me thinking that maybe we should discuss the topic of sharing a room permanently. Sure, his room was slightly smaller than mine, but it was where we slept night after night; I could move in there without a problem.

I opened my closet door to find a shirt to wear and was suddenly faced with "a problem."

In all the years that Willow and I had been friends, she had helped me build an extensive wardrobe. There was no way that all of my things would fit in Jensen's closet with his, and vice versa.

Then it occurred to me that the spare room at the end of the hall had an oversized walk-in. The room itself wasn't much larger—even if it was considered the master bedroom—and had once belonged to my grandparents. It wasn't that I was squicked-out to sleep in there, it was just *theirs*. Plus, with the ensuite half-bathroom, it made sense to use it as a guest room. Well, it made sense until now.

After pulling on my jeans and a fitted T-shirt, I went to the bathroom and brushed my teeth and hair before finding Jensen at the kitchen table. He had the paper open in front of him as he chewed a bite of his breakfast.

"Hey," I greeted, grabbing the coffee pot. "So, I was just thinking …" I heard the paper rustle behind me before I turned around to see Jensen staring at me inquisitively. "Well, we've been together almost a month, depending on when you start counting, and I've been sleeping in your room every night, only to have to go to my room every morning to get dressed …"

Jensen nodded, his lips curling up into a knowing smile. "Uh huh …"

"Well, what if all of our stuff was in the same room?"

Cocking his head to the side, he arched an eyebrow. "Are you saying you want to move in with me, Madison?"

With a laugh, I crossed the room and sat in his lap, setting my coffee on the table before wrapping my arms around his neck. "Don't be weird. We *already* live together; I'm merely trying to save valuable time in the mornings by cutting out a few steps. Literally."

"So, you want to move into my room?"

I shrugged. "No, actually I was thinking we could move into the guest room. The closet is bigger than both of ours."

"I think I love that idea. I can get started while you're gone today," Jensen announced happily.

I pulled my head back, my eyebrows knitting in confusion. "What about all the stuff that needs to be done around the barn?"

"No, of course. I'll wait until that's done." There he went again, acting all suspicious.

Luckily, Dad chose that exact moment to enter the house.

"Happy birthday, Madi!" he called out as he made his way to the kitchen. I stood from Jensen's lap and hugged my dad. "How's your morning been?"

"Really good. Jensen made me breakfast in bed and got me a card," I told him, letting my arms fall from around him before I took my usual seat around the table.

Dad laughed, making his way to the coffee maker. "Isn't that against the rules?"

"He got off on a technicality. A card was never on my list of what-not-tos." I glanced over at Jensen looking pretty damn proud of himself. "So," I said, turning my focus back to my dad. "What time did you want to head out? Jensen says he packed us a lunch ... Unless you don't want to be gone all day?"

Through my periphery, I thought I saw Jensen's head move quickly, but when I looked at him, he was absorbed in the paper again.

"No, I think an all day trail ride will be good. How do you think Halley will do? Will her leg give her any trouble?" Dad asked.

I shook my head. "No, she's been great. I think she'll be all right." Suddenly remembering last year, I narrowed my eyes at him. "Unless you plan to try and race us again."

Dad snickered, clearly thinking his attempt to race Halley and me last year was hilarious. Maybe he didn't remember we beat him. "Okay, well considering Halley's still getting back into the swing of things, maybe I'll wait to race you again. Speaking of Halley's injuries, I got a call yesterday wondering if you were still going to be attending the Masters this weekend. As a spectator."

"Oh," I said, caught completely caught off guard. "I, um, I don't know. I hadn't really thought about it." I looked over at Jensen, and the excited gleam in his eyes told me that he might be interested in going. "Maybe, if you guys think you can handle it without me and Jensen?"

"I think we'll manage," Dad assured me.

"Have you ever been to the Masters?" I asked Jensen.

His head shook. "Never. I've always wanted to go, but it just never happened."

"It's pretty great," I told him, remembering the atmosphere. It had been years since I'd attended as a spectator—since I was a teenager, actually.

"Look at the time," Dad said as he stood to take his mug to the sink. "We better hit the trails, Madi. Let Jensen get to work."

Jensen walked us to the door, watching as I pulled on my boots and grabbed my cowboy hat. Oh yeah, I went all out when trail riding with my dad. Jensen smiled his approval.

"Have a good day. I'll see you later." I stood on the tips of my toes and kissed him softly.

Nodding, Jensen held out the satchel that contained our lunches and refreshments. "You two have fun. Be careful."

That last part was directed at me.

I threw the saddle pack over my shoulder and walked with Dad out to the barn where I took Halley from her stall and tethered her up before I groomed her. Dad tethered his bay Thoroughbred gelding, Bandit, a few stalls down, and we talked, sharing a few memories of my past birthdays.

When the horses were brushed and ready for their saddles, Dad and I walked toward the tack room where I could grab one of the western saddles for today's ride. While I rode primarily English, I had initially started off in a western saddle. So, every year on my birthday, I went back to my roots.

After putting the thick saddle pad on Halley's back, I hoisted the heavy leather saddle up and adjusted it until it was in exactly the right place. Halley's ears flicked back, most likely curious about the weight difference. She was trained in both, but we only did this a couple times a year. When the saddle was in place, I lifted the fender, hooking the stirrup onto the horn while I pulled the cinch under her belly from her right side and up her left. Then, I looped the latigo through the large silver rigging dee, tightening it enough to keep the saddle in place.

"You ready, kiddo?" Dad asked as I unhooked the stirrup from the horn, letting it fall to Halley's side gently before I attached the saddlebags containing our lunches.

"Uh, yeah. I just need to get her bridle on and then we can head out."

Once Halley was bridled, Dad and I led our horses out of the barn and mounted up. There was no question of where we were going to go; every year we walked along the river. Today though, we'd stop somewhere along the bank and have lunch. It would be really nice to spend some quality time with my father again. We had both been so busy with the expansion that we never hung out alone anymore. I know I told Jensen no gifts, but this time alone with my dad could be considered one — and I couldn't be mad at him for it.

We walked single-file down the narrow path that led to the river, Dad leading the way and the conversation. "So, you and Jensen seem to be doing just fine."

It was a good thing I was behind him and Bandit, because my cheeks were probably redder than usual — and his comment wasn't even awkward or embarrassing. "Yeah. Things are great. He's great."

"It's good to see you so happy, Madi. I mean it. There've been very few times I've seen you this enthusiastic about anything. It used to be just when you were riding and teaching, but now? Well, it seems to be every hour of every day." His observations were only making my cheeks flare hotter.

It was time to take the attention off me. "How about you, old man?" I inquired. "When are you going to settle down?"

He laughed. "Aaah," he said. "You know I don't have time to meet women, let alone date."

"What are you talking about?" I asked incredulously. "You have seen how Lucy's mom looks at you, right? How she's always flirting with you? The woman's got the hots for you, Dad."

The trail widened, and I nudged Hails into a trot so I could move up next to my dad and Bandit. I fought to contain my laughter when I saw how red his cheeks were.

"Dad, are you blushing?" He didn't respond, instead changing the topic of discussion altogether.

"So, Tom was saying he'd like to go fishing again in a couple weeks. Think you and Jensen can handle things around here again?"

I nodded. "Sure. That shouldn't be a problem. Especially since you've offered to take care of our chores while we're away again."

About forty-five minutes had passed before we reached the river. We rode along, talking more about past birthdays and about how business was faring since taking on a few new clients.

"Did Jensen mention the idea of summer camps to you?"

I nodded. "Yeah. When he first moved in, we talked a little about some of his ideas for the ranch. I think they'd be great. Plus, they'd give us a little extra help and teach some of our students some responsibility. I don't think most of them realize just how much work goes into running this place. I mean, they own horses, sure, but they're not responsible for them. I think it would be good."

"Would you be willing to lead the campers? We'd all play our parts, of course. You could maybe do some of the classroom stuff, Jill could handle lessons, Tom and I could help them with the chores, and Jensen could take them on daily trail rides."

"Oh sure. Give Jensen the fun part."

Hearing the playfulness in my voice, Dad rolled his eyes. "Hardly. The entire time he'd be teaching them proper safety as well as about their surroundings."

"No, I actually think it's a great idea." I assured him.

We walked for a bit longer, discussing specifics like how many campers to each session, where we would put them up for the week that they stayed on the ranch. It was decided that we'd have to build another guesthouse near the main houses to accommodate them. That way, they'd have the privacy that they'd probably seek, but they'd be close enough to the three of us should something go wrong. Dad said he'd contact his builders and start discussing blueprints.

Just over two hours into our trail ride, Dad and I started to feel hungry. We dismounted and grabbed our lunches before sitting on a patch of grass near the river and digging into the sandwiches Jensen had packed.

After lunch, we remained on the river's edge, letting Halley and Bandit graze on the grass and drink from the river, neither of them wandering far from us. I couldn't have asked for a better day.

"What do you say we continue down the river for a bit longer before we head home? It's still pretty early," Dad suggested as we stood and collected our horses.

I was having such a good time with him that I almost didn't wait for him to finish before my head started bobbing. We mounted our horses and continued on our trail for another hour before deciding to head home.

By the time we returned to the ranch, it was nearly dinnertime, and all the horses had been brought in for the night. The entire barn was quiet as we entered, save for the sounds of the horses huffing to one another or eating their grain. While I brushed Hails, I hoped that maybe Jensen would appear from outside or somewhere in the barn as he finished his shift. But he didn't, which led me to believe he was probably already back at the house. Maybe preparing dinner.

Once we had Halley and Bandit brushed down and in their stalls, I looked at Dad. "Hey, did you want to come to dinner? I'm sure Jensen's cooking right now."

He smirked. Not smiled, *smirked.* "Anything for the birthday girl." As we walked back to my place, Dad lightly bumped me with his elbow. "So, did you have fun?"

"Yeah," I said, my smile stretching wide across my face. "I did. I liked spending the whole day with you. It's been a while."

We had just started up the walk that led to the house when Dad asked, "So, you're happy?"

I laughed and reached for the doorknob. "Yes. Very."

"Good," he replied. "Remember that feeling."

I furrowed my eyebrows at him, confused by his request, and pushed the door open. "What the hell are you talking abou—"

"SURPRISE!"

I nearly jumped out of my skin as the foyer lights turned on and voices assaulted my eardrums from all angles. My heart beat wildly, pounding a nervous rhythm that quickly washed out everything else. My eyes scanned the room to find everyone in my life gathered in my small entryway. Willow and Brandon had come all the way from Memphis. Jensen's parents as well as Lilah and Kyle had come to celebrate... Even Tom, Jeff, and Jillian were in attendance.

It would seem that my suspicions weren't completely unwarranted.

Willow was the first to rush forward and wrap her arms around me. "Happy birthday, Madi!" She squeezed me before whispering, "Don't be mad at him, okay?"

My eyes found Jensen standing next to his parents, a proud smile on his face for having pulled this entire thing off. His smile only widened when I narrowed my eyes at him briefly. "No guarantees," I muttered, finally hugging her back.

"Oh, come on," she said, pulling back. "You have to admit, getting everyone together like this? That's pretty amazing."

I didn't get a chance to fight her as Brandon cut in, accusing Willow of hogging "The Birthday Girl." Yeah, I'd been labeled. He wrapped me in his arms and kissed my cheek. "Happy birthday, Madi."

"Thanks, Brandon. I'm happy you guys could make it—even if this wasn't how I planned to spend my evening."

He laughed. "Come on. You haven't had a party in years. Don't you think it was time?"

"You do remember when I broke my arm at my last party, don't you?" I asked, bringing up my fifteenth birthday when we were all out on the trampoline, screwing around doing acrobatic tricks before I back-flipped right off and shattered my radius.

"That was eleven years ago, and nothing has happened since—"

"Yeah," I said, effectively cutting him off. "Because I *stopped* having parties."

Dad nudged me from behind. "Come on, kiddo. He put a lot of thought into this."

It wasn't that I didn't recognize just how thoughtful Jensen's gesture was; I just hated being the center of attention. That much pressure was likely what caused my klutziness to kick into high gear until I hurt myself in some way. It's absolutely why I fell while riding; Jensen had been watching me. There was all kinds of pressure that came with that sort of thing.

I shrugged and let a small smile form on my lips. "Okay, but if anything happens, I'm holding all of you accountable," I warned playfully.

Lilah and Kyle stepped forward next and wished me a happy birthday, Kyle's hold on me just as bone-crushing as it was at his wedding. Jill, Tom, and Jeff were next before Jensen's parents approached.

"Happy birthday, Madison," Janet said, pulling me into her arms. It was hard to stay mad at Jensen for not listening to me while I hugged his mother. A part of me wondered if he maybe knew that.

"Thank you both for coming," I said sincerely as I moved from Janet's arms to Henry's. "It's a good thing you're here, Janet. If today falls into step with any other party I've had, I'll be needing a doctor nearby."

Everyone in the room laughed—including me, even though I was almost one hundred percent serious. "Well, I smell like horses and feel slightly under-dressed," I announced, looking around at all the women in their party dresses and the men in their dress pants and button-up shirts. "I'm going to go and have a quick shower and change into something a little nicer."

Willow suddenly beamed, clasping her hands in front of her mouth, and I *knew* she must have gotten me a present; something she was hoping I'd wear.

"You didn't," I groaned. Willow knew the "no presents" rule was one I was always adamant about—well, I was adamant about them all, actually. It was simply a lesson in self-preservation that I took pretty seriously.

She giggled. "Well, I figured since the 'no party' and the 'no cake' rules were broken, no harm would befall me for buying you a little something. It's on your bed."

"There's a cake?" I looked around and into the kitchen where a multi-tiered cake sat on the kitchen island. It was official; every rule I had set for today was broken. Shaking my head, I moved through the crowd to confront the one person responsible. "You're pretty proud of yourself, huh?"

Jensen smirked, pulling me close. "Madi, you deserve

this," he said softly, wrapping his arms around my waist.

The minute I was pressed against his body, my discord faded. "You know, it's hard to stay angry with you for disregarding my wishes entirely when you say stuff like that," I grumbled, snaking my arms up around his neck to return his hug.

He chuckled softly, kissing the top of my head. "Happy birthday, baby. Go ahead and change. We'll hold off on the festivities until you're done."

I showered quickly before blow-drying my hair into waves and clipping the sides back so it hung loose down my back. When I entered my room, however, there was nothing on my bed like Willow had promised. Then I remembered Jensen was going to move us into our shared bedroom. My mood lifted a little more as I walked down the hall to the room that was neither "his" nor "mine." It was *ours*.

Jensen had made the bed in his fluffy bedding and moved the pictures and my laptop from my room into here along with a few of his own belongings. There, on our bed as promised, was a plain white box wrapped in a bright blue ribbon with a large tag that read:

To my bestie!

Don't be mad! I couldn't resist after seeing how much you loved it when we went shopping!

Love,

Willow & Brandon

I knew without even having to open it what was inside, and I'd be lying if I said I wasn't a little excited. I tore the ribbon off and saw the purple organza dress from our dress-shopping excursion. After grabbing a strapless bra and a matching pair of panties, I quickly dropped my towel from around me and got dressed. I was definitely feeling a little more party-ready, and my sour mood was fading more and more.

When I re-joined the party, all eyes were on me. An unsettling feeling wormed its way into my veins, but flitted away just as quickly when Jensen's eyes widened and travelled over me appreciatively. I crossed the room and took his hand, smiling up at him.

"You look beautiful," he said, lacing our fingers together and pulling me toward him. Leaning forward, he captured my lips with his in a soft, yet still passion-filled kiss that set my entire body on fire and curled my toes.

When our lips parted, I looked around at everyone mingling and smiled. Then I noticed my dad's absence. "Where's Dad?"

"He went to shower, too. He should be back soon," Jensen informed me. "So ... Exactly how much trouble am I in?"

I contemplated his question for a moment. "Well, I specifically said no party, cake, or gifts, and I got all three." I took in his expression, noting that he didn't seem *overly* anxious about how upset I might be. "But, I have to admit, it's nice to have everyone together and getting along. So, barring any mishaps, I'd say you might get off easy." Jensen's eyebrows waggled suggestively, and I realized that I maybe should have rephrased what I said. Thankfully, we were pretty isolated, and no one else (Kyle) overheard me.

"I may have to take you up on that challenge a little later," Jensen said softly, his eyes drifting up behind me as Dad entered the room.

I turned to see him head straight for Jensen's parents, who were talking with Tom and Jeff. I smiled at my dad, silently letting him know that I wasn't upset with him for being in on the whole thing. He seemed relieved.

"But first," Jensen whispered, drawing my attention back to him. "I'd like to give you something." Slowly, Jensen started to pull me through the room and toward the patio doors.

As we walked, I noticed everyone's eyes on us, turning in our direction as wide smiles formed on each and every one of their faces, only making me more and more nervous. "No," I argued, unsure what to expect. "You've already given me so much. This party is *more* than enough."

Laughing softly, Jensen slid the patio door aside, and I found myself stunned into silence. The entire backyard was decorated with white twinkle lights that must have taken hours to string up in the trees. There were vases of flowers on the patio, and off to the right was a —

"You bought a hot tub?" I exclaimed, my eyes focused on everything but him as he released my hand.

"No, I *rented* a hot tub, but that's not what I wanted to give you."

Slowly, I turned around and gasped when I saw Jensen down on one knee.

21
THINGS AREN'T AS THEY SEEM
Madison Landry

I wasn't entirely sure how much time had elapsed; all I knew was that Jensen was *down on one fucking knee*. Was he crazy? Had he lost his mind completely? We'd been together for a month. Four weeks. *Maybe* thirty days — give or take.

What. The. Actual. Fuck?

Frantically, I searched his eyes for answers — only to find absolutely nothing. What was I supposed to think, though? What other reason could he possibly have for being down on one knee? My palms were sweating, and I wiped them on the flowy skirt of my new dress as my brain finally registered the furious pounding of my heart in my ears. I could feel my chest tightening the more I thought about what Jensen was about to do. We weren't ready for this. *I* wasn't ready for this.

What I was, was on the verge of full-blown panic attack.

Swallowing what little saliva was in my increasingly dry mouth, I looked back to the house to find every one of my party guests waiting. Expectant smiles adorned every single face. They all knew this was going to happen, and I had been completely oblivious. Did Jensen think that this would guarantee an affirmative answer? Would it? I suddenly wasn't sure what I would do when the words finally left his mouth.

Slowly — or maybe it was quickly — I turned my eyes back to Jensen. The smile on his face was still wide and confident.

I cleared my throat, my eyebrows finally showing some small semblance of emotion — which emotion, I still wasn't entirely sure. "What are you doing?" I hissed, my voice raspy, trembling through every word.

The smile fell from Jensen's face, his own eyebrows pulling together in confusion. "I wanted to give you something."

My head started to shake in small, quick movements as I prepared to tell him I wasn't ready. We needed more time; there was still so much we had to learn about each other. Hell, we had *just* moved into the same room together. Why couldn't he just enjoy that one small step forward? Why did he always have to leap right after?

"Stop. Please ... Jensen, *don't* do this ..." I pleaded softly, hoping that I wouldn't have to out-right tell him no. I loved him—I did—and I wanted nothing more than to spend the rest of my life with him; to marry him and give him his three kids. I'd even consider his original five if I had more time. But not yet. Our foundation wasn't as strong as I knew it could be with a few more months—or years—under us.

Jensen reached around into his pocket, his eyes still locked on mine and registering his confusion with my pleas. "Madison," he started, his hand reappearing from his pocket, closed around something.

"Don't," I whispered, tears stinging my eyes because I hated doing this in front of everyone. I also didn't want to say yes and have him wonder if I only did it because people were watching. "*Please.*"

"Madison," he repeated, holding his hand out in front of him. Slowly, his fingers began to open. My eyes were locked on his hand, waiting to see some extravagant ring being presented to me.

Unable to tear my eyes away from his hand, I dropped to my knees on the cool wooden porch in defeat and awaited the inevitable. You know that saying, "a watched pot never boils"? Well, a watched hand never opens. Time actually seemed to slow even more as I came face-to-face with ...

"What the hell?" I asked, my eyes focusing on the contents of his hand. It wasn't a small velvet box with a ring inside. A confusing pang of disappointment swelled within me, but I quickly pushed it aside because, ultimately, I didn't have to turn him down. So, instead of focusing on how I wasn't being proposed to, I stared quizzically at the small, reddish ... dog biscuit?

That's when I heard it; the quickened steps of padded paws hurdling up the few steps to the porch before a long snout planted itself firmly in Jensen's palm. He wrapped his arm around the little fur ball, lifting it and coaxing my eyes to follow. The look in his eyes as they held mine was pure excitement as he held the German Shepherd puppy to his chest.

"Y—you got me a puppy?" I stammered.

"Us," he corrected me with a sly smirk. "I got *us* a puppy." He held the sweet puppy toward me, its squirming body trying to break free of his hold.

I complied and scooped the dog up in my arms like a baby, allowing a smile to form on my face. "We have a puppy," I whispered, looking down into the deep brown eyes of our first pet. He continued to wriggle and squirm in my arms, and I laughed when he stretched and licked my cheek. "What's its name?"

"Well, I hadn't named him yet. I figured since I picked him out, that you could name him," Jensen offered, moving forward until his knees brushed mine.

Looking down at the puppy as he moved his head back and forth between Jensen and me, I tried to figure out who he was. I always felt like naming an animal was more pressure than it should've been. Before, when I named an animal, it was just me that had to live with it if I didn't like it; but now I had to worry about whether or not Jensen would agree.

It was then that I realized there was really only one name for this sweet little ball of fur. "Bones," I said, moving my gaze back up to meet Jensen's. "His name is Bones."

Jensen laughed, the corners of his eyes crinkling slightly as his smile reached them. "I think it's perfect."

I was quickly reminded that there were other people still lying in wait just beyond the threshold when a small voice spoke up. "Bones?" Willow inquired. "He doesn't look too skinny. Or is it because dogs like bones?"

I giggled, standing up while still holding Bones in my arms. Jensen quickly jumped to his feet before assisting me so I didn't fall over. "No. Bones McCoy." Willow still didn't seem to connect the dots as Jensen and I made our way back into the house.

Kyle laughed loudly, stepping forward to scratch the top of Bones' head. "Dammit, Jim," he said in an uncanny impersonation of DeForest Kelley. "I'm a puppy, not a doctor!" Everyone laughed, and Willow simply groaned, finally understanding that this was another *Star Trek* thing.

"You guys are in serious need of a nerd intervention," Willow teased.

Once we were back inside, Jensen excused himself from my side. Bones continued to squirm in my arms, so I set him down. Happily back on his feet, he went from person to person looking for affection. As I watched him, everything still seemed kind of surreal; Jensen throwing all of this together really went above and beyond. While his total disregard for my wishes originally irritated me (but only a little), I couldn't deny the fact that I was starting to enjoy myself.

"Here, Madi," my dad said from behind me, tapping my shoulder with something to get my attention.

I turned around to see him holding out a small box topped with one of those shiny, green stick-on bows. "Dad, you know the rules better than anyone."

"It's not for you, kiddo," he said as I took the top off the box to find a brown leather collar with an engravable nameplate. Our phone number was on it, but the spot where our puppy's name would go was left blank. "It's for the dog, so I'm not breaking any rules here."

Arching my right eyebrow, I challenged my father. "You know, this whole 'technicality' thing that you and Jensen have going on right now is kind of losing its luster," I joked before looking at the collar again and smiling. "It's great. Thank you."

Jensen's hand found the small of my back just then, and a glass of red wine appeared before me. "Thanks," I said as he pressed a tender kiss to my temple. "Did you see what Dad got for Bones? I'm going to have his name added to it as soon as possible."

"It's great. Thanks, Wayne," Jensen said, acting like it was a gift for the both of us, not just for me. I was starting to feel like he really thought that all of these little technicalities would save him from a huge lecture later.

Oh, who was I kidding? He was probably right.

As we stood there, Bones came over and started sniffing at my ankle until I knelt down to pet him. Through my periphery, I saw Jensen drop down next to me. "So," he said quietly, reaching out and petting Bones' belly when he flopped to the floor clumsily and rolled over. "If you weren't expecting a puppy ...?"

Oh shit. He didn't have to finish his inquiry for me to know what he was getting at. In fact, I was pretty sure he knew already, he just wanted to tease me a little more. Yeah, on my birthday. What a prince.

Keeping my attention on the dog, I forced a quiet laugh. "I don't know what I was expecting," I lied.

Jensen knew me better than that. "Bullshit," he challenged, nudging me gently with his elbow and almost causing me to topple over since I was only balanced on the balls of my still-bare feet. Before I wound up on my ass, though, his left hand wrapped around my arm while his right gripped my waist, catching me and offering me an apologetic look.

Once I was balanced again, his right hand moved up the length of my back as I turned my head to finally look at him. "I thought ..." I let out a gust of air, totally embarrassed about what I was about to admit—especially since that wasn't even close to what he had planned. "I thought you were going to propose."

The look in his eyes told me I was right; he already suspected as much. That didn't stop the smug smile from crossing his face, though. "And you were going to say *no*?" he asked, pretending to be offended. At least, I *hoped* he was only pretending. "In front of all these people?"

I could feel my face warm, and I had to look away. Even though I knew deep down he was teasing, I was terrified of hurting him. He must have been able to pick up on it, because he placed his forefinger beneath my chin and gently coaxed me to look at him.

"Hey. I'm only joking."

I shrugged, offering him a small smile. "I know. I just ... I didn't want to hurt you. And it looked so much like you were."

"Baby," Jensen said, pushing himself to his feet and pulling me up with him. Bones whimpered, rolling back onto his belly before getting up and running off to find someone else to pet him. Taking my wine and setting it on the end table, Jensen turned my body to face his, cupping my face in his hands. "I love you. But I'm only just getting my life back on track after ... some incredible misfortunes. We're just not there yet."

"I know," I assured him, feeling relieved to know that he was in exactly the same place as I was. It made it easier to breathe again, not having to worry about him surprising me with an engagement ring any time soon. "Which is why I was so scared."

Something must have occurred to him right then because his smile widened. "Although, I bet I'd have gotten myself out of trouble if this had been an engagement party as opposed to a birthday party."

Unable to keep myself from laughing, I used both hands to push him away playfully. "Oh, you think so, do you?"

"Hey, I didn't make the rules," he said, trying to defend his actions as he pulled me into his arms.

I instantly stopped trying to push him away, instead wrapping my arms up around his neck. "No. But you sure as hell did a good job breaking them."

"Good job, huh? So, that means you're happy with this turn of events?"

I hummed, stepping up onto my tiptoes to place a feather light kiss on his lips. "I wouldn't be so sure of that just yet." I lowered my voice to just above a whisper, purposefully keeping my lips a hairsbreadth from his. My desire for him rose slowly as his grip tightened around me. Had it not been for Kyle's boisterous laugh, I probably could have gotten carried away.

Kissing him one more time, I smiled and pulled my face back to look into his eyes. "Let's see how the rest of the evening goes, shall we?"

Jensen was about to answer—with something cocky, I was sure of it—when I felt Willow's tiny hand wrap around my right wrist, forcing my arm from Jensen's neck. "You can't hog her, Jensen. You get to see her every day."

Chuckling, Jensen released me from his embrace, his hand sliding over my ass as Willow led me away. There was no way it was an accident, either—not with the way his eyes followed me as she pulled me to the kitchen where the rest of the women had congregated. It would seem that I was a little too wrapped up in Jensen because I hadn't noticed the crowd in the living room thin.

Lilah, Janet, and Jillian were all standing around the island picking at the trays of food that had been laid out. There was a little bit of something for everyone; crackers and cheese, fruit, veggies, some kind of pâté, and even a variety of finger sandwiches.

"Madison, sweetheart!" Janet greeted me excitedly, taking my hand once I was near and pulling me into her side before wrapping an arm around me. "Are you enjoying yourself, dear?"

Nodding, I mirrored her hold on me and gave her an affectionate squeeze. "I am. I'm so glad you're all here."

Willow joined us at the island within a few seconds, and in her hand was a bottle of Patron. Flashbacks to the night of Lilah and Kyle's rehearsal dinner flashed through my mind—as did the memory of the next morning's hangover—and I groaned.

"Will, I don't know if—"

She wouldn't let me finish as she scooted away and hopped up onto the counter behind me. Short girl problems. She was probably digging around to find shot glasses. There was really no use fighting her, because I knew that once I did she would pull out the *"Aw! But we never do this anymore!"* card, and I would feel obligated. This just saved me the grief.

"Shot glasses are on the top shelf, buried way in the back," I told her before removing my arm from Janet and opening the fridge. If Willow brought Patron, I was willing to bet she bought a few limes too. I found them sitting on the top shelf next to the milk and grabbed them, the cutting board and knife, as well as the saltshaker.

After returning to the island, Willow hopped down and brought the glasses over, setting one in front of each of us. I looked over at Janet, kind of shocked to see that her eyes were sparkling with what looked like excitement.

Was she going to do shots with us? Awesome.

I cut the limes into wedges and left the pieces on the cutting board, pushing it until it was central to us all as we circled the island. "Okay, ladies," I announced, grabbing the bottle and pouring shots. "Bottoms up."

All together, we licked the salt from our hands and slammed our shots. We each grabbed a lime wedge and bit into them before setting the remains off to the side.

Before any of us could recover, Willow was quick to pour another round for everyone. Laughing, Janet salted her hand again before passing the shaker clockwise around our little group. Never in a million years would I have imagined standing in my kitchen doing shots with Jensen's mom. Even more surprising, was how much I was enjoying it.

Conversation flowed, and soon everyone took turns sharing how they met their significant other—I gave the abridged version for Janet's sake. First, Willow chimed in about how her crush on Brandon when we were all teenagers evolved into an epic love story. Willow had been convinced that her feelings for him were unrequited, but I knew Brandon returned her feelings tenfold. No matter how many times I tried to tell her as much, it wasn't until he finally asked her out that she finally believed me.

Lilah then explained how she and Kyle met after she moved to Houston with Jensen. While she didn't go into specifics on why she left Chicago, she did say that she regretted none of her past, because without it, she'd never have met her soul mate. I noticed Lilah's eyes glisten before Janet reached across the island between them and grasped her hand, squeezing ever so slightly. It was almost as though she was trying to transfer some of her maternal strength to her daughter. Sure, Lilah might not have regretted her turbulent relationship with Robert, but that didn't mean it didn't still hurt to talk about it.

Willow poured another round of shooters, clearly picking up on the vibe that Lilah might be in need of one. We toasted to the past shaping us for our futures and drank simultaneously before Janet spoke next. "I'm almost ashamed to admit how Henry and I met," she admitted, setting her glass down in front of her. Why did her words suddenly make me nervous?

"Mom, you guys met in college. You moved across the Atlantic for him," Lilah said, grabbing her wine glass and taking a sip before reaching for a few crackers from the nearby platter. "It's romantic."

Janet laughed, and there was an impish glint in her eyes that told me her meeting with Henry might actually rival my own when it came to censorship. To say I wasn't morbidly curious for her to continue would have been a lie.

"I was a freshman at Oxford," Janet began, smirking slightly. "Henry and I met at a party."

Oh, I thought to myself. Was that all?

"I had just gotten out of a terrible relationship and wasn't looking to meet anyone else — let alone date ..."

Uh oh ... I was suddenly all too aware where this was going. Janet and Henry *hooked up* at a party. My morbid curiosity quickly dissipated, and I instantly picked up my wine glass and chugged the remainder of it, hoping to use it as some sort of stand-in brain bleach. My wine was gone before I knew it, and I had just reached for the bottle to refill when Lilah finally caught on to what her mother was implying.

"Mom! Ew!"

Janet laughed. "Oh please. We're all adults here," she said, trying to justify her story — or lack-there-of since she never *really* finished telling it. "Besides, nothing happened. Your father was a perfect gentleman."

It was a relief to hear. I couldn't imagine just how drunk I would've had to be to forget hearing otherwise.

Jillian didn't have a story to share since she was newly single, but said she loved hearing everyone's stories and that they gave her hope that one day she would meet the man of her dreams. She definitely deserved a nice guy. If only I knew any single m —

I hummed excitedly, my mouth full of wine. I quickly swallowed and reached across the island top to pat Lilah's hand. "We should introduce Riley to Jillian!"

Lilah loved the idea. "Yes! Oh, he would just love you to bits! You're *exactly* his type!"

Jillian beamed, listening raptly as Lilah told her all about Riley while Willow poured another round of tequila. After a few more shots, my body was starting to feel the effects, and soon enough the bottle was almost empty. The five of us were still circled around the kitchen island, laughing.

"Oh no!" Willow cried out as she tipped the empty Patron bottle completely upside down over her half-full shot glass. "Madi, do you have anything good to do shooters with?"

Pursing my lips, I turned to the cabinet where I kept my liquor. "Umm … Lemme check." Upon opening it, I noticed that I had a bottle of vodka and another bottle of Patron. "Ooooh!" I said excitedly, pulling the tequila from the back of the cabinet. It was official: I was definitely on my way to inebriated.

Willow gladly took the bottle from me so she could fill her glass, and we drank again. The rational side of my brain told me I was going to regret getting this drunk on tequila again, but the alcohol was effectively drowning her out. I was having such a good time; if my brain allowed for it later, I'd have to thank Jensen properly for not listening to me.

"Okay, ladies," Jillian announced. "If I plan to make it home tonight, I should probably stop drinking now."

"Oh psssh!" I protested animatedly. "You can stay the night! You can't go. It's my birthday, and I won't take no for an answer."

Jillian looked at me strangely. "That's really sweet, Madison. But I should go home tonight. Thanks, though."

"Fine," I grumbled. "But you're going to let me find you a ride or call you a cab or something. Now …" I slid her full shot glass toward her. "Drink up."

We had just set our glasses back down when I heard the clickety-clack of tiny claws on the tile floor. Turning around with a smile, I saw Bones join us from the living room where I could hear the guys talking and laughing up a storm.

"There's my little guy," I cooed, kneeling down to pick him up. His little tail wagged excitedly as he licked my face.

"Are you really going to give him a Trekkie name?" Willow inquired with an arched brow.

I kissed Bones on the top of the head, resting my cheek against the side of his face and looked at Willow. "Uh huh. It suits him," I replied through pursed lips, still using a cutesy baby voice as I spoke. It was probably safe to say that I had arrived to drunksville.

"And what is going on in here?" Jensen asked from the kitchen's entry. I smiled at him and watched his eyes drop to the empty bottle and discarded limes between us before he pieced it all together. "Are you ladies doing shots without us? Oh, Kyle will not be pleased with you at all."

"By all means," I said cockily, fairly confident I was slurring my words. "Invite him in. We found another bottle, *and* we have a full bottle of vodka."

My drinking partners all agreed that the guys should join us for a couple of birthday shots, and that's when Jensen looked at his mother. "Mom? Are *you* doing shots of Patron?"

"Of course she is," I announced, noticing for the first time that my words were slightly slurred. "It *is* my birthday."

"Jensen," Janet replied softly. "I'm not a child. I have done this before."

Shaking his head, he stepped farther into the room where he sidled up next to me and scratched the top of Bones' head. "You women are out of control," he teased.

"Mmm ... But having fun," I assured him. "And isn't that what's important? I mean, it's keeping you from getting in trouble for orchestrating this whole night."

My reminder seemed to please him, because he smiled and nodded like the good boy that he was. "Indeed. That *is* what's important. I'm glad you're having fun, baby." Slowly, he wrapped his arm around me, placing his hand on my waist before he tightened his grip slightly. Sparks of desire shot through me from the tips of his fingers as he leaned in to kiss my cheek softly.

His lips brushed the skin of my cheek before ghosting over my earlobe. "Make sure you don't drink *too* much. We wouldn't want a repeat of what happened in Memphis, now would we?" he whispered, and I expelled a breathy sigh, suddenly wanting to put the dog down and rush Jensen to our bedroom. The fact that we were entertaining guests was the only reason I wasn't doing just that.

"You two need to get a room," Willow chirped, causing the other three women to laugh with her. Jensen stood up straight and cleared his throat.

Suddenly, the kitchen seemed to be the most popular place in the house as the rest of our guests joined us. The girls and I backed away from the island to let the men and their growling stomachs through to get some food. That was when Kyle saw the tequila and turned to me.

"You're looking a little flushed there, Madikins," he announced. "You been doing shots without me?"

I shrugged. "What can I say, Kyle? I couldn't handle seeing you wallow after drinking you under the table again. I needed some *real* competition."

Kyle's booming laughter filled the room. "If you weren't already looking a little tipsy, I'd show you who'd reign champion."

Everyone grabbed a small plate of snacks before finding a place to stand or sit in the kitchen while we all talked. As I ate crackers and cheeses, munched on some fruit and drank the water that Jensen insisted on, I could feel the veil of inebriation slowly beginning to lift. I was still feeling pretty damn good, but I wouldn't be passing out any time soon. Bonus.

"Okay, who's ready for cake?" Janet asked when everyone had finished. No one answered, well, not with the usual "me's" or "I do's." No, they all broke into song instead.

I could feel my face growing warmer as the song went on, and I swore they were singing it at an agonizingly slow pace, just to draw out my embarrassment. "This is totally unnecessary," I mumbled, leaning into Jensen's side as he pressed his lips into the top of my head, breaking up his singing only momentarily.

As I cut the cake, Jensen told me it was from a new bakery in town that used only organic ingredients. It was absolutely amazing. First of all, Jensen and I had never had the "favorite cake" discussion, but when I cut into that top tier to find it was carrot cake with cream cheese frosting? Well, I almost *died*. My mouth watered as I cut slice after delicious-smelling slice for everyone before serving myself the biggest piece I thought I could eat. I had never tasted a more delicious cake in all my life.

Once everyone finished eating, Tom announced that he and Jeff had to go. Jeff had school the next day and Tom offered to come out to help on the ranch the next morning since Dad was giving me the day off to nurse my future hangover. Jensen and I walked Tom and Jeff to the door where I hugged them both and thanked them for coming.

It wasn't long after returning to the party that Dad said he needed to go home and get some sleep. It was almost ten by that point, and he had an early morning. When he announced his departure, Henry and Janet also decided they should be on their way.

"We'll leave you kids to have fun," Janet said, pulling me into her arms. "Happy birthday, honey. You make sure you and Jensen come out to the house for dinner soon, all right?"

"Of course. That would be great," I said.

Smiling, Janet nodded. "Jillian, dear?" she called over my shoulder.

"Yeah?" Jillian answered, entering the foyer.

"You live in town, right?" Jill nodded. "Well, Henry and I have to drive through town to get home. Would you like a ride?"

"Uh, yeah. That'd be great." Jillian turned to me. "I'll see about catching a ride into work tomorrow night since my car will be here."

I shook my head. "Nah, I'll be up at some point. I'll swing by your place and pick you up for work."

"You sure?"

Nodding, I wrapped my arms around her. "I'll see you tomorrow. Call if you want me to come and get you earlier."

She nodded against my shoulder. "Happy birthday, Madi."

The door had just closed behind Jillian when a loud clap was heard behind us. "Okay!" When Jensen and I turned around, we were met with Kyle's wide, dimpled grin. "Now that the parents are gone, let the real party begin." He extended an arm and pointed right at me. "You and I have some shots to do, little one. But first ... Hot tub time!"

22
HOT TUB BOOZE MACHINE
Madison Landry

"Here, let me help you with that," Jensen said softly, coming up behind me after closing the door and reaching for my zipper. The tips of his fingers brushed the skin of my neck, and my body erupted in goose bumps, tingling from head to toe at the completely innocent gesture. "I think I'm going to like this whole room-sharing thing." Okay, so I *thought* it was an innocent gesture; I really should have known better.

His hands slipped through the slackened fabric, palms gliding over my waist and toward my stomach before travelling down ...

Turning around quickly, I held my dress against my chest with one hand to keep it from falling down while I splayed the other hand across his chest and kept him an arm's length away. "Now, what kind of host would you be if I let you take advantage of me in my current state of almost-inebriation?"

Chuckling, Jensen moved my hand from his chest and pulled me against him. I crashed against his chest gently. "Baby, you're rambling. That's a sure sign that you're not *almost* inebriated."

I narrowed my eyes at him, trying to convey just how funny he wasn't. My ire was short-lived when his fingers started moving up and down the exposed flesh of my back between the open zipper, stopping at my bra and unfastening the hooks. Sighing breathlessly, I tilted my head up until my lips brushed faintly against his. Originally, I had only intended to tempt him before pulling away, but when his eyes locked on mine, I surrendered to desire, slowly pressing my lips to his.

With a deep groan, Jensen tightened his grip around me, his lips parting. My entire body tingled as the sound registered in my brain. I pulled the arm holding my dress from between us so I could wrap them both around his neck, and it didn't take long for the both of us to become completely shrouded in lust. Soon enough our tongues met, pressing and swirling around one another as Jensen backed me toward our bed.

Moaning into his mouth, I lowered my hands to the collar of his shirt and tugged on it until the backs of my legs connected with the cool, overhanging duvet.

A loud bang on the door forced us to stop kissing. "Come on, you two!" Kyle shouted through the thick door as Jensen and I tried to calm our heavy breathing. "Stop necking and get your asses changed!"

Jensen laughed, pressing his forehead to mine and nodding. "All right!" he finally responded, sounding more than a little irritated. "Give us five minutes."

"Wow," Kyle said, the smile on his face undeniably audible in his voice. "You're a lucky, lucky woman, Madi. Five *whole* minutes?" Laughing once more, Kyle's voice faded as he retreated down the hall toward the living room, leaving Jensen and I alone again.

"He's always such a smart ass," Jensen grumbled, parting our bodies and safely backing a few steps away.

Grabbing my dress before it could fall, I walked over to the long dresser and started opening drawers, still not sure which ones Jensen had designated to me. "In his defense, babe, you kind of walked right into that one," I teased, opening the middle drawer on the right side of the dresser to find my bathing suits.

After setting my black bikini on the dresser, I let my dress and bra fall to the floor before casting a coy glance over my shoulder to find Jensen perched on the edge of the bed. Just as I suspected, he was watching me intently. "Aren't you going to get changed?" I inquired, hooking my thumbs into the hips of my panties.

"In just a second."

"You're incorrigible," I informed him, playfully rolling my eyes and sliding my panties down my legs. Jensen hummed his approval, and I could feel his eyes still on me. Had it not been for the tequila, I probably would have been blushing for an entirely different reason.

"I don't know if I can let you go outside in that," Jensen said when I turned around, reaching behind me to tie my top.

Laughing, I crossed the room to stand in front of him, his face level with my bare abdomen. "Oh? And why is that?"

"Because I'd hate to have to gouge out Kyle or Brandon's eyes for having seen so much of you." There was only a slight lilt to his voice that indicated he was partially serious.

"Well, it's either this or a terribly unflattering green one-piece that I've had forever. I figured you'd like this a little more," I confessed, placing my hands on his shoulders while his ensnared my hips. "Come on. Get changed."

On our way down the hall, I grabbed a stack of towels from the closet. Willow, Brandon, Kyle, and Lilah were already in the hot tub, a fresh bottle of wine and six glasses on one of the edges as well as the remaining Patron and some shot glasses. Kyle smirked when he noticed my eyes fall to the tequila.

"That's right," he said. "You didn't think your little jab earlier about needing *'real competition'* would go unchallenged, did you?"

"I was counting on it, actually," I fibbed, hoping he wasn't as perceptive as Jensen.

As soon as my feet hit the grass, I heard an excited yip from the corner of our back yard before I heard Bones' heavy foot falls moving across the grass. "Hey buddy," I cooed, kneeling down to give him a quick pet, and then got into the water.

Kyle grabbed two of the full shot glasses, handing them to Jensen and myself, before divvying the rest out to everyone else. After our first shot was done, I accepted my glass of wine from Lilah and took a sip. "I want to thank you all for coming tonight. Even though a party isn't what I wanted ..." I glanced over to Jensen, glaring playfully "... I'm having a blast."

"Well, we're glad Jensen didn't listen to you," Willow informed me. "It's been far too long since you've had a party."

"You know I don't enjoy being the center of attention. It's just so much pressure, and then I get all clumsy and bad things start happening," I reminded her.

"And yet, you rode professionally with thousands of people watching," she challenged. The woman had a point, and she knew it.

Taking a sip of my wine, I nodded. "True," I said after swallowing. "However, you forget that I'm not alone out there."

Willow quirked an eyebrow. "So you're saying that you *never* buckle under pressure while riding?" I should have known she'd find a way to bring up my recent accident.

Jensen chuckled next to me, taking a sip of his own wine as he tried to mask his smirk. This birthday party may not have resulted in a physical injury, but my pride was sure taking a beating. There was no way I was going to sit back and take their teasing without at least trying to put up a fight.

"You know there were extenuating circumstances to what happened this summer," I replied, pointing my finger at Willow, who only smiled and nodded. "I was having an off couple of days."

"Mmhmm," Willow quipped. "I bet you were. Pretty hard to ride a horse when you can't stop thinking about riding—"

"Whoa!" I said, effectively cutting her off before she could say something that would tempt me to drown her—or myself. Everyone was laughing, and my face grew warmer. "I think that's about enough out of you. You've made your point. My logic is flawed. Parties from here on out. Happy now?"

"Elated," she said through her laughter.

"Kyle, I think I'm ready for another shot," I grumbled, keeping my eyes on Willow. I could only hope the look I gave her conveyed just how much she'd pay for this.

We had just finished our second round when Jensen's hand found my thigh beneath the water, and he leaned over, pressing his lips to my shoulder and smirked. "I knew you were checking me out."

Things had instantly shifted to playful between us as I pushed him away from me. "Oh please. Like you weren't doing the *exact* same thing," I argued.

"I check myself out every chance I get, so the odds are likely," he said with a wink as he leaned forward to kiss me.

What should have been an innocent sign of affection quickly escalated. The wine and tequila pumping through our veins plus the residual sexual tension from when we were in our room a little while ago, and I was swiftly overcome by my deeper desires. My fingers wove into Jensen's hair as I pulled his face closer to mine, our tongues meeting between parted lips and sliding languidly against each other. It wasn't until Kyle splashed us that I snapped out of it.

"You two wanna be left alone?" he asked, eliciting laughs from the others. "'Cause, we can leave."

Warmth spread across my face, and I reached for my wine. "Don't be ridiculous. We're not animals." A change of topic was needed, and fast. "So, what's everyone up to this weekend? Jensen and I are flying up to Canada to attend the Masters."

"Seriously?" Lilah exclaimed. "That is so cool."

That seemed to take the heat off of Jensen and I losing our senses and making out like a couple of horny fifteen-year-olds. Soon, Willow was sharing her story of when she accompanied me to Spruce Meadows the year before when I was competing, capturing everyone's attention. While it was odd to hear a second-hand account of the last time I competed, it was also strangely invigorating. Hearing her account of how graceful Halley and I were reminded me just how truly at home I was in the ring.

"You miss it." Jensen's soft voice pulled me from my silent reverie.

"Hmm?" I hummed, turning to him. "Oh, yeah, I guess I do. A little." It was true; I did miss it, but I enjoyed running the ranch with my dad and teaching lessons again. I wasn't sure if I could give it up. "I think a part of me will always miss it, but we have so much happening on the ranch right now, and I'm really enjoying how things are going."

Jensen nodded. "Okay, but you know if you wanted to go back, I'd support your decision, right?"

Placing my right hand on Jensen's cheek, I kissed him lightly. "I do."

As the night wore on, the wine and tequila bottles emptied. We were all pretty trashed, laughing at absolutely everything and nothing at the same time. It was just after midnight, and Bones had passed out on the porch after running around the yard for the last two hours. Willow and Brandon had retired an hour or so earlier — time kind of stopped making sense after my fifth glass of wine and a few more shooters. Kyle, Lilah, Jensen, and I stayed out a bit longer, exchanging dirty jokes. Okay, so maybe Kyle and Jensen exchanged dirty jokes while Lilah and I laughed or groaned or gagged — it depended on the joke, really.

"So, there was a construction worker on the fifth floor of a building who needed a handsaw. He spots another worker on the ground floor and yells down to him, but he can't hear him. So the worker on the fifth floor tries sign language," Kyle said animatedly through his laughter while Jensen, Lilah, and I still tried to rein in our hysterics from Jensen's last joke. "So, he pointed to his eye meaning 'I', pointed to his knee meaning 'need', then moved his hand back and forth in a hand saw motion. The man on the ground floor nods his head, pulls down his pants, whips out his cock and starts masturbating." Kyle was definitely loaded, because he starts miming the act above the surface of the water as he continues. "Well, the worker on fifth floor gets so pissed off, he runs down to the ground floor and says, *'What the fuck is your problem? I said I needed a handsaw!'* and the other guy says, *'I knew that! I was just trying to tell you I'm coming!'*"

I should have known better than to take a sip of wine when I did, because the instant the punch line to the joke was out there, I choked and sputtered on it in a very unladylike manner. In an effort to keep from spitting any out, and potentially spraying those who might be in front of me, I quickly covered my mouth while Jensen, Lilah, and Kyle howled with laughter. I hoped it was at the joke and not because I was aspirating—though, it was extremely likely to be a combination of the two.

"All right," Lilah declared as I stopped coughing. "I think we're going to turn in now. When Kyle tells that joke, I know he's about ten minutes from passing out."

"Wait," Kyle said, suddenly seeming confused and maybe a little bummed. "You've heard that joke before, babe?" The look on his face wasn't unlike that of a sad panda. I giggled.

Lilah smiled, placing her hand on his cheek. "Many, *many* times, honey. But it's still just as funny." That seemed to cheer Kyle up. "Come on, let's head inside and give Jensen and Madi some time alone. They've been entertaining guests all night."

There was no disagreement from Kyle as he stood and took Lilah's hand, helping her out of the hot tub before wrapping her towel around her. Bones lifted his head from his paws, his large ears perked forward as he watched them walk past him.

"Doctor McCoy," Kyle said, saluting the puzzled looking puppy as Lilah pulled his stumbling ass through the patio door, closing it behind them and leaving us alone.

In an instant, Jensen's hands found my thighs, and he pulled me toward him until I was straddling his lap. "I finally get you all to myself."

I sighed breathlessly when he started placing delicate kisses along my collarbone, letting my head fall back as his mouth moved across my throat and over the other shoulder. Slowly, I lowered my face and locked eyes with him as his fingers dug into my back, walking up my spine until they twisted into the tied strings of my bathing suit top. With one flick of his wrist, my top was undone and floating away from my breasts until he yanked it from between us and tossed it to the ground outside the hot tub.

Our mouths collided in a frantic kiss as Jensen moved his right hand around to grope and caress the swell of my chest, pinching and teasing my nipple. Ripples of pleasure flowed through my body, descending lower and lower until they settled between my thighs, and I thrust my hips forward again, seeking out some kind of relief.

Deep down, I knew what I really wanted was to get us both naked and have sex. Right there. In the hot tub. The rational side of my brain knew that we should probably take things inside; sex outside in a hot tub with our guests able to catch us at any moment seemed pretty risky. However, tequila had this tendency to bitch slap rationality into submission and my baser urges generally took the reins. So, instead of saying anything, Jensen and I continued to grope and paw at each other unabashedly.

"This is the best birthday ever," I whispered, allowing my fingers to tickle the nape of Jensen's neck.

He smiled against my skin. "Well, it's not over yet, love," he said, his gravelly voice vibrating through me until I rocked my hips against his. "Let me take care of you."

23
BLACKOUT
Jensen Davis

Soft, sweat dampened skin, pressed and slid sensually against mine. Kisses alternated from soft and feather-like to hard and ravenous, while her teeth nipped the flesh of my neck as she moved above me.

In ... Out ... In and fucking out... She continued to rock her hips above me, my orgasm quickly building as she increased her pace. The sounds she made were like music to my fucking ears as she broke her mouth away from my neck and moaned. Her body tensed above me, yet her movements were unrelenting as she continued to ride me at a steady pace.

Moving my hands up, I grabbed her hips savagely, pulling her against me. She cried out in ecstasy, her hands slamming down onto my chest and her short nails biting into the skin as she began to shudder, her orgasm crashing through her like a tidal wave. It wasn't long before I joined her, jerking my hips up off the bed until she collapsed on top of me, both of us completely spent ...

There was a soft groan beside me that pulled me from my deep sleep, the remnants of yet another sex dream hazy but still lingering in the depths of my mind. It was possible that the fog in my head was due to having just woken up, but the pounding was proof enough that I'd had too much to drink the night before. And the inability to remember crawling into bed at all only backed it up.

Madison's warm body shifted next to me, another groan coming from her as the blankets moved over me. Opening my eyes a sliver against the light filtering into the room, I saw her lying on her stomach with her pillow pulled over her head—probably in an attempt to keep the morning sunlight from making the headache she likely had even worse. While I couldn't remember much, I did recall Madison having a head start on the tequila; there was no way she wasn't hung over.

"Baby?" I asked, cringing at how hoarse my voice sounded.

"Hmmm?" Her response was muffled by the pillow over her head. Had it not been for the wrecking ball slamming around my skull, I would have laughed at how adorable she was.

I looked over her at the alarm clock and groaned when I saw it was almost eleven. "How's your head, love?"

"Oh, God. It's like Neil Peart in there beating the *shit* out of my brain," she replied into her pillow, her muffled voice sounding a little raspy as well.

"Who?" I queried, not quite understanding.

"The drummer from Rush, obviously."

I chuckled, rolling over and pressing my lips to her bare shoulder before pushing myself off the bed. "I'll go grab some Tylenol." Her pillow moved, prompting me to believe she was nodding beneath it.

It wasn't until I crawled out of bed that I realized I was completely naked—which shouldn't have shocked me considering how drunk I was. I crossed the room to our dresser so I could grab a pair of underwear, some jeans, and a shirt, and then locked myself in our bathroom to brush my teeth. After replacing my toothbrush, I ran my hands through my messy hair in an attempt to tame it and then down over my rough jaw. It had been years since I'd felt this trashed. Since college, probably.

As soon as I opened the bedroom door, I could hear low voices in the kitchen that only grew louder the closer I got. In addition to that, I caught the smell of fresh coffee and inhaled deeply. A little energy seeped back into my body, and I quickened my pace, eager to cure my hangover.

"Well! Good morning, sunshine!" Kyle boomed, causing my brain to throb painfully against the inside of my skull.

As I entered the kitchen fully, I heard the tiny clicking of claws rush toward me, and soon Bones was right in front of me, jumping up on my legs. "Good morning, buddy," I said, scratching his head before instructing him to get down so I could grab my coffee.

"I hope you don't mind," Willow said warmly, looking up at me as I turned toward the coffee maker. "I figured he'd probably have to go out. I didn't want him making a mess in your room. No one answered when I knocked on your door, so I just opened the door a smidge, and he came rushing out."

Nodding at her, I smiled. "No, I don't mind. Thanks."

"Sleep well?" Kyle asked from his seat at the table with the others, his loud voice making my brain pulse again.

Pressing the heel of my right hand to my temple, I groaned. "Uh, yeah. I think so. What the hell happened last night?" Upon looking at them again, I noticed that each of them had a fresh cup of coffee in front of them, and they were all smiling and staring intently as I moved toward the sweet, heavenly smell. It was almost like they were taking some kind of sick, sadistic pleasure in seeing someone suffer a hangover. How was it that Madison and I were the only ones who felt this way? They'd all had a lot to drink too ... right?

"You don't remember?" Brandon inquired, the grin falling from his face.

Opening the cupboard and grabbing two mugs and a glass, I wracked my brain. The smell of coffee surrounded me as I poured it into the two mugs, deciding to forego the cream and sugar just in case Madison's stomach was as upset as mine.

"Uh ..." Flashes of everyone in the hot tub came and went ... Laughing, shots, dirty jokes ... "Fuck, how much did we drink last night?"

Kyle laughed. "Dude, I had enough trouble remembering parts of last night, myself. Lilah had to fill in a few blanks for me this morning. I remember these two pansies heading off to bed and then your girlfriend goading me into another round of shots ... And then? Nothin'."

Well, it was comforting to know it wasn't just *my*

memory of last night that seemed to be missing. I reached for the bottle of Tylenol, shaking two into my palm before taking them, and then I shook out two more and set them aside to take to Madison.

"Is Madi up yet?" Brandon asked.

"Well, she was semi-awake before I came out here. I'm just going to run this in to her. We'll be right out, and I'll make breakfast for everyone," I offered, knowing that the only true cure for a hangover would be to rehydrate and feed our bodies. After picking up the pills, the glass of water, and Madison's coffee, I padded down the hall. Bones was hot on my trail, and I laughed when he quickly passed me, pushing the door open with his nose.

When I crossed the threshold, I found Madison sitting with her back against the headboard and the covers pulled up to her waist. She looked toward me and a faint smile spread across her incredibly pale face. "You're up," I whispered, moving to the bed and sitting in front of her before setting her coffee on the night table and handing her the pills and water.

"Yeah. I had to use the washroom and brush my teeth. My mouth felt all fuzzy and gross." A queasy look contorted her face before she popped the pills in her mouth and washed them down with some water. "Thanks. What happened last night?" Bones jumped up, placing his front paws on the bed next to Madison, and she acknowledged him with a smile and a quick pat on the head. "Seriously. I don't remember much ... and I woke up naked. Did we ...?"

While I'd hoped maybe she'd recall something, it wasn't really a surprise that she didn't—she definitely had more to drink than me or anyone else. "I'm going to assume we had a good time?"

She laughed, her face instantly twisting into a pained expression since her head was likely still pounding. Slowly, she set the water down on the bedside table before grabbing the coffee cup, sighing as she inhaled the rich aroma. "You're going to *assume*?" she asked before taking a small sip. She grimaced at the taste because she wasn't used to taking it black; I knew it would be best given our current state.

"Even Kyle says he can't remember much after Willow and Brandon turned in. Said you even goaded him into another round of shots," I told her, lying on my side across the foot of the bed.

Madison's brows pulled together. "Well *that* doesn't sound like me. I must have been pretty wasted." She took another sip from her mug before setting it next to her water. "Is everyone up?"

"Yeah. Willow let Bones out while we were still sleeping."

Smiling again, Madison leaned down and kissed the top of Bones' head since he was still up on his hind legs looking for attention. It was hilarious how his entire body moved as he wagged his tail excitedly. "Well that was awfully nice of Auntie Willow," she cooed to him.

"Oh, God. Are we *those* people?" I teased, pushing myself back up as I grabbed her lower leg gently. "Okay, get up. I'm making breakfast. And after, we should probably clean up the backyard. If we can't remember anything, I'm certain we were too drunk to even consider cleaning up before passing the fuck out."

"Ugh," Madison complained, shifting to the side to stand up. "That doesn't sound fun at all."

"Well, afterward, maybe you and the girls could go for a ride," I suggested, pulling her into my arms and kissing her softly.

Madison hummed in contentment against my lips. "Or," she said, pulling back slightly to lock eyes. "We could all go."

Nodding contemplatively, I kissed the tip of her nose. "That sounds perfect. Come on," I said, letting my hands fall to her ass and squeezing. I was sure everyone would agree that her idea was definitely better too. From what I had heard, Brandon knew how to ride, and I was pretty sure Kyle did too.

Madison pulled out of my arms, smiling sweetly. "You go ahead. I'm just going to pull on some jeans and a T-shirt. These shorts might be a little too scandalous for breakfast."

"Well, I like 'em," I assured her, letting my eyes rove

over her body appreciatively.

She arched an eyebrow and shoved me playfully. "Yeah, well, you're kind of a perv, remember?"

"I don't seem to recall you complaining about that before now," I countered with a smile as she rifled through her dresser.

"Not complaining. I was merely stating a fact."

Laughing, I backed toward the door, watching as Madison slipped her thumbs into the waistband of her shorts. She shook her head, silently telling me that she wasn't going to strip with me still in the room; she was such a tease—and I loved it.

After leaving her again, I made my way to the kitchen where I dug around in the fridge for everything I would need for breakfast. After scrambling the eggs, milk, veggie ham and diced vegetables, I put them into a casserole dish and waited for the oven to preheat before I put it in to bake. While it cooked, I washed and diced some fruit for a fruit salad.

"Well, there's the birthday girl!" Brandon exclaimed, his announcement causing me to turn to see Madison enter the room with Bones at her feet, his tail still wagging as he looked up at her every now and again.

"Good morning. Did you all sleep okay?" They nodded, telling her they slept fine as she crossed over to me. "Do you need a hand?"

I had just scooped the last of the pineapple into the bowl and shook my head. "Nope. You go and relax. Breakfast is in the oven. Should be done in about twenty."

"How are you feeling?" Lilah asked Madison.

She shrugged before answering Lilah as she grabbed her antibiotics from the counter and took this morning's dose with her last sip of coffee. "Okay, I guess. My headache's going away, but I feel a little queasy. I'm hoping breakfast will help."

"It will," I assured her.

Madison refilled her coffee mug, this time adding a smidge of cream and sugar to it and sat in her seat at the table. "So, Jensen and I were thinking that after we check on the condition of the backyard, we could all maybe hit the trails?"

She brought her foot up onto the seat of her chair and hugged her leg to her chest.

"You know how to ride, Kyle?" I asked, just to be sure.

Nodding, he spoke. "Yeah. It's been years, though."

"That's okay. I'm sure we'll find a good horse, plus it's not like we'll do anything faster than a walk or a trot," Madison said, her lips twisting up into an excited smile. Her headache must have been getting better, because she was definitely looking and sounding a little livelier.

When the fruit salad was done, I placed it on the table before grabbing plates and cutlery. Just as I finished setting the table, the oven timer went off, indicating that our brunch was finished. I quickly grabbed the two potholders, setting them on the table so I could place the casserole dish on them without fear of ruining the wood.

Out of courtesy, Madison and I waited until everyone else dished up, and I watched her closely to make sure she wasn't still feeling a little ill. The color seemed to be returning to her face, and thankfully she seemed all right as she scooped some of the breakfast casserole onto her plate. "Thanks for breakfast," she said before taking her first bite.

Based on the way everyone was devouring their food, it was clear that they must have been feeling a smidge hungover; they were just masters at hiding it.

Everyone pitched in to clean the kitchen before we all migrated outside to deal with the backyard. Upon stepping through the patio door, I noticed we'd forgot to turn off the lights the girls helped string up yesterday afternoon, and some of the vases of flowers had tipped over on the porch. That was about the worst of it, thankfully. The two empty bottles were tipped on their sides on one of the corner ledges of the hot tub, and all of our wine and shot glasses were scattered in the other three.

Madison had knelt down to pick up some of the toppled vases, saying how she was hoping to save the flowers so she could display them in the kitchen before they wilted, and Kyle offered to tidy up the glasses and bottles while Brandon and I helped the girls take the strings of lights down. Lilah and Willow laughed and joked around like they had known each other for years, and it pleased me to know that my sister and Madison's best friend were getting along. It made me optimistic that, by befriending Madison and Willow, the void Kaylie left could be filled.

Kyle and Brandon got along just as well as their spouses did. Of course, there was less giggling between them, and more dirty jokes and lewd behavior—typical guy stuff. Our lives continued to fuse in a way I never even realized was possible. It was new to me, and I couldn't believe I ever thought that what I had with Kaylie was in some way comparable.

I had just unplugged the main power source for the lights when Kyle's loud voice drew everyone's attention to him. "Well, well, well," he said, turning his head toward us and smiling smugly. "Do you two have anything to confess?" His eyes moved back and forth between Madison and me as we exchanged a confused glance, shrugging when we both came up with nothing.

Kyle's smile grew and he guffawed loudly, bending down to the ground and grabbing something at his feet. Through my periphery, I watched Madison stand slowly as we both inspected what he was picking up. At first, it didn't seem like anything, but the straighter he stood, the longer the item he held in between his thumb and forefinger got. Then, there was suddenly more to the skinny piece of black string that he was holding. Madison gasped loudly while my jaw fell to the ground, both of us instantly recognizing her bikini top.

24
DID WE...? DIDN'T WE...?
Jensen Davis

What. The. Fuck?

Willow hooted and hollered behind us, congratulating Madison on finally being sexually liberated enough for mild exhibitionism. "The backyard's always where it starts." She giggled, soon joined by my sister, and I didn't need to turn to Madison to know that she was probably the brightest shade of red she'd ever been.

My brain suddenly kicked into high gear, trying to remember how Madison's top wound up on the ground, only to come up empty again.

"Oh-ho-ho-ho!" Kyle boomed, sounding a little like Santa Claus. He was definitely a little too jolly about whatever he spotted next. "It would appear this skimpy piece of fabric isn't the only thing you two left behind last night."

He grabbed one of the empty bottles and dipped the neck into the hot tub, apparently afraid that whatever he was talking about might bite him. As his arm rose, and my swimming trunks came into view, I knew it was more likely about him being afraid of sticking his arm into water he now questioned the cleanliness of.

"What the hell did we *do*?" Madison whispered. Her voice was so quiet, I was sure she was talking mostly to herself. I had no recollection of anything either, so I didn't respond—mainly because I had nothing to offer in the way of an explanation.

My trunks hit the side of the hot tub with a loud *slosh* before he dipped the bottle in *again* and came back with Madison's black bikini bottoms. "Holy fuck," I muttered, raking my fingers through my hair, still trying really fucking hard to remember what the hell happened last night. I had completely blacked the fuck out.

"Did the two of you screw in the hot tub?" Kyle's dimples deepened as though he had already formed his own conclusion—not that it was a hard deduction to come to considering the evidence presented.

"I-I—" I stammered, still not quite sure how to answer that question. As arousing as the idea of hot-tub sex was, I couldn't imagine *ever* being so careless—drunk or not.

"Did we?" Madison was so quiet as she slipped her clammy hand into mine, and I had no answers, so I stayed silent. "Jensen?"

I shook my head and turned to her, being sure to keep my voice down as I responded. "No. We wouldn't have ... Right? I remember having a dream ... But, we were in bed. I think." I paused, suddenly trying to recall the still-foggy dream. Yeah, we were definitely in bed.

Madison let out a quiet, unconvincing laugh and shook her head. "Of course. I mean, if we'd have done anything, we'd remember." She still didn't sound so sure; it was almost like she was trying to convince herself more than anyone. "I'd remember."

It wasn't until Kyle cleared his throat expectantly that we realized he was still waiting for us to comment on the fact that we had stripped in the hot tub after everyone had retired for the night. While it wasn't *really* any of his business, I knew Kyle, and he wasn't likely to relent.

I had just opened my mouth to say something when Madison surprised me by stalking over to him and snatching her bikini top from his hand. "Since when is skinny-dipping a crime, Kyle?" she challenged, finding a bit of inner strength and narrowing her eyes at him.

He arched his eyebrows, not giving any indication that he was ready to back down any time soon. "Are you sure that's all that happened, Madikins?"

She didn't even flinch as she yanked my trunks off the

side of the hot tub and her bikini bottoms from where they still dangled on the neck of the bottle. "I'm pretty sure I'd know if I had sex in a hot tub, Kyle."

He looked like he wanted to say something else, but she didn't allow him to as she turned and walked back inside with our still sopping wet swimwear. It wasn't long before she returned, and everyone was still looking between the two of us, likely wondering if we were only trying to convince ourselves that nothing happened.

"All right," she said, drawing everyone's eyes to her. "We're all adults here. Can we get this place cleaned up and go for a trail ride? Or would you all like to talk this out a little more?" Willow started to raise her hand, a devilish smirk beginning to spread. "It was a rhetorical question, Will."

Dropping her hand back to her side, she grumbled, clearly picking up on something in Madison's voice that said the topic was to be dropped—immediately. Soon enough, everyone had gone back to his or her duties, and we had just finished bundling the last of the lights to store in the shed for future use.

"Okay, let's head out and find horses for everyone," Madison suggested, opening the gate to the backyard. "I'll see if Dad will watch Bones while we're out. Until he's trained to stay out from underfoot, I don't want him coming. It's too dangerous, and he could get trampled."

"I agree. I'm sure Wayne won't mind," I said, kissing her temple as we made our way down the narrow path that led to the gravel road between the houses and the barn.

Just as we stepped into the barn, Wayne was exiting his office and smiled upon seeing us. "Well good morning, kids," he greeted. "How was the rest of your night?"

Kyle chuckled, earning a very stern look from both Madison and me before he cleared his throat and held himself back.

"It was fun," Madison told him. "We actually just finished cleaning up the yard and were going to reward ourselves with a little trail ride. Would you mind watching Bones for a bit?"

Wayne smiled, looking down at the puppy as he sniffed

every nook and cranny in the barn, probably looking for some kind of trouble to get into. "I'd love to." Wayne's eyes suddenly drifted over us, and when I turned I saw Tom coming into the barn. "Oh, Tom's here so we can head to lunch. You kids have fun and we'll see you in a bit. C'mon, Bones." Already recognizing his name, Bones lifted his head, perking his ears forward and running after Wayne as he crossed the barn.

After a quick "hello" from Tom, Madison and I tried to figure out which horses everyone would be riding and grabbed several leads and halters. "Okay, Lilah, you'll be on Starla again. Brandon, I'll let you ride Bandit; Dad's made some real progress with him since you rode him last. Will, I'll put you on Miracle, and Kyle, I think Oliver would be a good fit for you based on how much experience you have. Jensen will be on Ransom, and I'll ride Hails," she instructed.

Miracle and Oliver were two of the ranch's newer additions from this past spring. From what I was told, Madison and Wayne had gone to an auction just outside of town and bought them to train as lesson horses since a few of their older ones would be retiring soon. In my first couple of weeks, Madison introduced me to each of the horses so I would know what to expect from each of them, and Miracle was troublesome. I was sure she didn't mean to be; it was just in her nature. She was this feisty little gray Arabian mare who, at eleven years old, acted like a yearling again. I remembered Madison telling me that it had taken a solid month to get her to calm down enough to actually get a smooth ride out of her. From what I could tell, having never ridden her before, she was great for the most part now, but still had quite a bit of get-up-and-go left in her—a perfect match for Willow.

Then there was Oliver; he was a solid horse. He was a nine-year-old Thoroughbred gelding who had actually been used as a racehorse until he blew his knee in a race last season. The vet checks that Madison and Wayne got upon buying him all said that he'd never race again. Not wanting to do anything to cause any horse harm intentionally, Madison told Wayne that Oliver would be strictly for Dressage, Western, and basic lessons. He would never race or jump while living at the ranch.

After catching our mounts, we brought them to the barn and began getting them ready for our trail ride. Once Madison and I checked to ensure that everyone's cinches were secure, we led the horses outside where we mounted up.

The girls took the lead while the guys and I followed them. Kyle seemed to have a pretty decent handle on things; he needed a bit of guidance in the beginning on reining, but overall, I was impressed.

As we walked the trails, the guys and I talked about planning a camping trip after Madison and I returned from Spruce Meadows, which sounded like a lot of fun. I knew my sister might be hesitant at first. She wasn't really an outdoorsy person—or she never *used* to be. It was quite possible that her love of the outdoors was being rekindled the more she hung out on the ranch. Maybe she'd be cool with it.

Brandon and Kyle loved the idea of a couples camping retreat. Thankfully, they didn't complain for long when I told them we'd have to wait until the week after next due to Wayne's fishing trip. Then they started asking if I knew of any good spots before they started talking about buying all sorts of camping gear.

We had been riding for almost an hour and a half before Madison suggested we head back. "I still have to head into town and pick up Jillian."

"Yeah, Brandon and I should head back to the city tonight. We have to go back to work tomorrow," Willow said. "I always hate leaving here."

"Well," Madison said coyly. "There's a very simple solution to that."

"And give up city livin'?" Willow quipped. "Nah. As much as I miss you and this place, I couldn't leave Memphis."

Madison pouted.

We continued back to the ranch with Brandon and Kyle still talking about this camping trip in a couple weeks. When Willow overheard part of the conversation, she squealed in excitement.

"We should definitely go camping before it gets too cold!

Hell, even if it does, I guess that's why they make those extra cozy, down-filled sleeping bags! Plus, you can buy them big enough for two people now." Even with my back to her and the girls, I could imagine her winking at Madison.

"I think that's a great idea," Madison concurred. "What do you say, Lilah? It would be a lot of fun."

There was a beat of silence as I assumed Lilah was trying to find a way out of it without knocking the idea entirely. "Well, I'm not really one for camping. I mean, I like toilets and showers, you know?" There was another moment of silence before she spoke again. "But, that was the old me. So, what the hell! Let's camp."

"Hey!" Kyle said excitedly. "We should check out that outdoor sporting goods store in town. Uh ... Hall's something-or-other, I think?" If I tensed upon hearing that name, I could only imagine how Madison reacted. Kyle noticed immediately. "What?" he asked.

"That store is owned by Madi's ex's parents," I explained, looking over my shoulder to see Madison scowling. "Maybe we could head into the city—"

"No," Madison interrupted. "It's fine. It's likely he's not going to be there anyway. Not to mention, Dad's known the Halls for years and has a standing account with them. They always give him the best deals on stuff. We should go there. Maybe sometime next week after we get back."

"You're sure?" I didn't exactly relish the idea of Madison running into that douche-nozzle again, but it comforted me to know that if she did, I would be with her to put him in his place—again.

"Yeah," she replied. "I'm sure. Plus, even if he is there, I doubt he'll come anywhere near me with you around ... not after what happened."

We finally made it back to the barn and groomed the horses down before turning them out and going home. It was already almost four, and Madison had to have Jill at the barn for her six o' clock lesson.

Soon, everyone was gone, and Madison and I had a few minutes alone. I pulled her into my arms and kissed the tip of her nose. "How are you feeling?"

She sighed, wrapping her arms around my waist. "That depends on what you're talking about?" I looked at her quizzically. "My head and stomach feel much better than they did this morning. However ..." She took a deep breath. "I hate that I can't remember what happened last night. I shouldn't have let Kyle talk me into a second round of shots."

I laughed. "Good luck there. He's relentless." I glanced at the clock behind her and groaned. "It's getting late, you should go. I'll see you back here for dinner?"

Giving me one last kiss, she nodded. "I'll see you soon."

I watched from the front porch as she backed out of the drive, and once she pulled out onto the highway, I stepped inside and closed the door. Now alone, the doubts about what may or may not have happened in the hot tub last night started to weigh on me. I still wanted to believe that neither one of us was careless enough to have sex without some kind of protection.

In our room, I searched for any kind of evidence that we'd been safe. The bed was still unmade, so I pulled the blankets up and fixed the pillows overtop of it, smoothing out any wrinkles in the duvet—because let's face it, I had a touch of OCD when it came to shit like that. With the bed made, I pulled open the nightstand drawer that contained our condoms.

I thought about counting them, but then realized that would be ridiculous because I'd have to have known how many were in there before last night. There was no empty wrapper on either of the nightstands, nor was there one in the bathroom trash can. I was starting to hope beyond fucking hope that the sex dream *was* just a dream, because if it wasn't, it was beginning to look like Madison and I would be playing a waiting game for the next couple of weeks, thanks to her recent strep diagnosis.

I had just stepped out of the bathroom, trying to come up with some way to apologize to Madison for being a total asshole and not being careful, when I saw a tiny glimmer of hope. Peeking out from beneath my side of the bed was the corner of a familiar foil package. I rushed over and dropped to my knees to retrieve it, rejoicing when I found it both open and empty.

Breathing easier, I discarded the empty condom wrapper and went off in search of Wayne so I could relieve him of puppy-sitting duties and start dinner for when Madison got home. He was in the barn, just grabbing a few halters and leads to start bringing the horses in for the night. Knowing I had a bit of time before Madison returned, I decided to help him and Tom out.

"Good evening," he greeted. "How was your ride this afternoon?"

"Pretty good," I replied. "We actually planned to go camping in a couple of weeks. We won't be far from the ranch if you still need us to come in for the morning chores."

Wayne laughed, clapping his hand down on my shoulder. "Don't you worry about it. You and Madison work so hard around here that you deserve a weekend off every now and again."

"Yeah, but we got the weekend off for my sister's wedding, and you're giving us this weekend off for the trip up north. We don't want you to work yourself into the ground," I told him, feeling guilty about taking advantage of his generosity.

"I've got Tom and Jeff to help out. Plus, Jeff said a couple of his school buddies were looking for an opportunity to make a bit of money and gain some work experience this winter," Wayne explained as we walked outside to start catching the horses. "We'll be fine. Go, have fun."

"As long as you're sure." One look from him told me to just accept his generosity, and I took two of the leads from him before we entered the paddock and caught the four horses Jill would need that night.

On our way back to the barn, I realized that the initial reason I came to find Wayne seemed to be missing. "Hey, where's Bones?"

"Oh," Wayne said with a laugh. "He was chasing a couple of the barn cats after lunch and passed out in my office while I was getting a head start on orders and invoicing for the month."

"Gotcha."

Knowing that Bones was tucked away, Wayne and I tethered the lesson horses before we brought the others in for the night. Wayne offered to gather the horses for the main barn if I was willing to start on the ones that occupied the new facility. Because there were only ten horses staying there so far, I was done before Wayne and decided to help with his last few before collecting Bones from the office.

When I opened the office door, Bones yipped, his tail wagging happily as he bounded toward me and tried jumping up. I coaxed him down, correcting his behavior and patting him once he obeyed, then I said a quick goodnight to Wayne so I could get home and start on dinner.

After dicing the vegetables and tofu for a new stew recipe I wanted to try, I put them in the pot of vegetable stock on top of the stove and turned the burner down to let it simmer. I had just put the last dirty dish into the dishwasher when I heard the truck pull up outside.

"Hey," I greeted as Madison came up beside me, wrapping her arm around my waist and leaning her head against my chest. "How was the drive into town?"

"Same old, same old," she replied with a yawn.

Stirring the stew in the pot before covering it, I pressed a light kiss onto the top of her head and inhaled lightly. "Tired?"

"Exhausted."

"Well, dinner should be ready soon. Why don't you go and relax until then?" Nodding, Madison stepped away, rounding the corner for the living room while I stayed to set the table and finish up dinner. I even lit a few candles and placed one of Madison's floral arrangements in the center of the table.

As I made my way to the living room to retrieve Madison from the couch, I found her curled up under her throw blanket on the couch, watching an evening talk show through heavy eyelids. Her head drifted in my direction and she smiled. "Dinner ready?"

Nodding, I crossed the room and took her hand, pulling her to her feet and then tugging her along to the kitchen. "You really didn't have to do all this," she said, eyeing the table's set up as I pulled her chair out for her.

"I know," I told her, taking my seat next to her. "But I wanted to." I grabbed her bowl from in front of her and started filling it. "How's Jillian?"

"Good. She was wise to go home with your parents; she felt great this morning."

There seemed to be something on Madison's mind as she stirred her dinner, her blank eyes staring into the stew. I was just about to ask what was troubling her when she spoke up. "I think I'm starting to remember what happened last night."

"Oh?"

"Yeah." She set her spoon down and placed her hands in her lap, her eyes following them. "I'm worried things got out of hand in the hot tub. I'm pretty sure I remember you taking my top off before we stripped the rest of the way ..."

I swallowed thickly; it wasn't sounding promising. "What else?"

Even with her eyes downcast, I saw her clench them shut in frustration. "Ugh! I don't know! That's all I can remember right now." Slowly, she brought her gaze to meet mine. "If I do the math, I'm about two-and-a-half weeks from my next cycle."

I nodded, suddenly nervous again because I knew how this shit worked.

"Normally I wouldn't be this freaked." Madison's eyes held mine, something akin to worry burning into them. "But I've been on antibiotics for just over a week. You heard what the doctor said." She shrugged. "Not really the best time to pull the goalie, if you know what I'm saying. We've been together a month. I was scared shitless when I thought you were going to propose last night, so *this* isn't any easier to process."

Taking a deep breath, she calmed herself a little. "I want kids, but not yet. What if ...?"

I reached over and clasped her hands in mine, bringing them out of her lap and onto the table. "Then we'll handle it," I told her softly.

She still didn't seem entirely convinced by my words, so I decided to tell her of my earlier findings. "I don't know if it helps, but when I was in our room after you left, I found a discarded condom wrapper that I know wasn't there yesterday when I moved us into the room. Maybe we knew things were quickly escalating and we moved inside."

"Yeah? You think so?"

"Anything's possible, love." I offered her a smile, which seemed to put her at ease while my panic returned.

It wasn't the possibility of us being pregnant that scared me stupid, it was because Madison was so upset, and I couldn't help but see the parallel to my past.

I smiled wider, squeezing her hands. "Let's just see what happens. If we dodged the baby-train, then we'll be more careful to avoid this from happening again. And if we didn't, well, like I said, we'll handle it together."

Madison's eyes glistened with tears as she threw herself onto my lap and wrapped her arms around my neck. "You're so amazing. Most guys would be freaking out about this, and you're handling it as though it's just another Friday afternoon."

Chuckling, I returned her embrace, trying my damndest to remain calm for her. "Baby, there's no sense getting upset until we know there's something to be upset about. As long as we stick together, there's nothing we can't handle."

Deep down, I knew my words to be true, but I couldn't help that one nagging thought from whispering, *What if?*

25
TWO-WEEK WAIT
Madison Landry

"You really mean that?" I asked, my voice muffled against his neck as I held him tightly.

The events of the night before in the hot tub were still really hazy, certain parts still missing entirely. Getting my memories back seemed to be the only thing I could focus on as I drove out to Savannah to pick up Jillian; honestly, I wasn't even sure what it was that triggered the ones that did come back.

I wrestled with the idea of telling Jensen at all, and initially, I decided not to. At first, I tried to tell myself it wasn't a huge deal; I was on the pill, after all. That was when I remembered the antibiotics and the doctor's warning. It wasn't until I started doing the math to make sure Jensen and I were at least in the "safe-zone" that I knew I had to come clean.

"Of course I mean it," he said, combing his fingers through the length of my hair. "Listen ..." He shifted until I pulled my face from his neck. My hair had fallen over the right side of my face, so he reached up to brush it aside. "The way I see it, we've got two choices. One, we can stress and dwell on the 'what ifs' for the next couple of weeks until we can take a test ..." I may have swooned when he said "we" and not "you." "Or, we can *not* focus on it; try to put it in the back of our minds until the time comes. Now, I know it's not that easy to just forget about it, but it has to be better than walking on egg shells for the next two weeks, right?"

Ultimately, he was right. While I knew I wouldn't be able

to forget about it completely, I didn't want it to control my every waking moment. How did people who were actually trying to procreate stand the wait?

I offered Jensen a smile, really willing to try and not stress. He was right; we really had no reason to believe that we had let things get out of hand. Maybe our drunk-selves had common sense after all. I mean, he did say he found an open wrapper in our room. Anything was possible.

"Okay. You're right. Let's not worry about it until we have to."

"That's my girl," he said, his famous crooked smirk returning before he kissed me sweetly. "Now, let's eat, and then I'll draw you a bath so you can relax. Let me take care of you."

That phrase ... There was something familiar about it, I just couldn't put my finger on it until something in my memory snapped, recoiling like an over-stretched elastic band. I gasped as the dam burst, and everything came rushing forward. I couldn't stop it, not even if I wanted to ...

Clothes came off, and the shameless moans of a wannabe porn star carried off into the night. Deep, guttural groans of pleasure and fingers digging into my hips, pulling me forward ... faster ... faster ...

My bottom lip stung with the memory of Jensen's teeth claiming it, and I could practically hear the water splashing over the edge of the hot tub as Jensen guided me onto him.

"Oh, God," I mumbled.

"What?"

"I know we said we weren't going to stress, but ... I think I remember what happened." Jensen's body went rigid beneath me, his eyebrows pulling up and in with worry. All I could do was nod.

"So we did? In the hot tub?"

"I'm pretty sure, yeah." Panic gnawing at me, I slipped back into my seat and picked up my spoon. Both of us were silent as we stared into our bowls, not particularly interested in eating.

"You know what?" he finally said, cutting through the quiet. "It doesn't change anything." I stared at him, letting the confidence in his voice soak into me. I took it in like I needed it to live. "We'll continue to wait. After dinner, I'm going to draw you a bath like I said I would, and you're going to try and relax."

"Okay," I agreed quietly, suddenly feeling like I didn't want to be alone. "But only if you join me."

"Well," he said with a light chuckle. "When you look at me with those big beautiful eyes of yours, it's kind of impossible to say no."

Which could explain how we might have gotten ourselves into this mess.

After dinner, Jensen left to go draw my bath as he promised, and I knelt to the floor and pulled Bones into my arms to snuggle him. I was placing dozens of kisses into the soft fur atop Bones' head until he started wriggling in my grasp, his tail wagging as he yipped and tried licking my chin. Laughing, I released him and watched him run over to his water and food dishes.

"Babe?" Jensen called from down the hall.

I hopped to my feet, leaving Bones to his dinner, and made my way for the washroom where Jensen was standing next to the tub. The lights were off, the natural light from the setting sun coming in from the lone window higher up on the wall. In addition to that, Jensen had lit the thick pillared candles I kept in here for when I felt the need for a relaxing bubble bath, and placed them on the floor on either end of the claw-footed tub. The bath looked so inviting with its steaming, bubble-topped water; I hadn't even hit the water yet, and I could feel the tension beginning to leave my body.

Extending a hand to me, he smiled. "Madi?"

I accepted his outstretched hand, and he pulled me to him before lowering his hands to my waist and slipping his fingers beneath the hemline of my shirt. As he crept the soft cotton fabric up over my waist, I raised my arms above my head to assist. His hands swept over my upper body as they made their way north, starting at my waist and moving over my ribs until they slid up my arms. He tossed my shirt to the floor beside us.

Wrapping his arms around me again, he slowly stripped

me of my bra; the look in his eyes assuring me that none of this was about sex. He was assuring me that, no matter what the future had in store for us, he would be right there with me. I shuddered, overcome with so much emotion between us as his hands moved down into the waist of my now undone jeans and panties before sliding them down my legs, the denim pooling around my ankles.

After stepping out of my jeans and pulling my socks off, Jensen held my hand as I stepped over the side of the tub and lowered myself into the hot water. I leaned forward, hugging my knees to my chest as I rested my cheek on them and watched Jensen discard his own clothing.

"Scoot up," he instructed.

I shifted forward in the tub, leaving him enough room to slide in behind me, and once he had nestled in and stretched his legs out on either side of me, he ran his hands up and down my upper arms, easing me back against his chest. With both of us in the tub, the water had displaced enough that it was only a few inches from the top, the bubbles covering me almost to my collarbone as I leaned against him. I could feel his heart beat against my back as his fingers trailed lazily up and down my arms and over my shoulders.

Every once in a while, he'd place a sweet kiss onto the top of my head, or on my temple, or the shell of my ear, while his hands slipped beneath the water so he could massage my lower back. "This is nice," I whispered, my eyes closing as the sensation of his amazing massage combined with the warm bubble bath caused me to melt into a puddle of goo. "Why have we never done this before?" I moaned when his fingers pressed deliciously into the muscles of my lower back.

"We bathed together in Memphis," he reminded me, his whispered words tickling my ear and making me giggle.

"That wasn't the same. That tub could have fit four or five people. This, though? Way more intimate," I explained, raising my hand and running it over his scratchy jaw until I found the back of his neck and teased the hairs there.

"We will definitely have to do this more often, then."

I nodded against his chest before tilting my head up to look at him. "Thank you," I said.

His eyebrows pulled together in confusion. "For what?"

There was so much I was thanking him for. For loving me, for being so patient with me when I had a tendency to be just a little bit irrational, but most of all, for being so great about everything we had been through today. My response to him was simple, hopefully summing up everything I was feeling in that moment. "For being you."

His smile widened, reaching the corners of his blue eyes, as he leaned forward and captured my lips in a kiss that told me he understood implicitly. "Right back at ya, baby," he whispered against my lips, pulling back slightly.

Exhaling a happy sigh of contentment, I lowered my head again and relaxed back into his arms, the raw emotions of the moment magnifying his embrace exponentially. It wasn't missed at all when his right hand flattened over my stomach, because now I wasn't just afraid of *the possibility* being too soon. Now my biggest fear was how disappointed he might be if I *wasn't*.

26
DISTRACTIONS NEVER WORK
Madison Landry

Over the next few days, we had acquired several new additions to the barn, and Jillian had to take some time off to go to Lubbock because her father had fallen ill. With her gone, I was picking up her lessons, which left little time for anything recreational.

With everything going on, Jensen and I offered to cancel our trip, citing that it wasn't really that necessary, but Dad assured me that things would be fine. Tom even offered to teach the weekend lessons until we returned. So we went, leaving Bones in the care of my father who was more than happy to take him in for a few days.

I was relieved to hear they could handle things around the ranch. This weekend away was just what Jensen and I needed to escape everything that was going on between the two of us—not that we talked about it—and would allow us to reconnect.

We had missed the first three days of the competition due to my birthday and work. It was a five-day event, but since I wasn't competing, it wasn't imperative I be there the entire time. Two full days were more than enough.

As the plane descended around nine-thirty in the morning, I felt the pressure in my ears changing and my stomach roll slightly. Take-off was never a problem for me, but landing was always a bitch.

The plane touched down on the tarmac with a slight bounce that had me gripping the arm rests on either side of me. Jensen chuckled, working my left hand free with his right and twisting our fingers together. His thumb moved soothingly over the back of my hand, relaxing me a little as the plane finally found its footing and the engine pulled back so we could taxi on toward the gate.

Jensen grabbed our carry-on bag as soon as we were stopped, and we made our way off the plane behind the people seated in front of us. I led the way to collect our luggage, and as we waited for the luggage carousel to start, Jensen set down our carry-on and wrapped his arms around my waist, his chin resting on my shoulder.

The carousel jolted to life, the motor and gears squealing slightly, and soon the first bag came flying down the chute. I turned in Jensen's arms and stood on the tips of my toes to plant a chaste kiss on his perfectly soft lips and smiled. "This'll be exactly what we need."

After a few minutes, our bags appeared and Jensen stepped out to collect them while I picked up our carry on and flung it over my shoulder. "Where's the rental car place?" Jensen asked when he came back to me.

"Oh, it's just this way," I said, nodding my head in the right direction.

We found the rental place and Jensen stepped forward to make the arrangements. "Will anyone else be driving the vehicle?" the rental guy asked.

"Yes, my girlfriend will probably be driving, too," Jensen replied.

"I'll need her information then, Mr. Davis."

I stepped forward and reached into my purse for my wallet where I grabbed my license. With one final keystroke, our documents printed, and both Jensen and I signed them before we followed the guy out to our weekend car, a black Audi TT. It was a pretty sweet car.

After doing our walk-around to make sure there was no pre-existing damage to the car, he handed Jensen the keys and wished us a good stay in Calgary.

After loading our bags into the trunk, I grabbed the front of Jensen's T-shirt and pulled on it until he closed the distance between us. "Come on, let's go check into the hotel and then maybe head to the grounds and watch the competition before you take me to dinner."

Jensen's eyebrows raised in amusement. "Oh, so I'm taking you out to dinner, am I?"

"A girl's gotta eat," I said with a shrug.

"I guess you've got a point," he conceded. "You want to drive? You know the city better than I do."

My eyes widened, my body vibrating with excitement. "Yes!" I snatched the keys from his hand as he raised it. I kissed him quickly and darted to the driver's side where I slid into the plush leather seats, moaning inappropriately as I allowed the smell of new car to register. "Ohhh, yeah ..."

I heard the passenger side door open before Jensen slipped in, chuckling at my pseudo-orgasmic reaction to the sexy car. "You going to start the car?" he teased.

"Mmm," I hummed contentedly. "Just give me a minute."

"I'm afraid if I do, you're going to want to spend the weekend with the car and not with me," he mock-pouted.

I turned to him with a smile. "Fine. But just know, if it was you in this seat, I'd have given you a minute."

Jensen leaned over the console until his lips were within inches of mine. "Baby, if it were me in the driver's seat, we'd be at the hotel already, and I'd be making up for the last couple days."

My breath shuddered, and I was milliseconds away from pressing my lips to his when he pulled back all of a sudden, leaving me aching to feel his mouth on mine. "You win," I told him breathlessly, turning back to the steering wheel and putting the key in the ignition.

Having driven in Memphis countless times, the streets of Calgary were easy enough to navigate, and soon we were checked into the Sheraton hotel. It was my hotel of choice when I came to the city because the staff was great and the rooms were a decent price for how luxurious they were.

I slid the key card into the lock and pushed the door open and stepped in with Jensen hot on my trail. We barely made it four feet inside, the door clicking into place, before Jensen had me pressed against the wall, his lips on mine in a fevered kiss that left me breathless. His hands moved under my T-shirt, palming my breasts and kneading them roughly as I shamelessly thrust my hips toward his.

Apparently there was something about hotel rooms that brought out the horn-dogs in us both.

I moved my hands between us and undid the buckle of his belt before pulling the button of his jeans free and reaching in to stroke his erection. With a forward jerk of his hips, he grunted into my mouth, his teeth gently nipping at my bottom lip before I pulled back panting.

"Did you—?"

Jensen didn't give me a chance to finish my question as he pulled away from my trembling body, my hand losing contact with him. He unzipped the suitcase and reached into the pocket on the top for a condom before returning to me and reclaiming my lips with his. Deftly, his fingers moved over the waist of my jeans, having them undone in a fraction of a second before he yanked them down my thighs. I frantically stepped out of them, refusing to break our kiss as our tongues twirled and slid over one another.

Jensen had a different plan of attack, however.

Pulling his mouth from mine, he pushed his own jeans down and kicked them off as he removed his shirt. Once he was completely disrobed, he returned his attention to me as I clumsily tugged my own shirt off and struggled with the hooks on my stupid bra. With a chuckle, he kissed me softly, reaching his hands around to relieve me of my efforts, having the bra on the floor in an instant like some kind of pro-bra remover. If it was a sport, he'd come in first every time.

His eyes danced back and forth between mine when he pulled back again, slowly moving down my body and eyeing my breasts. Instead of leaning his face down to my chest, he moved forward, his hard length pressing between us as his hands moved roughly down my body until he was cupping my ass and lifting me swiftly.

I squealed in delight as he raised me to face-level, dipping his head low and pulling my right nipple into his mouth. Weaving my fingers into his hair to hold him in place, my soft moans of pleasure filled the room, and I rocked my hips against him, feeling the tip of his length graze my opening. "Baby," I panted. Tremors of ecstasy raced through my body every time his tongue flicked my nipple and his erection moved back and forth through my sensitive flesh. "Condom." At first I wasn't sure he heard the word, because I was so overcome with bliss that my voice was something resembling a strained whisper.

He nodded against my tit before pulling us away from the wall. "What are you doing?" I asked.

"Taking us to the bed?"

I shook my head. "Mmm mmm," I said, shaking my head. "Here. I want you to fuck me against the wall."

He groaned, assumingly at my crass inner porn star coming out to play. His voice dropped to that raspy one he only ever used when he was turned on. "I have to set you down for a sec then." Slowly, he let me slide to the floor before he tore the condom wrapper open and rolled it down over him. I watched raptly, and let out a tiny, shuddering gasp when he squeezed and slid his hand back up his length.

In a flash, Jensen had me back in his arms, my back pressed against the cool wall while his warm chest was pressed to mine. At a steady pace, Jensen pushed himself inside me as we kept our eyes locked. I fought the urge to let them close as the sensation of him moving in and out consumed me. It took a few thrusts to find our groove in this new, more difficult position, but eventually we did.

Each one of Jensen's movements pushed me closer to the edge of pure bliss, and I knew I would soon be catapulting to the sweetest heights of rapture. Every muscle in my body tightened, and I swiveled my hips, pushing me further ... further ... *further* ...

I cried out as Jensen's own grip on me tightened, his hips jerking in a way that signaled his own release. Wave after wave of euphoria washed over us as we rode out the final swells of our climax until Jensen's legs began to tremble beneath our weight.

Jensen cursed breathlessly between labored breaths against my shoulder.

With hooded eyelids, I looked at him as he let me slip to

the floor. "Mmhmm," I agreed. "I'm not sure I want to leave the room now. I'm feeling the need to cuddle and maybe have a post-sex nap."

Jensen leaned forward and kissed the tip of my nose. "And while the idea of curling up with you—completely fucking naked—in that king sized bed you refused to let me *fuck you* on ..." The way he emphasized my earlier words made me shiver with excitement. "I've never been to Spruce Meadows, remember? I'd very much like you to show me this part of your life."

Smiling up at him, I nodded. "And I'd love to share that part of me with you," I assured him. "Come on, let's go get cleaned up, and then we'll head out."

27
THE MASTERS
Madison Landry

"Come on, baby. There's a Starbucks right there. I don't do well with change," Jensen whined, pointing to the third Starbucks we'd passed since leaving the hotel.

I shook my head. "Nope, sorry. You're in Calgary for the first time, about to go and see the Masters *live*. So, you're going to humor me and you're going to get an extra large double-double from Tim Horton's."

Jensen was silent as I turned to him, only to find both eyebrows raised in confusion, almost retreating beneath the crazy brown jungle of hair atop his head. "An extra large whaty-what?"

"Just trust me," I said, spotting the sign for the restaurant up ahead. I clicked the signal light on and prepared to turn off the road to hit the drive-through. As usual, there was a line-up of about six cars ahead of us and Jensen groaned.

"See, this wouldn't have happened at Starbucks," he grumbled.

I couldn't help but laugh. "And why do you think that is? There's a line-up here, but not there? Think about that for a minute, will you?"

Thankfully, we weren't in the line-up for very long before we made it to the speaker-box. I ordered both Jensen and me each an extra-large double-double, and they had our order ready as soon as we reached the window. After thanking the woman at the drive-through, I handed Jensen his coffee, put mine in the cup holder beside me, and pulled away so we could get to the grounds and watch the competition.

Jensen looked perplexed, so I finally asked. "What's wrong?"

"She didn't sound anything like a Canadian," he said, seeming completely serious.

I laughed—loudly. "What the hell are you talking about?"

"Well, on TV, they always say Canadians have an accent. Saying things like *aboot* or *eh*. But she didn't."

I shook my head in disbelief. "Are you stereotyping, Jensen Davis?"

"What?" he asked incredulously. "No! I just had this preconceived notion from the way TV shows and such depict their accent ..."

"You're ridiculous," I said with a laugh as he took a sip of his coffee.

I waited a moment for the "you're right" I knew would be coming any second and smirked when the left side of his lip quirked up in a smirk. "This is pretty good," he said quietly.

"Better than Starbucks?" I inquired. He took another sip, looking contemplative. It was almost like he was trying not to feed my ego by telling me I was right. "Say it," I told him.

With a sigh, he finally fessed up. "Okay, you were right. This coffee is amazing."

"Mmm," I hummed appreciatively as I prepared to tease him. "*You were right.* I think I like the sound of that."

Jensen's laugh was a little off, and soon I was able to differentiate it from his usual laugh; he was getting ready to tease me right back. "I was taught very early on to include those words into my vocabulary—regardless of whether they were true or not."

With my jaw now agape, I reached over and swatted his upper arm. "You were not!"

"Yes, dear. Whatever you say," he said through more laughter as he pressed up against the door to escape my playful attack.

"Stop that!" I cried, putting both hands back on the wheel, still giggling. "You think you're *so* funny."

Shrugging, Jensen moved his arm to over the console until his hand rested on my thigh. "Based on your laughter, I'd say *you* think I'm pretty damn funny, too."

"Whatever you say, *dear*," I mocked, keeping my eyes on the road as I turned one final time and reached our final destination.

I looked over at Jensen. His eyes were wide as he took in everything—and we weren't even inside the grounds yet. I navigated the parking lot until I finally found a spot, and Jensen was out of the car before I even had it in park.

"Whoa, tiger! Take it easy!" I said as he took me by the hand and led me through the lot. "We've got plenty of time to get there."

Jensen slowed slightly, falling into step with me before apologizing. "Sorry. I just wanted to get good seats."

I snickered. "You think I don't have good seats?"

His head snapped toward me. "You've got pre-assigned seating?"

"I may have a few connections," I said flippantly with a little shrug as we walked through the main entrance and onto the grounds. There were thousands of people walking around, horses being led by their riders—some I recognized as my past competitors and others as newbies to the ring.

"Holy shit!" Jensen exclaimed, his grip on my hand tightening and stopping me in my tracks. "Is that Ian Miller?"

Sure enough, Ian Miller was about twenty feet away. He hadn't competed in years. I still remembered the first time I had seen him compete live. It was back when I was five years old. My grandfather had taken me to Spruce Meadows for the very first time, and it was the year that Ian's mount of ten years, Big Ben, was being retired. The best part, though? As we were making our way through the crowd, I accidentally bumped into him. I was so flustered and my apology probably wasn't even understandable as I mumbled and shuffled my feet while looking at the pebbles I was kicking.

He knelt down before me, the reins to Big Ben's bridle still in his hands as the large gelding stood next to him. He held his free hand out so I could see it and introduced himself as though I didn't know who he was, and I finally looked up at him. He asked if I rode, and I, very enthusiastically, told him yes. Then he inquired as to whether or not I was having a good time—which I was.

Every trip to the Meadows never measured up to that one, and while I had seen him ride a few times in the years I had gone to the competitions, I never got the opportunity to talk to him again. Which was okay, because I was sure to be just as awkward as I was twenty-one years ago.

"Sure is," I said to Jensen. "He's super nice too."

"You've *met* him?"

I shrugged. "Only once; when I was five." Encouraging Jensen forward, we made our way past Ian and the crowd that had gathered around him to go and find our seats.

I pulled Jensen down to my left, and he placed his right hand on the top of my knee before sliding it slightly in—just slightly. Sipping our coffee, we waited for the competition to start when a few girls behind us started whispering and giggling.

"No, I don't think that's her," one said.

"Oh, it's totally her! I'd recognize her anywhere ... No! You ask her! I'm not going to!"

Suddenly there was a tap on my shoulder, and I turned around to see two bright-eyed young women in their twenties staring at me. They both looked as though they were holding back squeals of excitement as I looked between them, waiting for one of them to speak. Jensen turned with me, smiling almost proudly as he watched the three of us.

"I'm sorry," the blond on the left said. "But, are you Madison Landry?"

"I sure am."

"I knew it!" the brunette exclaimed. "We're big fans"

When they seemed to be having their own private conversation again, I looked at Jensen, wondering if we should turn around. Maybe all they wanted was confirmation that I was who they thought I was.

Then, the blond one spoke again. "Do you think we could have your autograph? Maybe a picture?"

Smiling, I nodded. "Of course." They both reached for their bags and started rifling through it for a pen before they grabbed their programs and held them out to me. "Who am I making them out to?"

"I'm Ellie, and this is my best friend, Sarah," the blond said as I started making out the first program to her.

"So," Sarah said softly as I started on hers. "Do you think you'll compete next year? I mean we heard that Halley's Comet was out of commission for the season due to an injury? Will you both be back? Or will you come back with another mount next season?"

"Um," I said as I signed my name and handed her the program back. "She's actually doing much better. I'd like to come back with Halley, but it'll depend on her training over the next few months."

"So, you won't come back without her?" Ellie interjected as I joined them and Jensen took our picture with her phone.

Honestly, it wasn't really something I'd ever considered. There were several riders who would compete with a few different mounts — essentially competing against themselves as well as others — but it wasn't something I ever did. "I don't know, to be honest," I confessed, the idea suddenly sounding appealing. Maybe it was the atmosphere, maybe it was having just signed my first two autographs of the season. Whatever it was, I realized that I missed it all. I longed to be in that arena, taking those jumps, feeling the wind on my face, and the adrenaline rushing through my veins as we raced against the clock for the prize.

The girls thanked me before letting Jensen and I turn back around before the competition started. With a sigh as I thought more about rejoining the circuit next season, I lay my head on his shoulder and looped my arm through his as his hand reclaimed its spot on my knee. He must have picked up on what I was thinking because he gave my leg a squeeze and kissed the top of my head.

"I want to come back," I confessed before he could voice his own thoughts. "To compete." He didn't move. "You said you'd support my decision," I reminded him quietly, tightening my grip on his arm, afraid he'd pull away.

"And I do," he said softly. "Baby, I want you to be happy, and I know that all of this" — he gestured around us with his free hand—"makes you happy. But maybe we shouldn't make any decisions until we have a handle on our current dilemma."

How had I completely forgotten about that? The last few days, it seemed like it was all I could focus on, even when we first arrived in Calgary. But getting caught up in the atmosphere of the sport I loved so much allowed me to momentarily forget. If I turned out to be pregnant, I'd have to put my career on hold for *another* year or so. "You're right," I whispered, turning my attention to the ring just as the first rider was announced.

"Madi—"

I nodded toward the ring. "It's starting. You're right. I'll drop it until we know." And that was the end of the conversation. I knew I was acting a little childish, which was why I was giving myself a time-out before I said something I would regret. It wasn't that I didn't understand what he was trying to say—I did—it just wasn't what I wanted to hear. Hence the childish behavior.

Sitting there in silence as we watched rider after rider complete the course, I felt my mood lighten again as my rationality started to return. Ultimately, he was right. Why get my hopes up when in two weeks' time I could have them crushed just as quickly? "I'm sorry," I whispered, turning to see him deep in thought as he watched Eric Lamaze start the course.

"Me too," Jensen replied, moving his hand from my knee and holding my hand.

I let a small smile form. "Let's just go back to not worrying about it?" I posed it as a question instead of a statement, giving him the option to go back to how things had been the last two days. Was it healthy to not talk about it? Probably not, but the way I saw it, we didn't know if there was anything *to* talk about.

With a smile, Jensen nodded and kissed my temple. "I never stopped worrying," he confessed, pressing his forehead to the side of my head and squeezing my hand. "And the only reason I worry about it is because, deep down, I know you miss this. And if we did fuck up, you'll be putting it on hold.

Because of me."

"Us," I corrected him, unable to let him take sole responsibility. "Because of us."

"We've only been together a little over a month, and I don't want you to resent me if things don't work out … *ideally* for us."

"I would never resent you, Jensen," I assured him before tilting my head up and kissing him softly. For the moment, everything between us was the way it should have been.

"Where did you want to eat?" Jensen asked when we got into the car after the competition ended for the day.

I thought about it for a minute after turning the car on. I wasn't as familiar with which restaurants were vegetarian friendly, so I knew I'd have to just pick one and hope. "I don't know," I replied. "Honestly, I'm still pretty wiped. I wouldn't mind going back to the hotel and ordering in."

Jensen nodded. "Sounds good to me. You drive us back, and I'll pay," he told me with a smile and a wink.

Traffic was a bit of a nightmare, but we finally reached the hotel and entered our room. Seeing the huge, luxurious king-sized bed in the room made the muscles in my body ache from exhaustion, but I was still starving.

"Why don't you go change, and I'll order room service?" Jensen suggested, unpacking my laptop.

My eyebrows pulled together briefly. "What do you want to do on the computer?"

He smiled sheepishly. "Well, I'm going to look up a list of restaurants for dinner tomorrow night. I want to take you somewhere special."

"Okay, but nowhere too fancy. I didn't bring anything super dressy. I've got some nice tops and dress pants, but that's about it for dinner apparel," I said, pulling out of his arms to grab my pajamas from my suitcase.

After agreeing, Jensen hooked up the laptop while I brushed my teeth, washed my face, and changed into my shorts and Star Trek tee. When I emerged from the bathroom, I found Jensen at the desk, scrolling through Google or some other search engine.

I stopped to wrap my arms around him, resting my chin

on his shoulder before kissing his cheek. "Did you order dinner?"

He nodded. "You bet. They had a veggie burger and fries option. I hope that's okay?"

"Sounds good. How long until it gets here?" I asked, sliding my hands down his chest and kissing his neck. He smelled incredible, and I was feeling needy again.

"About half an hour," he told me.

Smiling, I reached forward and closed the laptop. "I wonder what we can do to pass the time?"

FAIRYTALE DATE NIGHT
Madison Landry

No one could blame me for allowing my eyes to slowly wander over Jensen's body when he climbed out of bed and stretched. The black flannel pants he wore hung low on his hips. I sank my teeth into my bottom lip as I stared at his naked upper body, muscled and toned from years of taking care of himself. The muscles in his arm flexed beneath the vibrant tattoo on his right arm, and I sighed audibly.

"What are you looking at, creep?" Jensen teased with a chuckle after spotting me eye-fucking him.

There was no use denying it; I'd been caught, and I really didn't mind getting caught ogling him. He was hot, and he knew it. "I was looking at my sexy, half-naked boyfriend."

Jensen let his arms fall back to his sides, a devious grin suddenly starting to form on his face before he rushed around the bed and pounced on me, forcing me onto my back. His scruffy jaw tickled the bare skin of my neck as he nuzzled it, and I broke out into a fit of giggles as I struggled against him futilely.

"It's no use," he murmured against my neck, his warm breath causing goose bumps to arise all over my body as I tried to break free.

His scruff was soon joined by his soft lips as he planted deliberate kisses below my ear, along my jaw, and down my throat before he tugged at the neckline of my T-shirt to expose the swells of my breasts to him. He groaned in dissatisfaction when he was unsuccessful, and I stopped struggling, instead, running my fingers through his hair to gain his attention.

"If you want to make it to the grounds on time, you're going to have to get ready. It's a full day, and if you figured out where you're taking me for dinner tonight, then we'll need to make the most of our time. There'll be time for this later, baby," I assured him as I continued to stroke his soft hair.

Narrowing his eyes accusingly, he propped himself above me. "Et tu, Madison? What's with all the cock-blockage?"

I giggled. "Hey, if you want to miss out on an epic day of awesomeness to fondle my boobs, that's fine, too."

While I expected him to say that was definitely what he wanted to do, I was happy when he pushed himself to his feet and offered me his hand to help me up. "Shower with me?"

I arched an eyebrow at him skeptically. "Only if by 'shower with me' you actually *mean* 'shower with me.'"

His eyebrows pulled together and his mouth hung open, seeming taken aback by what I had said. "Madison Landry," he chastised, "I am *appalled* that you would even consider I implied otherwise. I'm not an animal."

Laughing, I dragged him behind me to the bathroom, where we showered and nothing more …

Kind of.

After a quick coffee run, we were on our way to the Meadows. We had made it about thirty feet inside the grounds when Jensen stopped us suddenly. "Oh! Did you grab the camera?"

"Shit. I left it in the car."

"That's okay," he said, freeing his hand from mine. "I'll go grab it."

Before I could even offer to go with him, he was jogging away from me. While I waited, I observed all the families walking by with their kids, and I felt a tiny bit of my worry over our possible situation slip away as I imagined what it might be like to bring my own family here one day.

I dropped my gaze to my clasped hands, glancing only

briefly at my abdomen and suddenly feeling a little silly. I mean, we weren't even sure what the hell was going on in there. Without warning, I was imagining a little blond-haired, blue-eyed girl, or a handsome little boy with deep brown hair and my hazel eyes. While Jensen and I hadn't been together long, I couldn't deny that these reflections weren't slightly appealing and worth putting my career on hold for.

"Okay, I'm back." Jensen's smooth voice drew my face up to him, and I must have looked distressed, because the smile fell from his lips as he dropped to his knees and clasped my hands in his. "Baby, what's wrong?"

Taking one of my hands back, I brought it to his face and smiled, leaning in for a gentle kiss. "Nothing. I was just thinking about some stuff. I'm fine." I wanted to tell him what I was thinking about, but I really didn't want to get him excited in case there was nothing to be excited about. Or worse, freak him the fuck out because he was just as aware as I was that it was far too soon for any of this.

"You're sure? Do you want to talk about it?"

I shook my head softly as he stood, pulling me with him. "It's nothing we haven't already discussed. My mind wandered." I paused, taking a tiny breath, and smiled. "I'm fine. I promise. Come on, we should go. We don't want to miss anything." I looked down at his hands, my eyebrows pulling together quizzically. "Where's the camera?"

Jensen shook his head. "Oh, it's in my pocket," he said, reaching into his left pocket for the slim device.

Once he had it in his hand, I took it from him and curled into his side as I turned it on. "Okay, smile." I snapped the picture, flipping the small camera around and checking out the picture before deeming it acceptable. There was still a hint of uncertainty in Jensen's eyes, but I wasn't ready to dissect my confusing thought process.

I needed to change the topic before I drove myself crazy. "So, where are we going for dinner tonight?"

Jensen smirked, and I could tell that he wasn't going to tell me. Damn him and his ability to keep secrets. "While I'd love to tell you, I can't."

Like yesterday, the competition was incredible. So many

talented riders that only made me long to be in the ring again. Naturally, this just awakened my inner conflict.

By five, Jensen and I were on our way back to the hotel to get ready for dinner. I was glad we got to see everything and that Jensen and I got a few more pictures together, and judging by the smile on his face all day, I felt it safe to assume that Jensen had a great time.

The second our hotel door closed, Jensen pulled me into his arms and lowered his face to mine. "Thanks for a great day, baby," he whispered, kissing me softly.

"You're welcome," I responded with a smile, right before my stomach growled quite audibly. "Sounds like I'm starting to get hungry again."

Cocking an eyebrow and smiling crookedly, Jensen looked at me suggestively. He didn't have to say anything for me to know *exactly* what he was thinking. With a laugh, I shoved him playfully. "You're incorrigible."

"You bring out the best and the worst in me, sweetheart," Jensen joked, sitting on the end of the bed.

"So you're blaming me?" I asked as we exited the parking lot. "Well, that doesn't seem right. I'll have to ask around about your character just to be sure."

"If you feel that's best."

"So, you're really not going to tell me where we're going?" I asked, rifling through my suitcase for clothes to wear to dinner.

"Nope." Jensen stood and walked toward the washroom while I dug though my suitcase.

I huffed in exasperation, prepared to admit defeat and request a quick trip to the nearest mall before getting to the restaurant. "Why didn't I think to bring something dressier than—" My words caught in my throat as I turned around to find Jensen holding up a white garment bag. "What are you...? What is that?" I asked, stepping toward him slowly and folding my arms across my body.

"Well, it's not new. I wish I'd had the time to go out and buy you something for tonight. I did know I wanted to take you out somewhere nice, so I grabbed this and put it in my suitcase before we left."

My eyes moved between the white bag and his eyes several times as he began to undo the zipper, revealing the blue dress I wore to his sister's wedding. "That was so sweet of you," I told him, taking the dress from him and tossing it to the bed before throwing my arms around his neck and kissing him.

He wouldn't allow me to deepen our kiss, his hands gripping my hips before smiling against my attempts. "Our reservations are for seven, so we should probably focus on getting ready."

"Right." I nodded, licking my lips and backing away a few steps to grab my dress and retreat to the bathroom to fix myself up for dinner.

I quickly washed my face and applied a little bit of makeup before pulling my dress on and curling my hair. After taking one last look in the mirror, I stepped out of the washroom to find Jensen fastening the last few buttons on his shirt. He turned to me with a wide smile, dropping his hands to his sides.

"You're a vision."

Even though he said things like that daily, hearing it still caused warmth to creep across my face. "Thanks." I looked down at my bare feet. "I don't have any shoes though." I should have known better; with another impish smirk, Jensen turned to the bed again and grabbed my black stilettos and a rectangular, blue velvet box.

"Willow was kind enough to help me pick out your shoes when I called her the other day," he told me with a wink.

"What's that?" I asked, taking the shoes and gripping his right arm as I slipped them on one at a time.

Jensen looked at the box in his hands, raising only his eyes back to me. The way his blue eyes burned into mine as he slowly opened the box made my heart skip a beat, and I was dying to know what was in the box. "Just a little something I did have time to pick up for you the other day."

As he opened the box, I saw a gorgeous sapphire and diamond, seven-stone pendant on a solid, white gold chain. "It's called a journey pendant," he said, holding the box out to me. I assumed he wanted me to take the necklace from the box, but I had seen *Pretty Woman* enough times to know that shit wasn't going to happen.

Chuckling, I raised my eyebrow, telling him with a look that I didn't trust him, and he lifted the delicate necklace from its box. "May I?"

Nodding, I turned and lifted my hair as Jensen reached around and fastened it around my neck. "Thank you," I said, looking down at the wavy line of gemstones. "It's beautiful."

When I felt his lips on the bare skin between my neck and shoulder, I shivered. "Only the best for my girl," he said, turning me gently and appraising the way the necklace looked. "You like it?"

My head bobbed lightly. "I really do. But you didn't have to buy me anything else. You've already given me so much this week."

Jensen shrugged. "I know, but I *want* to give you things."

"Okay," I said, poking the middle of his chest with my forefinger playfully. "But you realize that I'm starting to get used to this. You could be creating a monster."

"I'm willing to take my chances." He kissed the tip of my nose. "Come on, we should head out."

Because I had no idea where we were going, Jensen drove. I tried to do what he had done earlier and read the signs to try and figure it out, but he was apparently an expert when it came to distracting me, anticipating that I would somehow figure it out before we arrived. Sometimes he'd ask me a question about my lessons, other times he'd bring his hand over to rest on my bare knee—oh yeah, he was pulling out the big guns. Finally, I just gave up, deciding that I was enjoying the anticipation of the surprise for once.

I tried to figure out where we were going, but Jensen was really good at getting me talking. We talked about the weekend, the upcoming camping trip, and my plans for the ranch in the coming months. As he rounded a few more corners, our conversation came to an abrupt halt when he pulled the car to a stop. "Calgary Tower?" I turned to him, jaw agape. "You're taking me to Sky 360?"

"I take it you've never been?" Jensen grinned.

My smile grew until my cheeks hurt, and I shook my head quickly. "No, I haven't. Jensen, this is amazing."

The pride in planning the perfect dinner out was obvious as he smiled and leaned across the center console to kiss me. "Well then, Miss Landry, shall we?"

Inside the building, Jensen and I waited for the elevator to take us to the restaurant. The elevator ride was short, and when Jensen led me off and toward the hostess podium, I looked around at the gorgeous restaurant. It was unlike any other restaurant I'd ever been to, and the sight of the sky, alive with the colors from the almost setting sun over the mountains, was magical.

"Good evening," she said with a bright, cheerful smile on her face as she looked at both Jensen and me. "How can I help you?"

"We have a reservation for two. Under Davis," Jensen told her, pulling me closer to his side as she looked down at the book in front of her.

"Let's see," she said softly, clicking her tongue as she ran her pen down the length of her page. "Oh! Here we go. You requested a window seat?"

Jensen responded with a small nod. "I did."

Glancing at me once more and smiling a little wider, the hostess picked up two menus and walked around her podium. "All right, then. Come along."

It wasn't surprising to see how busy the restaurant was as we made our way through the sea of bustling tables, coming to a stop at a little two-seater table against the floor-to-ceiling window. "Here we are," the hostess announced, stepping to the side as Jensen pulled my chair out for me. "Marshall will be your server, and he'll be with you right away."

Jensen took his seat across from me while I turned to the right and took in the sight of the city below. I found myself completely entranced by the view of the mountains on the horizon.

"This is amazing," I whispered, turning back to Jensen and reaching across the table for his hand.

He lifted my hand and pressed his lips to it gently, and my entire body reacted with a light tingle that worked its way from my head to my toes.

Just then, our server showed up. "Hi, there," he greeted. "I'm Marshall, and I'll be your server for the evening. Can I offer you our wine list?"

"Thanks," Jensen said kindly, raising his eyes to Marshall. "But that won't be necessary."

Shaking my head, I gave Jensen's hand a squeeze. "Jensen, you don't need to do that. Have a glass of wine."

Stubborn as always, he ordered us some sparkling cider instead and a couple glasses of water. While his gesture was sweet, I couldn't help but feel a little guilty, but I wasn't about to let those feelings sully a perfect last night here.

"Anything on the menu appeal to you?" I asked, lifting mine again to have a better look.

"Actually, the Linguini Puttanesca sounds fantastic. And I'll probably start with a mixed green salad. You?"

I perused the menu again, being sure to bypass anything meaty, and found the pastas to be the only thing that catered to my personal dietary restrictions. Since Jensen was already getting the Puttanesca, I decided I'd get something different so we could try some of each other's if we wanted. "Oooh," I said, practically salivating as I read the description for the Penne alla Norma. "I'm thinking the penne and a salad."

Just then, Marshall arrived with a huge smile on his face. "So, how's everything here? Have we decided what we're having?"

"I think so," Jensen said, glancing to me and then ordering for both of us like the gentleman he was.

After Marshall left to put our orders in, Jensen and I fell back into conversation about the coming weeks of work, Dad going fishing, and the camping trip.

"So," Jensen said, his thumb brushing the back of my hand as we touched innocently across the table. "I was thinking we could take the ATV's when we went camping."

"We only have the two," I reminded him, reaching for my cider with my free hand.

"I could have Kyle stop by my parents and pick up theirs."

Nodding, I agreed. While it would have been nice to ride

out there, keeping the horses in an open field would be impossible; they'd be sure to wander while everyone was asleep. "That sounds great," I assured him. "I'd like to buy all new gear too. Everything I have is from ten years ago and it's crap now. I haven't been camping in forever, so I've had no need to buy new stuff until now."

Conversation then shifted to what was lined up for the ranch in the coming weeks; a few new boarders, Ransom and Starla's continued training, as well as beginning to rehabilitate Halley a little more. I needed to start figuring out if she'd be able to compete again, or if I'd have to find a new mount.

"So, you're going to ride?" I arched an eyebrow, his question confusing me. "It's just ... Do you think that's such a good idea?" My eyebrow raised a tad higher. "If you're ..." He let his words trail off, probably hoping I'd just pick up on what he was trying to say without actually having to voice it.

"I don't see how that should stop me from doing my job while I can," I told him honestly. "Besides, we don't know for sure if there's anything to worry about."

Jensen didn't seem appeased, but he also didn't argue with me. "Okay," he acquiesced, even though his tone gave me the feeling he wasn't finished. "But until we know we're in the clear, no jumps. Groundwork only, okay?"

While I knew he was just looking out for me until we had a conclusive answer, being told what I could and couldn't do was starting to wear my patience thin. "Jensen—"

"I'm just asking you to wait."

"And if I am? What then?" I asked, knowing the answer before he spoke.

Jensen sighed. "Then we wait to see what a doctor has to say. Is that something you can agree to?" I could tell he was frustrated, so I didn't argue any further. "I'm not trying to be controlling, Madi. I just want you to be safe."

The corners of my lips turned up into a tiny smile, and I squeezed his hands. "I know, and I appreciate your concern—I do—but you have to realize that no one other than my father has ever been so over-protective. It'll take some getting used to. Just, bear with me. Is that something *you* can agree to?"

With a chuckle, Jensen brought my hand to his lips and nodded. "I think I can, as long as you realize I'm never going to stop looking out for you."

"I wouldn't have it any other way," I told him with a shrug.

I was happy for the interruption when Marshall arrived with our food, knowing that this conversation had the potential to wreck the evening entirely. Not willing to let that happen, Jensen and I ate our meals, revisiting the topic of camping and what all we would need.

The food was absolutely incredible, and the view of the city as the sun continued to set beyond the mountains was breathtaking. All-in-all, our date was absolutely perfect.

"How is everything here?" Marshall asked, returning as Jensen and I finished our meals. "Would the two of you care for any dessert?"

Even though my appetite was sated, I couldn't help but remember seeing a delicious sounding dark chocolate and espresso cheesecake on the menu. I looked to Jensen expectantly and he nodded once before I turned to Marshall. "The cheesecake, please?"

"Two?"

Shaking my head, I amended his assumption. "Just one. We'll share."

"Perfect. I'll bring it right out." He was gone maybe five minutes before he returned with our dessert in-hand. "Enjoy," he told us before going to check on his other tables.

Jensen reached for his dessert fork and cut off a tiny bite, holding it out for me. In order to accept the bite, I had to lean over the table, lifting myself off my chair a few inches. I wrapped my lips around the fork, never breaking eye contact with Jensen, and slowly slid back with the rich cheesecake in my mouth.

I hummed seductively, sitting back in my chair and licking my lips. "That's good." I swear, I saw Jensen's Adam's apple bob as he swallowed thickly, watching my tongue swipe some of the graham cracker crust from my lips. I picked up my own dessert fork and mimicked Jensen's actions, holding my fork out for him before we started feeding ourselves.

"We should go," Jensen said after leaving me the last bite. I nodded, my stomach full and appetite sated, while he stood and pulled his wallet from his back pocket. He removed a wad of colorful Canadian cash to cover the bill and a very generous tip before pulling my chair back and offering me a hand to help me stand.

In the elevator, Jensen's hand moved from the small of my back to the exposed skin above my dress. He trailed his fingers up and down my spine before eventually fiddling with my zipper. Electric currents zipped through my body, and it took everything in me not to push Jensen against the back wall of the elevator and ravage him. When the doors opened with a soft *ding*, I almost broke out into a chorus of "Hallelujah," pulling him into the main lobby of the building and toward the doors. We half-ran to the car, my heels being the only thing to slow us down, and my hand had just barely touched the handle when Jensen turned me quickly and pressed me against the cool passenger side door. His lips descended on mine desperately, his fingers curling tightly around my hips as his tongue traced the line of my lips.

Sighing softly, my lips parted, and our tongues united frantically. Slowly, his fingers started moving over my hips and down my thighs, inching the hemline of my dress a little higher with every movement. The tips of his fingers caressed the bare skin of my upper thigh, carefully moving inward until the backs of his knuckles stroked the ticklish flesh just below the juncture of my legs.

"Jensen," I panted against his lips, my fingers finding purchase in his hair and tightening until he groaned with pleasure.

His fingers inched higher and higher as my breaths came faster and faster. Unable to take it anymore, I thrust my hips forward in hopes of forcing his hand where I craved it ... but he withdrew it before I could succeed. His lips slowed against mine before he nibbled on my bottom lip, and when I opened my eyes, he was looking at me, his forehead pressed to mine. "Get in the car," he ordered hoarsely.

I complied without breaking eye contact, reaching behind me and lifting the handle. The door popped open as Jensen placed another soft kiss upon my lips and ushered me away from the door so he could open it. After getting in, Jensen rushed around the front of the vehicle to climb in behind the wheel.

My eyes focused on Jensen's fingers wrapped around the steering wheel, imagining the pleasure I knew was coming — no pun intended. I fought back a whimper. My gaze continued to roam up his arms and neck until I finally settled on the profile of his face. When I reached his eyes, he turned to me, smirking as though he could read every filthy thought running rampant through my mind. And it thrilled me.

We arrived at the hotel a few moments later, and only one thing was on our minds the entire trip from the car to our room. Jensen wasted no time once the door was closed, pulling me into his arms and kissing as he pressed me against the cold wood.

Our kiss started off tender and sweet, our lips moving lightly against each other's and slowly deepening with every languid sweep of our tongues. Jensen pulled me farther into the room, his arms wrapped tightly around my waist until he sat back down on the bed and began to unzip the full-length zipper of my dress. Every clicking sound the zipper made while moving down my back made my heartbeat quicken, and my lips moved more enthusiastically while I tugged his tie from around his neck and tossed it to the floor.

Feelings of déjà-vu from our first time came flooding back, and I moaned into his mouth as my dress fell slack around me. Removing my hands from his shoulders, I let the satiny fabric flutter to the floor before I straddled him, forcing him to lie back on the bed. Keeping my bare upper body from resting flush against him, I slipped my hands between us and began undoing his shirt one button at a time. While I worked to rid him of his shirt, his hands moved down over my ass, resting just under it as his fingers dug into the flesh of my thighs, pulling me against him.

An intense tremor of pleasure shot up my spine and escaped as a breathy sigh against Jensen's lips. Once his shirt was undone, I ran my hands up and down the bare skin of his chest, tracing the waist of his pants and moving back up again. When my fingers ghosted over his nipples, causing them to harden immediately, I smiled against his mouth before trailing kisses down his jaw and over his throat.

His breaths grew uneven as I continued my way down his body, teasing one of his nipples with my tongue the way he always did with mine, and he responded by thrusting his hips up against me. "Fuck, Madison," he groaned.

"Soon," I murmured, raising my eyes to him.

My entire body felt like it was on fire—like one single touch would cause me to spontaneously combust. After lightly grazing his nipple with my teeth, I kissed my way down his body until I was forced to stand at the foot of the bed. His head shot up off the pillowy blanket, a look of confusion across his face as his wide eyes darted back and forth between mine.

"Where are you going?"

"I'm going to grab a condom." I turned toward his suitcase before tossing one sly glance over my shoulder and smiling. "Unless you aren't interested in seeing where this is headed?"

Jensen pushed himself until he was sitting, propping his body up with his hands flat on the bed behind him, and nodded his head in the direction of his suitcase to urge me on. After retrieving it, I made my way back to the bed, Jensen's eyes looking over my near-naked body as I walked back to him.

Standing before him, I braced myself on his shoulder, lifting my left leg to remove my shoe, when his right hand shot out to grip my wrist firmly. "Leave them on," he growled in a raspy voice that thrilled me to my very core.

"As you wish," I complied, tossing the condom next to him on the bed. He reached for it, and I shook my head. "Not yet."

He opened his mouth to speak, likely to ask me "why the fuck not?", but my motives were clear the second I sank to my knees in front of him and unfastened his pants. His breath shuddered as our eyes locked, and he lifted his hips off the bed so I could tug his pants down and remove them along with his socks and shoes. He tore his shirt from his body and added it to the growing pile of clothes before I placed my hands on his upper thighs and wet my lips.

"Wait," he said, lying back and reaching above his head for a pillow. "Kneel on this."

I stood up and smiled as he placed it on the floor before I resumed my previous position. "Always so thoughtful."

Jensen reached out and cradled my face with his left hand, his fingers tangling in my hair as his thumb stroked my cheek softly. That one look shared between us spoke volumes as I wrapped my hand around his length and sheathed the tip with my lips. Jensen groaned, his fingers tightening into my hair as I lowered my head until I felt him touch the back of my throat and moved up slowly. Using both my mouth and my right hand, I maintained a steady rhythm, moving up and down, swirling my tongue around the head on every upward pass before taking him all the way in again.

As I continued, I could feel myself getting more and more aroused. I wanted to stop and have Jensen throw me down on the bed and fuck me into oblivion, but the sounds he made encouraged me to carry on. Desperate for some sexual gratification of my own, I slipped my left hand between my legs and began stroking my fingers through the moisture that had gathered there.

I had just taken Jensen all the way into my mouth again when I swiped my fingers over my clit, moaning around him and pushing him that much closer to his release. Without warning, Jensen pulled my head back until I released his length. We were both breathing pretty heavily as he stared at me, his eyes dark and hungry.

"On the bed, now," were the only words he uttered, and I listened without pause, placing my hands firmly on his thighs and pushing myself to my feet, sidestepping and crawling toward the head of the bed. "So, how do you want me?" I asked coyly, turning my head to find him watching me raptly.

In a flash, Jensen grabbed my ankles and had me on my back. I squealed and was yanking my panties down my legs, careful to leave my shoes on the entire time. Before lowering himself, he rolled the condom on. He hovered inches above me, and it felt like the sweetest torture; heat radiated off of his body, but he wasn't touching me. And I *needed* him to be touching me.

Just as I lifted my head to kiss him, our lips barely touching, he pulled back a little. "Roll over, love," he commanded softly, his nose brushing mine.

I was probably a little too eager to comply. "Whatever you want," I said, sitting up and turning onto my hands and knees.

I felt his hands ensnare my hips, pulling me back onto him slowly. It took everything in me to not push myself back onto him like the shameless hussy that teetered on the edge of my awareness. We moaned with mutual satisfaction the second his hips rest against my ass, his fingers digging into my skin while I fisted the blankets. Soon, he was moving steadily behind me, each thrust making me see stars as I balanced on the brink of bliss.

It wouldn't have surprised me if the neighbors on the other side of the wall called in a noise complaint.

I moaned as he continued his manic thrusting, tightening my already strong grip on the blankets, and before I knew it, my orgasm crashed through my entire body.

Jensen groaned and murmured through his own climax, his hands gripping my hips and pulling me back to meet his own ferocious movements as he rode out his own final surges of pleasure.

My arms and legs trembled as Jensen leaned forward, placing delicate kisses onto my neck and shoulder while lowering us to the bed. "I love you," he whispered, pressing his lips to the hollow below my ear.

I hummed contentedly, my body sinking into the bed as numbness set in. "I love you, too." Turning my head to him, I smiled. "Tonight was amazing."

Jensen kissed the tip of my nose. "Only the best for my girl."

29
BACK IN THE SWING OF THINGS
Jensen Davis

I slammed my hand down on the alarm clock, silencing its insufferable buzzing, before turning back to Madison as she rolled onto her stomach and pulled her pillow over her head.

Smiling, I wrapped my arm around her waist and turned her back onto her side so I could press my body against hers as I kissed the top of her shoulder.

With a groan, she tossed her pillow to the foot of the bed, multiple strands of her hair standing on end as she turned to look at me through the corner of her eye. "It's too damn early," she grumbled, pushing her bottom lip out into a pout.

Smiling, I kissed her cheek. "Baby, it's no earlier than every other day this week."

We'd been home from Calgary for a week, and while Madison and I were hoping for a low-key weekend with Wayne and Tom gone, we actually found ourselves quite busy. We hardly saw each other except for first thing in the mornings, at lunch, and in the evenings. With Madison taking care of all the lessons, as well as her usual responsibilities, she seemed a little more stressed than usual, and was tossing and turning in her sleep almost every night since we returned as a result.

I moved my hand down her body, up over her hip, and traced my fingers over her bare thigh below the hemline of her shorts. She shivered. "Come on, we have to get up and get ready for work. I'll make you breakfast." I stood from the bed and entered the bathroom to brush my teeth. "What are you in the mood for?" I mumbled around my toothbrush, leaning against the doorframe to watch her.

Groaning again, she propped herself up on her elbows and frowned, shaking her head. "Um, nothing ... I'm not feeling very hungry, actually."

I laughed, rinsing my toothbrush off and watching her through the mirror. "Sweetheart, you have to eat."

Slowly, she pushed herself up before turning to put her feet on the floor. "I know. I guess just eggs. Plain though." She was acting odd, and I watched her carefully as she stood up, pulling her white tank down over her exposed midriff. "I'm just going to use the washroom, and then I'll be right out, okay?"

After pulling my T-shirt on, I nodded. "You okay?"

"Yeah, I'm just really tired." she said, placing a hand flat on my chest in passing, before closing herself in the ensuite.

Upon hearing the soft click of the washroom door, Bones woke up, his oversized ears perking forward and his tail wagging as he looked between the door and me from his dog bed. Finally, he decided I was the better option than the closed door, and he got up, clumsily running across the room with his tongue hanging out of his mouth.

After opening the patio door for him, I started on Madison's eggs. Thinking back on her change in appetite the last few days had me starting to worry about what fate might have in store for us. If I really thought back on it—not something I relished doing—Kaylie had shown similar signs right before I found out she was pregnant.

Lately, Madison wasn't overly excited about certain foods, even choosing plain buttered toast over a flavorful plate of pasta the night before. She assured me that it was her lack of sleep and stress that had cut her appetite in half, and that as soon as things settled down and Jillian returned she'd be back to normal. I was starting to think otherwise, however.

I was just scrambling the plain eggs when she entered the kitchen, seeming a little more sullen than before. "Madi?" I watched as she walked past me to grab her coffee. The lost look in her eyes as she stared blankly at the coffee filling her cup concerned me.

"I don't think we have to worry anymore," she said quietly. There was something in her voice that cut through my heart like a thousand knives: sorrow.

I turned the burner to low and turned to her. "What?"

Sighing, she shrugged. "I had cramps off and on all day yesterday—"

"You didn't say anything."

"Because I wasn't sure if it was worth mentioning. Anyway, I've started spotting. So, we can stop worrying. We're in the clear. Dodged the bullet." There was little to no inflection to her voice, making it harder to read her than usual. Dropping her eyes from me, probably in hopes that I wouldn't see what looked like sadness in them, she took a sip of her coffee.

"Hey," I said, crossing the kitchen and crouching in front of her. "Are you okay? This is what we wanted ... right?"

A lone tear fell from her eye, and with a laugh she brushed it away. "This is so stupid! We've been together a month." Shaking her head at herself she brought her coffee to her lips and took another sip. "I'll be fine." Slowly, she turned to me with a nervous look in her eyes. "How are *you*?"

I cradled her face in my hands. "I'm happy if you're happy. I knew this was tearing you up inside—what with wanting to compete again. We have plenty of time to think about kids. So, if you're okay with how this turned out, then I'm okay. Okay?" I tacked that last one on just to make her smile or even laugh.

It worked; she laughed genuinely, nodding and throwing her arms around my neck. "You always know just what to say."

As the days went by, Madison's mood seemed to return to normal. Her appetite was still touch and go, but she assured me that that wasn't too unusual during this time of the month. I took her word for it. How would I know any different? I wasn't a woman.

By Wednesday, the pregnancy scare didn't come up again. Madison adjusted back into her old work routines, taking Starla over a few low rails during their sessions. It was as though our little scare never happened.

I came out of our ensuite washroom to find Madison sitting up in bed, smiling. My breath faltered slightly as my eyes roved over her near naked form. The way her milky skin contrasted against the deep blue lace of the negligee she *wasn't* wearing when I crawled out of bed a few minutes earlier had my eyes practically falling out of my head. As she drew in breath after breath, I found myself ogling her supple breasts as they spilled over the top of her little outfit. They looked huge. I wanted to touch and kiss and lick and bite them. *A lot.*

"What are you doing?" I asked, leaning on the doorframe and trying to be cool, even if my groin instantly reacted to the sight of her and outed me.

Something mischievous gleamed in her eyes as she moved to her hands and knees, crawling seductively to the end of the bed.

"Where's the dog?"

Madison smiled. "I put him outside. Come here."

"Baby," I said, pushing off the doorframe and walking slowly toward her. "We should have breakfast and then head to work." I stopped at the foot of the bed where she was now perched on her knees, her almost-green eyes level with mine.

"So we'll be a little late," she said, slipping her hands beneath the T-shirt I had just slipped on. "Come on, you know you want to."

I was so lost in her eyes that I found myself succumbing to her sexual advances. She didn't even give me a chance to respond before crushing her lips to mine, and that was pretty much the end of me convincing her we shouldn't carry on down this road. I slipped my arms around her, laying my palms flat against her lower back and running them over the curve of her ass until I gripped her upper thighs. In a flash, I pulled her upward, eliciting a squeal of surprise from her as she fell back onto the bed.

After pushing myself between her legs, I began lightly biting at her throat as my right hand moved up over her blue lacy nightie, palming her amazing tit. *Fuck* ... It felt even better than it looked. So soft and full ... *perfect*.

"I want you," She whispered through panted breaths as I teased her nipple through the thin fabric.

I growled. "I want you t—"

Suddenly there was a knock at the front door, and our heads both snapped toward our open bedroom door, our eyes wide, just waiting for Wayne to let himself in.

"Oh shit! Get off! Get off! Get off!" Madison hissed, pushing at my chest until I stood at the foot of the bed. She rolled over the mattress until she fell behind the bed, her head popping back up over the top with her hair in disarray. If I wasn't so terrified, I might have laughed. "Go to the bathroom and take care of"—she gestured to the pop-tent I had sprung—"that." After scrambling to her feet, she rushed to the dresser and quickly changed into a pair of yoga pants and a tank top before bolting from the room.

Not surprisingly, the father of the girl you were about to bone showing up instantly killed a person's erection. I stayed hidden in the washroom for a few more minutes, washing up and running my hands through my hair—not that it did anything. When I thought it might be safe, I emerged, changed into jeans and a fresh shirt, and made my way out to the kitchen to find Madison scrambling some eggs while Bones lay under the table chewing on his rawhide bone.

"Where's your dad?" I asked, looking around the room as I made my way to the coffee.

Madison turned to me with a smile. "Oh, he was just wondering if I was heading in to town to do some grocery shopping this week. He's got a busy couple of days lined up, and asked if I'd mind picking some things up for him. I planned to go later today, I'll just need to stop by his place and see what all he needs beforehand."

Turning the burner off, Madison removed the skillet and plated our eggs just as the toaster popped. She quickly buttered the toast and brought breakfast to the table. I was pleasantly surprised to see cheese on the eggs, because it meant she must have been feeling better.

With breakfast finished, we started taking the horses out

so we could muck out the stalls. By nine, Madi's first lesson was to begin, so she excused herself to make her way over to the arena. Wayne and I finished up the stalls, filling the water buckets and laying a few flakes of hay in each one before I grabbed the broom and swept up the aisle. Bones hopped sideways beside the broom, snapping his jaws at it every time it would pass him; he apparently thought it was all a big game.

"I've got a bit more invoicing and paperwork to do this morning, and I need to call the farrier for a few horses that need their hooves trimmed. Oliver threw a shoe last week. Plus, I have to call your dad to come and take a look at Hails today. Madison wants to see if she's ready for some low rails. Can you manage things for a bit?"

"Definitely. Let me know if you need anything," I told him before he left for his office. "Well, Bones. What should we do?" Sitting down, he looked up at me with his ears perked forward and his head cocked to the left. "No suggestions?" His tongue flopped out the side of his mouth as he panted. "Well, let's go for a walk around the grounds, then. And after, we'll go watch a lesson or two."

Bones hopped to his feet and trotted beside me as we exited the barn. Along one of the paths, I found a large stick. I picked it up, waved it in front of Bones until he seemed interested, and then tossed it. He dashed off after it, retrieved it and then stood waiting for me. Clearly, he didn't understand the game yet. I stopped, knelt down and called him to me. He came running back, stick in mouth, and gave it to me with very little fight. Standing back up, he kept his eyes glued on the stick in my hand, his paws dancing in place as he waited for me to throw it again. We continued to play for a while longer as we circled the grounds and made our way back to the barn where his attention was quickly drawn to one of the barn cats as it raced through the long grass.

My whistle brought Bones' focus back to me, and I nodded toward the door of the new barn as I walked through it. He looked torn on whether or not he should come with me or chase the cat. When the cat hissed at him, he decided I was the safer option.

Earlier, as I finished up the stalls, I noticed that our grain and alfalfa cube levels were running low, so I knew a trip to the feed store was in order. While I made my list, Bones barked and chased a few birds away. I was just on my way to the storage shed for a few bales of straw to restock what had been used this morning when I saw Madison standing outside, talking with her client. Her eyes caught mine, and she smiled before returning her attention to the woman.

By twelve-thirty, I had finished trimming the overgrown grass around both barns and was feeling pretty damn hungry. Lunch was still a half hour away, and that seemed like forever to me as my stomach protested loudly, so I decided to stop in the viewing gallery and see if maybe there was something behind the snack bar. Luckily, I found a protein bar and hoped it would tide me over.

After taking my first bite, I wandered back outside to search for Bones. His absence wasn't too surprising as he had a tendency to hide out in Wayne's office or follow him back up to the house.

I continued to search the empty grounds for any sign of the dog, and was just passing by the open main door to the new barn when a slender hand wrapped around my wrist, pulling me roughly inside. Before I could question what was happening, Madison had me pressed against the wall, her lips ravaging mine while her hands rapidly worked to undo my pants.

I mumbled against her voracious mouth. "Madi, what are you doing?"

She pulled her face back and smiled up at me. "I've been watching you all damn morning, and I just can't take it anymore," she confessed, her voice soft and breathy as she yanked my pants open and slipped her hand inside.

My head fell back against the wall with a soft thud as her delicate fingers wrapped themselves around my cock and began to move up and down ... up and motherfucking down. "Shit, baby," I moaned, my hands reaching out and cradling her face to draw her mouth up to mine.

Our lips united passionately as my fingers worked their way into her loose hair, pulling her closer to me in an effort to deepen our already fevered kiss. She moaned and whimpered into my mouth, each one sounding even more glorious than the last. My hands slid from her hair, travelling down her body until I was cupping her ass to lift her off the ground and turn her around. Having no other choice when her feet left the floor, she withdrew her hand from my pants.

Her legs wrapped around my waist as I pressed her against the wall, and I pushed against her. Panting breathlessly, she broke our kiss as she rocked her hips eagerly against my straining erection and pressed her face into my neck to release a moan. Her hips continued to move persistently against my ever-hardening cock. The only thing keeping our bodies from joining was my boxers and her yoga pants, and I was hoping to rectify that right fucking quick.

As the sounds of her pleasure echoed in my ears, her long, precise movements against me changed slightly, and her arms tightened around my neck. Prickles of pleasure shot through my entire body until they settled in my groin as her fingers tugged at my hair before moving down my back and clawing desperately at my shirt.

"Yes," she whimpered. "Mmm ... Oooh ... Yesyesyes!"

I couldn't believe what was happening; save for my jeans now being around my ankles, we still had most of our clothes on, and I was pretty sure Madison just fucking came.

I pulled my face back to look her in the eyes. "Did you just—?"

She didn't give me a chance to finish before she turned to me with this needy little whimper that caused me to thrust my hips against her again. Her lips landed squarely on mine as she held eye contact, and there seemed to be remorse lingering in her eyes as I continued rocking my hips—which was ridiculous since I was feeling pretty damn smug about getting her off fully clothed

Common sense soon kicked, in and I remembered exactly where we were while we groped each other. "Baby," I groaned against her lips. "We shouldn't do this here." While my brain was telling my mouth to say one thing, it was sending an entirely different signal to my dick as I continued to thrust against her, causing her eyes to roll back as she tried to stifle her cries by kissing me harder.

Even though it took everything in me, I pulled my lips from hers. "What if we get caught?"

"We won't," she said, sounding pretty damn sure. "Now shut up and fucking kiss me."

"I don't have a—" before I could even get the rest of my sentence out, she reached into her bra and pulled out a condom.

"I ran back to the house," she informed me, her voice breathless and thick with lust.

Against my better judgment, I let her slide to the floor and yanked her pants down her legs. I knew the only way we'd avoid being busted was if we made this quick, which meant a majority of our clothes would have to stay on.

With her pants around her ankles, I smirked. "Turn around," I ordered gruffly, getting a small, excited nod from her in return before she faced the wall.

Now that her back was to me, I pulled my own boxers down and rolled the condom on. The longer I kept her waiting, the more I noticed she seemed to be squirming and craning her neck to see what was going on. Unable to take it any longer, I closed the space between us, my cock resting against her ass as my hands ran over her shoulders and down her arms. When they reached her hands, I clasped them and brought them over her head, effectively pinning them against the wall beneath my own.

"Is this how you saw this going down?" My lips trailed down her neck and back up again, my teeth nipping at her earlobe.

"N-not exactly," she stammered. "It's far, *far* better than anything my twisted mind cooked up." I bit down on her neck lightly, careful not to leave a mark, and she whimpered.

Keeping my left hand over hers on the wall, I brought my right hand down, being sure to grope her breast roughly over her shirt before I moved south to align my cock with her pussy. Stepping up onto her toes, she arched her back so her hot little ass stuck out, and I pushed forward slowly, enjoying the sensation of her warmth as it sheathed me entirely. We moaned simultaneously as my hips lay flush against her ass.

Knowing we could be caught at any minute, I pulled out before burying myself in her just as quick. A long string of whispered profanities blew past her lips as I continued to move my hips behind her, my free hand squeezing her waist firmly and pulling her against me roughly.

Pressure started forming inside me, tightly coiling like a spring just waiting to release. I was barely balanced on the edge of an intense orgasm when Madison's moans increased. The volume of her voice was bound to attract some unwanted attention should anyone be passing by, so I released my hold on her hands to cover her mouth while leaning next to her ear and shushing her quietly.

With her second orgasm ebbing, I continued my manic thrusting, hoping to join her when a third orgasm ripped through her unexpectedly and she bit down on my hand. What the fuck was going on? Wait ... Why did I care? I was clearly doing something right.

That was when I felt that coil inside me release, and I buried my face in her neck to keep from crying out as I came. After a few short jerks of my hips, I raised my head, placing tender kisses to her damp skin as I removed my hand from her mouth, and pulled out of her.

Madison's hands trembled as she lowered them and turned around. "Wow," she said, still out of breath. "Just ... *wow.*"

Chuckling, I removed the condom and quickly zipped up my pants while Madison readjusted her pants and smoothed her hair. "We should stop by the washroom in the main barn before going to lunch," I suggested.

When the coast was clear, we exited the barn together and ran across the yard to the other building. We were both laughing like a couple of high-schoolers who just snuck away to have a nooner in the parking lot when they should have been in class. Which, I guess wasn't too far from what actually happened.

When we reached the main door, Madison poked her head in first. "Hello?" There was no response, so she nodded, indicating that we were safe.

Madison and I parted ways for a few moments, going into the separate washrooms to wash up before we headed over to Wayne's place for lunch. We'd barely walked through the door before we were acknowledged.

"Well, there they are! We thought maybe you two got lost or something," Wayne announced, kindly drawing Tom's attention to us as we entered the kitchen. The two men were sitting around the table playing a hand of poker while they waited for us to arrive.

Not wanting to suggest in any way what the two of us were actually up to, I looked around the kitchen and found Bones lying under Wayne's chair. "Oh, well we were just looking for Bones. I hadn't seen him in a little over an hour." I looked to Madison for her to back up my fib, but the way her nose scrunched up, I knew that wasn't going to happen.

"Well, that's odd. Madison knew he was coming with me to the house," Wayne said.

I could hear the smirk in his voice, and I wanted to fucking die.

Thankfully Madison had enough sense to change the topic, not that Wayne would ever, *ever* forget this. The man had a mind like a steel trap; nothing escaped. "What do you guys want for lunch? Tomato soup and grilled cheese? I'll head to the market tonight, Daddy."

"Sounds good, Madi." Wayne turned his attention to me. "Jensen, why don't you join us and we'll deal you into the next hand."

With a smile from Madison before she opened the fridge to grab what she would need for lunch, I walked over to the table for what I expected to be the most awkward card game in the history of man.

30
SOMETHING IS AMISS
Jensen Davis

"I won't be long," Madison told me as we entered Wayne's place after closing up the barn for the night. "I just need to make a quick list of what all he'll need for the week."

With Bones on our heels, we walked into the house, and the smell of Wayne grilling his food in the backyard hit me. When I recognized Wayne's dinner as steak, I grew concerned — especially considering her stomach was still a little sensitive.

She looked up at me with a smile, though. "Guess Dad's about to eat. Come on, this'll only take a second." She tugged me into the kitchen and opened the fridge. "Dad! I'm here!"

"Hey, Madi! I'm just out here cooking. I'll be right in," he replied.

"No, that's okay. No rush. I'm just checking to see what all you need from town. Is there anything non-food related? Razors? Shaving cream? Shampoo? Anything?" she inquired, bending over to rifle through the fridge a little.

"Nah, just groceries, kiddo. Thanks."

Madison closed the fridge and pulled a pad of paper and a pen from the drawer next to it so she could jot a few things down. Then, she moved to the pantry and looked around in there. As she started writing a few more things on the pad in her hand, Wayne entered the room with a plate in one hand and a beer in the other. "Hey, Dad."

"Evenin'," he replied, setting his dinner on the counter. "I'm just going to go wash up before eating. Feel free to leave the pup here. If I don't see you kids when I get back, you have a good trip into town."

I noticed Madison's eyes wander to the very rare steak, and I feared the worst. "Madi, why don't you go grab the truck? I can finish the list," I suggested, in hopes to get her out of the house before she threw up all over Wayne's meal.

"Hmm?" she asked, almost as though she wasn't really focused on anything. "Oh, um. No. I'm almost done. You can go grab the truck, though. I'll meet you out there."

"You're sure?"

"Mmhmm," she hummed, offering me a smile that seemed off.

Nodding, I backed out of the kitchen, watching her the entire time and hoping that she didn't get sick. Once I felt certain she was okay, I walked out the front door and toward our place to grab the truck. I pulled to a stop outside Wayne's place minutes later and waited for Madison to appear. She didn't. Guessing that she probably got caught up in a conversation with her dad, I went back inside.

Nothing could have prepared me for what I witnessed upon entering; Madison had just shoved a forkful of dripping red meat into her mouth and was chewing eagerly while she cut into another slice.

"Madison, what the hell—?" both Wayne and I said in unison as he entered the kitchen from the other entrance.

The silverware clattered to the plate as Madison brought her right hand up to her lips, swallowing the masticated piece of meat in her mouth. "Oh, God," she mumbled through her fingers, her eyes darting back and forth between her father and me like she had no idea what she'd just done. "I—I—" She dropped her gaze to the steak on the counter. "Sorry?"

Wayne seemed concerned as he stepped closer to Madison. "You feeling okay? You know that's real beef, right? Not like that ham you try to pass off as real pork?" Even though I was still really fucking confused and worried about what we just walked in on, I smirked.

Madison's hand fell from her lips, her eyebrows pulled together in confusion. "You know about that?" she asked, evading the first half of what he said.

"Never mind that …" He picked up the steak, and I watched Madison eye it, licking her lips and then looking ashamed. "What's going on?"

Frowning, Madison shook her head. "I don't know. It just smelled so good. Maybe my iron's low? I'm so sorry."

It wasn't iron; there was something much deeper to blame here.

"We should go," I suggested as my mind ran rampant with thoughts that maybe we hadn't actually dodged the bullet like we originally thought this week.

Madison smiled sheepishly at her father before dropping her eyes to the floor as she crossed the room to me. She seemed almost disappointed in herself for indulging in a little red meat, when she really had no reason to be. Clearly, her body was craving something it needed. Probably for a good reason.

We drove in silence for about fifteen minutes before I finally spoke. "Do you want to talk about what happened back there?"

"I honestly don't know. One minute, I'm finishing up the list, and the next, I'm staring at Dad's steak, practically salivating. I'll make an appointment with my doctor to have my iron levels checked. I'm sure that's all it is," she said, but there was something in her voice that told me she might not believe her own theory.

"What if it's not?" I said, tightening my grip on the wheel and waiting for her to get angry.

Through my periphery, I saw Madison turn to me. "Well, what else could it be?" she asked with a light laugh.

"What if you're pregnant?"

Her laugh died in her throat. "Pregnant? Maybe you've forgotten, but I got my period on Sunday. I'm not pregnant."

She sounded pretty convinced. Who knew; maybe it was just low iron and *I* was over-reacting.

"You're sure?" I asked. "Should we pick up a test? You know … just to be sure?"

"Jensen. I'm not pregnant. I think I'd know by now." Honestly, it sounded more and more like Madison was in denial. "While we're in town, we need to pick up some food for camping too. Ice for the cooler, food, drinks." She was changing the topic, probably hoping I would let it go.

"Drinks?" I asked, still ninety-nine percent certain I was right.

She nodded slowly. "Yeah. Water, maybe some tequila — because you know Kyle's going to want to go there."

"I'd really feel better if we just picked up a test," I tried to suggest, only to be shot down again. She told me that because her period was earlier than she expected that a test probably wouldn't even give us a conclusive answer, and that she would talk to her doctor the following week when she went to discuss her iron levels.

If she wasn't willing to pick up a test today, then I would have to take matters into my own hands. No matter the consequences. I knew I ran the risk of pissing her off, but I had to know. *We* had to know …

How the fuck did women choose between all of the different pregnancy tests?

I stood in the Family Planning aisle of the pharmacy late in the afternoon on Friday — the day we were to go camping with everyone. Madison still didn't want to believe that she could be pregnant, and I couldn't seem to think of anything else. So, after feeding her a line about needing to pick up a few last minute supplies for camping, I was able to sneak out of the house.

True, I probably should have been forthcoming with her and told her that I went out to grab a pregnancy test, but I didn't want to risk a fight in front of her dad. While I knew I would probably still face Madison's wrath, I was hoping that she'd just laugh it off and pee on the damn stick to prove me wrong — it seemed like something she would do. I hoped.

To make this never-ending situation even worse, my dad showed up that morning to check on Halley and update a few of the horses' inoculations. He told Madison that Halley's leg was much better and that she'd be safe to start training her.

He didn't see any reason anymore why she might not be able to compete, contrary to his findings after she first hurt herself.

Madison and Wayne were over the moon to hear it, and she couldn't wait to start working with her and Tom next week. How was she going to react if this test turned out positive and she wouldn't actually be able to start training for next season?

Feeling hopeless, I placed my face in my hands and groaned. She was going to fucking hate me for doing this to her, and I was fairly certain I wouldn't be able to handle that.

Sick of my own indecisiveness, I looked up and grabbed the first box I saw. It was pink and the caption read "results five days sooner."

I took my purchase to the front counter where a young woman glanced at the box then up at me before cocking an eyebrow questioningly. Unable to think of anything witty to say—and realizing that now might not be the time for shenanigans—I simply smiled, making her giggle and blush, before paying. She put the receipt in the bag, and I grabbed it before climbing on my bike.

The entire ride home, I tried to play out every possible scenario so I wasn't caught off guard. In some, Madison would smile and take the test from me before retreating to the bathroom. I liked that one best. The others varied from her being so pissed off she would storm away upon my pleading with her to just humor me, to her huffing exasperatedly, but complying regardless. I tried not to think of anything worse. I wanted to believe Madison wasn't capable of murder.

After pulling into my parking spot next to the truck, I sat on my bike in silence for a few minutes before heading into the house. My nerves were shot as I walked through the front door to find Madison at the kitchen island with her back to me. I watched her pack a bunch of food into the cooler while Bones lay at her feet, breathing deeply as he slept. As she continued to add food and bottled water to the storage container, I noticed that she was quietly singing to the soft rock station that was playing on the radio, swaying her hips in time with the quiet music.

When I closed the door, she turned around, her smile

bright as it stretched across her face. "You're back." She looked down as Bones woke abruptly and skittered across the kitchen floor to greet me as I entered the room. "Did you get what you needed?"

I swallowed my fear. "I did," I replied with a nod, my voice hoarse as I held out the small brown paper bag.

Madison eyed the bag, her eyebrows pulling together with confusion as she looked back up at me. "What did you buy me now?" She took the bag from me, still smiling wide, which only made my response more difficult to voice.

"A pregnancy test."

Her eyes snapped up to mine, and she kind of laughed. "What? Why? Is this because of yesterday? I told you, it was just low iron. I get weird cravings after my period all the time. This is just the first time I've ever acted on one."

Well, so far, so good, she wasn't pissed. So I pressed a little harder. "I know, and I want to believe that, but I'm just not so sure anymore. I mean, it's not only the steak, baby. What about in the barn the other day?" I asked, hoping to remind her of how she came at the slightest touch.

She smirked. "Are you doubting your mad skills?"

This time I laughed. "Not at all," I replied, moving forward and gripping her hips. "I just want us to be doubly sure before we head out with everyone, okay?" I looked deep in her eyes, hoping she would just agree. "Please?"

There was heavy silence between us before she exhaled softly. "Fine. But you better be prepared for a world of '*I told you so's,*'" she warned.

"I am," I said, relieved. "So, you'll take it now?"

"Yes, I'll take it now."

Together, we made our way toward the main bathroom where she stopped in the doorway and pushed me back. "You can stay here. There's a little added pressure here. I don't want to get stage fright," she joked lightly before closing the door.

I paced back and forth in front of the door, time creeping along at a snail's pace, my anxiety climbing with every second that passed. I stopped in front of the door several times, stopping myself from asking how everything was going because I was pretty sure only ten seconds had passed.

I should have read the box to see how long this was supposed to take and then set the timer on my watch. Actually, that probably would have been like watching a pot of water until it boiled. It would seem I wasn't cut out for stressful situations.

When I heard the toilet flush, I rushed the two inches to the door and gripped the casing tightly as I waited for it to open. When it didn't, I groaned quietly and pressed my head against the cool wood. I didn't want to rush her, but I couldn't help but feel a little impatient. Okay, *a lot* impatient.

After what felt like forever, Madison walked out. Her expression was unreadable, and I wasn't sure if that was a good thing or a bad thing.

Nervously, I ran my fingers through my hair, tugging slightly out of impatience the longer she remained silent. "Well?" I asked.

With what looked like a subtle hint of a smile, she held the test out for me to see. Desperate to know, I grabbed it — not once thinking that she just pissed on it — and looked at the little window that would tell us our future. I stared for a length of time I knew to be entirely too long, especially considering the response was as clear as day, before raising my eyes back to hers.

"How accurate is this?" I asked.

31
UNDER WRAPS
Madison Landry

So many feelings rushed through me in that one moment. Mild irritation that Jensen went out and got a pregnancy test without telling me, relief that he had done it, and finally a strange combination of confusion and happiness upon seeing the second line appear in the results window.

I shrugged. "I've heard false positives are rare. Like, really rare."

"So ...?" Jensen let his word trail on for a moment as his eyes fell back to the test.

"We're going to have a baby," I finished for him, letting my lips curve up into a small smile—even if I was still a little scared about how fast this was all happening.

Not another word was spoken as Jensen swept me up into his arms and twirled me around the room. It then became clear that my previous assumptions of him being disappointed earlier in the week were correct. And, if I was being honest, I was a little upset about it too; I had really warmed to the idea of a perfect mix of Jensen and me.

Jensen let me slide to the floor, the smile on his face bright and so full of love. He must have seen a tiny flicker of my conflict, because his smile fell. "Are *you* okay with this?"

My eyes blinked several times as I let his question really sink in. "What?" I brought my hands from around his neck and cupped his jaw. "Yes. I'm okay with this. It's sooner than I'd have liked, but we're not exactly known for taking things slow, are we?"

Jensen seemed to relax before me, leaning forward to press his lips to mine. In that moment, everything seemed all right; he was right when he said as long as we were together we could tackle anything our lives threw at us. Our embrace was cut short when there was a soft knock on the front door.

"That'll be Willow and Brandon," I whispered, our noses still brushing as I looked up at him through my eyelashes.

"God," Jensen sighed softly. "I can't wait to tell everyone."

Quickly, I placed my hands flat on his chest and pushed back a little, my eyes suddenly hard and serious. "No. We're not telling anyone yet. It's too soon."

"Baby," Jensen said, his hands resting on my hips.

I shook my head, cutting his argument off at the pass. "Please. Just give me time." A look of worry flashed in his eyes before I smiled again. "I'm going to go and put this away. Will you get the door?"

"Yeah," he replied, his voice low and wavering.

As I made my way toward our room, I couldn't get the look on his face out of mind. It wasn't that I didn't want to tell our friends and families, but *we* just found out. Shouldn't we be allowed a little time to adjust to the news ourselves? Not to mention, what if something happened and we lost the baby? It would be hard enough for Jensen and I—especially Jensen, after everything he'd been through—to deal with. I couldn't do that to our families as well.

After making sure the box and test itself were well stashed away in the trash bin of our bathroom, I made my way back out to the kitchen to see Willow and Brandon sitting at the table with Jensen.

"Madi!" Willow hopped up from the table and rushed over to me. She had her arms around me for maybe half a second before she pulled back and looked up into my eyes. "How was Calgary?"

"Amazing, as always. It was the perfect weekend. Just what we needed." I led Willow to the table where we sat and talked about the trip until Kyle and Lilah showed up.

Jensen kissed me on top of the head as he passed. "I'm going to go and help Kyle unload the ATV. We'll be right back."

"Sounds good," I told him, placing my hand on his when it rested on my shoulder.

"I'll come and give you guys a hand," Brandon offered, standing up and stretching. "I could use a stretch after that three hour drive. That way it'll give the ladies a chance to visit."

As soon as the door closed behind the guys, Willow turned to me. "Okay, seriously, are you okay? You and Jensen seem tense."

Lilah nodded. "Yeah. I only just got here, but even I can tell something's going on."

"I assure you everything is fine." I offered them my most convincing smile, pushing my chair away from the table. "C'mon. Let's make sure we have everything."

Once we confirmed we had everything, we headed outside to find the guys were just closing up the trailer attached to Kyle's Jeep after unloading the ATV.

"So, we're pretty sure everything's accounted for," I tell Jensen. "Did you need a hand securing it to the quads?"

Jensen smiled, walking toward me. "That's okay, sweetheart. I got it."

The excitement in the air was electric as we all climbed on our quads. It didn't take us long to reach the site, and we decided to start setting everything up before making a safe fire pit.

Kyle suggested a friendly competition was in order to see who could get their tent set up first. I laughed and was just about to tell him he was being ridiculous when Jensen confidently accepted his challenge. Jensen and I totally dominated the whole thing; we had our tent standing and secured to the ground in about fifteen minutes—not too bad considering we'd never set it up before. Of course, Bones was helpful in distracting the others by jumping on their tents as they tried to set them up. He was a good boy.

"I'll go and gather some firewood," I offered as the guys started clearing an area for our fire pit.

I gave Jensen a quick kiss before turning to the girls who had made themselves a cozy little seat out of a couple of old blankets. "Ladies? Care to join me on a nature walk?"

Willow narrowed her eyes at me, keeping them locked on mine as she leaned over to Lilah. "*Nature walk* is code for *gathering wood*," she translated. "She wants us to *work*."

Shaking my head, I stalked toward them and laughed. "Willow, get off your ass and come help me," I mock-threatened.

With a salute, Willow hopped to her feet. "Fine," she huffed with a tiny smirk. "Let's go. The sooner we find wood, the sooner we'll all be warm."

Kyle snickered again, and we all knew what was coming before he said it. "That's what she said."

That was our cue to leave.

Together, we trekked through the brush gathering kindling and any bigger pieces of wood from fallen trees that we could find. We only grabbed enough for the night since the sun was beginning to set and the temperature was dropping; there'd be plenty of time to gather more the next day.

"Madi?" Willow asked as I picked up a larger chunk of wood, inspecting it to make sure it was dry enough.

"Hmm?"

"If something were wrong, you'd tell me, right?" she asked, seeming nervous.

I stopped in my tracks and turned to face her. "Of course I would." I felt awful for keeping anything from her—she was my best friend—but I just wasn't ready to tell people.

"Okay." She still didn't seem convinced that nothing was wrong.

"Look," I said, walking toward her and Lilah. "If it seems like I'm acting ... *odd* ... just know that everything is fine, I've just got a lot on my plate right now."

Willow and Lilah accepted that, and we all went back to our search. A little while later, we emerged from the thin brush and started toward our campsite where the guys were just finishing up with the fire pit.

We were about twenty feet away when I started to feel faint. Willow and Lilah hadn't noticed that I stopped walking for a minute to deal with the fog in my head, but Jensen did. He immediately got up and walked over to me, capturing the attention of everyone else.

"Here, let me help you carry that," he said loud enough for everyone to hear, and when he was next to me, he leaned in to take the wood from me before adding, "What's wrong?"

"I feel a little light-headed. I need to eat," I told him.

With a nod, Jensen turned and carried the firewood, keeping me close. "We'll just get the fire started and then we can start dinner. Is there something in particular you want?"

I could feel heat rise in my cheeks. "Um, yes. But we don't have it, so I'll have a veggie dog ... or two."

"What do you want? I'll go get whatever it is." It made me smile that he was so willing to dote on me.

"Thanks," I told him. "But if you were to bring me what I really wanted, I think people would start to catch on."

Comprehension flashed in his eyes. "Oh. Steak again?"

I nodded. "I don't know if I can handle that though," I confessed. "I mean, nine months of this? Just the thought of it makes me ... well, hungry, but also incredibly sick."

"If it's what your body needs, then we'll figure something out," he assured me, kissing the side of my head.

When we were within hearing distance of the other four, we stopped talking about what was going on, and I joined Willow and Lilah on their cozy little blanket set-up while the guys started the fire. Within fifteen minutes, the fire was roaring, and we were all holding hot dog sticks over the fire.

"I'll prepare the buns," Jensen offered.

Before Kyle had a chance to say anything, Willow, Lilah, and I spoke together. "We know, we know; that's what she said."

Pushing his bottom lip out, Kyle pouted. "You girls just sucked the fun right out of it."

I choked on the sip of water I had just taken, holding out the hand that held my bottle, and pointed at him. "And *that* is what he said!" Everyone, including Kyle, roared with laughter.

"Okay!" Kyle's booming voice tore me from my happy place, and I focused all of my attention on him as he pulled out a bottle of Patron and some shot glasses.

My eyes instantly fell to Jensen across from me, and my brow furrowed with worry. Pushing myself up and stepping over Bones as he slept on the blanket at my feet, I walked over to Jensen. He leaned back against the huge fallen tree we had set up camp around and crossed his legs. With a wide smile, he offered me his hand and pulled me down onto his lap. Once I was situated comfortably across him, I wrapped my arms around him and he nuzzled my neck, making me giggle and squirm against him.

"Madikins?" Kyle said, bringing my attention to him.

"Hmm?" I said, turning to see the full shot glass he was offering me. "Oh, um ... I don't think that's a good idea."

His eyebrows shot up. "And why not?"

I had to think fast. "Because after how drunk I got on my birthday, I've decided to lay off for a while." I purposefully avoided Willow's eyes because I knew she'd see right through me. Instead, I turned back to Jensen and he smiled at me while running his hand up and down my back soothingly. Supportively.

Thankfully Kyle seemed to understand and didn't push me. He was a little suspicious and tried to tell me I'd give in soon enough.

"Wouldn't it just be easier to tell them?" Jensen asked quietly, his eyes pleading with me.

"Not yet," I whispered, casting my eyes around the fire to see that everyone else was deep in a conversation, the bottle of Patron momentarily forgotten.

Jensen sighed, running the fingers on his free hand through his hair. "Okay." There was something in his eyes that concerned me, but it quickly disappeared when Kyle engaged him in a conversation about a paintball outing he was trying to organize.

I was relieved that the focus seemed to have shifted from drinking. Brandon had even passed beers out to everyone. I politely declined, telling him that I really did plan to take it easy since I got so out of control on my birthday. He accepted my reasoning easily and didn't pressure me; he was good like that.

The night wore on, and I could tell everyone was feeling

a little tipsy. It was funny to see just how silly they got when drinking. Having always partied with them, I'd never really noticed this side of things before. Jensen took it easy on the drinking, choosing to be supportive of the fact that I couldn't partake without giving our little secret away. While he wasn't drunk, I could tell he was loosening up.

I was still sitting across his folded legs, my arms draped around his neck. A shiver ran from my scalp, down my spine, and out through my toes when Jensen's fingers glided through my hair. Our eyes remained locked, and in an instant, we were transported into our own little bubble, the voices around us hushed as we focused on each other. I watched, in silence, as the shadows from the flames of the roaring fire danced over Jensen's rugged jaw, how his eyes blazed brighter than the glowing embers. I sighed contentedly.

Swept up in the moment, I leaned forward and pressed my lips to his, hoping that my kiss could convey just how happy I was—even if still a little nervous about the timing and having to put my career on hold for another year. The hand moving through my hair moved down my back until it rested on my hip, squeezing gently as he opened his mouth to deepen our kiss. With a soft moan, I complied, sinking down into his lap a little more and bringing my left hand up to cup his face as his right hand slid up my inner thigh …

"Okay, you two, let's make s'mores," Kyle suggested excitedly.

Jensen must have been out of his mind, because he thought it would be sexy to feed me one of the delicious treats, but in reality it was a gooey and crumbly affair. I laughed when he offered to retrieve the bits of graham cracker that had fallen down my shirt, and slapped his hand away when he weaseled his fingers down the collar and between my boobs. This only spurred him on until he had me pinned on the ground, tickling me mercilessly, and it wasn't until Kyle threatened to dump cold water on us both that he stopped.

By midnight, I was pretty damn exhausted. It had been a pretty huge day for the both of us. With a yawn, I stood up and stretched. "Okay, you party animals, I'm heading to bed."

Jensen hopped up. "Me too," he announced a little too eagerly.

Everyone seemed to be in agreement that it was time to pack it in, so after extinguishing the fire, we all went to our tents. Once inside our tent, Jensen and I changed while Bones circled the little blanket we had set up for him before flopping down. I pulled on my tank top and a pair of flannel pants while Jensen pulled on his own pajamas and pulled the top of the double sleeping bag down for us. I waited for Jensen to get situated before I joined him, rolling onto my side away from him so he could curl himself around me.

It didn't take long before sounds I really could have gone without hearing started coming from the other two tents, and even less time before I realized Jensen had the same idea.

"Mmm," he hummed against my neck, placing sweet kisses along the skin there and inhaling deeply. The way his fingers tickled against my lower belly as he worked them beneath the bottom of my shirt caused me to shiver.

Before he could get too far, I turned around and placed a hand on his cheek. "Hey," I said softly. "Would you be upset if I said I'm tired? It's been a pretty big day and all." Nervously, I bit the inside of my cheek and awaited his reply. I hated disappointing him.

Jensen leaned forward and kissed my forehead. "Not at all, love," he assured me, wrapping his arms around me and pulling me into his side.

I rested my head on his chest and let the steady *tha-thump tha-thump* of his heart lull me to sleep.

32
CAMPFIRE TALES
Madison Landry

I don't know when I finally fell asleep, but when Kyle started shaking our tent, I awoke with a startled gasp.

Grumbling, Jensen pulled me back into his warm body. "Fuck off, Kyle!"

"Dooo-ooode!" Kyle responded, his shadow moving around to the front of the tent. Bones was on his feet in an instant, waiting at the door of the large tent with his tail wagging manically. "It's nearly noon. You two are going to sleep the entire day away."

The sound of the zipper moving forced Jensen and me upright. "Kyle, I swear, if you open that door ..." Jensen threatened.

"It's okay, we should get up. I'm kind of hungry, and we should go and gather more firewood for tonight," I said, kicking the blankets toward the end of the bed. My pants had twisted up around my calves, and I was pretty sure Jensen may have been copping a feel in his sleep because my shirt was showing more skin than it should have been.

Thankfully, I had just fixed my tank top when Kyle's head popped into our tent through the small opening he'd made in the door. "Come on! Get up. We made breakfast!" And then he was gone, Bones right behind him through the opening.

After quickly getting dressed, Jensen and I emerged from the tent to find Kyle playing fetch with Bones while Willow and Lilah helped Brandon cook over the fire. I recognized the smell of pancakes immediately, and my stomach rolled.

"I think I'm going to be sick," I whispered, covering my mouth and running as far away from the campsite as possible.

I hoped that no one else would notice my abrupt departure, but I heard both Willow and Lilah calling after me as I disappeared into the brush and dry-heaved a few times. My legs trembled, threatening to give out, so I rested my hand on a nearby tree to steady myself. I felt a hand on my lower back, and the relief it brought could only mean it was one person.

"Are you okay?" Jensen asked, moving to my side as I pressed the back of my hand to my mouth and nodded. "Is there anything I can do?" I shook my head, feeling the nausea still rolling around in the depths of my belly.

When my stomach finally settled, I pushed myself upright and wrapped my arms around Jensen, tears from the energy I'd expended almost getting sick slipping from the outer corners of my eyes. Jensen placed his right hand on my lower back while his left held the back of my head softly, and he tried to calm me down before we faced everyone.

"I told them you had to pee. I don't think they suspect anything," he told me.

I forced a smile on my face as we neared the group, and he was right; it would appear that they were none the wiser about what was going on.

"Hey! Feel better now that your bladder's empty?" Willow asked before taking a bite of her pancakes.

"Uh, yeah. Much." I looked around at everyone's plates. "Hey, are there any eggs?"

Everyone shook their heads, looking at me apologetically, but Jensen came to my rescue. "You know, I could go for some eggs, would you like me to make you some too?"

Nodding, I smiled up at him. "Yeah, thanks. I'm going to go and brush my teeth." Bones decided to follow me back to the tent where I retrieved my toothbrush and a bottle of water before heading back over to the bushes. After brushing my teeth, I rinsed my toothbrush with the bottle of water and turned to the dog. "Bones? C'mon, boy," I urged before heading back to camp.

The eggs Jensen made really hit the spot, and because he had them with me, no one asked any questions or seemed suspicious. Willow looked at me a little strangely, especially since she knew I had crazy-mad love for pancakes, but she didn't say anything.

"Should we maybe gather some more firewood for tonight?" I suggested after we got the dishes and campsite cleaned up. "It would probably be wise to do it during daylight hours rather than waiting until the sun goes down."

We wound up gathering quite a bit of wood for our fire and decided to head back. I was thankful for that because I was feeling pretty wiped out and ready for a nap—at three in the afternoon. I had only known I was pregnant for less than twenty-four hours and my symptoms had hit me like a freight train.

Jensen started stacking the firewood when I knelt next to him. "I'm going to go and lie down for a bit, okay?"

"Are you feeling all right?" he asked, concern appearing in his eyes.

I nodded. "Yeah, that walk just kind of zapped all my energy." Smiling, I leaned forward and kissed his cheek. "You know, you could always come and snuggle with me."

"You don't have to ask me twice. Let me just finish up here, and I'll be right there."

With a smile on my face, I started to make my way toward our tent when Willow stopped me. "Hey!" she exclaimed. "Where are you off to?"

"I'm going to go and take a little nap. That walk through the woods really took a lot out of me," I explained.

There was something in Willow's eyes that told me she suspected something, but she didn't say anything. "Okay. Well, have a good nap. We'll see you when you get up."

"Thanks."

I had just finished changing out of my jeans and climbed into our sleeping bag when Jensen slipped into our tent alone. "Where's Bones?" I asked.

"He stayed with everyone else. Kyle was playing fetch with him again, and I didn't want to break up their fun," he explained, shedding his jeans and T-shirt before crawling into bed next to me. "How are you feeling, baby?" he asked, rolling onto his side and propping his head in his right hand as he used his left to tuck my hair behind my ear.

"Um," I said quietly. "I feel okay."

The smile he gave was sympathetic. "Only okay? You're sure there's nothing I can do?"

"Nope." I sighed. "I'm not sure, but I also don't think there's anything anyone can do. We'll just have to wait this part out."

When I yawned, Jensen chuckled. "Okay, sweetheart. Let's get some sleep." He moved until his warm body was pressed to mine, and I rolled onto my side, placing my head on his chest and sighing when I felt his lips against my forehead.

I was lying on my belly with my arms tucked up under my pillow when I opened my eyes slowly, still groggy. The light canvas of the tent wall came into focus as I reached for my cell phone with a groan. Based on the time, it would appear that my "quick nap" wound up being three hours long.

"Hey, we slept longer than inte—" When I turned my head to my right, I found myself alone, and I sat up quickly. "Jensen?"

There was rustling from outside the tent before the zipper moved upward and Jensen stepped in. "Is something wrong?"

Shaking my head, I tossed the sleeping bag off my legs. "No, I just woke up and you weren't here." I looked up at him with sad eyes. "Why didn't you wake me up?"

Laughing softly, he dropped to his hands and knees over my stretched out legs and kissed me sweetly. "I tried, but you were non-responsive. I figured I'd let you sleep. I'm sorry."

He kissed me again, and I found it impossible to stay upset. "I guess you're forgiven. Did I miss anything?"

Jensen hopped to his feet and offered me his hands to help me up. I changed back into my jeans and long-sleeved tee from earlier and took his hand, following him outside.

"Kyle and Brandon are trying to think of what to do tonight. The girls want to play charades while Kyle would love to scare the shit out of you all with ghost stories." He laughed. "I feel like a camp counselor mediating for a bunch of children."

I joined in his amusement and bumped into his side lightly. "Well, we're going to have to practice that if we're going to have camp sessions next summer," I reminded him.

"Excellent point."

When we made it back to the fire, Willow and Lilah stole me away from Jensen and pulled me down onto the log between them. I watched as Jensen rejoined the guys, taking a fresh beer from Brandon and smiling at me while Kyle talked to both of them.

"How was your sleep?" Lilah asked, offering me a wine cooler.

Holding up my hand, I shook my head. "Oh, no thanks. I just woke up."

Smiling, she traded the cooler for a bottle of water and handed it to me with a shrug. "No worries."

"I can't believe I slept that long," I said, still a little upset with myself for missing the last few hours.

"No worries," Willow replied. "Jensen filled us in on how stressed you've been with work. I remember how hectic it gets this time of year."

"Yeah, it's been trying, that's for sure."

"Ladies?" Jensen asked across the flames. "Should we be thinking about dinner anytime soon?"

The words had barely left his mouth, and my stomach started rumbling. "I don't know about anyone else, but I'm famished."

While the guys cooked, they continued to argue about what to do after dinner. Kyle was still hung up on this ghost story thing while Willow and Lilah were still lobbying for something a little more *fun*. Along with suggesting charades, Willow recommended truth or dare, which made Jensen and I laugh, remembering our game on the way to Lilah's wedding a few weeks ago. After a bit more bickering, they finally decided that we could do both—not that I was looking forward to being scared shitless right before bed.

After dinner, we regrouped around the fire, settling in so we could begin our first game of charades, which was pretty fun—probably because Jensen and I kicked ass. The sun had long set, and we were in the lead with seven wins while our competitors each had four. It was my turn to act out the clues, and I felt like a tool—just like the first three times I had to do it.

After Jensen and I won again, Kyle admitted defeat and suggested we make s'mores and tell scary stories. My nose wrinkled at the thought of telling ghost stories out in the middle of nowhere, but I complied, snuggling up close to Jensen as Kyle began.

"So, there was this guy and his wife who lived in Memphis, like, five years ago ..." The light and shadows from the flames of the fire danced eerily across Kyle's face, chilling me to the bone as he continued. "They had this huge Doberman in a little house just outside the city limits. One night they went out for dinner and dancing. By the time they got home it was late and the husband was more than a little drunk. They got in the door and were greeted by the dog choking to death in the family room.

"Well, the husband passed the fuck out from all the alcohol, but his wife called the vet, who was actually an old family friend of hers, and got her to agree to meet her at her clinic. The wife drove over and dropped off the dog, but decided that she'd better go home and get her husband into bed."

I was freaking out as he continued, pushing myself closer to Jensen until I was practically sitting on his lap. My eyes searched frantically for Bones, only to find him huddled between Willow and Lilah as they hugged him for dear life.

"Well, she arrived home and finally slapped her husband into consciousness, but he was completely shit-faced. Because he was about twice her size, it took her almost half an hour to get him up the stairs, and then the phone rang. She was tempted to just leave it, but she decided that it must be important or they wouldn't be calling that late at night. As soon as she picked up the phone, she heard the vet's voice screaming out: *'Thank God I got you in time! Leave the house! Now! No time to explain!'* Then the vet hung up."

I shivered, but not because I was cold.

"Because she was such an old family friend, the wife trusted her, and so she started getting the hubby down the stairs and out of the house. By the time they made it all the way out, the police were outside. They rushed up the front stairs past the couple and into the house, but the wife still didn't have a clue what was going on. The vet showed up and said, *'Have they got him? Have they got him?'*

"*'Have they got who?'* the wife asked, starting to get really pissed off. And the vet answered, "*'Well, I found out what the dog was choking on – it was a human finger.'* Just then the police emerged, escorting a dirty, stubbly man who was bleeding profusely from one hand. *'Hey Sarge,'* one of them yelled. *'We found him in the bedroom.'*"

I was deeply regretting this idea and definitely wanted to hear a funny and light-hearted story. No luck though; apparently Kyle either thought it was funny to tell all these dog-centric urban legends – the poodle in the microwave, the one where the girl was getting her hand licked by what she *thought* was her dog under her bed – or he just wasn't thinking how freaky it might be. I shuddered again.

It was getting late, and I was terrified. There was no way I was falling asleep. I needed to change the topic.

Sensing my distress, Jensen started telling jokes, which got Kyle onto a dirty joke tangent. The mood in the air had shifted, and soon I felt comfortable enough to let my fatigue settle over me. I pushed myself to my feet. "Okay, it's after midnight, and I'm feeling like I might be able to sleep peacefully now, so I'm going to turn in."

Jensen was on his feet next to me instantly. "Me, too. Have a good night, guys." He turned to the dog. "C'mon, Bones."

Bones followed after us as we made our way to our tent and got ready for bed. We crawled into our sleeping bag, and I snuggled up to Jensen, closing my eyes and preparing for sleep.

Jensen took a deep breath, almost like he was steeling himself for something big, and I looked up, trying to make out his expression in the dark. "Madi, if I ask you something, will you promise to be one hundred percent honest?"

"A hundred and *ten*," I assured him.

He seemed to choke on what he was trying to say. "Do you want this baby?" I opened my mouth to speak when he interrupted with more. "It's just ... you don't want to tell anyone, you say things sometimes that worry me ..."

Scooting forward carefully, I coaxed his face up so our eyes locked. "Listen to me," I ordered. "Yeah, it's all happening really fast, but I love you, and I'll love this baby. You have nothing to worry about."

Even though I spoke the truth, there was something in his eyes that told me he wasn't entirely convinced. Regardless, he smiled, nodded, and kissed my forehead.

"Goodnight, Jensen," I whispered. "Sleep well."

33

TRIPPED UP BY DEJA VU

Madison Landry

As promised, I called and made a doctor's appointment the Monday after our camping trip. The soonest I could get in was in three weeks and Jensen seemed even more impatient about that than me. We kept ourselves busy with work, though. Jillian was still away, but she called and assured us things with her dad were looking up and she should be back within the next couple of weeks. Extending her stay in Lubbock worked out well for me since Jensen was refusing to let me do basic groundwork, and it saved me from having to explain why I couldn't train in the afternoons. Dad seemed a little suspicious, but he hadn't said anything outright.

"Madi?" Dad called from the office when I'd come in from releasing Starla into her paddock after our session.

Popping my head into his office, I found he was buried up to his eyes in paperwork. "Yeah, Dad?"

Running his hands over his weary face, he sighed. "I was going to head in for feed and a few other things this afternoon, but as you can see, that isn't going to happen. Would you mind running in?"

"Not at all. It'll be nice to get away for a bit," I told him with a smile.

He nodded. "Okay. Well, I called everything in earlier this week, so just tell Ken I couldn't make it."

Since my dad knew where I was going, I didn't think to tell Jensen; I knew he and Tom were busy fixing a few fence rails that some of this spring's foals had rubbed and chewed on. My truck roared to life, and I was suddenly reminded that with Jensen and I now expecting, I would probably have to start looking for a new vehicle soon.

I had barely been driving for ten minutes before my cell phone vibrated. Smiling at seeing Jensen's name on my caller ID, I held it to my ear. "Hey, what's up?"

"Where are you?" Jensen demanded, sounding frantic.

"Um, heading into town for feed, why?" I inquired, confused by his frenzied state.

There was an aggravated sigh on the other end, and I could just imagine Jensen fisting his hair with his free hand. "Why didn't you tell me you were heading into town? I'd have offered to come with you."

"Don't be ridiculous. You and Tom have to get that fence done. How's it coming along?" I asked, knowing I needed to change the subject.

"It's fine. When will you be back?"

"Soon, I promise. I'll see you in a bit, okay?" I told him.

"Sure. I'll see you soon."

As I made my way into Savannah, I thought back on how Jensen had been behaving the last couple weeks. For the life of me, I couldn't think of how to assure him that everything would be fine, nor could I think of how to help him relax. Yes, I was pregnant now—but barely—and I was fairly certain that alone shouldn't impede my ability to do any aspect of my job.

His offer to drop everything to run an errand with me wasn't the first; it happened almost daily. In fact, I was surprised I was allowed to pee by myself most days. While I loved him, there was so much going on (and so quickly) that sometimes I just needed a minute alone to breathe. His constant hovering made that difficult.

Most couples so early into a relationship had the luxury of going to their own houses for time apart, Jensen and I had been living together since before we even became a couple, making it hard to find a minute to be alone. Telling him that would upset him, though. And I had done enough of that since it was confirmed we were expecting. My foot-in-mouth syndrome seemed to be flaring up a lot lately, and everything that came out of my mouth was sure to be tainted in some way. It was probably best to just keep my feelings to myself for a bit.

Needless to say, this errand for Dad was the perfect opportunity for me to sneak away for some alone time and maybe pick up something special for Jensen. I started juggling ideas of how I could help him see that I was just as happy about our situation as he was.

I had just hit the outskirts of town when I had a great idea for what to do for him. The only problem with my plan was that I could potentially risk outing the pregnancy. Deciding it was a risk I was willing to take, I grabbed my cell phone and dialed Lilah's number while trying to figure out how to word my question to guard our secret as best I could. I still wanted to have the doctor confirm everything was fine before we told anyone else.

Not surprisingly, the phone only rang twice before she picked up. "Madi, hey. How's it going?"

"Really good," I answered. "Listen, I don't have long to talk as I'm just driving into town, but I just wanted to ask you something…"

"Shoot."

Running the question through my mind once more, I decided to just ask. "Well, you see, Christmas is coming up, and I was wondering what Jensen's favorite book as a child was. Do you know by chance?" I asked, nervously awaiting the *why's* that were likely to follow, because "Christmas" just didn't seem plausible enough.

There was silence on her end before she hummed quietly. "Oh!" she said suddenly. "I think I remember when we were younger, Mom used to read him *The Velveteen Rabbit* all the time. Like, *all* the time."

"Yeah? Thanks, Lilah. Hey, are you still coming out this weekend to ride?" I asked, quickly changing the topic so she wouldn't think too much about my odd question.

"You bet. I can't wait. Oh, and Madi?"

Shit. "Yeah?"

I could almost hear her smile. "I think the book is a really sweet idea. He'll love it."

"Thanks. I'm grateful for your help," I told her. "Well, I'm going to have to let you go, but I'll talk to you later?"

"For sure. Drive safe."

The first stop I made after hanging up with Lilah was for a cheeseburger—because I couldn't seem to get enough lately. After our camping trip, Jensen took me into town where we stocked up on ground beef and steak to satiate my cravings. He was so great about it, never once making me feel worse than I already did about it.

After eating my lunch in my truck, I decided to check out a couple of the local bookshops—not the ones where they sold the new shiny books, but the ones where they sold older ones. Some of the books were usually pretty pricey, but usually just the rare ones.

I pulled to a stop in front of one of my favorite shops and got out of my truck. Just as I was stepping through the doors, my phone rang, and I looked down to see it was Jensen again. It had maybe been thirty minutes.

"Hey," I said softly, gaining a welcoming smile from the lady behind the desk. I waved at her and continued on my way toward the children's books.

There was a sigh from Jensen's end before he spoke. "You on your way back yet?"

"Uh, not quite. I stopped for a quick snack, and I had a couple of other things I needed to do in town. I won't be long."

"What other things?" he asked, and for a minute, I thought he sounded terrified.

Finding myself in the children's section, I smiled as I perused the titles, really hoping I could find a copy of *The Velveteen Rabbit*. "Don't you worry about it," I told him through my grin, knowing for sure he had to know I was up to something—he always did. Even though I knew he'd probably see right through me, I told a tiny fib so that I could get him off the phone. "Look, I'm driving through town now, and don't want to risk an accident. I'll see you soon."

"Oh, uh, okay," Jensen stammered slightly.

With my phone tucked back in my pocket, I continued to read the titles of the books. There were so many classics; it was hard to abstain from buying them all for the baby's book collection. That thought of course got me to thinking of converting my old room into a nursery. The crib would go where the bed currently sat, the dresser along the other wall and the rocking chair would remain right by the window where we would rock our child to sleep night after night. Maybe even reading him or her *The Velveteen Rabbit*. My vision blurred as tears welled in my eyes before I blinked them back to refocus on my search.

Unpredictable hormone surges? Check.

When my eyes finally settled on the title I was looking for, I held back an excited squeal that bubbled to the surface. I snatched the book off the shelf and started to look it over carefully to be sure it was in decent shape and that no pages were missing. It wasn't a first edition, but it was old and still worth a pretty penny. Price didn't matter. I'd happily pay double if it meant showing Jensen in some way that I was happy. I just hoped this book would do that as well as make it easier to have a conversation I knew was long overdue.

With my book by my side in the truck, I drove over to the feed shop to pick up our order. On the way, I heard my phone vibrate on the seat next to me. I waited until a red light before reaching for it, knowing that Jensen would shit bricks if I read my text messages while driving. Not that this was any more legal or safe.

"Speak of the devil," I said quietly.

> Hey. Just finished the fence. How's it going?

I quickly tapped out my response.

> I can't wait to see your handiwork. Light's about to turn green. I'll talk to you soon. XX

Setting my phone back on the seat, I drove forward when the light turned green and proceeded down the street. I made it maybe a half block before my phone vibrated again.

> Ok. Well, let me know when you're on your way.

What was with his strange behavior? He was hovering

unnecessarily again, and I couldn't figure out why. This wasn't the first time I'd run an errand by myself, and it certainly wouldn't be the last.

A half hour later, Ken was helping me load the feed into the bed of my truck, and I was finally on my way home. Because of my two unscheduled stops, I was going to be a touch later than anticipated, but I was sure Jensen would forgive me when I gave him the book. Since it was already after six, I knew he'd probably be at home starting dinner by the time I unloaded the feed. I may have dawdled a little, hoping I'd make it back a little closer to dinner actually being ready.

"Hey, you're back," Dad greeted, exiting and locking up his office. "Jensen's been asking if I'd heard from you for the last hour. He must really have it bad for ya." When he winked, I couldn't help but laugh.

"Apparently. I probably should have texted him to let him know I was on my way." Inwardly, I scolded myself for forgetting to tell him I was leaving the feed store. "Oh well. I'll just get this unloaded and head home."

"Don't be ridiculous." Dad approached the tailgate of my truck, forcing me off to the side. "I'll handle this, you go on to dinner and put your beau at ease. He's so anxious when you're not around lately."

"Yeah?" I asked. Dad nodded once. "Okay, thanks. See you in the morning."

I quickly grabbed the brown paper gift bag with Jensen's book in it before running off toward the house. The excitement pumping through my veins had me feeling as though I wasn't going to be able to make it to dinner to give it to him — and I was pretty certain I was okay with that.

I was barely through the door before Jensen's arms were around me in an almost bone-crushing hug, his present forgotten.

"I'm so glad you're back," he breathed into my neck, kissing below my ear several times before lifting his head to look at me. "Why didn't you call?"

"I forgot?" Something definitely wasn't right with his behavior.

"I asked you to let me know when you were on your

way home," he stated firmly, his eyes flashing with mild irritation. He turned from me and headed for the kitchen where it looked like he was only just starting dinner.

Following him, I set the bag on the island and crossed my arms across my body defensively; my frustration had finally reached its peak. "I said I was sorry. Had I known it was such a big deal, I'd have called." Were we seriously fighting about me not calling when he knew I wasn't going to be gone long?

I was staring at his back as he placed his hands flat on the counter in front of him, slumping his head and shoulders almost like he had been defeated. "I was just ... worried," he confessed, his voice soft and barely audible.

"About what? You knew where I was." I was growing more and more confused as time went on.

He snapped his head around, his eyes narrowed. "Did I?"

Whoa. *What?*

"What the hell is that supposed to mean?" I demanded with an evil glare.

"It doesn't take almost three hours to pick up feed — especially if your dad's already called the order in."

"Now hold on just a minute," I demanded. "Are you accusing me of something?" Pausing for a beat, I gave him the chance to respond. When he didn't, I continued. "Do you think I'm ... *cheating* on you?" He turned to face me completely. Tears stung my eyes and my chin trembled. "You don't trust me?"

He continued to stare at me, his face completely void of any kind of expression that indicated he was just grouchy. It was his eyes that startled me most; the sparkle that usually lit them was dull. If it was possible, they looked darker than usual as he stared at me almost accusingly.

In an instant, my heart clenched and my stomach rolled with nausea as I realized what was really going on here.

"You think I ..." Uncrossing my arms, I placed my hands over my abdomen protectively, choking on the words before they came to rest on my tongue and burned like acid. The first of my tears fell from my eyes, and I cursed my raging hormones for making me appear weak in the wake of his heinous accusation.

Mustering up the courage and piecing together what little control I had left over my own body, I drew in a large — albeit shaky — breath and marched up to him. I refused to let my eyes or my voice reveal just how hurt I was in that moment. Knowing that he was comparing his past with Kaylie to his present with me broke my heart, though.

Yes, at first I had been terrified — wasn't everyone when something this life-altering happened unplanned? We hadn't been together very long. Was I not allowed to be scared? I realized I'd behaved poorly, saying things without first thinking how they might affect him, but had I really been so awful these last couple weeks to deserve these allegations? How could he possibly think I could *ever* do what she had done?

"I'm. Not. Kaylie. You have no *idea* what I'm feeling." No matter how hard I tried, my voice still betrayed me, trembling on *her* name and following through to the last word.

"Because you won't fucking talk to me about any of this!" he shouted.

A single, humorless laugh escaped accidentally. "Oh, and you're just a fountain of fucking feelings since this all started?" I countered, yanking the paper gift bag off the counter and thrusting it at him as more tears spilled down my cheeks. His hand came up to hold the bag against his chest, brushing my knuckles as I pulled mine back. It wasn't how I envisioned giving the gift to him, but maybe he needed to know I was in this with him — that I was *never* against him and I never would be.

Unable to say another word, I stormed from the room and down the hall, turning into my old bedroom and slamming the door behind me.

34
IMPULSIVE DECISIONS
Jensen Davis

I wasn't sure what the fuck just happened, but I was sure, it all could have been avoided if I could have found the strength to pull my head out of my own ass and tell Madison how I was feeling. I understood just how fast everything was happening, and I could tell that she was working toward acceptance, but it still worried me a little. I could sense how stressed she was, and I didn't want to make it worse by unloading my own shit on her. Honestly, I figured things would get better and we'd find that perfect moment to talk about our fears soon enough.

Days went by, and there just never seemed to be a good time between work and Madison being so tired afterward. Before we knew it, two weeks had passed and we still hadn't been able to clear the air between us. Madison assured me she was "fine" whenever I would ask, and she seemed happy. Other times, though, I could see the elation fade from her eyes, and her apprehension seep back in. I knew that if we didn't talk about it soon, the smallest thing would trigger an explosion between us.

And I was right.

The day was no different than any other. We got up, ate, worked, had lunch and went back to work. We didn't talk about the pregnancy in the company of others, but I was starting to get used to it. Then, everything seemed to get a little hazy. One minute, I was working on the fence with Tom because it was a day, maybe two, from falling apart, and the next I heard Madison's beast of a truck roar to life. By the time I made it to the side of the barn, she was already gone. Just ... *gone*. Without a fucking word. I panicked.

No. Scratch that. I lost my fucking mind.

Trying my best to contain the whirlwind of emotions I was feeling, I ran into the barn to find Wayne hunched over his desk. He told me that Madison had run into town for him, and I believed him — I did — but that damn nagging motherfucker I had been trying to keep buried these last couple weeks resurfaced, telling me that all women were the same. That Madison was showing all the signs I should recognize. The voice poked and poked and then poked some more, reminding me about Madison's apprehensions. It told me she wanted to go back to competing and that she would do anything to get there.

Anything, it said

When I got a hold of her, she confirmed what Wayne had already told me: that she was headed into town to pick up an order for him. So, why didn't that make me feel any better? Why couldn't I get the *ridiculous* idea that Madison was capable of the same betrayal Kaylie was out of my fucking head?

It could have been the fact that she was adamant about keeping the pregnancy a secret. It could have been that, just before finding out she was pregnant, she had made the major decision to restart her training so she could compete next season. Whatever it was, it only served to add fuel to the raging inferno of emotions inside me.

After going back to help Tom with the fence, I hit my thumb with the hammer at least half a dozen times, cut my hand with the hacksaw and gotten four splinters. I was a fucking mess. It was a wonder how Tom and I even got the fence done. Actually, I was pretty sure Tom did a majority of the work, and I was just getting in the way and being a hazard to the entire project.

Unable to focus on anything, I found myself dialing her number again. Unfortunately, talking to her that second time didn't help put my mind at ease either. She was acting secretive, and it only served to spike the anxiety I harbored for my past coming back to bite me in the ass again.

I was pretty sure Wayne was starting to get annoyed with me every time I asked what all Madison needed to pick up, or if she'd given him a time that she'd be back. He would just look up at me from his desk and shake his head before telling me she'd be back as soon as she picked up the order. Finally, he just sent me home.

"This time will be different. This time will be different," I repeated over and over to myself. I knew it wasn't fair to just assume what Madison might have been up to, but I couldn't stop.

In an effort to try and take my mind off things so I didn't wind up going even crazier, I opened the fridge to look for tonight's dinner. Food was the last fucking thing on my mind, though. I started pulling random vegetables out, not really paying attention to what they were or what I could make with them. That was when the door opened and Madison walked through it. Relieved beyond words, I barely registered her joyful expression or the brown bag in her hand as I wrapped my arms around her.

What happened next could only be described as an out of body experience. It was as though I had lost complete control of who I was, and that soulless monster scratched and clawed his way to the surface, completely taking over while I was forced to watch helplessly as he spewed hurtful accusations on her.

Things turned ugly fast, and Madison was all too quick to realize why I had been acting like a complete control freak these last couple of weeks. When she questioned my trust in her, I felt a sharp stab of pain in my chest. I had been so badly burned in the past that it was hard to see clearly sometimes. I *knew* she wasn't Kaylie, and I had heard her weeks ago when she told me that she would never do what Kaylie did, but none of that seemed to matter in that moment as we faced off in the kitchen.

In my defense (and it wasn't a strong defense), I didn't outright accuse her of anything, but she didn't exactly jump to conclusions, either. No, she followed the trail of breadcrumbs to the root of what was going on, and I could almost hear her heart shatter upon realizing it.

Watching that first tear fall down her cheek destroyed me; *I* made her cry. Madison wasn't someone who cried often, and to know I was someone who made it happen destroyed me. I wanted to reach out and pull her to me, but I still wasn't in control of my own body.

When I raised my voice at her, I wished the floor would have opened up and swallowed me whole. It was our first fight, and I hated every fucking minute of it.

It wasn't until she thrust that paper bag against my chest that I finally snapped out of it, blinking rapidly before raising my hand to clutch it. Her hazel eyes — now a vibrant green as she cried — were usually so warm and soft, but now they were cold and hard as she stared up at me, more tears threatening to spill. I brushed her hand lightly, that electric spark between us faint but still there when our skin touched.

I wanted to say something, apologize for my outburst so we could reconcile and move on — talk about this rationally, like adults — but before I could even open my mouth her tears fell, staining her pink cheeks, and she fled the room. The sound of our door slamming echoed through the house, startling me.

So, there I stood, in the middle of our kitchen, clutching a small brown paper bag to my body as Bones sat at my feet, looking up at me with confusion. My mind was reeling from the maelstrom of emotions that we'd just stirred up, and it took a few minutes to realize there was a reason she gave me the bag: there was something inside. For me.

I was an ass ... a jerk ... an insensitive prick. While I couldn't help my insecurities given my past, I could have worked harder to show her just a little trust.

Knowing just how undeserving I was of anything she had to give me — emotionally and materialistically — I looked down at the bag I held to my chest. I contemplated putting it back on the counter, knowing this couldn't have been how she intended to give it to me. My curiosity got the best of me, though.

Slowly, I lowered the bag and opened it, reaching in with my free hand and pulling out a book. I inhaled a sharp gasp as my eyes fell to the cover of the book in my hands, and I was suddenly inundated with even more guilt than I ever thought possible.

The bag fell to the counter as I ran my right hand over the age-weathered cover. I couldn't believe she had gone to all the trouble of finding out my favorite childhood book. Then, to find an early publication—one that had to cost a shit-load of money …

I was an ass … a jerk … a fucking insensitive prick.

I could only imagine what she thought of me now. Fuck.

Setting the book down, I gathered all the courage I could to go and apologize. There wasn't a doubt in my mind that she might try to castrate me on sight. Bones was on my heels as we made our way toward the hall, veering off and out to the backyard with an excited yip when he heard the birds in the backyard.

It was down to just me now.

I was halfway down the hall when I looked up and stopped dead in my tracks to find our door wide open. The sight before me shocked me because I could have sworn I heard it slam. Running my hands through my hair, my gaze shifted to the left and my stomach rolled when I saw that it wasn't *our* room she escaped to, but *hers*. That couldn't be good, considering she hadn't been in there much at all since the incident with Dane.

My hands shook as I reached for the knob, turning it and easing the door open slowly just in case there were any flying objects I needed to be shielded from. But the room was silent. Too silent. Then I heard her quiet sniffles. The scene before me as I pushed the door open the rest of the way made me feel as though I had been punched in the gut.

Madison was lying on the far side of her old bed with her back to me. Her breathing was uneven as she cried quietly in the darkness of her room.

I needed to make things right, and the only way to do that was to apologize and hope to God we could talk about everything we'd been holding back from each other. We couldn't keep going on like this.

Slowly, I walked into the room, carefully crawling up onto the bed. When it dipped beneath my weight, Madison's body stiffened, but she didn't glance back at me, nor did she say a word. That could have been either good or bad. I wanted to believe it was probably somewhere in the middle—maybe a little closer to the good side of the spectrum—and continued toward her. There was no way to be certain how she might react to my next move, but I wrapped my arm around her in my first act of surrender.

I laid a gentle kiss to her shoulder as she moved her hand to rest over mine—a pretty fucking fantastic sign, if you asked me—and sighed. "Baby, I'm so sorry," I whispered, tightening my hold around her. "I don't know what came over me. I didn't mean to hurt you."

The longer Madison went without speaking, the more the world fell apart around me. What if I had ruined everything? What if she never forgave me?

"H-how could you even think I could *do* that?" she asked, her soft voice cracking. "Do you have any idea what it felt like to have you look at me that way?" A tear I hadn't even felt form fell from my eye and trailed over the bridge of my nose as I listened to her hoarse voice. "It fucking sucked, Jensen. It broke my heart."

I quickly tried to think of a way to explain everything I was thinking. It was all one big jumbled fucking mess in my head, and I was having trouble finding the right words.

Madison interjected before I had a chance to speak. "Look, I know you didn't actually *say* anything outright, but I could see it in your eyes, Jensen. You compared me to *her*. To Kaylie. Since you and I started seeing each other, I *never* compared you to Dane." She paused to take a breath, and it shuddered as it filled her lungs before she exhaled smoothly. "When I saw Kaylie all over you at your sister's wedding, I *trusted* you—not her so much, but you? Yeah."

I opened my mouth to speak, but she apparently had more to say—and I was in no position to interrupt her.

"It would have been nice if you'd shown the same level of trust in me."

Fuck, she was right.

"I'm not saying your past with Kaylie hasn't affected you—it's only natural that it did—but I'm not her. I told you from early on that I would *never* do what she did if we found ourselves in this very situation," she continued quietly. "So, what changed?"

I sighed, dropping my head to the pillow behind her. "At first, I guess I was scared that your love of competing would be more appealing to you," I confessed. "And then, when you took the test and it came up positive, you didn't want to tell anyone and that terrified the shit out of me. I guess what Kaylie did only made dealing with your apprehensions that much harder."

For the first time since I joined her in the room, Madison turned her head, glancing at me from the corner of her red, puffy eyes. "Why didn't you tell me any of this?"

"Because you seemed so stressed about it already, I didn't want to make it any worse," I told her honestly, realizing just how stupid it sounded saying it out loud for the first time.

"That's stupid," she said, mirroring my thoughts. Sniffling, Madison turned her head forward again and squeezed her hand around mine as her body pressed back into me. "I'm sorry, too, you know."

Shocked by her apology, I lifted my head to look down at her. "What do you have to be sorry about?" I asked.

She shrugged. "For not talking to you about any of this." She turned her face to me again, her eyes glistening with tears that rested on the brim and threatened to fall. "I was scared, and I handled it poorly — I know that now — but I would never —" She sobbed again, effectively cutting herself off as she directed her face away from me again, holding my arm tighter to her chest as though she were afraid I'd let her go.

"Shhh," I whispered, kissing the bare skin of her neck and squeezing her just a little tighter to let her know I had no intention of going anywhere. "I know." I couldn't even say the words out loud. "I let my stupid insecurities get the best of me, and I thought the absolute worst. Fuck, I hate that I let *her* poison this." I placed a hand over her belly.

Madison shook her head adamantly. "Not just her," she whispered. "If I hadn't been so secretive about everything, you'd have understood that, while scared, I am happy. You wanted to tell everyone, and I didn't because I was afraid that if something happened, if we miscarried, then we'd have to put your parents through that again. I couldn't bear it, Jensen. There was never a doubt in my mind that I would have this baby. Fear of the unknown? Hell, yes. But never any doubts."

That was what she meant when she said it was too soon to tell anyone? Had I ever misinterpreted that. Kaylie really had fucked me up.

Madison turned to face me again, her tears gone—hopefully for good. "We can tell them, though, if that's what you want. I realize now how selfish it was of me to ask you to keep it a secret given everything you've been through."

"If it makes you more comfortable to wait, then we'll wait. I'm sorry for thinking the worst," I told her.

"Only if you're sure, Jensen," she said, her eyebrows raised and pulled together. "I don't want this to be the source of anymore discord between us."

"It won't be," I assured her. "Now that I understand why you wanted to wait, I can see your point." Feeling the need to show her with more than words just how happy I was that we had been able to discuss our feelings with each other, I leaned in for a kiss.

Before my lips could make contact though, Madison turned her head away from me and pulled herself out of my arms. "I'm sorry. I'm still just kind of … reeling, you know?" It physically pained me when she started for the door, and she must have sensed my unease because she turned to me. "I'm just going for a walk. I need some time to think about everything. I'll stay on the grounds. I promise."

Even though I didn't want her to go anywhere, I nodded, hoping to show her a little of that trust that I seemed to have been lacking earlier. "Okay. I'll be here." Just as she moved for the hall again, I called out to her. "Madison?" She turned back, meeting my nervous-as-fuck stare. "Are we okay?"

The right side of her mouth turned up, and she nodded. "We will be …" She paused, looking at the floor and then back at me on her bed. "I'll be back in a bit."

Inhaling a deep breath, I smiled. "I love you."

"I love you, too."

I remained frozen as Madison disappeared from the doorway. Time didn't seem to matter as I lay on her bed, staring up at the ceiling. I wasn't thinking of anything in particular, just running our conversation over and over in my mind. It wasn't until Bones whimpered that I turned to find him with his paws up on the bed, his head resting on them as he looked at me.

"How's it going, pal?" I asked him, causing him to perk his ears forward. I scratched his head and it lolled to one side, his eyes closing as he seemed to enjoy the affection. "Come on," I ushered quietly, pushing myself off the bed and heading for the door. "Let's go and start on dinner before Mama gets back."

Forty-five minutes later, dinner was ready and Madison was still nowhere to be seen. I tried not to worry, but I couldn't help it. Instead of letting dinner get cold, I put the food in the oven's warming drawer and decided to do a bit of light tidying to keep from focusing on when she'd return.

I wandered through the house, picking up Bones' toys that he'd left lying in the middle of the living room or halfway down the hall before grabbing our hamper and taking it to the laundry room. After putting a load in, I went back to our bedroom to tidy up a bit more. The room seemed a little stuffy, so I opened the window to let the cool fall breeze in while I cleaned.

Madison still wasn't home by the time I finished, and I had to fight every impulse I had to call her and make sure she was all right. I checked the clock and realized that Madison had been gone for over an hour. While I wanted to give her the space she needed, I also needed to be sure she was okay. Just as I picked up my phone, the front door swung open.

"I'm back," Madison announced.

I wanted to race to her, but I didn't. I waited for her to come to me. "Dinner's warming in the oven." Turning toward the stove, I grabbed the oven mitts, removed the two dishes from the oven, and set them on the stovetop.

"Smells amazing," Madison said, her soft voice right behind me. I didn't even get a chance to turn and face her before I felt her arms wrap securely around my waist.

Basking in her affection, I placed my right hand over hers and held her there a moment longer before I patted it and twisted in her embrace, forcing her hands to rest loose on my hips. Something had changed from the time she left the house until now; she definitely seemed happier, yet still a little timid about something.

Ensnaring her waist, I tentatively leaned forward, our eyes locked the entire time, and pressed a gentle kiss to her lips. I could feel her smile against my mouth, and I felt an overwhelming sense of relief as I wrapped her in a tight embrace and exhaled. "How was your walk?" I asked.

"It was fine. Thank you."

I wanted to tell her it was no trouble, but that would have been a lie. Instead, I just nodded. "Come on, let's eat."

A moment of calm fell over us as we took a few bites of our dinner, occasionally looking up into one another's eyes and silently admiring each other. As we ate, I remembered her gift to me; there were really no words to express just how much I appreciated the gesture, but I was sure as hell going to try.

"Thank you, by the way." I inwardly rolled my eyes at myself for just how lame my gratitude sounded.

"For what?" Madison said, lifting her eyes to mine.

"My gift," I explained. "I really don't deserve it after tonight."

"True," she said, her lips fighting a cheeky grin. "But I'm sure you'd have redeemed yourself."

"It was a lucky guess ... figuring out what my favorite book was." The grin that she finally allowed to appear on her face was one I had seen before: she had outside help. "How did you know?"

She shrugged. "Your sister." I was stunned, and I was pretty sure that was evident by the way my mouth fell open. "Oh, I didn't tell her. I said I was thinking of Christmas gifts already."

I chuckled. "And she bought that? I'm a little disappointed by her naïveté."

"I don't know," Madison said, sounding serious again. "I'm sure she suspects something. There was something in the way she told me how perfect the gift was that had me questioning if she hasn't known for a couple of weeks. She and Willow were far too interested in what was going on between us while camping."

We finished our dinner before I started cleaning up—I had a lot of making up to do, and I intended to do whatever I could to make sure I did it right. After suggesting Madison retire to the living room, I did the dishes and wiped the counters before sweeping the floor. When the kitchen was in pristine order, I found Madison sitting on the couch. Her legs were tucked to the side with Bones nestled into the crook of her knees. She was awake, but barely.

Grinning so wide my cheeks started to hurt, I walked forward and joined her, pulling her into my side. Madison snuggled in a little closer, her hand coming up to clutch my shirt as I draped an arm around her. There seemed to be something in the way she was holding onto me that told me she was upset.

"Love? Is something on your mind?" I asked softly.

Madison didn't move except when she inhaled deeply and sighed. "I stopped by to see Dad when I went out for my walk."

"Oh?" Hearing that she went over to see her father caused me to panic a little—okay, a lot. While I felt good about airing things out between us, I knew she would still be upset. Had she told Wayne about the fight? If so, did that mean she told him about the pregnancy?

"Yeah. It wasn't originally my intention, but I just kind of found myself there." She took another deep breath. "I didn't tell him about the pregnancy yet; I figured we should do that together. But he knew something was wrong, and I told him that you and I had a fight."

The man was going to kill me. The day I found out that he knew about us, he told me never to hurt her, and I had done just that. Yeah, it was pretty much guaranteed that I was going to incur his wrath in the very near future.

"He suggested some time away," Madison said in a voice so quiet I almost didn't hear her.

My fear was momentarily forgotten, and I laughed softly, feeling a little relief. "Baby, we've already taken advantage of his generosity and taken so much time away. I don't know—"

Madison pushed herself up, looking nervous as she tucked her pale hair behind her ear. "No," she interrupted. "Just me."

"For how long?" I asked, trying to keep the hurt from my face when she turned to look at me.

"I'm guessing a couple of days?" I had to drop my eyes. I couldn't hide my true feelings any more. She shifted against me before saying, "I'm not going, though. I can't. Not after everythi—"

I interrupted her, wondering if maybe she needed this so much that her father had seen it before we had. "Maybe he's right?"

Madison shook her head firmly. "No. He's not. Jensen, we just made a huge breakthrough in our relationship, and I'm not going to risk taking four giant leaps back over something like *running away*."

"Madison, I know I can trust you," I whispered softly, my voice unsteady as I tried to convince myself.

"And I know you want to, but can you honestly tell me that if I went away for even a *day* you wouldn't be out of your mind with worry?"

There was a beat of silence where we just stared at each other. "Madi, I know I've been pretty overbearing these last couple weeks," I said with a small smile.

"You had your reasons, and I shouldn't have been so closed-minded to miss the signs. I was so wrapped up in my own shit that I failed to acknowledge how my behavior was affecting you. It won't happen again. I won't let it."

My expression softened, and my smile widened. "You realize what's happening right now, right?" I asked, causing her to drop her hands to her lap and look at me with a puzzled expression on her face. "We're *talking*. Pretty big step, don't you think?"

She shrugged flippantly, almost like she was pretending it was no big deal. "If you say so." The smile that slid across her face gave her away.

"Always a smart ass, huh?" I teased. "Seriously though, I want to thank you for talking to me about this instead of just doing it. I really appreciate it. Can you do me one favor?" She nodded. "Take tomorrow."

"What do you mean?" she asked, slightly confused.

"Tell Wayne you won't be in for work—I'll cover your workload. Go get a massage, shop, do whatever it is you need to in order to unwind. The only thing I'll ask is that you be home for dinner," I explained, my tone wavering slightly between conviction and doubt.

"Will you be able to handle that? I don't want to cause any undue stress on you."

Sighing, I turned to face Madison completely. Bones decided we were both far too restless and hopped onto the floor before heading outside. "Madison, I need you to do this. I'm not saying I won't have my moments, but I think it will be good for both of us. I need to learn how to let go of my past, and you need some alone time. I think this is the best way to accomplish both of those things. Please?"

"I just don't know if *now's* the time to be messing around with something like that."

"Baby," I whispered, cupping Madison's slender face in my hands this time. "I'm only asking you to go pamper yourself, and when you come home, I'll have dinner waiting."

Nodding in my grip, she agreed to the offer. "Okay. I'll take tomorrow off." She turned her face into my left hand and kissed the palm, bringing her right hand up to cover it. She paused when she noticed the bandage.

"What happened?" She pulled my hand down to inspect it.

"I had a minor disagreement with a hacksaw this afternoon while you were gone. I may have been a little distracted," I explained, pulling my hand back so she'd stop fussing over it. "It's fine, I promise."

"See. This is why I shouldn't go anywhere tomorrow. You're going to be too focused on me to work safely."

Chuckling, I pulled Madison into my arms and kissed the top of her head. "The difference between today and tomorrow will be that we've discussed everything, so it won't come as a big surprise."

With a hesitant nod, she agreed. "Okay."

"Okay," I parroted. "So, what do you want to do?"

"Honestly?" My head bobbed up and down. "I'm exhausted. I'd like to have a shower and hit the sack."

A much better idea came to me, so I hugged her to my chest and whispered, "How about a nice soothing bath? I'll give you a neck rub and then we'll go to bed together?"

While I started the bath, Madison called Bones in and closed the patio door. The dog ran straight to the bedroom while she entered the bathroom to climb into the tub. With a contented sigh, Madison relaxed back against my chest, and I wrapped my arms around her, placing tender kisses along the shell of her ear, down her neck, and over her shoulder. Starting at her neck, I massaged, moving my hands in firm strokes down her shoulders until I reached her lower back and hips.

I leaned forward until my lips brushed the shell of her ear. "I love you."

Madison hummed softly tilting her head back to look at me. "I love you, too."

I placed a tender kiss on her lips before continuing my massage. We were silent for a moment as my hands moved over her waist, coming to a stop on her abdomen. Soon, her belly would begin to grow as our baby did, and I couldn't wait for that to happen. When she placed her hands over mine, I twisted my wrists until we were palm-to-palm, lacing our fingers together as I lifted them from the water and kissed her left hand.

The minute my lips touched the warm skin of her hand, my eyes fell to her naked ring finger and my thoughts shifted. What if there was no "right moment?" I was pretty sure our relationship would attest to the fact that things always just happened for a reason and that you can't always plan them out to the letter. What would make this any different?

Keeping her hand within sight, I continued to stare at the bare skin of her ring finger where I knew a ring should sit. Madison deserved more, and I wanted to give it to her. My thumb grazed over the back of her hand, causing her arm to break out in goose bumps as she giggled and turned to press a kiss to my neck before snuggling in and inhaling deeply.

It was then that I realized that *this* was the perfect moment. We were alone and together; it didn't get more perfect than that. Sighing against the top of her head, I whispered, "Marry me, Madison ..."

BREAKING REIN
a horse play novel ~ book three

I had just lifted about three rolled pairs of socks when a tiny, black velvet box tumbled into my line of sight. I froze, my breath catching in my throat as I tried to tell myself I was seeing things. Unable to turn my head away, I clenched my eyes shut for a few seconds before opening them and still seeing the box.

"No," I whispered to myself, dropping the socks I now held in my hand to the floor as I reached for it. The box looked aged, so I tried to tell myself that maybe it was his high school or college grad ring—a totally reasonable explanation for the mystery box I now grasped in my hand, right?

Swallowing thickly, I opened the box with a soft *click* and gasped when the square solitaire diamond stared back at me, it's thousands of tiny facets glittering in the remaining sunlight that spilled in through the windows. *Nope, definitely not a grad ring.*

Unable to stop myself, I lifted the delicate ring from the cushion that held it in place before setting the box down. The white gold band was in pristine condition, leading me to believe that the ring could have been new, but the box was aged as well as the antique looking setting the stone was in. While it was a simple ring and no more than a half-carat in weight upon first glance, the claws that held it in place weren't entirely modern. Realization hit just then: this was what he was keeping from me on our way back from his parents' place.

It wasn't enough to just hold the ring between my fingers, apparently; soon enough, I was sliding the delicate ring down my left ring finger and marveling in just how *right* it felt sitting there. My heartbeat quickened, and I could feel my lips turning up into an excited smile as I stared at the sparkling diamond. While I knew I was worried about what others would think if we got married *now*, I couldn't help but wonder if Jensen was going to ask me again soon or why he hadn't tried giving it to me in the last few weeks…

"*Front door*," the alarm panel chimed before I heard the beeping of our code being entered.

"Madison?" Jensen called out. "Baby, I'm home."

Panicked, I looked from my finger to the bedroom door, and then back to my finger before I realized I had to take the ring off so he wouldn't find out that I discovered it! I quickly tossed the socks back in his drawer, not worrying about tidying them because I now understood why they were disorderly. Once I had them all picked up, I lifted my hand and pulled gently on the ring…

"Fuck," I muttered when it didn't move past my knuckle. How could I have been so stupid? I continued to twist and pull the ring, hoping that I'd be able to get the friggin' thing off before Jensen reached me.

"Love?" Jensen's voice was getting closer, so I pulled again to no avail…

I was so screwed.

Coming Soon

ABOUT THE AUTHOR

A.D. Ryan resides in Edmonton, Alberta with her extremely supportive husband and children (two sons and a stepdaughter). Reading and writing have always been a big part of her life, and she hopes that her books will entertain countless others the way that other authors have done for her. Even as a small child, she enjoyed creating new and interesting characters and molding their worlds around them.

To learn more about the author and stay up-to-date on future publications, please look for her on Facebook and her blog.

https://www.facebook.com/pages/AD-Ryan-Author

http://adryanauthorblog.wordpress.com

Sign up for my **NEWSLETTER** to receive updates & exclusive content!

Made in the USA
Charleston, SC
17 July 2016